THE FLAG OF FREEDOM

THE FLAG OF FREEDOM

a Nathan Peake novel

Seth Hunter

McBooks Press, Inc.
www.mcbooks.com
Ithaca, New York

Published by McBooks Press 2016

First published in Great Britain by Headline Review, an imprint of Headline Publishing Group, a Hachette UK company, 2012

Cover illustration © collaborationJS
Typeset in Sabon by Avon DataSet Ltd, Bidford-on-Avon, Warwickshire

The Nathan Peake Novels, book five:

ISBN 9781590137178 (softcover)
ISBN 9781590137185 (mobipocket)
ISBN 9781590137192 (ePub)
ISBN 9781590137208 (PDF)

Visit the McBooks Press website at www.mcbooks.com.

'From the halls of Montezuma
To the shores of Tripoli'

US Marine hymn

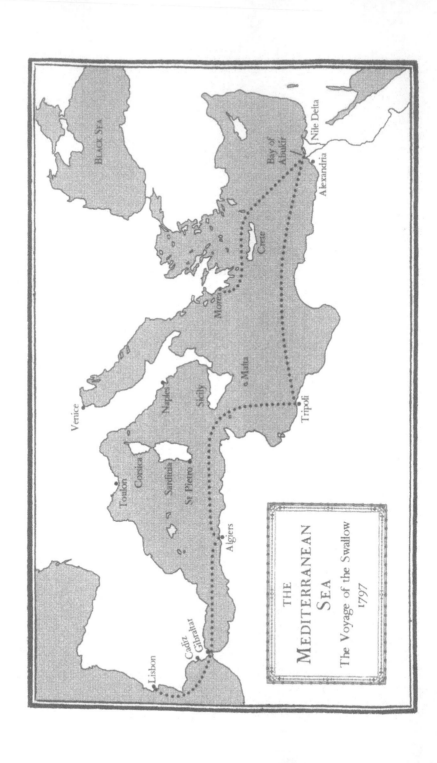

BLACK SEA

Nile Delta

Bay of Aboukir

Alexandria

Crete

Morea

o Malta

Tripoli

Venice

Naples

Sicily

Corsica

Sardinia

Toulon

St Pietro

Algiers

THE
MEDITERRANEAN
SEA
The Voyage of the Swallow
1797

Lisbon

Cadiz
Gibraltar

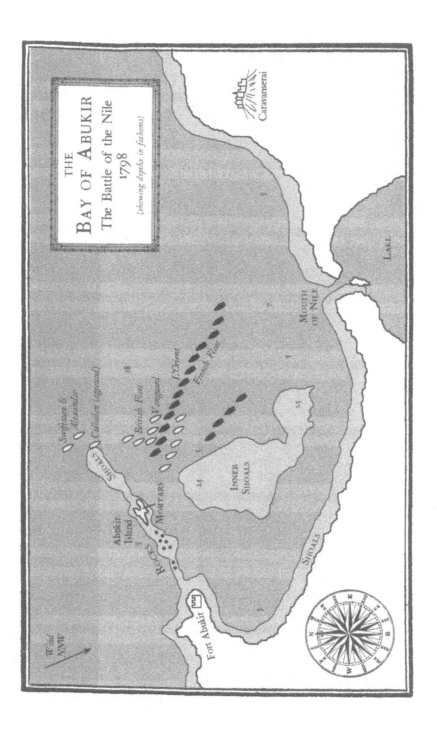

The Corsairs

——————•◆•——————

April, 1797

*I*t was the last ship out of Venice before the French landed. Caterina was lucky to find a berth. She had never seen such panic. The harbour was crammed with people trying to flee the city by the only means remaining to them. Pushing, shoving, shouting, swearing . . . it was like the worst days of Carnival. Some even wore masks, presumably to avoid being picked out by the French agents among the crowd, or more likely so they could push and shove and shout and swear without much risk of being recognised by their neighbours.

Everybody who was anybody was here. Masked or not, Sister Caterina identified some of the most illustrious names in the Golden Book: the noble elite of the Serene Republic of Saint Mark reduced to the status of refugees or brawling fishwives in the marketplace. Anyone with the means to make their escape before the arrival of the invaders was doing so – with good reason to fear the fury of the mob if they stayed behind.

Caterina was ashamed. Ashamed of Venice, ashamed of her fellow Venetians, ashamed of herself. As a leading member of the Patriot Party, she had played an important role in the fight against the French – and had publicly announced her intention of continuing that struggle, even in a city under occupation. The Doge, however, had persuaded her to think again. It would, he said, invite reprisals.

And the French were very good at reprisals.

'We must greet them with dignity and restraint,' he had told her – shortly before announcing his abdication and making off with whatever he could salvage from the wreck of the Republic. The last Doge of Venice.

So Caterina had gone, too, in her plainest, drabbest attire and without so much as a single servant to accompany her. She left the convent and her nuns to make what accommodation they could with their conquerors, and parted with a not insignificant portion of her savings for a passage on the *Saratoga*, an American ship, homeward bound for Philadelphia after a profitable cruise in the Levant.

Caterina had no intention of going so far, of course. There were some things worse than the French. For an additional outlay the Captain was prepared to land her in Naples, where she had influential connections. People who shared her political sympathies. People who would help secure the defeat of Bonaparte and restore her beloved Venice, if not to its former greatness, then at least to a position which would sustain a life of luxury and elegance for those with the wit and the charm to embrace it.

In the meantime, she did not get a great deal for her money. Her cabin was the size of a small wardrobe, which she was obliged to share with one other passenger; her bed a cot which resembled an instrument of torture in the Doge's prison; the sanitary arrangements would have disgraced a hovel in the poorer parts of the Veneto; the food was unspeakable.

Caterina made no complaint. Some level of inconvenience was inevitable in the circumstances, and it was nothing to the discomfort she would have had to endure at the hands of the French.

Her only real concern was the flag.

She ventured to mention this on one of her rare encounters with the ship's Captain on that restricted area of the upper deck where she and the other passengers were permitted to take the air.

It was their second day out of Venice. The wind was from the north-west – or so Caterina had been informed by an admiring officer who mistook her casual enquiry for passionate interest and embarked upon an elaborate discourse on the subject of winds and compass points. It did, however, reassure her that they were heading more or less in the right direction. The flag in question was streaming from a rope or some such fixture halfway up the mast – an especially large flag of vibrant design and colouring, not unlike the wrapping on a fruit candy.

'A fine spectacle, is she not?' the Captain remarked, as he noted the direction of her gaze. 'And a fine history, for all that it is a short one.'

Or something of the sort. Caterina spoke adequate English – as well as French, Spanish, Latin and the Venetian dialect – but it was not English as the Captain spoke it. In fact, Caterina was not at all sure that what the Captain spoke was English at all. Certainly it was very different from that of the English Ambassador and those of his compatriots whom Caterina had encountered in Venice. She inclined her head politely, but something in her expression alerted him to a measure of doubt.

'Or do you not think so?' his tone was challenging.

The Americans were a sensitive race, Caterina had observed, especially where their nationality was concerned. Possibly because their independence had been so recently and violently wrung from the English, for whom they were loath to be mistook. And they displayed a particular reverence towards their flag. The one outside the American Consulate on the Grand Canal had been the biggest in Venice, bigger even than the flag of St Mark which had flown from the Doge's Palace – before it was flung down and trampled underfoot by the Revolutionists.

Caterina hastened to explain that she had nothing against the flag *in principle* and was appreciative of its history. But was it wise to flaunt it so openly, she wondered, in such perilous waters?

'Flaunt?' he enquired, tilting his head and scratching his jaw. 'Perilous?'

He was a large man, his features gaunt and leathery from long exposure to the elements and his long greying hair unbound and unpowdered in the fashion of the French regicides. He looked a veritable ruffian, but then so did most Americans of her acquaintance, and yet she had heard it said that he was a Quaker and serious in his devotions. Captain Fry.

Might it not attract the attention of certain *undesirables*, she persisted, shading her eyes to gaze up into his face and assuming an expression of anxious regard.

'Undesirables?' the Captain repeated with a frown.

She put it in the vernacular. 'Pirates,' she said.

The frown cleared. He chuckled agreeably. She was given to understand that she should not worry her pretty head about such things, which were more properly the concern of those with intimate knowledge of the maritime world.

'Say an Ave Maria, if you wish,' he advised her, being aware of her status as a nun. 'Myself, I will rely upon those objects there,' indicating the twin rows of cannon upon the main deck, 'in the unlikely event that we will have to use them. Ha ha.'

Caterina was not impressed. It would take more than eight small cannon to deter the undesirables she had in mind. But the Captain made it plain that he considered her opinion to be of little value. She was a nun; what did she know of the sea and those who sailed upon it?

Caterina was tempted to inform him that she knew a great deal more than he imagined – and a great deal more than she wished, in fact, for her last lover had been an Admiral and was inclined at times to be dogged in his instruction. But, of course, she did not tell the Captain any such thing. Americans, she had discovered, adhered to a strict moral code and were intolerant of any lapse in others. And though for the most part heretics, they appeared to have a far greater expectation of those in Holy

Orders than most Catholics of her acquaintance – certainly in Venice where her activities had achieved some notoriety over the years.

As Deputy Prioress and effectual head of the Convent of San Paolo di Mare, Sister Caterina Caresini had presided over one of the most successful and profitable casinos in the Serenissima. Indeed, it had been described, by detractors and admirers alike, as a 'den of iniquity' where almost every vice known to man or woman might be indulged – for the right price – and where the Devil himself would have blushed at some of the excesses permitted within its walls.

This was something of an exaggeration.

Whilst the convent did possess a magnificent gaming room and the Sisters had been known to grant their favours to chosen admirers, some of the entertainments reportedly on offer were extremely fanciful. Suora Caterina prided herself on her high standards, in vice as in any other indulgence of the flesh. Under her guidance, the nuns of San Paolo di Mare would never be guilty of lapsing into the supreme sin of bad taste.

Though widely revered as a woman of fashion and distinction, Caterina had, in fact, risen from the most humble of beginnings. Her father had been a shepherd on the hillsides of Treviso in the Veneto, and their family name was not Caresini but Chodeschino – Sheep's Head. He had died of the ague when Caterina was ten years old, and her mother had sold what was left of his flock and contrived to keep the wolf from the door by practising as a herbalist. There were some who called her a witch – Strega Rosa. From her, it was widely believed, Caterina had inherited an extensive knowledge of love potions and poisons. This was another nonsense. Caterina had not yet resorted to the use of poison and had no need of love potions to attract an admirer. Her face had always been her fortune and she had done what she could to make the most of it, initially as an actress in Verona where she had first announced herself to the world as Caterina Caresini – leaving Chodeschino back in the hills with her father's grave and the sheep. Her success had been spectacular. She had soon established herself as the most beautiful, the most famous actress in Verona. And the most notorious.

Scandal, of course, was grist to the actor's mill, but there had been one too many – Caterina had been less circumspect in those days – and the Inquisitors had become involved. Caterina had bribed her way out of a flogging or worse, but she could not obtain a complete remission. She was given the choice of prison or a convent.

Strange that she had needed to think about it. For in the event, the Church had proved even more lucrative than the stage. So much so that even after her recent troubles Caterina was in possession of a considerable fortune, the bulk of which was invested in the English banking house of Coutts & Company. But for travelling expenses – and she knew she might be travelling for some time – she carried about her a small purse of gold coins, and another of cut diamonds, cleverly set in wax and disguised as rosary beads. Having saved them from the French, she was not minded to hand them over to the Beys and Bashaws of the Barbary Coast, especially when such an event might so easily be avoided by flying a different flag.

Caterina was as well-versed as any Venetian concerning

the perils of the Barbary Coast. Named after the Berbers who had been its original inhabitants, it extended from Tripoli in the east to Morocco in the west, and since the time of the Crusades it had been ruled by a succession of Regents or satraps, nominally under the control of the Grand Sultan in Constantinople, but in reality answerable only to themselves and their warlike followers – and, of course, God and the Prophet.

In pursuit of their war against the infidel, these princes had given licence to a particularly rapacious breed of pirates known as the Barbary Corsairs, who had become the scourge of Christian shipping the length and breadth of the Mediterranean. The prizes were brought into the ports of Algiers and Morocco, Tunis and Tripoli, where the ship and its cargo were impounded – and the passengers and crew either ransomed or sold as slaves.

Naturally, this provoked a measure of protest – and in some cases violent retribution. The corsairs found it advisable to steer clear of vessels flying the flag of any nation possessed of a large enough navy to exact revenge for any transgression. And they bestowed immunity upon the ships of several other nations who were willing to pay them an annual subsidy. But for the rest it was open season – especially for those flying the flag of the United States, which was notoriously reluctant to pay the necessary bribes and had neglected to build a single ship-of-war to protect its maritime interests.

Thus it would have been expedient, in Caterina's view, to fly the flag of some other country, preferably that of France, Spain or England, which would give the marauder pause for thought. Having failed to impress the ship's

Master with this argument, however, she sought backing from her fellow passengers, not least the young woman with whom she was obliged to share her cabin, and who happened, coincidentally, to be the daughter of the American Consul in Venice.

Although Caterina would have preferred the cabin to herself, Louisa Jane Devereux was as amiable a companion as she could have wished. She was young, charming and lovely. She did not snore, she did not smell, and she did not take up too much room. And she showed Caterina almost as much respect and admiration as the novices at the Convent of San Paolo di Mare. Had Caterina still been Deputy Prioress there, she could have put her in the way of earning a considerable stipend.

Of course, being American and a Protestant, Louisa had little knowledge of the diversions available in the convents of Venice. She had, by her own admission, lived a sheltered life. Her mother had died within a few months of her arrival in Venice, and since then Louisa had rarely left the American Consulate, her only excursions being a weekly visit to the Lutheran church and the occasional trip along the Grand Canal to attend a concert at the house of Carlo Goldoni. The rest of her time was devoted to study and prayer – and providing a comfort to her poor father. She was just seventeen.

'Bless you, my child,' sighed Caterina. 'There are many nuns who do not live so reverent a life.'

Louisa was now bound for England to stay with a cousin, her father having deemed it safer for her than remaining in Venice during the present disorders. He would send for her when some measure of normality was achieved, he promised; and if the turmoil continued, he would join her in London and they would return to Virginia where she had been born and raised.

Louisa did not seem overly impressed by this prospect. Her life in Venice, for all the restrictions placed upon it, had given her a taste for the exotic. She would like to see more of the world, she confided.

'Be careful what you wish for, my child,' Caterina warned her – she had assumed an armour of propriety for the duration of the voyage, there being little else to amuse her – 'or the Devil might be tempted to indulge you. There are parts of the world, not so very far from here, which are a great deal more "exotic" than you would care to imagine.'

But, of course, she then proceeded to supply the child with enough material for her imagination to run riot. So much so, that after listening with rapt attention to Caterina's tales of corsairs and slave-masters, eunuchs and concubines, and asking a great many supplementary questions concerning the conditions she might be expected to endure *should the worst happen*, Louisa was moved to voice her concerns to the ship's Master – a consequence which Caterina had foreseen and which had, to some extent, motivated her narrative. She considered that the gentleman in question might prove more receptive to the petition of an American Consul's daughter than he had been to the former Deputy Prioress of the Convent of San Paolo di Mare.

This proved unduly optimistic.

He did, however, deign to give Louisa a more fulsome explanation for his confidence, which she dutifully reported to Caterina in the privacy of their cabin. The American government had apparently swallowed its pride and its principles to the extent of paying a subsidy to the worst and most dangerous of the corsairs. The remnant possessed nothing more startling than a few lightly armed galleys manned by starving slaves. The *Saratoga* could see them off with a stout broadside, he assured her. Besides which, her present course, down the western edge of the Adriatic and through the Strait of Messina, would keep them well clear of the danger zone. As for the practice of flying under false colours, this was a stratagem more to be expected of the English and the Venetians.

And so, much to Caterina's irritation, the Stars and Stripes continued to fly from the masthead. And for four days the *Saratoga* continued her steady progress towards the heel of Italy.

And then the wind changed.

This was not immediately apparent to Caterina, but she was informed by the first officer that it was no longer possible, with the wind in its present quarter, to navigate the Strait of Messina. Instead, they were obliged to sail much further south and would not be able to land at Naples as promised. Caterina and several of the other passengers would be put ashore in Sicily and obliged to find another vessel to take them to the mainland.

Caterina was sorely displeased by this information, but in the event she was spared the inconvenience it would almost certainly have caused her.

On the morning of the fifth day, she and Louisa were taking the air on deck when a sail was sighted some little distance to the south-west. This appeared to cause som agitation among the officers and crew, and the Captain's steward shortly came over and advised them to return to their cabin. The approaching vessel was thought to be an Algerine, he confided, and 'purely as a precaution', the Captain had determined to run for the port of Masala, some several leagues to the north-west. As the women were ushered below, they saw the guns run out.

They remained in the gloom and stench of the lower deck throughout the ensuing encounter, news of which was conveyed to them by the dull report of cannon fire, initially at some distance but growing increasingly closer. Louisa was now quite fearful, Caterina only slightly less so, though her annoyance far outweighed her apprehension.

'Idiot,' she berated the Captain. 'I'll give him an Ave Maria. I hope they bend him over one of his precious guns and take turns.'

Certainly the guns did not seem much use for any other purpose. Possibly the ship was heeling too far over for them to bear – a mishap of which her Admiral had warned her during one of his weighty expositions – but for whatever reason they remained silent. The only sounds that carried to the two women were the wails of their fellow passengers, the occasional drumming of feet upon the upper deck, and, of course, the distant guns of the enemy. They became less distant as time went by and finally there was another, sharper report, and the crash of something large and solid hitting the hull. Shortly after, the vessel made a violent lurch and appeared to stop dead in the water.

Caterina climbed irritably to her feet. 'Be damned to his,' she said.

Among her possessions that were not stowed out of reach in the hold of the ship was a travelling bag containing a pair of pistols which had been given her by the English Ambassador shortly before his own flight from Venice. Caterina began to load them, ramming home the wadding, powder and shot with the tool provided for this purpose and distributing the required measure of powder into the firing pan.

Louisa observed these preparations with some astonishment.

'What are you doing?' she enquired at length.

'I am doing whatever may be necessary to defend our honour,' Caterina replied, more to shut her up than anything, for the loading of a pair of pistols required considerable attention.

'You do not consider that a prayer would help?'

Caterina detected the irony in this remark and was impressed.

'It would do no harm,' she conceded, in a similar spirit, 'if you feel the inclination.'

She cocked each of the pistols in turn and sighted along the barrels. Then she took one in each hand and led the way to the upper deck with Louisa following close behind.

She had reached the top steps when the hatch cover was thrown back and she saw a man staring down at her. His face was bearded and swarthy and he wore a turban. She raised one of the pistols and had the satisfaction of seeing the face withdraw.

Her satisfaction did not last long. There were shouted commands in a foreign tongue and the barrels of severa' guns appeared over the edge of the hatch. Then she heard a voice she recognised.

'Whoever you are, you must come on deck – and without your weapons.' It was the voice of the Captain, though somewhat more subdued than usual. 'I regret to have to inform you that the ship has been taken.'

Caterina swore an oath.

'What are we to do?' Louisa hissed in her ear.

'There is not much we *can* do,' Caterina admitted. 'Save to make the best bargain that we can.'

She mounted the last few steps of the ladder. In spite of Captain Fry's instructions, she kept the pistols with her.

To her considerable annoyance, she discovered the deck to be filled with men in beards and turbans, all staring at her and waving an assortment of weaponry. Their vessel was drawn up alongside. It was smaller than the *Saratoga* but more men lined the rails and clung to the rigging, all similarly attired and armed to the teeth.

Caterina caught the eye of the *Saratoga*'s Captain. He looked suitably contrite. 'I am truly sorry,' he informed her, 'but to avoid bloodshed I have surrendered the ship. Do please give up your pistols.'

There was another man at his side. Though he wore a turban, his face was fair-skinned and his beard was reddish-blond. Caterina kept her pistols levelled.

'Kindly inform him, in whatever language he speaks, that I am a nun,' she told the Captain. 'A woman of God,' she added, in case it lost something in the translation. 'And that I will be treated with respect – or I will blow his brains out.'

The man grinned widely. 'A nun, is it? Then I am Sinbad the Sailor.' He turned and said something in a foreign tongue which caused some amusement among his fellows. Then, turning back to Caterina, he told her: 'I'd be the more inclined to believe ye, lass, if you was to put those irons down and conduct yourself as befits a woman of God.'

Caterina frowned with displeasure, for she was not used to being laughed at.

'I take it you are English,' she addressed him sternly. 'And a renegade.'

'English be damned,' said he, 'and as to t'other, ye may take me for what ye like. Now put them down like a good lass, afore ye do yourself some harm.'

'Only when I have your assurance,' she insisted, 'that we will be treated with respect.'

Ignoring this request but giving a wide berth to her pistols, he peered past her into the shadows below the hatch and reacted with exaggerated astonishment when he saw Louisa peering back up at him. 'Well, damn me for a bampot,' he declared obscurely, 'there is another of them.' And then, stepping back a pace and bowing low to Caterina, 'Ye have my word on it, lass. If the word of a renegade has any value to ye.'

Caterina considered for a moment, but in truth she had little choice in the matter. She raised her right hand high into the air and pulled the trigger. The subsequent explosion rather surprised her. She had not been at all sure that she had loaded them properly. She did the same with the other. A little theatrical, admittedly, but then she was still, in her heart, an actress – and besides, she had not been too confident about handing them over fully loaded in case they went off by accident.

When the smoke cleared she saw that the renegade was grinning at her, but now in something more like admiration than mockery. She tossed the empty pistols on the deck. She had made as much of a point as was available to her and was under no illusions that it would make a great deal of difference.

She was in the hands of the Devil – again – and the future would require some very hard bargaining indeed.

Part One
The Prisoner of The Rock

Chapter One

The Black Sheep

———— ◆●◆ ————

The British Mediterranean fleet off Cadiz, 7 July 1797. A Sunday, and the ships were rigged for church, though it was not the chaplains who read the lesson, nor was it from *The Book of Common Prayer*:

If any person in or belonging to the fleet shall make, or endeavour to make, any mutinous assembly upon any pretence whatsoever, every person offending herein, and being convicted thereof by the sentence of the court martial, shall suffer death.

The solemn voice of the Flag Captain rang out across the sluggish waters, and in the silence that followed, other, more distant voices could be heard, as if echoing down the long line of fighting ships.

. . . shall suffer death . . . death . . . death . . . death.

The Articles of War, as devised by the Lo

Commissioners of the Admiralty, left little room for compromise, and as if to emphasise the point, the four corpses hanging from the yardarms of the flagship twisted a little on their ropes to provide a creaking chorus to the sombre lesson from the book of *King's Regulations*; the ships gently rising and falling on the slight swell like bobbing gulls, and the men standing grim and silent at their divisions.

The main deck of the flagship was unusually crowded, for the Admiral had ordered that every ship in the fleet should send two boatloads of seamen to witness the punishment meted out to their former comrades. And so they had. But no one looked at the bodies swinging from the yardarm. As if by common consent, every eye was averted from the bloated and discoloured faces. Instead, the gaze of a thousand men was fixed upon the quarterdeck where the Admiral stood at the side of his Flag Captain with the rest of the ship's officers in support – and four ranks of red-coated Marines providing a solid wedge of bayonet and muscle between rulers and ruled.

Among the officers stood a man wearing the uniform of a Post-Captain. It was an ill-fitting uniform, for it had been borrowed for the occasion from one of slighter build, and this, together with certain other of his features, gave him an air of slightly awkward individuality. He was a month short of his twenty-ninth birthday but looked younger – younger than many of the lieutenants and even some of the midshipmen aboard the flagship. His hair was dark and his countenance more swarthy than was the norm among those honest, red, perspiring English faces: might have been a Spaniard or, worse, a Frenchman – a misfortune of which he was more than usually aware at this critical moment in his career.

His name was Peake. Nathaniel Peake. But his friends called him Nathan, and despite his appearance he was an Englishman – or at least half of one on his father's side – and as loyal a subject of King George, at least in his own estimation, as any man afloat. (He could not speak of those ashore, being but little acquainted with the breed.) Despite the uniform, he was at present without a command: his ship, the *Unicorn*, having run upon the Rock of Montecristo and foundered with all hands while he was on business ashore – a circumstance which could also be construed as an offence under the Articles of War.

He had been summoned to the flagship for an interview with the Admiral, and while it was unlikely to turn out as badly as it had for the four men swinging at the yardarm, he could not help but consider that the present occasion was not auspicious. Being ashore upon the King's business should not, in all fairness, be regarded as either wilful or negligent, but there were certain ambiguities, certain subtleties, in the nature of that business which gave the Captain especial cause for concern. Besides which, he was not overwhelmed by the capacity of a naval court to dispense fairness, or even justice – the recent trial being, in his view, a case in point – and while he had every confidence in the judgement of his fellows when it came to seafaring, he was less sure of their reasoning in the finer points of the law.

As the lesson drew to a close, it was an earlier article that occupied his private thoughts:

If any officer, mariner, soldier, or other person of the

fleet, shall give, hold or entertain intelligence to or with any enemy or rebel without leave from the King's Majesty or his commanding officer, every such person so offending, and being convicted by the sentence of a court martial, shall be punished with death.

The Captain had, during his short career, entertained a great deal of intelligence with the King's enemies, and though in his opinion he had always had the King's leave to do so – or at least that of his commanding officers – he was not entirely sure that the present company would see it in quite the same light. Particularly not his present commanding officer, Admiral Sir John Jervis.

Nathan glanced towards this godlike figure as he gazed down upon the ship's company – as God Himself might gaze down upon His ungrateful Creation, Nathan considered, in the days and centuries following the Fall.

Fanciful though this notion was, it could not be denied that the Admiral was in a most ungenerous mood.

A few months previously, he had presided over the defeat of the Spanish fleet – the fleet presently locked up in Cadiz by the British blockade. Nathan had played his part in this, albeit as a passenger, and was proud to have done so. He was not convinced that it was as great a victory as the British government had subsequently proclaimed – only four Spanish ships in total having struck their colours – but it was an opinion he wisely kept to himself in the present company. Back home, he had been assured, the church bells had been rung from one end of the country to the other in honour of the brave boys in blue, and there had been a mood of popular rejoicing. For a time the Admiral and his men had basked in the approval of Parliament, press and public – a rare concordance. But then Parliament, press and public were united in their hunger for victory, no matter how insubstantial.

There had been precious little to celebrate since the start of the war, back in 1793, when the great powers of Europe had also achieved a rare unity in their bid to crush the forces unleashed by the French Revolution. But Paris had stood; the Revolution had endured. And as the years went by, the tide of war had swung against the monarchists. New French armies – raised by a *levée en masse* – had stormed across Germany and Northern Italy. The Pope had been forced to pay tribute to keep them out of Rome. The ancient Republic of Venice, mistress of the seas, had been torn apart, the British fleet driven from the Mediterranean. Holland and Spain had even gone so far as to change sides, if only in the hope of claiming a share of the spoils, and even the Hapsburg Emperor in Vienna, brother of the murdered Queen Marie Antoinette, was now thought to be seeking a humiliating compromise with the regicides in Paris.

Little wonder that the news of a single naval victory off Cape St Vincent had caused such rejoicing back in England.

But it had not lasted long.

Early that month, news had arrived of a mutiny at Spithead, the home base of the Channel fleet. The brave boys in blue had apparently refused to sail until the Admiralty agreed an improvement in their pay and conditions. The contagion had spread to the North Sea fleet at the Nore, where by all accounts the hands had turned on their officers and refused to join the blockade of the D fleet. Instead they had elected a committee of represen on the French model, imposed their own blockade of London and threatened to sail up the Thames and lay siege to Parliament.

A terrible fear had spread through the commanders at sea. Sir John Jervis had resolved to stamp out the first signs of mutiny as soon as they appeared. And a complaint against excessive punishment had provided him with what he would doubtless consider to be just cause.

Which was why four dead bodies were now swinging from the yardarm of the flagship and the word 'Death' echoed down the long line of warships off Cadiz.

The shrill wailing of the boatswain's pipes signified that proceedings had come to an end. The off-duty watch was dismissed for dinner. The visiting seamen returned to their own ships. The Admiral and his entourage disappeared below.

Having nothing else to do, Nathan tarried on the quarterdeck. No one spoke to him. He had begun to suspect he was regarded as something of a pariah, a black sheep. His fellow officers had sympathised with him over the loss of his ship, but being as superstitious as any of the foremast jacks, they no doubt thought that misfortune was catching and wished to avoid too close a contact with a source of infection.

He did not have long to wait. A lieutenant presented the usual respects and begged to inform him that the Admiral would be happy to see him as soon as his duties permitted. The words were a mere courtesy. Bracing imself for the worst, Nathan followed the officer below.

Admiral Jervis was at his desk, its surface entirely d in papers. He was not alone. His secretary,

Benjamin Tucker, was in attendance, and there was another man in civilian dress, unknown to Nathan, who looked upon him keenly as he entered the cabin.

The stern windows were open to the sea but the air was humid and the Admiral's ruddy countenance was slick with sweat. He had taken off his wig, and what little hair he had was plastered thinly across his scalp. He looked older than he had on the quarterdeck and less imposing, but no more amiable. Nathan had seen a portrait of him in his youth when he had appeared every inch the dashing young officer, but there was little of that dash now. His eyes had shrunken in his skull and grown hooded, and his nose, which had always been large, now appeared more like to a beak than ever, so that Nathan, who may well have been biased, had the impression of a malevolent old buzzard glowering over the corpse of his prey.

When Nathan entered, the Admiral was dictating a note to his secretary. The part that Nathan overheard was in Jervis's usual forthright style:

'Furthermore, I am pained to note that all the lieutenants are running to belly. They have been too long at anchor. I have therefore issued a general order to block up the entering ports that they may be obliged to come and go by climbing over the hammocks. I have the honour to be, sir, your most obedient et cetera, et cetera ... Ah, Peake, so there you are.'

It was the first time Nathan had engaged with the Admiral at close quarters and he had good reason to feel apprehensive. Jervis was a fierce disciplinarian, famous f treating officers and men with the same harsh seve Hangings might be uncommon, but lesser punish

were meted out with a frequency – and a disregard for
human dignity – that disturbed not a few of his officers.
Just a few days since, he had ordered a young midshipman
to be courtmartialled for allowing his boat's crew to
plunder a Spanish fishing vessel. Nathan had no objection
to that – the midshipman was entirely out of order – but it
was not enough for Jervis that the court had ordered the
officer to be deprived of his rank and stripped of his uniform before the whole ship's company. He had personally
intervened to order the man's head shaved and a notice
hung around his neck describing the crime – and then, as
a further humiliation, made him solely responsible for
cleaning the ship's privies until further notice.

But he could be extremely generous at times, and was
said to be entirely unmoved by rank and privilege. You
were as like to suffer a withering rebuke if you were the
son of a cowherd or a peer of the realm.

'Well, sir,' he growled when Nathan had made his bow,
'I hope you are not another of these fools who think a
rogue should not be hanged upon a Sunday.'

Nathan was well aware that the timing of the execution
had aroused further disquiet among the officers. The
men had been condemned late on Saturday night and it
had been widely anticipated, even by the President of the
Court, that their sentence would be deferred until the
Monday, out of respect for the Sabbath. The Admiral,
however, had begged to differ.

Nathan assured him that he had no strong views on the
matter and was rewarded with a dismissive grunt. But at
t he was invited to sit.

do not believe you have met Mr Scrope.' Jervis

indicated the civilian, who acknowledged Nathan with something between a nod and a bow. 'He is sent by their lordships on a special commission – to keep us up to scratch.'

This riposte was greeted with a thin smile. The Admiral was noted for his wry sense of humour.

Nathan viewed the stranger with renewed interest. Shortly after rejoining the fleet he had sent a confidential report to their lordships of the Admiralty detailing what he had learned, while on his 'business ashore', of French intentions in the Eastern Mediterranean. He wondered now if Scrope had been sent to discuss the implications of this, perhaps even to propose a plan of action. Jervis had given no indication of the fellow's status, but it was reasonable to suppose from the Admiral's remark that he was no mere clerk.

He was probably in his early thirties, Nathan estimated, modestly dressed but with the look of a man who has a considerable opinion of himself. It was difficult to perceive the reason for this, certainly in his appearance. His face had the unhealthy pallor of a civil servant who rarely sees the outside of a room in Whitehall and then only when it is dark. Even his eyes seemed drained of colour, though there was the merest hint of blue in them, like a dying promise in a wintry sky, and the long, sandy lashes had something of the appearance of a web.

There was much about him that reminded Nathan of one of those *représentants en mission* that the National Convention in Paris sent out into the provinces from time to time to ensure that the populace there kept to the path of righteousness, with the help of a large contingent of soldiers and a portable guillotine.

These reservations apart, his presence at this interview was encouraging. Nathan dared hope that it might presage a new mission for himself, either to learn more of the French plans or to forestall them. But the Admiral's next words swiftly dispelled this conceit.

'Their lordships have been debating how we might persuade the Dons to come out and fight,' he said. 'And they have hit upon an ingenious plan. I wonder that I had not thought of it myself. Perhaps Mr Scrope would be so good as to explain it to you.'

It was difficult to know if the Admiral's tone was sardonic or not. A great many officers had made the mistake of misjudging his mood and suffered the consequence. Scrope clearly took no chances but gave another of his meagre smiles and replied that he was simply the bearer of a proposal – *a mere suggestion* – and that neither he nor their lordships would presume to direct the victor of the Battle of St Vincent in matters of strategy.

'Oh come, sir, you are too diffident, too retiring by half. Tell the Captain what is proposed.'

Mr Scrope turned his pallid countenance upon Nathan. 'It behoved their lordships to suggest that the Spanish fleet might be induced to leave the shelter of Cadiz and engage in battle if the port were to come under some form of a *bombardment*,' he confided.

His voice was courteous enough but there was something in those pale blue eyes that suggested an element of disdain, as though he resented the necessity of an explanation, especially to one whom he clearly considered an underling.

Nathan inclined his head in the pretence of deliberation.

In fact, his mind was entirely engaged with the question of why *he* was being consulted in the matter when there were several Rear-Admirals and above a score of Post Captains – considerably senior to himself – who might be summoned by means of a simple signal, if not a modest hail.

Perhaps it was a test. The kind of hypothetical problem he had dreaded when obliged to undertake his examination for lieutenant.

Let us suppose that you are close-hauled upon the larboard tack under a full press of sail when a line of breakers is reported at a distance of less than a mile about two points off your starboard bow. What is your immediate reaction?

But Nathan was no floundering midshipman. He could speak now with all the authority and presence of a Post Captain, having the benefit of several years' experience in command of a King's ship.

'Interesting,' he said.

A sound issued from the Admiral that could have been laughter or the violent clearing of his throat.

'I dare say you would find it a lot more interesting to be on the receiving end of it,' he said. 'Or even to be firing the bombs.'

This was true, though Nathan had not experienced either of these misfortunes. Naval bombardments were highly specialised operations requiring the use of a bomb vessel and trained artillerymen, either of the Marines or the Army. Nathan was inclined to deplore them, both from a military and a moral standpoint, since the bombs were highly unreliable and tended to explode at the wrong time, and the mortars that fired them were notoriously inaccurate. Directed against a port, they could land almost anywhere and were almost certain to cause a number of civilian casualties.

He saw no particular reason to point this out, however, for it seemed to him that the Admiral had called him in merely to witness his own demolition of the plan.

In which supposition he was entirely mistaken.

'I anticipate, as you are presently without a command, that you might care to be involved in the operation,' the Admiral proposed with only the merest hint of a question in his tone.

'By all means,' agreed Nathan, wondering quite what Jervis had in mind. He had only the vaguest notion of how to fire a mortar. Besides, so far as he was aware, the fleet had no such weapon at its disposal.

But once more he was in error.

'They are sending us a bomb vessel from Gibraltar,' the Admiral confided. 'Also a gunboat with a howitzer.'

Nathan inclined his head once more, in appreciation of this intelligence, but ventured to point out that he had very little experience of either mortars or howitzers – or indeed the vessels that carried them.

'That is of no consequence,' the Admiral assured him. 'Rear-Admiral Nelson will be in overall command of the operation, and it is to be assumed that the individual commanders know what they are about. Your role will be to command the guard boats. Unless you have an objection, of course.' He raised his shaggy brows like a pair of gunports.

'Not at all,' replied Nathan. Anything less would have been to invite a broadside. 'Indeed, I am grateful for the honour.'

'Then you may take one of the launches and report to
Admiral Nelson with the inshore squadron. I am persuaded
that the pair of you will devise a suitable plan of attack
and that we will shortly see some fireworks. It will, of
course, be a night attack.'

Nathan returned to the upper deck in an even more
subdued frame of mind than when he had left it. Despite
what he had said to the Admiral, he felt neither gratitude
nor any sense of honour in his new commission. Indeed, it
was close to being the least honourable assignment of
his career. In effect, he was to assist in the shelling of the
civilian population in the hope that it would so incense
the Spanish authorities they would order their fleet into
battle.

Nathan had no illusions about the nature of warfare.
He had studied enough history to know that civilians often
bore the brunt of it. And yet in recent years, wars between
European nations had become rather more civilised than
in the past. They had become wars of manoeuvre between
professional armies or navies, rather like games of chess.
Attacks on civilians had been seen more as an aberration
than the norm – a crime punishable by hanging or the
firing squad. But not in this war. The French Revolution
– and the reaction to it – seemed to have engendered a new
kind of savagery, even among people who normally commanded Nathan's respect. The bombing of a city to make
its defenders come out and fight fell into this category, as
far as he was concerned. And he wanted no part of it.

The consequences of refusal, however, were likely to be
severe. It would mean disgrace, even a charge of cowardice
And cowardice in the face of the enemy, as the *Articles*

War had so recently assured him, was a hanging offence.

When he came on deck, he saw that the bodies of the four men had been taken down and were being sewn into canvas bags for burial. He doubted they would be granted the distinction of a Union Jack, though the chaplain might say a few words before they slid off the plank into the waiting sea.

From what Nathan had heard, they had led a protest when two of their shipmates had been condemned to death for sodomy. It was said that they had planned to seize their ship and sail her back to Spithead, but the evidence at their court martial had been fairly inconclusive. It seemed to Nathan that their execution was yet another sign of the savagery to which they had all succumbed. And for what? Everyone said there would be peace before the year was out. Nothing had been resolved by the last four years of war, except to make the French stronger.

Perhaps that was the problem. A sense of frustration – and fear – had spread through the English upper classes. Frustration at their failure to crush the regicides in Paris. Fear that the Revolution might spread to their own shores. That was why they were so merciless at the first hint of disaffection in the ranks.

Nathan wondered what he felt about this. He had witnessed the Terror in Paris at first hand. He knew what revolution could mean and had every reason to fear and loathe it. But he was sickened by the violence it had provoked in his own side. He needed to feel not only that he was fighting in a just cause, but also that he was fighting in a just *manner*. He knew that many of his fellow officers would regard this as pathetic, deluded. They were fighting for their survival – or at least they thought they were; they could not afford to be sentimental. And yet ... how could Jervis punish an officer for allowing his men to plunder a few fishermen, on the grounds that they were non-combatants – and yet order his fleet to bombard a city full of them?

Jervis would probably say it would help to end the war. But Nathan was not convinced.

Even so, he dutifully passed on the Admiral's orders and waited for the boat crew to prepare the launch for his journey to the inshore squadron. He had no belongings to take with him, besides the borrowed clothes he wore. Even his sword was borrowed. He had lost everything when the *Unicorn* went down – even, it seemed, his self-respect.

'Well, sir, I am very happy to have you aboard. With a bit of luck we will finish what we started at Saint Vincent and may sail home trailing clouds of glory – and a string of prizes.'

Rear-Admiral Sir Horatio Nelson greeted Nathan on the quarterdeck of his flagship, the *Theseus*. It was the first time they had met since Nelson's promotion for his part in the British victory. That, and the knighthood that came with it, were richly deserved in Nathan's opinion, for it was Nelson's single-minded action in breaking out of line, without orders, and driving his ship into the heart of the enemy fleet that had prevented the Spaniards' almost certain escape, unscathed, into Cadiz.

As it was, the Spanish navy had lost four ships in the resultant action. Nelson had taken two of them himself, boarding the second prize from the decks of the first – an unheard-of feat which had won the acclaim of the nation.

Nathan remembered the joy on Nelson's face as he led the attack.

'Glory – or a tomb at Westminster!'

Had he really said that at the time? The newspapers said he had, so it must be true. All Nathan could remember now was the dash and fury of the attack and the sense of being led by a schoolboy in Captain's uniform, for Nelson was slight of stature and led men into battle with all the eagerness and energy – and contempt for personal safety – of a house captain on the school playing-fields. As a result, he now wore an Admiral's uniform, with the Star of the Garter stitched to the left side of the breast. He was about ten years older than Nathan but looked surprisingly young for one so senior in rank – and appeared as keen as ever to take the fight to the enemy.

The inshore squadron consisted of ten ships of the line – enough to take on the entire Spanish fleet in Nelson's view, before Jervis could come up with the rest of the fleet. He had them drawn up in a crescent – or a drawn bow – just out of range of the batteries on the shore and in the direct path of the enemy fleet, should the Spanish Admiral choose to lead them out from the fortified area known as the Diamond and risk another battle. The fact that Nelson's squadron would be outnumbered by more than two to one did not seem to trouble him in the least.

'Depend upon it,' he assured Nathan, 'the moment they stick their noses out of the Diamond, I will make the most vigorous attack upon them.'

Clearly, he did not share Nathan's doubts about the bombardment of civilians, or if he did, he kept it for his more private reflections.

'If that fellow there don't bring them out, then nothing will,' he observed, indicating the bomb vessel sent up from Gibraltar which was now lying at a cable's length off their stern – the arrow to their drawn bow. The *Thunder*.

Nathan observed her with a professional detachment. As he had told Admiral Jervis, his knowledge of such vessels and their weaponry was not great, but he knew a little of their history and structure. They were originally a French concept, built for the wars of the last century. The plans for their design had been brought to England by the Huguenots – French Protestants fleeing the oppressions of Louis XIV – and the first to be made in British yards had been ketches with their two masts stepped further aft and the mortars mounted side by side on the foredeck, firing forward. But they had been awkward sailors, particularly in a rough sea, and since the last war the British versions were all ship-rigged, with the weapons mounted along the centreline on a revolving platform.

The *Thunder*, however, was not a British design. She had been captured from the Dutch, shortly after their surrender to the French and their decision to declare war on their former allies. From where Nathan stood, she looked much like a ship-rigged sloop, her sides pierced with gunports for ten 24-pounder carronades. He could see no sign of her more lethal armament, which he assumed must be carried below decks and somehow winched into position for whenever it was required.

Nelson had already explained the basic plan. Careful soundings had been taken of the waters around Cadiz an⌐ a position had been located in what was said to be a b⌐ spot for the Spanish batteries.

'It will be like lobbing stones into a hornets' nest,' he told Nathan, 'and if we make them mad enough, I dare say they will overcome their natural reluctance to come out and fight.'

In Nathan's experience, Spaniards were no more reluctant than hornets to take on a perceived aggressor. But from what he had been told, their ships were manned mainly by soldiers who might have been steady enough on land but had little notion of how to sail a ship or fire a gun at sea. Besides which, their superiors seemed to be convinced that it was only a matter of months, if not weeks, before a general peace was declared, and so they had no particular desire to risk their lives for nothing.

Hence the decision to bring on the *Thunder*.

'Depend upon it,' said Nelson, 'even if they do not care a fig for their own people, they will not stand idly by while their precious cathedral is brought down around their ears, for they have been more than a hundred years building it, and their priests have doubtless assured them they will spend ten times as long in Purgatory if they permit it to be destroyed by heretics.'

Nelson was the son of a country parson and maintained a proper Anglican contempt for Papist superstitions.

'Never trust a Spaniard,' he had warned Nathan, even when His Most Catholic Majesty was an ally of King George, and he considered the current ascendancy of the French Party in Madrid to be the complete justification of this prejudice. It was said that Nelson hated a Frenchman more than the Devil. In taking their part, the Spaniards d clearly invoked the wrath of God – which the *Thunder* bout to dispense.

The main problem, it appeared, was moving her close enough to the port to do some real damage. Her draught was shallow enough to go closer inshore than any of the other ships in Nelson's squadron, but she would need protection from the Spanish gunboats. This was where Nathan came in.

'You may take your pick of the ships' boats,' Nelson told him. 'And we will give you whatever backing we can from out in the bay.'

Nathan had studied the position carefully on the map and he could already name most of the salient features of the port and its defences, but he begged leave to go aloft with a borrowed telescope so he might view the real thing at close hand – or as close as the *Theseus* was likely to get. Nelson kindly lent him his own.

Nathan climbed high into the crosstrees of the main topmast. From this lofty perch, a good 180 feet above the upper deck, he had as perfect a view of the port as he could have wished. It was at the end of a long, narrow peninsula, surrounded by a massive seawall and guarded by the fortress of San Sebastian with over eighty heavy guns at its disposal. Just beyond the fort, Nathan could see the mosque-like dome of the cathedral, still under construction, and the church of Santiago on the opposite side of the same square. He could even see a number of the citizenry walking out on the mall – women mostly, judging from their parasols. And on the far side of the peninsula, in the channel Nelson had called the Diamond, he could just make out the masts of the Spanish fleet – twenty sail of the line. A formidable number, even if they handicapped by their lack of trained seamen.

He was about to return to the deck when he noticed something else. Closer to the port, right under the guns of the fort, there was a fleet of much smaller vessels. These must be the gunboats – and there were a great deal more than he had imagined. There must have been at least a score of them, and he could see a few more in the dockyard beyond, apparently being equipped with heavier cannon.

Nathan slid the glass shut and made his way back to the deck, a little more slowly and thoughtfully than he had made his ascent.

Nelson was no longer to be seen, but in his place stood another officer of Nathan's acquaintance, a stout, ruddy-faced individual who had been appraising him with the amused air of a spectator at the monkey-house in the zoo. He, too, wore the uniform of a Post Captain, though rather more elegantly tailored than that of his associate.

'You're slowing down a bit,' he observed, as Nathan joined him on the quarterdeck. 'Quite the staid old gentleman. Thirty next month, is it not?'

'Twenty-nine, as a matter of fact,' Nathan replied, trying not to breathe too hard from his exertions. 'How are you, Thomas? You look even fatter than when I last saw you. And even more pleased with yourself. Must be marriage.'

'Cannot speak too highly of it,' the Captain replied contentedly. 'You should try it yourself, Nat, if you can find someone who will have you. I'd change your tailor, though, if I were you. He ain't doing you any favours, you now.'

homas Fremantle was Nathan's senior on the Post
n's list by several months and they had served

together in the Gulf of Genoa under Nelson. Both had been involved in the evacuation of Leghorn in '96 and Fremantle had profited from the experience by acquiring a wife – Betsey Wynne – the daughter of an Anglo-Venetian gentleman whose family he had evacuated to Corsica from under the guns of the French. He and Nathan were friends, of a sort; Nathan thought of them more as old protagonists. He would not trust Fremantle further than he could throw him – which was not very far, given his propensity for rich food and fine wines – but their shared experiences had bonded them somewhat and they both enjoyed being able to say pretty much what they liked to each other. Most of the time.

Nathan flicked at the fibres of hemp adhering to his sleeve.

'It's one of Miller's cast-offs,' he said. 'Lost mine. I expect you heard the *Unicorn* went down with all hands off Montecristo.'

'I did. I did.' Fremantle looked properly grave. 'Fortunate you were not aboard at the time.'

Though his tone was sympathetic the elevation of his brow added a questionmark.

Nathan dropped his voice. 'As you know, I had official business in Venice. The authorities decided to extend my stay with a spell in the Doge's prison.'

He had been advised by the Admiral not to discuss the circumstances of his absence from the *Unicorn*, but Fremantle was well aware of his mission to Venice. The two men had been serving together at the time of his despatch there and it would have been pointless, as well as pompous, to say nothing of it. However, Fremantle was

notoriously indiscreet and Nathan had no intention of
being drawn any further on the subject.

'So, Thomas, what brings you aboard?' he said. 'You've
missed dinner, I think.'

'I am here for the same reason as you, I expect. To help
push the boat out. See some fireworks.' He flicked his head
in the direction of the bomb vessel.

'What – are you to lend a hand at the oars?'

'Good God, no! I leave all that small-boat stuff to you
younger fellows these days.' Fremantle was all of three
years older than Nathan. 'No. My role is to give support
with *Inconstant*, in case they send something bigger out –
and you take fright at all the noise.'

The *Inconstant* was one of the new, heavy, 36-gun
frigates of the *Perseverance* class. Her name was as much
a joke in the fleet as the irony of Fremantle's commanding
her, for he was known to be somewhat random in his
attachments to the fairer sex. Or had been before his
marriage.

'Well, that is good to know,' Nathan remarked vaguely.
'I thought it was just the *Theseus*.' He dropped his voice
again. 'Tell me, Thomas, what do you make of the scheme?'

'What do *I* make of it?' Fremantle looked more
deliberately over towards the *Thunder*. 'Well, it seems
simple enough to me, m'dear. We lob a few firecrackers
over the wall and wait to see what happens. Used to do it
at school. Nothing to it. Get a hiding, of course, if you're
caught.'

He spoke with the smug assurance of one who knows
that he is a lot less likely to be caught than the object of
his wit.

'It don't bother you, then, making war on women and children?'

'I say, coming the Quaker a bit, are we not?' Fremantle recoiled with mild indignation. 'When did you go all sanctimonious on us?'

'I imagine I took your lead, Thomas. When you were sounding off about the French, do you remember? When they were lobbing "firecrackers" into Leghorn and the place swarming with refugees. "Typical Frogs," you said. "Spineless Johnny Crapaud. Making war on women and children." I must have thought you had a point. Or was it only because the future Mrs Fremantle was there?'

'Well, if the Dons would only come out and fight, we would not be put to such an extreme, would we?' But Fremantle had clearly been stung into a more reflective mood for, after a moment's silence, he added: 'It ain't the most honourable course, I grant you, but then . . .' He shrugged. 'Nelson was talking about storming the place. Doing a Drake on it. Singeing the King of Spain's beard and all that.'

Francis Drake had led a raid on Cadiz in 1587 – the year before the Armada – and carried it off with his usual panache, looting and burning to his heart's content and taking or destroying three dozen Spanish sail. But then the Spaniards had not known he was coming.

'He asked my advice, as a matter of fact,' Fremantle confided modestly.

'Drake?'

'No!' An irritable frown. 'Nelson. We had a look at the charts together. I reckoned if we landed a few men on the isthmus, we could hold off a small army.'

'What about the men in the fort?'

'Well, obviously, one would have to take care of them. But if we could storm San Sebastian, you would have the whole Spanish fleet at your mercy. They would come out then, all right – else we could take them at their moorings.'

'So what happened?'

'Oh, Jervis sent back to London for approval and their lordships took against the plan. Said it ain't feasible. And Spencer came up with this instead – as you might expect.'

He kept his voice low but there was no disguising the contempt in it. Earl Spencer was the First Lord of the Admiralty. A political appointment to buy off those Whigs who continued to support the war. Not a Navy man; nor even a soldier like his predecessor, the Earl of Chatham. He was not widely liked in the fleet, and not only because he was a Whig.

'Even so, I'm surprised Jervis went along with it,' Nathan observed. 'And Nelson, too.'

Fremantle eyed him doubtfully. 'Thought they might share your scruples, did you?'

'I did, as a matter of fact – certainly in Nelson's case.'

'Well, let me put your mind at rest, young man. Nelson sent to Mazarredo a few days ago to tell him what to expect.'

Mazarredo was the Spanish Admiral.

'He did *what*?'

'Thought that would interest you. Told him we were preparing to burn Cadiz to ashes and that he might be advised to remove the civilian population to a place of safety.'

'Dear God.'

'I trust that restores your faith in the man? Of course, Mazarredo has done no such thing. But he cannot complain he was not forewarned.'

'So the Dons know we are coming.'

'They do indeed.' Fremantle eyed him complacently. 'I am told the harbour is full of gunboats. And they have armed every ship's boat with carronades.' He clapped Nathan on the shoulder. 'So you need have no fear, my friend. Your Quaker scruples need not be troubled by the venture. You may greet your Maker with a clear conscience.'

'Thank you, Thomas, I am touched by your concern. It is reassuring to know you will be in close support.'

'I said nothing about close, Nat. Nothing at all. We shall be staying well out to sea. Lot of rocks about, I am told. No, you had better put your trust in God and hope He ain't turned Papist. The Dons, I have heard, are not averse to shooting a sitting duck, especially when it is intent upon spreading murder and mayhem among their own chicks. You had better pray for a dark night, m'dear. Plenty of cloud cover, and no moon.'

Chapter Two

Fireworks

———◆———

*G*od had indeed turned Papist. Or asserted His privilege of remaining neutral and letting Nature take its course. It was a clear, moonlit night, the sky a sea of stars. So clear, Nathan could see every one of his little fleet of ships' boats as they pulled gamely towards the shore. Almost as clearly, he supposed, as the Spaniards must be able to see *them* from the ramparts of the city wall or in the gunboats that lay in wait for them at the edge of the harbour.

He tried not to take it personally, but for all the advantage it gave them, he considered they might have given the darkness a miss and attacked in broad daylight.

But the sea was as calm as a lake, that was the main thing. Or so he had been assured by Lieutenant Gourly, the somewhat overbearing – *bombastic?* – commander of the *Thunder*, for in the slightest swell, he said, their bombs tended to go awry. They could land anywhere, he said. And they did not want that.

No, they did not want that.

Looking astern, Nathan could see the bomb vessel making its slow but steady progress towards the port, towed by half a dozen boats from the fleet, for there was not a breath of wind, a circumstance that added somewhat to Lieutenant Gourly's satisfaction. 'Steady' was his favourite word. In the half-hour or so of their acquaintance, Nathan had heard him say it many times.

The *Thunder* was a platform for the delivery of Death and Destruction, and Lieutenant Gourly's job was to deliver it to the right place at the right time. Steadiness was all. Though a lack of imagination probably helped.

About a cable's length to starboard was the gun brig *Urchin*, also under tow. And behind them, a good way behind for fear of the shoals, were the *Goliath*, 74, and the frigate *Inconstant* – as insurance against a sortie by some of the larger elements of the Spanish fleet moored in the Diamond.

But in the event – the almost certain event – of an attack by gunboats in the shallower waters off the peninsula, the task of protecting the bomb vessel belonged to Nathan and his fleet of auxiliaries. His sitting ducks.

He had eight ships' launches under his command and two barges. Also a cutter, the *Fox*, which he had made his flagship. Each boat was commanded by a lieutenant or midshipman, and Nathan had a young sailing master, Prebble, as his Flag Captain. Most of the boats had 24-pounder carronades mounted in the bows, and the cutter had a pair of swivel guns besides. And every boat

was packed with men – seamen, not Marines – armed with
the usual assortment of weaponry. Nathan had issued no
particular instructions on the matter but he noted with
grim satisfaction that they had followed their brute
instincts and favoured the simple over the sophisticated.
Pistols and cutlasses, tomahawks and bludgeons, even a
sledgehammer: weapons ideally suited to murderous,
close-quarter encounters in the dark. Though drawn to
the tomahawks – he briefly saw himself ducking and diving
and slashing out like an Indian, with one in each hand –
Nathan had pitched for a pair of pistols and a cutlass, on
the rather depressing grounds that they were more appropriate to his rank. He had placed them in the scuppers
beneath his feet where they rested more comfortably than
in his belt, which he reserved for a dirk he had borrowed
from one of the midshipmen, but he touched them from
time to time for reassurance.

He was missing his own men – the men who had gone
down with the *Unicorn*. On occasions such as these he
normally had three self-appointed bodyguards: a giant
Irishman called Michael Connor, an equally impressive
African called George Banjo, and, most of all, his manservant, the former highwayman Gilbert Gabriel – known
ironically as the Angel Gabriel – who had been his father's
servant before him and who had been looking out for him,
more or less, since Nathan was a boy. Gabriel had accompanied him to Venice and there was a chance – a faint
chance – that he had avoided the fate of the rest of the
crew, though it was as likely he had been strung up as a
spy by the agents of the Serene Republic, shortly before it
was overrun by the French. Connor had died in a fight

very much like the one promised for tonight, watching Nathan's back as they boarded a French corvette in the dark. Banjo was the most likely survivor of the three, for he had deserted, with Nathan's connivance, off the island of Corfu. It was unlikely, however, that Nathan would ever see him again and if he did, he would probably be obliged to hang him.

Nathan dragged his mind back to present realities. The night air was humid; the rowers already gleaming with sweat in the moonlight. Nathan sweltered in his tight uniform coat, but he had found a pair of loose canvas ducks in the slops store which made him more comfortable below the waist, at least, and a pair of seamen's pumps, the better to keep his footing in the close-quarter encounters he anticipated before the night was much older.

It was already a little after ten o'clock and the sky did not seem to be getting any darker. From where he sat in the stern of the cutter, he could see along the entire length of the peninsula, which extended in a long, straight line for five miles into the Bay of Cadiz – rather like the needle of a compass, he had reflected earlier when he had studied it on the charts. It pointed exactly NNW, except that at the very end it turned itself into a phallus and swelled impressively before falling away to westward, as if too heavy for its slender stem. At the very tip of this engorgement was the lighthouse of San Sebastian – their main reference-point for the attack.

They were heading for a spot about 2,500 yards south of this marker, and the same distance west of the peninsula. This, it had been determined, was a blind spot for the batteries defending the city wall. *How* this had been determined, Nathan had yet to discover. However, he was not overly concerned by the shore batteries. He could do nothing about them – they were not his responsibility – and even on a night as clear as this he doubted if they would hit the smaller boats, except by accident. His sole concern was the fleet of Spanish gunboats waiting for him in the shallows and creeks of the peninsula.

There was, at present, neither sight nor sound of them. But there were no lights on in the port – no streetlights, no lights in the windows of the houses or taverns: a uniform darkness which could only have been ordained by the Spanish authorities, who clearly knew what was coming. Nathan suspected that most of the gunboats were lurking in the even darker patches below the city walls and the brooding fortress of San Sebastian. He could almost feel the eyes of their crews staring out at him from their invisible vantage as they waited for the order to attack.

He twisted in his seat again to look back at the *Thunder*. Lieutenant Gourly had conducted him on a tour of the vessel before they set out and had indicated its salient features with a paternal pride. These, essentially, were the two guns: the 12.5-inch mortar, up forward, and the 10-inch howitzer amidships.

Normally, the lieutenant had explained, they would carry a pair of mortars. The howitzer was a recent innovation. Something in his tone suggested to Nathan that he did not consider it an improvement.

'But ours is not to reason why,' he observed coolly.

The remaining mortar was his particular delight. It was the only naval weapon designed to fire an explosive shell, rather than solid shot, he informed Nathan impressively.

This was detonated by a smouldering fuse which could be cut to length depending upon the range required. The maximum range was about a mile and a half, about the same as the 24-pounder long guns of a ship of the line, but unlike these more conventional pieces, the mortar fired in a high trajectory, so high it could clear the most form-idable of defences and carry the shell into the heart of the enemy camp – or in this case, city.

Nathan privately recalled that an earlier term for a mortar was a 'murtherer', or murderer.

'So you will be firing at maximum range,' he had mused in a neutral tone that disguised his earnest wish that every one of the lieutenant's murdering shells would drop well short of its target. He entertained the insubstantial hope that the mere sound and fury of the attack would succeed in its stated ambition of encouraging the Spanish fleet to put to sea without the loss of a single civilian life.

But the range was not a problem, the lieutenant had assured him – not in a flat calm. At 2,500 yards they should be able to fire every shot into the heart of the city. No, his main concern was the length of the fuse. Exact precision was required to ensure that the shell exploded when it landed, he explained, and not in mid-air. If it exploded in mid-air, the shattered pieces of casing would fall harmlessly into the sea, or onto the rooftops and towers of the port. And if you made the fuse too long, it might be put out by a bucket of water or even by the rubble as it smashed through the roof or walls of a building.

And we did not want that.

Ideally it should explode on impact, or within a second or two afterward, distributing the full force of the explosion and a lethal hail of shrapnel into the immediate vicinity.

This was why bombardment was a highly specialised art of war, he told Nathan. It required a team of trained artillerymen, supplied by the Army, who had the necessary expertise to aim and fire the weapons. The Navy's job was simply to sail or tow the bomb vessel into position.

The mortar itself was a short, round weapon, not unlike a carronade but with a much wider bore. It was mounted in a pit on a revolving platform that enabled it to fire in any direction not obscured by the rigging, which was made of chain to withstand the blast of the muzzle. But because it fired at such an acute angle, there was no cabling to harness the recoil. Instead the entire force of the explosion was absorbed by a stout framework of timbers extending deep into the hull.

The howitzer was more like an ordinary gun, firing solid shot, save that it was designed to fire at a much higher trajectory than a normal gun – though not as high as a mortar and not at so great a distance.

Nathan had nodded gravely when these details were expounded to him, while disguising his personal disquiet. He knew his feelings were irrational, even hypocritical. Every weapon of war was designed to kill. But somehow, it seemed to him, it was more acceptable to kill someone who was trying to kill you. Raining death and destruction down upon unarmed civilians at a safe distance smacked more of massacre than of honest conflict. But then he supposed its proponents would argue that it was the swiftest way of bringing a conflict to a successful conclusion – and thus saving life in the long run.

Besides, in this case it was debatable whether the murder would be carried out at a safe distance. Not that he found this especially consoling as he led his little fleet closer and closer to the shore.

The first shot was fired a little after half past ten. And it did not come from the bomb vessel.

It was a testing shot from one of the guns mounted on the city wall, and though it fell well short, it came skipping across the water like a stone, marked by several white splashes before it finally sank about a half-cable's length off the *Thunder*'s larboard bow. The defenders clearly considered this a satisfactory result, for about a minute later the entire battery erupted in smoke and flame.

For the next few minutes the shot fell thick and fast. Whoever had determined that this was a blind spot for the city defences had clearly not calculated on the weather conditions, for the combined effect of a near-flat trajectory and a flat calm was to send almost every shot skimming towards the approaching attackers, greatly extending the range of the guns. Spent of its force, the shot could have had little effect upon the solid hull of the *Thunder*, but it played merry havoc with the boats that were towing her into position.

So far as Nathan could see, only one of the launches was hit – the round shot ploughing into the bank of oars on the larboard side – but to his consternation he saw that several boats were casting off the tow and heading back out of range. By his calculation the bomb vessel was still some several hundred yards short of the position that had been agreed upon, but whether from choice or necessity, both anchors splashed down into the sea. Moments later, a great gout of flame illuminated her lower rigging and a massive explosion shook the still waters. The *Thunder* was in action.

Nathan turned to observe the flight of the projectile, marked by an impressive trail of fire – rather like the tail of a comet. Its descent, though, was less spectacular. It fell into the sea about a quarter of a mile short of the lighthouse. Nathan swore he could hear the hiss. This was shortly followed by another spurt of flame – longer, thinner – from amidships, and the sharper report of the howitzer, but the shot left no trail and Nathan had no idea where it fell. Within seconds the *Urchin* opened fire, with much the same result.

And so the fireworks continued. Nathan watched them with interest, his feckless conscience slumbering upon his shoulder, for there was a childlike fascination in seeing the sudden red and orange flash illuminating the rigging and lower yards of the *Thunder* and watching the trail of sparks ascending into the heavens before plunging down towards sea or shore. One or other of the guns fired every minute or so, and Nathan counted two definite hits as the rooftops and steeples of the city flared into brief incandescence and the sound of the exploding shells rumbled back across the still waters. But the flash of the guns blinded him to his own peril, and the first he knew of it was from the startled shouts of his crew as it bore down upon them. He glimpsed the white surge of water below the blunt, black bow a moment before it ploughed into the starboard bank of oars, hurling the rowers onto their backs and sending him sprawling into the scuppers. From this undignified position he saw the single mast of their assailant against the starlit sky and the twin banks of oars that must have been raised an instant before impact – and the long bowsprit jutting out across the waist of the cutter with a writhing figure impaled upon the end of it like a gaffed fish.

As he scrambled up, groping for his sword and pistols in the dark, cursing his idiocy in not keeping them about his person, the Spaniards came leaping aboard, screaming their exultant battle cry of '*Sant' Iago!*' Nathan found his pistols, cocked and fired them one after the other, but it was like throwing stones into the advancing sea. There was no visible effect and the sea kept coming.

The British sailors in the bows were buried under the first wave, but the rest of his crew had dropped their oars and taken up their weapons. Pistols flashed in the darkness, their loud reports providing the percussion for the frenzied clash of steel and the harsher cries of the men. One man, almost as big as the late, lamented Connor, was wielding a broad axe like a Saxon warrior of old, while emitting a great roar, rising and falling with each stroke. Nathan threw his pistols one after the other at a man seeking unfair advantage by climbing up the rigging, and had the satisfaction of seeing the second bounce off his head, causing him to lose his hold and fall backwards into the sea. Then he took up his sword and hurled himself into the fray.

It was his second mistake of the night, for their attacker, after backing oars, had come at them again from astern. Half a dozen Spaniards had leaped aboard before Nathan realised what was afoot. He turned to meet them but was taken aback by the fury of the attack and could only retreat, desperately parrying with sword and dirk as he tried to keep his footing on planks now greasy with blood. He saw the pike thrust coming, but as he twisted to avoid it, he felt a savage stab of pain in his left hip. It was violent enough to bring him to his knees but he parried the next blow with the metal guard on his sword and stabbed upwards with his dirk. A scream of pain and his assailant fell back.

Nathan struggled to his feet but was knocked down again in the rush of his own men as they moved to tackle this new threat in their rear. By the time he found his feet again, the remaining Spaniards had been forced back into their own boat or swept into the sea. Then there was a flash and a roar at his shoulder and he whirled round to see the young sailing master, Prebble, bent over the starboard swivel gun. He had fired at point-blank range into the Spanish boat and was already leaping across to its twin on the opposite gunwale, heaving it around across his startled shipmates. They threw themselves down across the thwarts an instant before he fired and Nathan, who had sensibly dived with them, heard the wind of the grapeshot above his head before his ears were assailed by the roar of the explosion. The canvas bag of shot, torn in shreds, distributed two dozen leaden musket balls down the length of the crippled Spanish vessel, and what was left of her drifted away into the darkness.

Nathan put a hand to his hip and felt the sticky mess of blood, but at least it was not pumping out of a severed artery and the bone felt sound enough. He tugged off his stock and pressed it against the wound. Then he looked about him. All along the line of his miniature fleet, battle was joined. A tangle of boats and oars, struggling figures

– in the water and out – a wreath of smoke like a sea fog, palely gleaming in the moonlight. And through it, the stabbing orange flash of pistols and muskets and occasionally something more substantial.

And in one of these brighter flashes, to his complete astonishment, he saw Nelson. He was standing in the stern of a barge, a sword in one hand, a pistol in the other, his teeth bared in a snarl of rage. Then the darkness closed on him and Nathan wondered if it was some spectre of his imagining. But no. Another flash and a roar and he saw him again, hatless now, his hair streaming about his ears. Nathan felt a momentary exhilaration, then wonder. What in God's name was he about? An Admiral hurling himself into a fight like this, like some young midshipman anxious to make his name.

He had brought up reinforcements, but so had the Spaniards. There must have been more than fifty small boats engaged in this frenzied, vicious brawl off the shores of Cadiz, like some ancient battle of the fighting galleys: Greek against Persian, Roman against Phoenician, but without the elegance, its authenticity betrayed by the flash and roar of the explosions.

And it was by their light he saw Nelson's barge assailed by a much larger vessel, a gun brig under sweeps, its decks crowded with men waving swords, pikes and pistols, and yelling their frenzied invocations to St James. Gathering his shattered wits, Nathan made a swift appraisal of his remaining strength – above a score of men, though several like him, clutching wounds. He stumbled back to the helm and issued a stream of orders that had them falling to the oars, most still, marvellously, hanging from the rowlocks.

Setting his teeth against the pain, he folded the mess of
skin and cloth back over his wound and stood with one
hand on the tiller, the other at his hip like some mincing
fop on the Haymarket, save that fops did not normally
mince with one leg soaked in blood from hip to heel; he
could feel it squelching in his ill-fitting shoe. They rounded
the stern of the brig and swarmed up the side that was not
engaged. Nathan was past swarming, but he heaved
himself laboriously aboard, helped by an undignified push
from the mad axeman.

Prebble, he noted, had taken the lead with the inspiring,
if surprising cry of 'God and Saint George!' which clearly
marked him as a gentleman of breeding and religious
inclination. Nathan's own exhortations were of a less
devout nature but he suspected his men needed no officer,
pious or profane, to teach them the basics of this bloody
business. They cleared the decks of the brig in the first wild
rush and followed the boarders into the Admiral's barge.

Pausing at the rail, Nathan glanced down and saw
Nelson again. He was still on his feet but hard pressed, his
face wild and bloodied; and in that instant he saw him
fall, swamped by a horde of charging men. Then Nathan
jumped –

– into a heaving, slashing, kicking, swearing, brutish
brawl of bodies. God, St George and St James were buried
under a stream of Saxon and Spanish profanity. It was too
frenzied, too one-sided to last. The Spaniards, caught
between two fires, sought refuge in surrender, or the sea.
Nathan fought his way through the press of wounded or
exhausted – or exhilarated – men, thinking to find one
dead Admiral, only to find two living ones: Nelson, with

two swords now, and a man he introduced, with whimsical formality, as the Spanish Admiral Don Miguel Irigoyen, who had taken charge of the gunboats. He was curiously amiable, and as over-excited as his captor, and they were bowing and exchanging compliments like a pair of dowagers at a ball. Suddenly sickened, Nathan turned away, and found a thwart to sit upon, poking gingerly at his wound.

After a moment he became aware that something was amiss – something other than his damaged hip. The *Thunder* had stopped firing. He could see her masts against the sky but they were no longer illuminated by the flash of mortar or howitzer. And the *Urchin*, too, was silent.

Nathan was not the only one to have noticed. Nelson was looking decidedly less cheerful. Wearily, they took the Spanish brig in tow and rowed across the intervening stretch of water to the dormant volcano, where a distraught Mr Gourly confessed that his precious mortar was dismounted and could no longer be brought to bear, while the howitzer was useless, he said, as he had always known it would be, at such a range.

Nelson was clearly unimpressed.

'And can you not advance any closer?' he demanded coldly.

For answer another shot skimmed off the surface of the water and smashed into the hull of the battered vessel. Her timbers were sprung, the lieutenant explained, and they were taking water – already above a foot in the well. And without the mortar . . . he shrugged helplessly.

And so, with obvious reluctance, Nelson called off the attack.

'We will try again tonight,' Nathan heard him say. 'If your damned mortar can be brought to bear.'

It was dawn when Nathan climbed aboard the *Theseus*. The effort opened up his wound again but he was not the first to soil those holystoned decks with blood. He followed a trail of it to the cockpit and found it groaning with the night's harvest, most in far worse shape than he.

In the cut and thrust of battle there was little thought of the damage that you might inflict on another human being – any more than of the damage he might inflict on you. It was kill or be killed, a frenzied shambles of an affair; there was even a fierce kind of joy in it. If you thought of anything at all, it was not life or death; it was of victory or defeat.

But here it all was. Laid out, as if for his inspection, by the light of the smoking lanterns: the faces slashed to the bone, the missing ears and noses, the severed and half-severed limbs, the bleeding stumps . . . The men who, if they lived, would never be whole again.

Nathan stood for a moment taking it in: a detail from a painting of Hell by one of the Dutch masters, even down to the demon winding someone's entrails round a stick, or was he merely some loblolly boy trying to stuff them back in again? Then he found a corner with a patch of still unbloodied sawdust and lowered himself carefully to the floor, his left leg stretched out stiffly in front of him. He felt desperately tired and depressed – a deflation that came to him in the wake of every battle. Victory or defeat, it was all the same afterwards. Blood on his hands, blood on his clothes, the stench of it in his nostrils, and an infinite self-disgust.

He leaned back against the solid oak timbers and closed his eyes, and despite the pain of his throbbing hip, the ache behind his eyes, the images in his head and the screams of the men under the surgeon's knife, he was instantly asleep.

It was not a bad wound, the surgeon told him, he had seen far worse – as he sniffed it and swabbed it and sewed it up. 'Report sick,' he said. 'Do nothing for a few days, rest up.'

It was wise advice. Nathan wished he had taken it, and not only for the sake of his wound. But some stubborn wilfulness or pride led him to report for duty. Perhaps because he had seen so many worse wounds than his own. Perhaps because he was on Nelson's ship and it seemed like the right thing to do. Though later he did wonder if he was entirely in his right mind. Men were maddened, it was said, by the noise of battle alone, never mind the sights they saw, the things they did. Their minds were numbed, incapable of rational thought. He should have drunk a pint of rum and slept for a day or two.

But he was pure gunpowder from the neck up, and it was the news from Cadiz that lit the fuse.

The attack had been a failure. Only a few shells had landed on the port. A few houses had been demolished, and a convent. Several priests had been killed. Also a child, a baby girl. And the child's mother had lost an arm.

Nathan was appalled.

So was Admiral Jervis, though for a different reason. He was appalled that the *Thunder* had not gone closer inshore, appalled that the boats had cast off the tow, appalled that the mortar had failed. He had ordered a new attack as soon as it was mended. The honour of the service demanded no less.

'Be damned to him,' Nathan swore, 'and his honour. I'll have none of it.'

'Well, you have done your bit,' declared Fremantle, when Nathan's decision was imparted to him, 'and may safely plead incapacity on account of your wound.'

But this would not do for Nathan, not in his present mood. Whether from light-headedness due to loss of blood, or weakness of intellect, or some deeper, more pervasive cause, he must needs write a letter to the Admiral protesting that his own sense of honour – and the honour due to his country – would not permit him to make war upon women and children, or even priests of the Church of Rome, and that he respectfully declined to take any further part in the action.

He regretted the impulse almost as soon as the letter was despatched.

It was wildly out of character. He had been long enough in the service to know that if there was one thing worse than an official protest, it was an official protest on a matter of principle.

But it was too late.

By way of reply came a sergeant of Marines and four men with an order for Captain Peake's immediate arrest and his detention upon the Rock of Gibraltar until such time as arrangements could be made for his court martial, lest the honour of his country be further tarnished by his continued association with the loyal subjects of King George.

Chapter Three

The Castle of Blood

——◆◆◆——

The port of Tripoli baked in the heat of the afternoon sun. All along the waterfront, nothing stirred. Flea-bitten curs sprawled comatose in the shadows. The flags drooped limply from the mastheads of the corsair galleys moored in the harbour. Even the flies were moribund.

And Spiridion Foresti lay in a darkened room in the English Consul's house, dreaming of Ithaca. Spiridion was, in fact, a native of Zante, one of the neighbouring islands of the Ionian Archipelago, but Ithaca was the home of his latest paramour whose affections he sorely missed. It was also, according to legend, the island of Ulysses, and Spiridion had been wondering, just before he dropped off, if the victor of Troy had been happy when he finally arrived home. Or had he missed his adventures, his siren voices, even his monsters? In his dreams Spiridion saw the old warrior – or it might have been himself – sitting under a tamarind tree in the cool of the evening with his favourite dog at his feet, drinking wine from a glass that was at least half-full and watching a distant ship approaching from the sea. He was, he thought, content – but there was a stirring of hope in his breast that the ship might bring change or challenge.

Spiridion was roused from this idyll by a sudden loud explosion, the preliminary to a series of explosions, which he quickly identified as gunfire. This was not infrequent in Tripoli. It was usually no more significant than some minor celebration, such as the birth of another child to one of the Pasha's wives, or the death of one of his many enemies, or the anniversary of some massacre or other atrocity perpetrated by either himself or one of his ancestors. What was not usual was to embark on such jollification in the afternoon, when most people were asleep. Spiridion lay for a moment thinking about it. But the continuing gunfire and the clamour of the seagulls making it impossible to continue this process, let alone to resume his slumbers, he threw a loose-fitting robe over his Persian *pajamas*, snatched up his spyglass, and hurried up the stairs to the roof.

The British Consulate was on the waterfront in the merchant neighbourhood of Zenghet-el-Yehud, close by the Marine Gate, and from its flat rooftop, shaded by canvas awnings, he was able to look out over most of the city and across the natural harbour which had established Tripoli as one of the great ports of antiquity. It had flourished under Phoenicians, Romans, Byzantines and Arabs alike, but its importance had diminished over the long years of Ottoman rule, and of late, in Spiridion's opinion, it had become little more than a nest of pirates and a den of thieves. But it was home to some 30,000 souls of various ethnicity and denomination – Turks, Moors, Sephardic Jews, Moriscos, even a few Christians – most of whom found some means of profiting from its pariah status. Also, some several thousand Christian and Negro slaves who profited not at all.

As soon as he stepped onto the roof, Spiridion detected the source of the disturbance, though he had already fingered the obvious suspect. It was the castle. Or to be more precise, the battery of 18-pounders on the ramparts facing out to sea. On this occasion they appeared to be firing blanks, almost certainly in salute to some important government or foreign vessel approaching the harbour. Spiridion shielded his eyes from the glare off the water and was rewarded by the sight of two vessels under a full press of sail at the very outermost of the series of reefs which extended from the harbour mole far out into the bay.

Even without the glass, he was able to identify the first of these by its fore-and-aft rig as the *Meshuda*, the flagship of the Pasha's fleet. The other was ship-rigged and, despite the evident gunports, almost certainly a merchant vessel which the *Meshuda* had taken as prize. Lest there be any doubt about this, the flagship fired a rippling broadside in the familiar *feu de joie* that announced a profitable voyage and a triumphant return.

Spiridion took up his glass and focused it upon the captive. There were two flags at her masthead, and though they flapped limply in the scant wind, he was able to identify them as the flag of the Ottoman Navy, also used

by the Pasha's corsairs, and beneath it, denoting its
surrender to the forces of Islam, the flag of the United
States of America.

Spiridion closed the glass, his expression thoughtful.
He knew what would happen next and was thankful it
was none of his business. Though he had represented
British interests in various parts of the Mediterranean,
Spiridion had no official function in Tripoli. As far as the
authorities were concerned – and anyone else who enquired
during his frequent trips to the port – he was a ship-owner
of Greek origin with trading interests in the Levant,
currently staying at the British Consulate as the guest of
the Consul-General, Mr Lucas. Unofficially, however, he
was here on behalf of the British Admiralty to keep an eye
on the French, whose recent activities in the region had
given their lordships cause for concern. The capture of
an American merchant vessel by the local corsairs, while
deplorable, could have no possible bearing on this.

But then he thought again.

The arrival of a foreign prize in Tripoli invariably
triggered a meeting of the Pasha's Council – the Divan –
under the supervision of the Pasha himself, to congratulate
the victorious Captain and divide the spoils. All the foreign
consuls were expected to attend, either to represent the
captives and begin the laborious process of agreeing a
ransom, or to remind the Pasha of his obligations to release
those whose governments had had the foresight to pay in
advance, as it were, with an annual subsidy. Even if the
carrying vessel was American, some of its cargo might be
owned by British merchants or some of its passengers
subject to King George. In which case, the British Consul-

General would be expected to make a powerful representation on their behalf, backed by the threat of force.

Mr Lucas, however, was ill and abed with one of the mild stomach upsets to which he was prone, and he would no doubt take kindly to an offer from Spiridion to represent him. Not least because the prestige of the British Crown, and therefore its representative in Tripoli, had been considerably diminished by the enforced absence of the British fleet from the Mediterranean. If there was a humiliation in store, much better to confer it upon a relatively unknown Greek, rather than the representative of His Britannic Majesty.

Besides which, it was always useful to know the current mood at the castle. Who was in, who was out; what were the current state of relations with the Great Sultan in Constantinople. How much the French had increased their influence since the British withdrawal. It would give Spiridion an official pretext to do some nosing around. All he would need was the Consul's authority in writing, and the services of his dragoman, that particular functionary of the region who acted as translator and guide and general mediator with officialdom.

Spiridion suddenly became aware of a presence behind him. A large presence. George Banjo was an African of impressive physical stature and considerable intellect who acted for Spiridion in the official role of manservant and bodyguard. In fact, he was rather more than that. Spiridion invariably introduced him as 'my associate, Mr Banjo'. He had until quite recently been a seaman – a gun captain – in His Britannic Majesty's Navy. Having become involved in an altercation with one of the junior officers, who had had the temerity to instruct him in the art of firing a cannon, he had been obliged to jump ship at Corfu, in which crime he had been aided and abetted by no less a personage than the ship's Captain, who was anxious to avoid hanging him. This, with a recommendation to Spiridion, who was then British Consul in Corfu, to assist the fugitive in making his way in the world.

Spiridion had done more than that. He had taken Mr Banjo into his service, for the former gun captain had many talents besides that of aiming and firing a gun, and Spiridion had many duties besides that of British Consul in Corfu. In fact, he was known to a select circle of officials in the British Admiralty – and regrettably to a small but growing number of Frenchmen – as the best source of intelligence in the Eastern Mediterranean. He had more need of accomplices than of servants, and George Banjo had proved his worth in a number of tricky situations, mostly in the role of bodyguard, but also as a courier and confidant. They conversed mostly in English, which Banjo had picked up during his time aboard the *Unicorn*, but he had since learned something of the Venetian dialect and even Greek.

'I think we might make a visit to the castle,' Spiridion confided in him now. 'Please give my compliments to Nassif Malouf and ask if he would be good enough to attend to me in my rooms.'

Nassif Malouf was the Consul-General's dragoman. A Lebanese by birth and a Muslim by religion, he could converse fluently in Turkish, Arabic, English, Greek and Persian. He also spoke reasonable French and Spanish and several of the Italian dialects. Mr Lucas had a very high opinion of him. Unfortunately, it could never be as high as Malouf's opinion of himself. Like many men Spiridion had known who had a facility with tongues, he had an equal facility for deceit. Thus far the two men had masked their mutual suspicions with an elaborate show of *politesse*, but Spiridion found it a considerable strain at times and he detected the same tension in Malouf.

He appeared a little taken aback by Spiridion's offer. But after a brief interval he returned with the Consul's grateful thanks – and a letter of authorisation. It was no more than Spiridion had anticipated. Simon Lucas was not the most active of His Britannic Majesty's representatives that Spiridion had ever encountered, and usually only bestirred himself if there was a prospect of significant personal gain. Which in this case there was not.

'It would be useful to know something of the captured vessel before we present ourselves before the Divan,' Spiridion instructed the dragoman. 'Do you have someone you can send down to the harbour to discover what we can?'

By the time Spiridion had dressed in his official uniform, Malouf was able to supply the news that the prize was the *Saratoga* brig of Boston, taken off the south-western tip of Sicily, and laden with the produce of her recent cruise in the Levant and the Adriatic. He added that her most recent port of call had been Venice, where she had picked up a number of important passengers fleeing from the French.

This latter was of considerable interest to Spiridion, but it also struck a cautionary note, for his various business and official activities had obliged him to spend a great deal of time in Venice over the years, and there was a possibility

that one or other of the passengers might recognise him as
the former British Consul in Corfu, which was not, at this
present moment in time, to be welcomed. His curiosity got
the better of his caution, however – as it usually did – and
as soon as the dragoman was ready, they set off for the
castle with Mr Banjo and a pair of Janissaries as escort.

They were not the only ones. The streets of the harbour
were crowded with dignitaries, merchants, and other
interested parties making their way towards the castle by
horse, donkey or on foot. Spiridion being new to the port,
most of them were unknown to him – but he did recognise
several of the foreign contingent who had, for various
reasons, been brought to his attention. Among them,
Father Maurice, Prior of the Catholic Fathers – a French
Order who concerned themselves with the religious
wellbeing of the Christian slaves – the Danish Consul,
Monsieur Nissen, who normally represented the United
States' interest in Tripoli, and the French Consul Monsieur
Pellatier, accompanied by one of the newcomers from
Toulon whose presence in the port had so aroused
Spiridion's suspicions.

Elsewhere in the crowd, distinguished by their ornate
ceremonial uniforms and as often as not by the elaborate
plumage of their headgear, would be the representatives of
Spain, Portugal, the Papal States, the Two Sicilies, Genoa,
Sardinia and several of the lesser trading nations of the
Mediterranean, all of whom might have reason to fear
that their own nationals were among the passengers on the
captured vessel, thus involving them in protracted and
expensive negotiations for their release.

Among this flow of ubiquitous diplomacy moved the

local interest groups: the Moors in their white woollen cloaks, Janissaries in muslin and silver embroideries, Jews in their obligatory black robes and hats, *marabouts* or holy men with the inevitable following of beggars and urchins. A jostling, bickering, braying, sweltering, itching horde of supplicants and officials, each with their attendant household or hangers-on, picking their way through the piles of rubbish and ordure, swatting at flies, swearing at the packs of scavenging curs that snapped at their heels and the heels of the donkeys on which they rode. A typical afternoon stroll in Tripoli, Spiridion reflected wryly, as he climbed the sandy track towards the castle, past the whitewashed, windowless walls of the houses, the open doors of the mosques and the dark, mysterious archways that led to the bazaars and bordellos. Past the coffee houses, where the old and the idle sat, smoking their pipes in the shade of fig and pomegranate trees and smiling wisely at all this activity, all this human progress, all this wasted energy, when all a man desired was at hand.

Upwards and onwards until, with the grim persistence of human progress, even in Tripoli, they reached their objective: the fulcrum and focus of it all, the source of all honour and the fount of all wisdom. Al-Saraya al-Hamra. Otherwise known, from its reputation as much as the colour of its stones, as the Red Castle.

Built by the Arabs and the Ottomans between the sixth and sixteenth centuries, but resting on much older foundations, al-Saraya al-Hamra was one of the great citadels of the Eastern Mediterranean. Its towering walls and bastions defended it from land and sea, foreign invader and rebel insurgent. Its outer ramparts encompassed a vast, sprawling labyrinth of chambers and courtyards, covered passageways, stone stairways and archways, armouries and barracks, kitchens, stores and dungeons. It was the Pasha's principal residence, the centre of his administration, the prison and chief execution place of his enemies, and the main barracks of his Janissaries – the *Yeniçeri* or 'New Soldiers' who had been the spearhead of the Ottoman advance across Asia, Europe and Africa. Formerly drawn from Christian children captured or bought from Asia Minor, converted to Islam and trained as crack infantry, they were now almost exclusively recruited from the slums of Constantinople and the seaports of the Levant where they were known colloquially, though not to their faces, as the 'scum of the people'.

Only two narrow entrances gave access to the interior of the Red Castle. One, the Main Gate, was reached over a slender causeway that crossed the deep ditch separating the castle from its shabby protectorate; the other, the Marine Gate, which was used chiefly by the Pasha himself and his *Taiffa*, the Corporation of Corsairs, connected directly to the inner harbour where the fleet was moored and might, in extremis, be used for a swift getaway in the event of a military coup or popular uprising.

Both of which events were daily predicted by the sages in the coffee houses.

It was towards the Main Gate of this fortress that the various processions and less official assemblies made their slow and fractious progress. While the Consuls perspired and fretted in their official uniforms, their dragomans engaged in heated exchanges with the guards to establish their precedence over all the local suppliants and each other. On the walls above, more guards peered down and occasionally spat onto the heads below, especially if they recognised someone – and above *them*, the seagulls soared and swirled and shat – and added their fiendish chorus to the already hellish din.

Spiridion caught Mr Banjo's eye. Neither spoke or betrayed by the flicker of an expression what they were thinking, but both knew. For they enjoyed a curious rapport, these two, despite all the distinctions of race and birth and background. Spiridion was a native of Zante, one of the seven islands of the Ionian Sea, which had until recently been a part of the Venetian Empire. His father had been a local merchant, trading mainly in sponges. As a young man Spiridion had assisted him in this enterprise but had soon tired of its limitations and branched out on his own. He had become the skipper of a small schooner, trading with the Levant, and by the time he was thirty he was the owner of a small fleet. His association with the British had originally been a matter of self-interest, for the British had succeeded the Venetians as the foremost mercantile power in the region. But he had soon been drawn into something else: something that was more difficult to define. A combination of power and profit and piracy, perhaps. The British, of course, had no wish to define it. They would keep it as vague and as ambiguous and as unthreatening as possible, until suddenly the world would wake up and find itself entirely occupied by their trading posts and their garrisons and their factories and their ships. Most of all by their ships.

Spiridion knew what they were up to – he was part-Greek and part-Venetian – but he was not immune to their

charm. Or the sense of being a valued ally in some elusive
enterprise that transcended commerce and religion and
politics and even nationality: the Great Adventure –
everyone can join in, unless you are French.

And George Banjo, he was ... what? George was not
his given name, nor was Banjo, though it might be a rough
translation of it, a seaman's cheerful rendition of the
unpronounceable. He was a native of Yorubaland, on the
western coast of Africa, a chief's son who had been taken
as a slave and transported to Spanish Louisiana until his
freedom was bought by the same British Captain who had
assisted in his desertion off Corfu. Flotsam, really, swept
by the tides of Empire. He rarely spoke of his past, even
less of his future. He did not seem to want to go back to
Africa, not the part he had come from, at any rate. He
liked the sea. It represented a kind of freedom for him,
even on a British man-of-war which was more often than
not a floating prison. He liked guns. He liked food, and
women and good company. And for the time being he
liked Spiridion Foresti. Mr Banjo, too, had developed a
taste for adventure.

Like all adventurers, the two men preserved a certain
objectivity, a feeling of detachment from their surroundings
and situation. They did not consider themselves to be
above their fellow humans or even that much apart from
them. On the contrary, their various experiences – George
as slave and seaman, Spiridion as seaman and spy – had
obliged them to adapt to many different environments and
circumstances. They had a gift for survival, for making the
best of things, for falling on their feet. With this came a
wry sense of the absurd, not so much the absurdity of their

fellow humans, but more of the situations in which they so often found themselves. So that as they lingered among the madding crowd at the barbican, under the remorseless sky, and the spitting guards, and the shitting seagulls, they felt rather like the readers of a book who had unexpectedly found themselves projected as characters and participants into the story they were reading.

That is what the exchange of glances meant as they waited outside the castle gate.

Admitted at length through the narrow entrance, they followed the dragoman into the office of the Grand Kehya, the Pasha's chamberlain, where their papers were examined. These being approved, though not without the usual objections and protestations, the scarcely veiled insults and threats, the inevitable exchange of currency, or the promise of future favours, they were conducted by guards through a labyrinth of dark passages that led into the secret heart of the Pasha's castle.

As a citizen of Venice and a Greek who had spent most of his life trading in the Levant, Spiridion probably knew as much about the workings of the Ottoman Empire as any man in Europe, but he still did not know *why* it worked. Its methods and practices were so bizarre, so apparently self-destructive, it was a wonder to him that it worked at all.

From their origins as nomadic horsemen on the plains of Anatolia, the Ottomans had expanded across Asia and North Africa and up through the Balkans to the very gates of Vienna. They had long since lost this momentum. The Empire had been in decline for at least 100 years. However, the Great Sultan in Constantinople still ruled over a vast

territory of some 30 million peoples, from the Caspian Sea
to the shores of the Atlantic. Except that he did not rule in
any real sense of the word. Some said he did not even rule
in Constantinople, or even in his own palace of Topkapi,
where the real rulers were the court eunuchs, or the women
of the harem. And beyond the walls of the palace, the
Empire was ruled by hundreds, perhaps thousands, of
individual officials – satraps, beys or warlords, pashas and
regional governors. Officially, they were appointed by
firman, or decree, of the Sultan. In practice, they often
seized power by military coup or assassination, ruled by
extortion and the threat of more violence, and were
confirmed in office by the Sultan – or more likely his court
eunuchs – on payment of a large bribe. It was a kind of
formalised brigandage. But then most governments were,
Spiridion reflected, as he followed his guide through the
corridors of the Red Castle.

He was aware of its sinister reputation. It was here,
among these dark corridors, and the haunted chambers
that led off them, that most of the political murders which
characterised the Karamanli dynasty were committed.
Many a guest, invited to a banquet or reception, had met
a grisly end in one of these gloomy passages. A shadowy
figure would step out of some recess or doorway with
knife or garrotte, and after a few moments of futile struggle
the corpse would be dragged to one side ready for the next
victim. It was said that as many as 300 of the Pasha's
enemies had been disposed of in this manner, *at one sitting*.

It was unlikely to happen on this occasion, however,
for the main purpose of this particular summons was
extortion, and though the Pasha could, and frequently did,

extort money from the dead, it was a once and for all withdrawal, whereas the payment of ransoms could continue for some considerable time.

Even so, it was an essential feature of the Ottoman system that anyone entering the presence of the ruler should fear that he would never emerge from it alive. It was part of the mind torment that ensured the complete subservience to his will. Thus, the walls of the buildings themselves were pervaded with such an air of gloom and despondency, such a sense of betrayal and treachery, of unseen suffering and secret murder, that the courtier, supplicant or foreign ambassador invited to enter such a web would feel himself to be completely in the power of the monstrous spider at the heart of it. And grateful to him if, on this occasion, he was merely spat out, like a pip, without his skin.

Thus Spiridion was led through a network of passages, twisting and turning this way and that, up stairs and down stairs, through heavy, iron-plated doors – locked at sunset, Spiridion had been told, to divide the castle into a myriad different compartments – into tiny courtyards, open to the sky but barred with iron gratings that only emphasised the resemblance to a prison, until he arrived at length – at unnecessary length, he suspected – into the audience chamber of the Pasha.

The contrast was startling, as indeed it was meant to be. A large, almost cavernous room, with beams of light filtered through narrow arched windows set very high in the walls; the walls themselves gleaming with tiles and mirrors in ornate designs; sweet-smelling herbs burning in long-legged holders, the smoke twisting and turning like phantom snakes in the beams of sunlight; the great expanse of floor covered with sumptuous Turkish carpets and cushions and – unusually in the Levant – chairs: carved and gilded chairs from France, a sign of status in the Orient, like the mirrors, as if in some reflection of the Sun King in distant Versailles. Before the Revolution.

The centre of all this magnificence was the throne, a simple enough affair padded out with tasselled cushions and raised on a dais at one end of the room. It was currently empty. On each side of it and all around the walls stood heavily armed guards. Opposite the throne but at a healthy distance from it, sat the members of the Divan, in their finery, with the Grand Kehya occupying a table in the centre with his clerks and his paperwork. And huddled in a group at the far end of the room were the captives from the *Saratoga* – in chains and under close guard.

There were about 100 of them, by Spiridion's reckoning, including a number of women and children, presumably the passengers the Consul's dragoman had told him about, who had fled Venice after its surrender to the French. Spiridion kept his head down, near the back of the hall, but his covert surveillance established that several of them were indeed known to him personally. He recognised two senators and a judge – also one wealthy merchant with whom he had done business from time to time. But so far as he was aware, none them knew him as anything but a merchant from Zante who acted as British Consul in the Seven Isles. Even so, he was subjecting them to a more intense inspection when he was distracted by the dragoman whispering in his ear. Most of what he said was unintelligible but Spiridion picked up the words 'Murad Rais'.

Murad Rais. Yes. There he was, the Captain of the *Meshuda*, standing to one side of his captives with several of his officers. Spiridion had heard of Murad Rais from various sources both within and without the British Consulate, where Rais was also known as Peter Lisle, or Lilly, the Scottish seaman who had turned renegade.

According to one story, he had been a master gunner who had deserted from a British frigate visiting Tripoli. Another story had him as the mate of a British merchant ship. Yet another, the mate of the *Meshuda* when it was an American vessel, a schooner called the *Betsy*. Whatever the truth of the matter, he had converted to Islam and so impressed the present Pasha that he had appointed him Captain of the *Meshuda* and later, when his exploits had made him famous – or infamous – throughout the Mediterranean, he had promoted him to Admiral of the Fleet.

Murad Rais was a smallish man with a red beard and earrings – every inch the pirate. He could have been Drake or one of his fellow Elizabethan seadogs, Spiridion thought, had it not been for the turban and the flowing robes and baggy trousers, a curved dagger at his belt – or at least the sheath, for weapons were forbidden in the court of the Pasha. He looked a little troubled, Spiridion thought, for a man who had just returned to the port in triumph. He kept glancing towards his captives as if they were a burden to him and not a supplement to his already considerable fortune.

A deep and rhythmic drumbeat announced the imminent arrival of the Pasha. Was it Spiridion's imagining, or did it send a shiver of apprehension running through the crowded room? Certainly, there was a tension, a collective stiffening of fibres, a nervous adjustment of dress. The drumbeat grew louder and with it the shriller sound of pipes and timbrels. Moments later the musicians marched in, closely followed by a file of Janissaries in their steel helmets and breastplates. Then came the *Agha* carrying the Pasha's staff of three horsetails – in homage to the nomadic origins of the Ottoman Turks and a mark of the Pasha's dignity as a senior potentate of the Empire, equal in rank to the Governors of Baghdad and Budapest.

Then finally, as the music ceased and the courtiers and ministers and supplicants prostrated themselves, and the foreign representatives bowed as low as was possible without actually touching the floor with their heads, the Pasha himself entered the hall.

Yusuf Karamanli was a short, fat man of about thirty, and though he wore the bejewelled turban, the embroidered robes of an Ottoman satrap, he had a fair, almost rosy complexion, with pale blue eyes and a thin blond beard. To Spiridion he looked like one of those young men from England or Germany when they turn up in Venice, the highlight of the Grand Tour, wearing the costume they have bought for Carnival.

It was said that he took after his mother, who had been born in the Ottoman province of Georgia, in the Caucasus – at least, in his appearance. Unhappily for his subjects, he had nothing of her gentle, passive nature. For although he exuded an air of humorous and relaxed charm – quite the jolly prince, in fact – he was frequently possessed of violent rages. Spiridion, when they were described to him, had wondered if it was all part of the act, the elaborate subterfuge of a man who knew himself and his people very well and was well-versed in the power of theatre to impress them. For Yusuf Karamanli, appearances to the contrary, was, in fact, a cold and calculating killer.

He came from a long line of what were known in Tripoli as Khuloghlis – literally, in Turkish, *the sons of slaves*. In reality, they were the sons of Turkish officials who had taken Arab wives, and they formed an elite warrior caste similar to the Janissaries. But unlike the Janissaries, who fought on foot, the Khuloghlis were horsemen – splendid horsemen for the most part – who lived under the control of their own elected Aghas, mainly in the oases outside the towns.

Yusuf's grandfather, Ahmed, had been one of their leaders. He had seized power in a military coup, which was not unusual in the outer provinces of the Ottoman Empire. What was unusual was that shortly afterwards, he had invited several hundred of the country's most eminent chieftains and notables to a state banquet and had had them murdered, singly or in groups, as they shuffled through the corridors to the dining room. There was still some debate in the coffee houses over whether he had had them garrotted or cut their throats. The majority favoured garrotting, to avoid any telltale signs of bloodshed. Either way, none of the victims returned to shed light on the matter. The Pasha used the money from their confiscated estates to bribe the Sultan into confirming him as Regent.

Whether Yusuf had learned from this admirable example, or inherited the same ruthless sense of survival, his own route to power was just as merciless, if rather more personal.

As Spiridion had heard it, the story was this:

The previous Pasha, Ahmed's son, Ali, was a drunk and a profligate, who rarely moved beyond the castle walls and left the management of the country to his Grand Kehya, while for the more subtle business of managing the court he relied on his women – 'those casual instruments of mischief', as Spiridion's informant had described them. Ali had many women, but in the Khuloghlis tradition, only one wife, the Georgian, Lilla Kebierra, by whom he had three sons, Hassan, Ahmed and Yusuf.

The eldest, Hassan, was widely regarded as a man of intelligence, charm and courage. Spiridion's informant, who was the sister of the previous British Consul and clearly enamoured, had described him as 'a fine, majestic figure of a man, a born ruler, much beloved by his people'.

Always a curse in the Ottoman world.

In his early twenties, as was customary with the eldest son, Hassan had been appointed Bey, Commander-in-Chief of the Janissaries. He took this role more seriously than most and spent a great deal of his time and much of his money on military campaigns against the brigand tribes of the interior, which was mostly desert the size of France and Spain combined. Unfortunately for Hassan, his obvious qualities of leadership, together with his prolonged absences from court, proved fatal. The first provoked the jealousy of his two brothers and aroused the fear that he would have them disposed of the moment he assumed power; the second provided them with the opportunity to do something about it.

The middle son, Ahmed, was a nonentity – a drunkard and a coward who took after his father and made himself scarce at the slightest hint of danger. Hassan had nothing to fear from *him*. But the youngest son, Yusuf, was a talented and ruthless conspirator, with a devotion to his own interests uninhibited by considerations of family, friends, country, honour or religion. Everyone expected him to go far.

His main problem was catching Hassan off-guard.

Such was the hatred and suspicion that existed among the three brothers, they rarely moved without a coterie of armed retainers and loyal followers. The one exception to this was their mother's harem – a traditional place of sanctuary in the Ottoman world, where no violence was tolerated, and no weapons or male followers were permitted.

From what Spiridion could gather, Yusuf persuaded his mother that he wanted to be reconciled with Hassan. So she had summoned them both for a meeting – in the harem.

Hassan had just lost his two young sons in a recent plague which had decimated the population. He was in a mood for reconciliation with his brothers, but being a Khuloghli he took his sword with him, hidden under his robes. Unfortunately, his mother detected it and made him take it off and leave it on a windowsill.

She then sat her two sons down beside her and joined their hands together, begging them to swear an end to their enmity. Yusuf appeared willing. He even proposed that they swear on the Qur'an. Hassan being agreeable, Yusuf crossed to the door and called loudly to the servants to bring him a copy of the Holy Book. This was a pre-arranged signal. One of his slaves promptly appeared and handed him two loaded pistols.

Hassan was still seated beside his mother on the sofa. Yusuf had his back to them at the door. When he turned, they both saw the pistols and Lilla Kebierra gave a scream and threw herself in front of her eldest son. Yusuf fired anyway and the ball pierced her hand and struck Hassan in the side. He was still able to reach for his sword, however, and make a lunge at his younger brother. Whereupon Yusuf discharged the second pistol, killing him instantly.

Lilla Kebierra draped herself across the body, wailing piteously. The door opened and Lilla Ayesha, Hassan's wife, came running in. She, too, hurled herself upon the body. In her wake came five of Yusuf's slaves who pulled the two women away and hacked the corpse to pieces with their swords. Then Yusuf and his followers, covered in blood, made their escape, killing the Grand Kehya on the way.

As Spiridion's informant eloquently put it: 'Hamlet ain't in it!'

But whatever Shakespeare's audience might have made of it, the population of Tripoli, after a short period of pleasurable horror, anarchy and Turkish intervention, gave Yusuf a standing ovation. He was widely acknowledged to have that elusive spirit of *bashasha* – a combination of charisma, charm and the capacity for unrestrained violence – which marked him as the coming man: a man with all the qualities necessary to rule a turbulent province on the fringes of the Ottoman Empire. When he emerged from his exile among the Berbers and the Bedouin of the interior, he returned in triumph to take his place on the throne. His grieving mother uttered no word of rebuke, his surviving brother fled to Tunis, and his subjects kept their heads down and refused all invitations to dinner at the castle.

They were wise to do so. At his first full Divan, the new Pasha announced the death penalty for everything but the most trivial of offences. Thieves were seized by snatch squads of executioners – a profession reserved, in Tripoli, for members of the Jewish faith – and instantly hanged or strangled. Raiding tribesmen were beheaded. Women convicted of adultery were tied in a sack and throw into the sea. Yet it was said that Yusuf could be merciful. He had a tendency, it was reported, to be swayed by a transitory emotion. This, too, was part of his *bashasha*.

His personal life was simple. He had two wives, one black, one white, and thus far no concubines; his alcohol consumption was moderate; he had no other known vices. Spiridion had been told he had a lively and penetrating knowledge of events in Europe and that he spoke fluent Italian, in the dialect of Sicily. He was on good terms with the Spanish and the French and until recently, when there had been a certain cooling of relations, with the British. His main problem, as a ruler, was lack of money. For which reason he had resorted, as had so many of his predecessors, to the licensing of piracy.

Yusuf adhered to the traditional policy, practised all along the Barbary Coast, of being in a permanent state of war with Christendom. This conferred the right of his seafaring subjects to embark on a *corse*, or cruise, with the purpose of raiding isolated Christian communities throughout the Mediterranean and of seizing any Christian ship incapable of defending itself.

It being forbidden by the Qur'an to enslave the followers

of Mohammed, the sole purpose of this enterprise was the harvesting of slaves and plunder.

In practice, however, the states of the Barbary Coast made exceptions for all those nations powerful enough to exact retribution for such atrocities or prudent enough to pay an annual subsidy. One of Yusuf's first acts on assuming office had been to declare all existing treaties to be null and void and to demand additional payments from the tribute nations, most of whom had reluctantly paid on demand. But not the United States.

Which was why the *Saratoga* now languished in the Pasha's harbour and her passengers and crew were assembled in his castle with chains around their ankles.

The language of the court was Turkish and Spiridion was able to follow most of what was going on without the help of the dragoman. The Grand Kehya sat at a table with his paperwork while one of his officials read out the names and nationalities of the crew and the passengers. Spiridion knew the form. Crew members, whatever country they came from originally, were considered to be of the same nationality as the ship and were disposed of in the same way as the cargo. A tenth of their number belonged to the Pasha, the rest would be sold in the slave-market to the highest bidder and the profits divided by the corsair Captain, the ship's owners, and those of his crew who were not slaves already.

The passengers were treated more individually. If they were not covered by treaty they, too, were enslaved – unless they could raise sufficient funds to buy their freedom. The actual amount varied but it was usually as much as they could afford to pay. There were a number of

Jewish merchants in the port who acted as brokers, assessing exactly how much might be raised from the family and arranging the transfer of funds with other Jewish merchants in Europe. The whole process tended to take months, if not years, during which time the prisoners were employed as slaves.

If any of the passengers were from a country covered by treaty, however, their Consuls would promptly petition for their release – and usually it was granted.

On this occasion most of the passengers were Venetian – and their legal status, so far as their captors were concerned, was ambiguous. The Most Serene Republic of Saint Mark had ceased to exist. Something else had taken its place, but it had not yet been recognised by any of the nations of Europe, let alone by the Great Sultan. Nor did it have any consular representation. Venice being under French occupation, it was possible that the French Consul might speak up for them. Possible, but unlikely. Not when they had been fleeing from French control.

Spiridion glanced towards the French delegation. His particular interest was in a man called Xavier Naudé, who was, like Spiridion, keeping well in the background. For he was, like Spiridion, a spy. He had formerly been the leading French agent in Venice, acting on behalf of the notorious Jean Landrieux, head of Bonaparte's intelligence service in Northern Italy. What he was doing in Tripoli was anyone's guess. Mr Lucas had heard that he was here on behalf of the Directory to renew the peace treaty, but he was far too important an agent to be concerned with such an issue. Something else was afoot, and Spiridion intended to find out what it was.

He assumed that Naudé's interest on this particular occasion was in the Venetians. If they were fleeing the French they probably had good reason to do so. Very likely they had considerable funds at their disposal, almost certainly stashed away in a bank vault somewhere. It was as much in the French interest as it was in the Pasha's to lay their hands on it. Naudé did not look particularly interested in the proceedings – he looked quite bored, in fact – but this was the normal expression of a spy.

Spiridion was about to turn away and resume his study of the Pasha when Naudé's expression changed. It was nothing dramatic and he had it under control in an instant, but not before Spiridion had noticed. It had been an expression of surprise – and something more. He had seen someone in the crowd, someone he knew. Still looking, he leaned his head towards the French Consul standing next to him and murmured something in his ear.

Spiridion followed the direction of his gaze – and the shock of recognition drove every other thought from his head.

He was astonished now that he had missed her. Perhaps someone had moved, or she had been brought forward. Yes, that was it, they had brought her forward to the front of the crowd of prisoners, and now Spiridion could detect the quiver of interest that ran through the room. More than a quiver. It was like the sudden change of temperature that heralds an earthquake or an approaching storm. For though her face was without the artifice of rouge or powder and her hair was unkempt, she was stunningly beautiful.

And then there was an audible gasp of astonishment.

For the court official had read out her name and rank.

'Sister Caterina Caresini, Deputy Prioress of the Convent of San Paolo di Mare in Venice.'

The fact that Spiridion shared this astonishment was not because of her beauty. He had seen her before, many times, and though he was not inured to it, nor indifferent, he viewed it with the same circumspection as he might the beauty of a tigress, or a bird of prey. Nor was it because she was a nun. He had known that, too.

The reason for Spiridion's interest, and almost certainly that of Naudé, was that in her previous existence, Suora Caterina Caserini had been the foremost British agent in Venice.

Chapter Four

Of Apes and Swallows

---

*I*t was the final week of October and Nathan was watching the last of the swallows heading out towards Africa. At least, he had been told they were the last, for the weather had grown noticeably cooler over the past few days, and for the first time on his afternoon walk, though the sky was clear, he wore an overcoat – a Spanish army greatcoat that he had purchased from one of the local stores. He suspected its previous owner had died, possibly during one of the long sieges to which the outpost was prone, but there were no suspicious holes or obvious bloodstains to cause him embarrassment in fashionable circles, inasmuch as these existed upon the Rock of Gibraltar.

Nathan had been here for nigh on three months. At first he had been confined to his quarters in the Moorish castle, now used almost exclusively as a prison, but the

Lieutenant Governor – General O'Hara – had generously conceded him the freedom of the peninsula, at least between the hours of sunrise and sunset, in return for his parole.

There was little chance, in any case, of escape. From his perch on the highest point of the Rock, Nathan had a perfect view of the surrounding area – most of which was sea. The Bay of Gibraltar lay to the west, with the port of Algeciras, almost lost in the haze; the Alboran Sea to the east; and the Strait of Gibraltar to the south: very still for once and very blue, like shot silk under the crisp autumnal sky, and a distant smudge on the horizon that could be cloud – or Africa.

Where the swallows went.

To the north, much closer, was the great Spanish fortress of San Felipe, whose battlements and towers stretched across the mile or so of land joining the Rock to the mainland. A barrier of stone and iron, armed for war. Gibraltar had been in British hands now since 1704, and under an almost constant state of siege. But every attack had failed, broken on the guns and ramparts of the invincible Rock.

'I expect you think we are all mad,' Nathan remarked to his solitary companion, who had found something of interest behind his ear and quite sensibly put it into his mouth. 'Fighting to the death over a chunk of rock that you cannot even eat.'

There was no reply. His companion was not inclined to comment on the affairs of men, though his silence, accompanied by a certain look from under his heavy eyelids, could be eloquent at times. Although Nathan had twice referred to him as 'Johnny', and once, more formally, as 'Sir John', he was, in fact, an ape. A Barbary ape from Africa. Mature, male, and usually morose, though he had his more amiable moments when there was food at his disposal.

Nathan had named him after the Admiral – Sir John Jervis – less on account of his temperament than his appearance, though in truth, it was not a resemblance that many others would have noted, and in any case, Sir John – the Admiral – had lately been ennobled and taken the title Earl St Vincent, after the battle he had won. But the ape had thus far made no complaint at the comparison. Or even to being called an ape when he was, in fact, a monkey or macaque.

This information, and indeed Nathan's recent knowledge of swallows and suchlike, had been imparted to him by his only other regular associate on the island, the garrison chaplain Dr Moll who was a keen naturalist and ornithologist and who was wont to accompany him on these walks, when not about his duties.

He had informed Nathan that the swallows, which had been landing on the Rock for some weeks past, had in all likelihood flown from England, and that contrary to general belief, it was their normal practice to winter in Africa, returning to more northerly shores in the spring.

Nathan had not previously given much consideration to the travel arrangements of the swallow, nor any other kind of bird, but he had watched them as a child, swooping across the skies over Sussex in pursuit of small insects, and he had noted their sudden disappearance at the end of the summer. He had supposed they hibernated, like bats, possibly in barns or hollow trees, a belief widely shared by most country folk of his acquaintance, although old Abe Eldridge, who had been his main informant in such matters when he was a child, claimed that they spent the winter under water, either in the mud at the bottom of a pond or among the rocks off the Sussex coast. He based this theory on his observations as a shepherd on the Sussex Downs, having seen them diving into the sea many times, he said, and sometimes finding their bodies washed up on the shore during the months of autumn. And as if this were not enough, his view was shared by no less an authority than the Bishop of Chichester, who had suspended the creatures in a fish bowl by way of an experiment to see how long they could hold their breath, and had declared that they went into a kind of comatose state, very like hibernation, that could last some considerable time.

Dr Moll had ridiculed these suggestions. Far from spending the coldest months of the year at the bottom of the English Channel, or a pond, or even the Bishop's fish bowl, they headed for the tropics, he claimed, flying across France and Spain and choosing the shortest sea crossings, usually at the Straits of Dover and Gibraltar, until they reached Africa.

During his stay on the Rock, Dr Moll had watched great flocks of them as they arrived from the north in the early autumn, and then proceeded southward across the Strait, making the return journey in the months of April and May when the skies over England were once more filled with sunshine and insects, or at least insects.

'But how do you know the birds come from England?' Nathan had challenged him, early in their acquaintance.

Well, of course, he didn't, the chaplain had confessed; it was purely hypothesis, though based on detailed records kept by naturalists in England, France and Spain during the years of peace. They had noted that every year, in early September, great flocks of birds, including swallows, could be seen heading out to sea across the Straits of Dover in the direction of France. And French naturalists had reported the arrival of similar flocks about an hour or so later in the Pas de Calais.

It was possible, of course, that the English birds dived into the sea and the French birds took their place, but informed opinion considered this unlikely. Nor did they stay in the region of Calais for more than a day or two. Usually they resumed their journey within a matter of hours – and were tracked by dedicated ornithologists across France and Spain to the Reverend Moll's own perch on the Rock of Gibraltar.

Unfortunately the chaplain had been unable to find reliable correspondents who could report on their safe arrival in Morocco, and chart their subsequent progress across the desert. But it was his belief that they continued flying south until they came to the more fertile regions of Central Africa where the vegetation – and the insect life – was more to their liking.

Nathan was not entirely convinced by this hypothesis, any more than he had as a child been convinced by Old Abe's. It seemed a preposterous notion that a small bird with a brain the size of half a walnut could navigate across 1,000 miles of land and sea when he himself, with all his advantages, was barely able to make the same journey with a compass and sextant and the best charts the

Admiralty could provide. And even then, as often as not, he got it wrong.

Another thought occurred to him, equally wonderful, though somewhat disturbing. He had always assumed that the swallows and other birds he saw in the skies of Sussex were English. As English as he was. And presumably that those on the other side of the English Channel were French, as committed as their human counterparts to ceaseless enmity. But if Dr Moll was right they were of a more international breed, flying freely across borders and making their homes wherever they pleased. How wonderful was that! What freedom! To flit about the globe and settle where you pleased, and give no thought to borders or the restrictions of language and custom and the horrors of war. And how fascinating to think that the very swallows he had seen in the skies of Gibraltar had been swooping over the fields and downs of Sussex only a few days previously. They might even have perched on the trees surrounding Windover House, his family home in Wilmington.

It was a pity they could not be trained to carry a letter.

Nathan had received scant news from home. Just one despatch from his mother, written on the occasion of his twenty-ninth birthday, on 1 August, and delivered a little over a fortnight ago. Her news was not entirely welcome, but then news imparted by his mother rarely was.

He took it out of his pocket now – his last surviving link with home – and opened it with care, for the folds were fragile with overuse.

It started promisingly enough. She had paid off most of her debts and was no longer troubled by the bailiffs. She had even taken on an extra servant *to relieve the burden on poor old Izzy* and had quite reconciled herself to living in Soho, *which is not quite as deprived or as like to the Wilderness as I had first imagined.*

It might be imagined – and was no doubt stated in no uncertain terms by several of her acquaintance – that Lady Catherine Peake, having been born and bred in New York, and thus being no stranger to the Wilderness, had no business to be particular about living in Soho, or indeed any other area of London, deprived or otherwise. But she was the daughter of wealthy Huguenot immigrants who had made their fortune in trade, and for most of her life she had lived in the lap of luxury. At the time of her marriage to Nathan's father she was one of the most sought-after heiresses in New York, and the Peakes of Wilmington, though nowhere near as rich, were by no means poor. Nathan's father, though a mere sea Captain at the time of their meeting, was himself the proud possessor of some 3,000 acres of prime Sussex downland.

Unhappily, the marriage had not endured. It had foundered, Lady Catherine was fond of saying, upon the rocks of political incompatibility: she supported the rebellious American colonists while he did his best to repress them in the service of King George. Since when, he had retired from the sea and devoted himself to the rearing of sheep, whilst Nathan's mother gave her life to politics and fashion – which were not, apparently, so very far removed.

Indeed, for a time, Lady Catherine – or Kitty as she was known to her intimates – had run one of the most fashionable political salons in London, though tarnished in some eyes by its association with such degenerates as the Prince of Wales and Charles James Fox and other members of His Majesty's Disloyal Opposition. But the war between France and the other great powers of Europe, and the inevitable disruption to commerce, had played havoc with the family fortune. Several of her father's ships had been seized by one or other of the warring parties on suspicion of running contraband, and to make matters worse, Lady Catherine's London bank had collapsed, and while this had not plunged her into absolute poverty, it had obliged certain economies of scale.

She had moved out of the house in St James's Park and into a smaller and far less fashionable residence in Soho Square with a dwindling band of servants and followers. But her debts had mounted. The last time Nathan had visited her she was under siege by the bailiffs and had retained just one servant – the redoubtable Izzy, whom she mentioned in her letter, and one follower – her friend Mrs Imlay, better known as Mary Wollstonecraft, author of the infamous treatise *A Vindication of the Rights of Women*, who had also fallen upon hard times.

Nathan had been obliged to come to their rescue, using the proceeds of a profitable cruise in the Mediterranean to pay off his mother's debts and providing sufficient funds to keep her, if not in her former splendour, at least off the streets. Lady Catherine, albeit reluctant to share in the profits of what she was pleased to call 'piracy', had managed to overcome these scruples to such an extent that Nathan was now rendered almost as penniless as she had been.

Although he tried not to resent this, he was somewhat irked to read of her continuing involvement in opposition politics.

For although Lady Catherine no longer mixed with the likes of Prince George and his friend Mr Fox, she continued to give comfort to those of the King's enemies as could bring themselves to venture into Soho. Among those who had enjoyed the benefits of her patronage – or Nathan's, as he thought in his crabbier moments – were such reprobates as Francis Place, Thomas Hardy, William Blake, the brewer Samuel Whitbread and the poets Wordsworth and Coleridge, whenever they laid aside their verse and came to London in search of more practical nourishment.

Consequently, the greater part of his mother's letter was taken up with an account of the present grievances of these worthies and their vigorous if vain attempts to bring down His Majesty's Government.

London, she represented, was in a state of siege. Not, as Nathan might have imagined, by the French, or even the mutineers at the Nore, but by hired mercenaries in the pay of 'the Scoundrel Pitt' and his 'Devil's Cabinet', who were bent on suppressing the people's liberties and reducing them to the status of serfs or eunuchs, according to whichever condition the Satraps of Tyranny favoured at the time.

Using the excuse of imminent invasion by the French, His Majesty's Government had arrested many of Lady Catherine's friends and subjected the rest, including herself, to relentless persecution. They found themselves under constant surveillance by spies and informers, she told Nathan; their houses were raided, their confidential papers seized and their servants threatened and abused. They were already in fear of their lives because of the hysteria worked up by the popular press; now leaked documents had revealed that, in the event of a French landing, all known critics of the government were to be rounded up and shot.

Nathan had read this intelligence with more scepticism than alarm, for he knew how much his mother valued her notoriety. But it was not reassuring to know that she was seen as a prominent critic of His Majesty's Government. Apart from his fears for her safety, it could not help his own tarnished reputation.

Indeed, there was little in the letter that could console him for his present misfortunes. And very little of what one might call the personal, until the final page.

Then it came.

He turned to it now, smoothing the creases and screwing up his eyes in the still bright, if ineffectual October sunshine.

I am sorry to rattle on so much about Politics, my dear, knowing of your Indifference to such matters, but now that Sara has moved in with Godwin and Mary, I have little else to distract me and indeed have become a veritable Hermit, alone with Izzy and nothing but the occasional bottle of gin to comfort me.

Sara. It was the only mention of her in the entire letter – and so casual a reference that Nathan was persuaded his mother must have written about her in an earlier missive which had failed to reach him. She must know what Sara meant to him, for even if Nathan had not troubled to inform her, Mary almost certainly would have.

They had met in Paris in '93, when Nathan had been sent there on an assignment by William Pitt. She was the widow of a French aristocrat – an ancient roué called Alexander Tour de l'Auvergne, Count of Turenne, who had died in exile with the French court at Koblenz – and she and Nathan had become lovers, only to be separated by the politics to which his mother thought him 'indifferent'. Sara had endured a great many hardships and had narrowly escaped death on the guillotine, but now she and her young son, Alex, had found refuge in England.

Though Nathan had not formally asked her to marry him, there was an understanding between them. But he had heard nothing from her for almost a year.

He was certain she would have written, if only to assure him of her wellbeing, and had persuaded himself that her letters must have gone astray – his own movements being somewhat erratic – and, of course, any that had been sent to the *Unicorn* in his absence would have been lost with the ship.

But it had been a nagging concern. And now there was this solitary, infuriatingly brief reference to her in his mother's letter.

It was so typical of his mother that it was only with the greatest restraint that he had prevented himself from tearing the letter up in a fury of frustration and scattering the pieces to the wind.

Instead, he had carried it around with him ever since, reading it over and over again and tormenting himself with his imaginings. What did his mother mean by *now that Sara has moved in with Godwin and Mary?*

By Mary, she must mean Mary Wollstonecraft, who

had known Sara in Paris. But who was this Godwin? Could he have taken up with Mary? It seemed unlikely, for poor Mary was fatally attached to an American called Gilbert Imlay, who was, not to put too fine a point on it, an adventurer, a scoundrel and a spy. He and Mary had gone through some form of marriage ceremony, of doubtful legality, in Paris, and they had a child – little Fanny. But when Mary had discovered that Imlay was involved with another woman – an actress from a strolling theatre company – she had tried to kill herself. Twice. If she had now taken up with another man – this Godwin – he could hardly be worse than Imlay. But what part had Sara to play in the ménage?

Nathan knew he had no right to be jealous, but he could not help himself.

Not that he could do anything about it, of course, stuck here on the Rock of Gibraltar, with the apes.

There had been no news of his court martial, nor indeed of any formal charge brought against him, either by the Admiral or anyone else. It was the opinion of Dr Moll that no such charge would be brought. There was a widespread feeling in the fleet that he had been made a scapegoat for the failure of the attack on Cadiz. And that far from being guilty of cowardice or mutiny, he had acquitted himself with considerable merit. In the chaplain's opinion, the Admiral would not risk putting his judgement to the public inspection of a court martial. Doubtless, after leaving Nathan to kick his heels for a few weeks on the Rock of Gibraltar, he would quietly permit him to resume his duties.

But the chaplain knew a great deal less about Admirals than he did about swallows. And this particular example

of the species was as well-known for his obduracy as for
his severity especially when he considered his authority to
be in question. Besides, Nathan had no duties to resume,
not as the Captain of a ship. He might stay kicking his
heels in Gibraltar until the end of the war.

And if he was not guilty of cowardice, he could certainly
be accused of disrespect.

He had taken the reluctant step of sending a letter to
the Admiral, expressing his contrition for having written
to him in such a manner. Thus far, there had been no
reply. And as the weeks dragged into months, he began to
feel he had been forgotten.

These melancholy thoughts were interrupted by the
report of a cannon. Nathan stood up and walked to the
edge of the cliff. He saw the situation at once. A vessel had
entered the Bay of Algeciras and appeared to be heading
towards the Rock, a cloud of smoke in her wake indicating
that she had just fired one of her sternchasers. She was
under a full press of sail to catch what little there was of
the wind, but her obvious difficulty in this regard had
attracted the attention of the Spanish gunboats based in
Algeciras and they had put out to intercept her.

Another gun – and another puff of smoke from her
stern. Then an answering discharge from the gunboats.
Three of them. No, four, for there was another emerging
from the haze to the west.

A great cloud of gulls rose from the Rock and set up a
riot of complaint, and from down below among the
fortifications along the harbour, Nathan heard the sound
of a bugle and saw the red- and blue-coated figures of the
garrison hurrying to their posts.

He was joined at the top of the cliff by Sir John and several of his fellows, who had emerged from their haunts within the Rock to watch the developing battle.

'I think it is the *Fly*,' Nathan instructed them tersely. The *Fly* was the regular packet which plied between Gibraltar and Lisbon with despatches and mail and the occasional passenger. It also brought news from the Mediterranean fleet off Cadiz. Every time he saw her, Nathan hoped she would bring an order for his release. Or at least news from family and friends.

'She is not going to make it,' he informed his companions, for it was clear, from the vantage of his great height, that the gunboats were gaining on her. 'She will have to come up into the wind and bring her broadside to bear.'

The apes bowed to his greater expertise; certainly there was no observable sign of dissent. Sir John nodded gravely, and his followers emitted a series of frenzied hoots in anticipation of the manoeuvre that Nathan had predicted. He did not disclose to them his serious doubt as to whether the broadside of the *Fly* would be sufficient a discouragement to four determined aggressors.

Fortunately, help was at hand. Two British gunboats were issuing from the harbour to provide an escort. Nathan watched as they came up on each side of the brig, engaging her assailants with the 24-pounders in their bows. After a few more shots for the sake of appearances, the Spanish withdrew, helped on their way by a series of scornful hoots from the audience upon the heights – and the *Fly* scurried, with a maidenly swirl of her skirts, into the shelter of the harbour.

Nathan took a polite leave of his associates, and made his way down into the town via the Douglas Path. Even if the packet had letters for him they were unlikely to be delivered for at least a day or two, but she would almost certainly have brought some more general news from the fleet. And besides, it would soon be sunset, when he was obliged to return to his adequate, but by no means cheering accommodation in the Moorish castle.

He was in no particular hurry, however, and stopped to exchange pleasantries with two of the local labour force he encountered along the way, for he was putting his time on the Rock to good use by learning Spanish. So he was still some way from the foot of the hill when he saw the tall, gangling figure of the Reverend Dr Henry Moll climbing towards him. His face betrayed a measure of anxiety and he was out of breath.

'I am sent by the Governor to find you,' he announced. 'There is a gentleman come by the packet – an official of the Admiralty in London – who is most anxious to make your acquaintance. He is waiting for you at Governor House.'

Nathan tried to question him further but Dr Moll, normally the most garrulous individual Nathan had ever encountered, appeared strangely reluctant to engage in conversation. All he would say was that the Governor was in 'a rare state' and had been ready to call out the guard until he himself had volunteered to find Nathan and bring him in.

Then, just as they entered the High Street, he said: 'Be mindful of what you say, and whatever happens, do not lose your temper.'

Chapter Five

The Grand Design

—◆—

*G*overnor House had once been a convent, built for the Franciscans during the Spanish occupation. Nathan had been here on two previous occasions to dine with the Governor, who had until now showed him every courtesy, having made it clear that he thought the charges against Nathan were absurd. But there was another, more personal reason for his sympathy. They had both been prisoners of the French in Paris during the time of the Terror: Nathan on suspicion of being a British spy, General O'Hara after being taken captive during the Siege of Toulon. For a time they had even shared the same prison – the old Luxembourg Palace on the edge of Paris.

But there was no sign of the Governor now, only one of his less charming aides, who was pacing at the main entrance, clearly anxious for Nathan's delivery and accompanied by two Marine sentries with muskets and bayonets. His greeting was terse and he hurried Nathan through the corridors and left him to kick his heels in a small, dark room with bars on the windows while he scurried off to 'see if the Commissioner is ready to receive you'.

Nathan was left to brood on the significance of this development. It was clearly not auspicious. Fortunately he did not have long to wait. Within a few minutes the aide was back.

'Follow me,' he snapped. It took all Nathan's self-control and his memory of the chaplain's injunction not to kick the man.

Another brisk march through the corridors and up a flight of stairs, the Marines clumping along behind in their heavy boots, as if Nathan might attempt escape. The aide knocked on a door and upon being given an invitation to enter, ushered the prisoner in before him.

'Ah. Captain Peake.'

It was the man he had met in the Admiral's flagship. The *représentant en mission* with a face like the guillotine. Mr Scrope.

He was standing at the fireplace, still wearing his travelling cape and taking some refreshment, but at Nathan's entrance he crossed to the solitary desk and sat down, waving Nathan into one of two chairs set before it. His cape was a little stained with salt spray from his passage on the *Fly* but he still looked like a man who did not get out much.

'I had expected to find you at the castle,' he said, 'but I am told you are in the habit of taking a stroll at this time of the afternoon.'

Nathan chose to ignore the sarcasm and answered with his own.

'I take what exercise I can,' he said. 'In the circumstances.'

The meagre fire in the grate did little to take the chill off the atmosphere. Unless Nathan was much mistaken, this was known as the Nun's Room. He had been shown it by the Governor on his last visit here. According to legend, it contained the ghost of a nun who had been bricked up alive in one of the walls as punishment for attempting to run off with her lover – one of the Franciscan friars.

'We reserve it for our more unwelcome guests,' the Governor had informed him, with a smile.

And yet the Commissioner's opening words were encouraging.

'I am sent by their lordships to enquire into your recent report concerning French intentions in the Eastern Mediterranean,' he began, fixing a pair of spectacles upon his nose and searching among the papers set out on the desk. 'Specifically, that General Bonaparte intends to invade Egypt – and use it as a stepping stone for an attack upon British India.' He looked up and fixed Nathan with his penetrating stare.

'That is correct,' said Nathan. It was six months since he had sent the report but the wheels of the Admiralty moved slowly at times. It was not too late to act upon it. Bonaparte was, so far as he knew, still occupied with the Austrians in Northern Italy.

'And the source of this information was a Colonel Junot, according to your report, an officer on the staff of General Bonaparte in Italy?'

'He was under the impression that I was an American sea captain by the name of Turner,' Nathan felt it necessary to explain. 'And sympathetic to the cause of the Revolution.'

Scrope still looked puzzled. 'But I do not understand why he would disclose such a confidential piece of information to a mere acquaintance – do you?'

'He was under a sense of obligation to me,' Nathan pointed out. 'I had – inadvertently – saved his life. It is all in the report I sent to their lordships.'

What was *not* in the report was the fact that he had saved the life of General Bonaparte, too – when the latter was a penniless nobody in Paris. But this was not something that Nathan wished Scrope, or anyone else at the Admiralty, to know about. Bonaparte had achieved almost demonic status in London. His victories in Italy had shattered the coalition against the French. They had wrecked Pitt's careful diplomacy, left Britain almost isolated, and France as the dominant power on the continent. Nathan would hardly achieve the thanks of a grateful nation by admitting that he had once saved the man's life. Even inadvertently.

Scrope was shaking his head. 'And when did he say this remarkable plan would go into effect?'

'As soon as Bonaparte concluded his campaign in Italy. He planned to use the Ionian Islands as his base, and the Venetian fleet to ferry his troops to Egypt.'

'And then march overland to India.'

'That was the plan, yes.'

To march in the footsteps of Alexander the Great. That was how Junot had put it.

'And this had met with the approval of the Directory in Paris?'

'Apparently so.'

'So it would surprise you to know that Bonaparte has negotiated a truce with the Austrian Emperor, shortly to be announced as a peace treaty, and is now in Paris preparing to march – not on India, as you suggest, but on London.'

Nathan stared at him. 'Yes,' he began uncertainly, 'it would, but—'

'And it would be considerably to his advantage,' Scrope continued, 'if a large portion of the British fleet was despatched to the Mediterranean – in the belief that he was planning to invade Egypt.'

So that was it. Nathan struggled to take in the implications.

'You met this Colonel Junot in the Veneto, I understand?' Scrope was shuffling about among his papers.

'Yes. That is also in my report.'

'Pray remind me – what precisely was your business in Venice?'

'I was under orders to enter into negotiations for the surrender of the Venetian fleet – to prevent it from falling into the hands of the French.'

Scrope observed him in his clinical way. 'Orders from whom?'

Nathan was taken aback. 'You must surely know.'

'If I knew, why would I enquire?'

'But their lordships must be aware of the nature of my mission to Venice!'

Scrope said nothing. The room had grown darker. It

was difficult to read his expression. In his black cape he looked like a hooded crow, a raven.

'I had a direct order from the Viceroy of Corsica, Sir Gilbert Elliot,' Nathan insisted. 'Given me in the presence of Commodore Nelson, who was then my commanding officer. I had assumed that their lordships knew of this. And that if they did not, then Admiral St Vincent had been informed.'

'And these orders were given you in writing?'

'Yes, but . . .' Scrope inclined his head in a pretence of patient enquiry '. . . naturally I did not take them with me to Venice.'

'So where are they now?'

Nathan was beginning to lose his temper. He recalled Dr Moll's advice. 'I left them in my cabin in the *Unicorn*, but—'

'Ah yes, the *Unicorn*.' Scrope turned over another paper. 'Which we were given to understand was sunk with all hands off the Rock of Montecristo.'

'What do you mean "given to understand"?'

'We now have information that she was taken by the French.'

Nathan stared at him. 'But – it was reported that she had run upon the rocks. That – that she was fleeing from a Spanish squadron and—'

'That is as may be. The details of the action are confusing. All we know for certain is that the *Unicorn* is now in the hands of the French. In Corfu, to be precise.'

'In Corfu?' Nathan tried to make sense of this. He had been totally convinced that she had been lost on the rocks of Montecristo. Lost with all hands.

'And her crew?'

'Are held as prisoners of war. Those that have not already been exchanged.'

So they were alive. All those men he had thought were lost. Men he had served with for the best part of two years.

'Where . . .' he began, but then he took in the last part of Scrope's reply. 'There has been an exchange of prisoners, you say?'

'Of certain of the officers, including your first lieutenant, Mr Duncan, who was in command during your unfortunate absence.'

His unfortunate absence. Nathan let this go for the moment. 'And the others?'

'I have no idea,' Scrope replied indifferently. 'They are not my concern. However, I am told that Lieutenant Duncan had no knowledge of your reasons for going to Venice.'

The significance of this was lost on Nathan.

'But why should he? My orders were marked *Most Secret.* I had specific instructions not to discuss them with anyone – not even my first lieutenant.'

'So it is to be assumed that – if they exist – the French now have them?'

'I suppose they must, but what do you mean, "if they exist"?'

'I mean that it would be difficult for you to *prove* that they exist in a court of law,' Scrope replied smoothly, 'if they are in the hands of the French.'

'I am sure Admiral Nelson can confirm the order,' Nathan assured him coldly.

'Unfortunately, we are unable to consult with the Admiral at present, the seriousness of his injuries having obliged him to return to England.'

'His injuries?'

'Admiral Nelson was badly wounded in the attack on Tenerife. It was necessary to amputate his right arm.'

'No.' It was a groan deep in Nathan's throat. 'But he is recovered?'

'As to that, I cannot say. But he is a very sick man and is unlikely to continue in active service. It is certainly impossible to consult with him at present about any orders he may or may not have given to a junior officer in Corsica over a year ago.'

The shock of this news deprived Nathan of rational thought for a moment. He put his hand to his head. Dimly he was aware that Scrope was still talking.

'However, these "confidential orders" – whether they were given or not – are not the most pressing of the matters that concern us here. What concerns us is the advice you gave to their lordships that the French were contemplating an invasion of Egypt as the preliminary to an attack on India. Their "Grand Design", as you called it in your report.'

Nathan looked up. 'You think that I was duped?'

'Either that, or you were a willing partner in the conspiracy.'

It took a moment for this to sink in.

'You are accusing me of being a French agent?' Nathan's voice was dangerously calm. Even in the gloom he could see the hint of a smirk on the man's face. It was enough. He launched himself forward.

He was not precisely sure what was in his mind. Probably nothing more than to seize the man by the scruff of his neck and shake him like a rat. But the desk proved a serious obstacle to this intent. That, and the fact that the Commissioner, in his panic, threw himself to one side, upsetting his chair and precipitating himself to the floor. The inevitable delay while Nathan climbed over the desk to get at him permitted him to utter a frantic cry for help.

The guards must have been posted at the door. They came crashing in with the Governor's aide close behind. Nathan found himself in the ludicrous posture of standing on a desk while two Lobsters levelled their bayonets at him. Scrope climbed unsteadily to his feet. He pointed a shaking hand towards Nathan.

'Do you see this man!' It was clear that they did, even in the gathering gloom, for Nathan's position was somewhat exposed. But the Commissioner repeated the question, his voice rising hysterically. 'Do you see him? He tried to kill me!'

'Nonsense. I intended only to teach you some manners.' Nathan climbed down from the desk, taking care to avoid the bayonets.

'Watch him!' Scrope urged the guards. 'Do not take your eyes off him for a moment. If he moves, kill him.'

'This is ridiculous.' Nathan appealed to the Governor's aide, who looked at something of a loss.

'What am I to do with him?' he enquired of the Commissioner.

'Take him back to the prison, and hold him under close confinement.' Scrope was still tugging at his collar, his voice trembling.

'On what charge?' Nathan fought to keep his own voice steady.

'Treason,' declared Scrope, with all the considerable venom at his command. He flapped a hand in dismissal. 'Take him away.'

Chapter Six

The Division of the Spoils

———◆◆◆———

Caterina had played a great many parts in her life, but never a maiden in distress. Cleopatra was more in her line, or La Donna di Garbo in the play by Goldoni. The haughty beauty dangling her lovers on a string.

But vulnerability was not beyond her capabilities as an actor.

She took as her model St Catherine of Alexandria, her namesake in the famous painting by Caravaggio, leaning against the wheel they were about to break her upon. She did not have a wheel, but the chains helped.

She had been advised by her captor, Murad Rais, on what to expect.

'They will call out your name,' he said, 'and the foreign consuls will have an opportunity to speak up on your behalf.'

He thought there was still a Venetian Consul in Tripoli. But if there was not, then as a woman of God – he smiled sardonically – she might appeal to the Catholic Fathers.

Caterina knew of the Catholic Fathers. They were one of the charities supported by her convent with the profits of their various commercial enterprises. They worked among Christian slaves on the Barbary Coast and raised money to buy their freedom if they had no resources of their own.

It would be only just for them to donate something on her account.

She did not possess the formal habit of a nun – it was not quite the style in the Convent of San Paolo di Mare – but she wore the most modest of her robes and ensured that the crucifix was displayed prominently on her bosom. She also carried her rosary, though not solely for the purposes of deception. They had taken her purse but the diamonds were still concealed beneath their black blobs of wax.

Louisa stood next to her, similarly attired. Caterina had considered casting her as a nun, or at least a novice, but as the entire crew and most of the passengers knew her as the American Consul's daughter, one of them was bound to blab. And if her captors thought Louisa's father had the means of paying a large ransom to have her restored intact, it might protect her virtue rather more effectively than the cloth.

She had intended to position both Louisa and herself in the front ranks of the prisoners where they could not fail to be seen, but she had not reckoned on the misguided honour of Captain Fry. This tiresome man, not content with having plunged them into this catastrophe in the first place, now ensured that the female passengers were corralled within a circle of his officers and crew, as if to protect them from the prurient eyes and grasping hands of the natives.

So to begin with she was hemmed in by broad male shoulders and obliged to crane her neck to see what was going on. She noted the foreigners, of course, by their distinctive dress. And the priests. Four of them, in a huddle near the back of the hall in their black cloaks.

When she heard the official call out her name, Caterina grabbed Louisa by the arm and began to force her way through the male phalanx, making judicious use of her elbows and dragging her chains after her.

She was about to make a direct appeal to the Catholic Fathers when she became aware that someone else had already appealed on her behalf. It did not take her more than a moment or two to realise that it was the French Consul.

Although the discussion was conducted in Turkish, she caught a few words of the translation that was afforded for the Consul's benefit. He was apparently claiming that the Venetian passengers should be regarded as French citizens, on the grounds that the French Army was presently in occupation of the city and the new government had yet to be recognised. Initially, Caterina was inclined to favour this approach – for the French Consul in Tripoli was unlikely to know of her activities in Venice on behalf of his country's enemies. But then she noticed the man standing next to him.

It was a considerable jolt. For she had last seen him at

the head of a mob of Revolutionists on the Piazza San Marco.

His name was Xavier Naudé and he had been one of the leading French agents in Venice.

But what was he doing here – in Tripoli?

For a moment Caterina wondered if he had followed her here. But it was impossible. He had no means of knowing she had been taken by corsairs. Unless he had arranged it.

It said much for Caterina's high opinion of herself – and of him – that she seriously considered this possibility.

For the last six months they had been deadly adversaries. Caterina on behalf of the Venetian Patriot Party, Naudé for the pro-French faction. He posed as a French diplomat but everyone knew he was a spy – an agent for General Bonaparte whose army was then sweeping through Northern Italy. She was not sure if Naudé knew of her own work as an agent for the British and the Austrians, but it had to be regarded as likely. And even if he did not, he knew her as a dedicated enemy of France.

He was a youngish man of thirty or so, and strikingly handsome. Perhaps she could appeal to his sense of honour. Honour among spies.

Better not. Better by far to put her trust in the Church.

But the Church did not appear to be interested. There were mutterings among the four priests but no attempt to intercede for her. But then, of course, she remembered that they were a French Order and no doubt susceptible to the pressure of their countrymen, even since the Revolution. The Papacy itself had been forced to make peace with

Bonaparte and pay an enormous tribute in gold and works of art to avoid occupation.

Caterina considered whether to throw herself at the feet of the Reverend Fathers and appeal for sanctuary. She was quite capable of doing so. The chains were somewhat of a hindrance but they could only add to the effect.

But now the Pasha had decided to intervene. He was in consultation with one of his officials. The Grand Keyha was invited to approach the throne.

Looking about the crowded room, Caterina caught the eye of her captor, Peter Lisle – or Murad Rais as his men called him. He looked troubled.

He had warned her about the Pasha. Not a man to be crossed, he had said. But at the same time he had told her that if she was to be taken into custody for a time, and this was almost a certainty, then the Pasha's harem was not the worst place to be.

'And what is?' she had enquired coolly.

'Well, it is a lot better than being farmed out to some Bedouin goat thief,' he confided, 'and spending the next few years in a tent or on the back of a camel.'

She agreed that this was not a future she could look forward to with any equanimity.

'So your conscience would be at an ease, were I to end up as one of the Pasha's concubines?' she goaded him.

'Who said I had a conscience?' he retorted. 'I just want you to fetch a good price. But no doubt the wives will see to it that you're kept out of the Pasha's clutches,' he added, puzzlingly.

Finally an announcement was made. Again it was in Turkish but this time a translation was given in French.

The Pasha would consult with the Divan, but his interim judgement was that when the *Saratoga* had sailed, the passengers had been citizens of Venice. The Doge having abdicated, the Republic no longer existed in its previous form and no treaty had been made with its successor. Therefore the passengers were prisoners of war and at the disposal of the Pasha. The men would be held in the dungeons under the castle, and the women and children would be housed in the Pasha's own harem until a figure was agreed for their release.

It could, Caterina supposed, have been a lot worse.

Chapter Seven

The Prisoner of the Tower

———◆———

They gave Nathan a room in the Tower of Homage. Four paces long and two paces wide with a single window, barred, through which he could see a small patch of sky.

And not so much as an ape for company.

Otherwise, as prisons go, it was not unbearable. There was a wooden pallet with a straw mattress, even a table and a chair, one bucket for washing, another for his more basic requirements. Some would call it luxury.

The first night there he thought about all the other prisons he had been in. A fair tally, given that he was still under thirty. A hardened criminal might have blushed. He rated them in order of preference, as some men rate inns, or the women they have known.

There was the Luxembourg in Paris, where he had

spent three months during the Terror. Formerly the Luxembourg Palace, it had been built for Queen Marie de Medici early in the seventeenth century and still retained traces of its former grandeur; it even had a fountain in one of the courtyards where you could bathe or wash your clothes, and a theatre which had been turned into the prison store. You could buy most things there if you had the money, even the use of an old mattress and a few minutes with your loved one. The main problem with the Luxembourg was that for most of the prisoners, it was a staging post on the way to the guillotine, which tended to take the shine off things.

Even so, it was better than the Grand Châtelet, the ancient fortress on the river guarding the Pont au Change, where he had spent a few wretched nights shortly after his arrival in Paris, or the *Maison d'Arret*, where he had been hung in chains and flogged with a cane.

The Bridewell in Holborn, where he had whiled away a night after a duel in Lincoln's Inn Fields, was hardly worth a mention. Nor was the cell in Fort Felipe in Cuba, where he had been detained by the rebel slaves known as the Army of Lucumi. But by far the worst was the Doge's Prison in Venice, his last experience of prison life before this. He had been given one of the cells on the ground floor, below sea level, always damp and half-filled with water when the tide was in, sewer rats when it was not.

His present accommodation probably rated the best so far, had it not been for the charge of treason hanging over him.

And the loneliness. For he was allowed no visitors at all. Not even the prison chaplain. If Dr Moll had tried to see him, Nathan had no knowledge of it. During his time on parole, he had encountered other prisoners in the corridors or the courtyard where they were allowed to exercise – French or Spanish naval officers for the most part, awaiting an exchange. But not now. Now, in his new role as enemy of the state, he was held in total isolation, like a plague victim in the *lazaretto*. He must be held apart for fear of contagion. He was the prisoner in the tower.

The castle had been built by the Moors, back in the eighth century when Gibraltar was the springboard for the Moslem conquest of Spain. Over the 700 years of Moorish occupation it had grown into a vast fortress. But all that remained when the British took the Rock was the single ornate gatehouse, a few battlements and terraces – and the tower. The Tower of Homage.

Nathan was in a cell near the top. If he pulled himself up by the single bar in the window – which he did at least twenty times a day, for exercise as much as for the view – he could look down into the courtyard, where he was permitted to take the air once a day in the company of two guards. His few comforts – the table, the chair, the buckets – were presumably by order of the Governor, in deference to their shared experience of the Luxembourg. He had even sent a couple of books: the King James Bible and Book Two of Newton's *Principles of Mathematics*. Nathan would have preferred lighter reading, but they helped pass the time.

And there was a great deal of time.

For one who had spent a good part of his life on a ship-of-war, with more than two hundred people crammed into a few hundred feet of space, the loneliness was devastating.

And though a ship-of-war was not unlike a prison at times, you had only to step out onto the upper deck, or climb into the crosstrees, to enter a world of vast horizons. Here, there were just the four walls and the window.

He felt as if he had been buried alive. The panic was like some great beast that shared his tiny cage and threatened to consume him. He had to resort to numerous mental and physical exercises to fight it.

He spent a lot of time thinking.

He thought a lot about Sara. Sara in Paris, Sara in Provence, the short time they had spent on the *Unicorn* together before she left for England.

What was she doing now – and who with?

He reflected that it was not just distance and circumstance that had separated them, but his own inability to come to terms with what she was, or had become. The truth was, he had great difficulty coping with a woman of her maturity and experience – the fact that she had been married before, to an older man who was a notorious roué, and that she had almost certainly been in love with someone else. He wished he could accept that. Dear God, there were worse things one had to accept. But the thought of it was a constant torment to him. A not uncommon failing in men. Which was why most men of his acquaintance chose virgins of unimpeachable reputation and good family, he reflected: young women in their teens, or barely out of them, who could be moulded into the dutiful and charming wives and mothers of their heart's desire, studiously trained to manage a large household but with very little experience of the world outside it. No wonder Fremantle had fallen for Betsy Wynne, a young woman with just enough experience of foreign travel to be deemed romantic, but still, fundamentally, an innocent.

He thought about his own life, and where it had taken him, and what he had learned from it. He thought, time and again, of that conversation in the Veneto with Junot about Bonaparte's plans. Could it be possible that Junot had known he was a British agent and had deliberately set out to deceive him? He could not believe it. It was just possible, he supposed, that someone had given false information to Junot, knowing he would disclose it to Nathan. But then this someone – whoever it was – would have had to know that Nathan was a British naval officer.

He would drive himself mad thinking about it.

Christmas came and went. The Governor sent him a bottle of wine and half a capon.

And so he entered the New Year. 1798. The fifth year of war.

Soon the swallows would be back, flying northward now. He wondered if he would see them in his meagre patch of sky – hunting insects in the fading light of evening, or rising on the air, finding their bearings, if that is what swallows did, as they gathered for the next stage of their journey back to England. Sometimes he lay awake at night and he could have sworn he heard them – the flapping of wings overhead, hundreds of wings, as the birds set off on their journey. Not just swallows and martins, but every species that follows the sun, cleaving the air above his lonely tower. The warblers and flycatchers, nightjars and nightingales, the doves and the raptors, beating the wind with their strident wings, making their way northward, through the night, to England.

And then it would stop. And all he would hear was the silence.

This was his world.

He had attempted to enlarge it, converting his cell into a kind of planetarium, with the principal planets and constellations scratched on the walls with a bone rescued from the Governor's capon. It was executed from memory, for he was a keen astronomer and had, from adolescence, devoted a large proportion of his leisure time to the study of celestial bodies. He was much taken with Newton's concept that their motion was governed by a set of natural laws; that everything moved in a precise and pre-ordained relationship to everything else; that this was also true of objects on Earth – and that an individual was as much governed by these laws as an apple on a tree.

Newton had believed in God. In a Master Creator. But Newton's God was not an interventionist God. He was a God Who had designed the world along rational and universal lines. These principles could be discovered by application, by study, by experiment. They could enable people to pursue their own aims and ambitions in life. But you could not change them, even by prayer.

This had a natural appeal to Nathan, as a mariner, as a navigator, as the Captain of a ship. Sometimes he wondered if 'God' was just a word for the whole complicated system that Newton had defined, and that when he looked at the stars in the sky or in their cruder version on the walls of his cell, he was looking into the eye of God. Or even His brain.

A heresy, no doubt, a blasphemy, even by Newton's standards.

But if Nathan believed in any kind of a Creator, it was in a Creator Who conformed to His own rules, and Who would not change those rules for the convenience or advantage of His creations. The best you could hope for – or pray for – was that you might understand them and use them to your advantage, much the same as the means by which you sailed a ship.

You could not change the ebb and flow of the tide, nor the currents of the sea, any more than you could change the direction of the wind, but you could trim your sails to that wind; you could choose your course; you could make choices based on what you knew of the elements that surrounded you – and hope, and pray, that they were the right ones.

As in sailing, so in life. There were no miracles, only choices.

His problem at the moment was that he had made the wrong choices – in his relationships and in his career. Dashing this way and that, blown by the wind, hither and thither, with no great objective in view, nor even a small one.

How much more sensible to be a swallow. To know where one was going and why. And to go there – to go straight there – with no diversions in pursuit of fame, or wealth, or women. Or in the service of one's country.

At times he was angry. He had done what was required of him, at great risk to life and limb, and they had rewarded him by charging him with treason and locking him up in a prison cell on a rock.

His anger was fairly wide-ranging but there were some individuals for whom he felt a particular resentment. One was Admiral Jervis, or St Vincent, as he now was, who had ordered his arrest, when a severe dressing-down would have been more in order. Then there was Earl Spencer, the First Lord of the Admiralty, who must have launched the enquiry against him – and the Commissioner, Scrope, who had been sent to execute it. But he could not help but think that there were others, in the shadows, who had their own sinister agenda – such as Sir Gilbert Elliot, the former Viceroy of Corsica and a member of the Privy Council. Even William Pitt, the King's chief minister.

It was impossible to believe they could think him a traitor. For what? For reporting what he had heard of French plans to invade Egypt?

Even if the rumour was untrue – even if it had been fed to him deliberately – it did not amount to treason. Rumour was the stuff of intelligence. There must be hundreds of rumours passed on to the British government, from hundreds of informants. It was the job of government to sift through them, to decide which were true and which were false, and to act upon them accordingly. Not to punish the messenger.

Not that this stopped them, of course.

But he could not believe this was why he was in prison.

There had to be something else. Something to do with his mother, perhaps, and her dissident friends in London.

Nathan had always tended to be dismissive of Lady Catherine's cherished role as unofficial leader of His Majesty's Disloyal Opposition. But what if he was wrong? What if she was regarded as a serious problem for the government, and in their vindictiveness, in their resolve to shut her up, they had turned on her son?

It was something to consider. Particularly as she seemed to have used the money he had made in the King's service to fund the most outspoken of the government's critics. If that was known to Billy Pitt and his friends in the Admiralty, they might have every reason to vent their displeasure upon Nathan.

The government had always been wary of moving against his mother personally. This was probably less because she was a woman than because she was an American. Pitt was known to foster a rapprochement with the United States, if only to increase the prospects of British trade with the new nation and to bring it into the coalition against Revolutionary France. He was doubtless wary of bringing a charge of sedition against a woman who was known to be a close friend of the American Minister to the Court of St James, and whose family were personal friends of President Adams.

But her son was a different matter, particularly as he was a serving officer in His Majesty's Navy.

And there was something else. Pitt's government had brought in the most draconian measures against civil liberties: freedom of speech, freedom of the press, freedom of association. They had suspended habeas corpus and locked up many of their opponents. They had even hanged a few. All on the grounds that the nation was in mortal peril – faced with the threat of imminent invasion by Revolutionary France. Pitt was hardly likely to welcome a report that the threat did not exist, and that the French were planning an assault upon Egypt – a country over 2,000 miles away. Especially when that report came from the son of a woman who had devoted a great deal of her time and money to denouncing him as a tyrant.

But it was one thing to decide what had brought him here; quite another to decide what to do about it.

He had written to his father begging him to use what influence he had with the Admiralty and Parliament, but he did not know if the letter had been sent, much less delivered. There had, of course, been no reply. He supposed that the Governor, for all his kindness, was under orders to prevent him from engaging in correspondence.

He felt forgotten. As the New Year began its weary plod through January, with only his artificial cosmos for company, he began to sink into despair. The real sun brought neither comfort nor heat, and as he huddled in his Spanish greatcoat, nursing the aching wound in his hip and the greater wound in his heart, he felt his own inner light grow dim.

Then one day the swallows came.

They were disguised as aides of the Governor. The first brought gifts: a fish pie with a bottle of Portuguese wine, still chilled from the Governor's cellar, and a cake fresh-baked by his pastry cook. The second brought a change of quarters – from the top of the tower to the bottom. With a log fire and a carpet – and a real bed. The third brought a bath, carried in by two of the Governor's own servants and filled with hot water, heated in a great vat on the fire. And when Nathan had bathed and wrapped himself in the robe provided, one of them shaved him and cut his hair. He was left to ponder the reasons for all this, but many years in His Majesty's Service had taught him not to look a gift horse in the mouth. He slept well.

The following day, the first swallow returned with the full-dress uniform of a Post Captain in His Britannic Majesty's Navy and an invitation to dine with the Governor. Nathan had lost so much weight that it almost fitted; it was just a little tight under the armpits and across the shoulder. The hat was too big and fell down over his eyes. The servants offered to pad it but Nathan elected to carry it under his arm.

They walked to the Governor's House without an escort, the aide making polite conversation about the weather. It was mild, in fact, just the slightest suggestion of a breeze, more refreshing than not. The sky was blue, the sun sliding across the north-west corner of Africa towards the Atlantic. A crescent moon rising in the east. It would be an excellent night, Nathan thought, for stars.

He asked no pertinent questions regarding his present situation or status. They would have been a waste of time. Even depressed, numbed from the neck up, he had enough sense to appreciate that this was no mere whim on the part of the Governor. It was either a softening up or the prelude to release.

He was inclined, by nature, to suspect the former.

But what were they softening him up *for*? If they wanted him to retract his report about the French intentions towards Egypt, they only had to ask. He was not going to go down with the ship. Not over Egypt. Nor even for India. There were other ways of proving his patriotism. Let them give him another ship.

He could say he had misheard. It was England Bonaparte planned to invade. Or Ireland. Not Egypt. *Angleterre, Irelande, Égypte.* It was a mistake anyone could make. Or else Junot had become confused. He had meant to say England, but he had said Egypt. He had always been a scatterbrain and the head wound had not helped.

Nathan was rehearsing this submission as the aide led him past the sentries outside Governor House and up the broad staircase to the Governor's private apartments. No dismal cell this time, no haunted guest room. The Governor's own study, with the candles lit, though it was not yet dusk, and a blazing fire in the hearth. And the Governor himself to greet him.

He was posed, as Scrope had been, by the fireplace, a glass of wine at his elbow, but as soon as Nathan was announced, he crossed the room towards him with his hand extended. Nathan had to hide his surprise at the enthusiasm of the Governor's clasp.

'My dear Peake!' he enthused as he peered intently into Nathan's face. What he saw there seemed to reassure him a little. 'You look well. Yes. Remarkably well in the circumstances. Can I offer you a glass of wine? Or would you prefer something stronger?'

Charles O'Hara was a bluff, still handsome man in his late fifties. He had been born in Lisbon, the bastard son of an Irish baron and his Portuguese mistress, but had spent his entire life, from the age of twelve, in the British Army. These days, he wore the look of an old campaigner who has found himself an easy berth at last and is determined to make the most of it, before it kills him with drink and soft-living.

O'Hara had been commissioned as a lieutenant in the Coldstream Guards twelve years before Nathan was born, on the eve of the Seven Years War. Since when he had fought in three wars on three continents and attained the rank of Lieutenant-General – but his great fear, as he had confessed to Nathan when they had last dined together and he had taken rather too much in drink, was that he would be remembered as the officer who had surrendered his sword to General Washington at Yorktown, thereby effectively surrendering America.

Although it was hardly in the same category, he had also surrendered Toulon, when the British had been briefly in occupation of the port in the first year of the present war. The officer to whom he gave up his sword on that occasion was Napoleon Bonaparte, then a mere Captain of Artillery in the Revolutionary Army.

'A scruffy-looking bugger,' O'Hara had reported to Nathan, when he recalled the incident. 'You would not have given him a second glance. Not like Washington. No presence about him – unless I was missing something. And I suppose I was, given what he has achieved since.'

But at least Bonaparte had treated him as a fellow officer. The Revolutionists in Paris had a different view. It was a time when the whole of Europe was against them, and the Committee of Public Safety under Robespierre had resorted to wholesale repression to save the Revolution – or at least, his own narrow view of it. Toulon had sided with the enemy, had given up the French Mediterranean fleet to Britain. In their fury, they turned on O'Hara. A British officer or not, he had supported the rebels – and he must suffer the fate of rebels. So they called him an 'insurrectionist' and locked him up in the Luxembourg, where he was in serious danger of being executed at the guillotine. He and Nathan had met several times there, though O'Hara had been under the impression that Nathan was an American called Turner, and it must have taken considerable restraint on his part not to question Nathan about this whilst he had him in his charge. But in those days, there had been many in Paris who were pretending to be people they were not.

That shared experience under the shadow of the guillotine was a powerful bond, however, and O'Hara appeared genuinely upset that he had been obliged to confine Nathan to his quarters for the best part of three months.

'I hope you understand that it was not of my own choosing,' he assured him now. 'I have written numerous letters on your behalf to Admiral St Vincent, Earl Spencer and others in positions of authority, up to Mr Pitt himself, requesting that you either be charged with an offence or released.'

'So what is it to be?' enquired Nathan with a smile, as if it were of no particular consequence. He was having difficulty in coming to terms with his sudden change of circumstance, and had expectations of having it snatched from him at any moment, like a child with a new toy.

'Why, you are to be released, of course,' the Governor assured him, as if in surprise that the question should arise. 'Admiral St Vincent has written to withdraw the charge of insubordination. I am told that when Nelson heard of your confinement, he wrote immediately to the Admiral extolling your conduct at Cadiz and stressing that if it were not for you, he would be either dead or a prisoner of the Spaniard.'

'That was very good of him,' Nathan acknowledged, genuinely moved. 'And how *is* Admiral Nelson? I had heard he was seriously wounded at Tenerife.'

'I am afraid he suffered the loss of his right arm,' the Governor confirmed, 'and given that he had previously lost an eye, I fear he may no longer be suited to active service.'

They relapsed into silence, staring into the fire and sipping their wine.

'There was talk of another charge,' said Nathan after a moment.

The Governor looked at him, his expression troubled.

'A charge of treason, I believe,' Nathan prompted him.

O'Hara shook his head, but it was more in anguish than denial. 'It was never . . . I do not believe such a charge was ever made. Not – formally. It was more, I believe, in the nature of a vague – and entirely unmerited, of course – accusation.'

'And yet I would not like it to go unanswered.'

'Of course not. Of course not.' O'Hara frowned, his jowls wobbling like a jelly. 'If such a charge had been made against myself, even in the heat of the moment, I would feel exactly as you do. And yet, I do not believe there were any witnesses to the incident.'

'On the contrary. One of your aides was present – and two Marine sentries.'

'I see. Yes. Well, all I can say, sir, is that if you wish to take the matter up with the . . . the *person* involved, I am sure no one would blame you. Though my private view, sir, is that he won't stand up to the mark. However,' he wiped a fierce hand across his nose as if he wished to eradicate a bad smell, 'from my own point of view, I was instructed to hold you in close confinement pending certain *investigations* into your conduct in the Adriatic. Again, we have to thank Admiral Nelson for coming to our assistance.'

He stood up and crossed to his desk, returning with a sheet of paper which he handed to Nathan.

'I understand that your written orders were lost with the *Unicorn*. Fortunately, Admiral Nelson had a copy made which the Admiralty has seen fit to forward to me. Would you be good enough to tell me if they are as you remember them?'

Nathan held the document to the light of the nearest candles. He did not recognise the handwriting – it must have been copied out by Nelson's secretary, John Castang, probably that same sultry evening back in July, aboard the flagship after Nathan's discussion with Nelson and Sir Gilbert Elliot.

It was headed *To Captain Peake,* Unicorn *(Most Secret)* and the first part did nothing to relieve Nathan's anxiety.

Sir,
You are, in pursuance of instructions from the Lords Commissioners of the Admiralty, to proceed with the ships etc under your command to the Adriatic, for the purpose of protecting the vessels engaged in the transfer of troops and supplies to and from the different places where the said troops may be required during the ensuing campaign. Further to which, their lordships having received intelligence of the possession of Ancona by privateers in the French

service, you are to cruise for the annoyance of the enemy off the coast of that port or any part of the Adriatic where they may be operating, taking care not to be surprised by a superior force.

But then it came . . .

Further, you are to seek intelligence of the British Consul in Corfu with regard to the condition of the Venetian ships-of-war in that port and any communications he might have received concerning their future deployment. Depending upon the form of that intelligence, you are to proceed to Venice by whatever means are available to you and in whatever guise should prove necessary – and to communicate directly with His Majesty's Ambassador, Sir Richard Worsley, with a view to taking such action as may seem appropriate to you both in the circumstances.

Given at San Fiorenzo, April 1796
Horatio Nelson

The wording was peculiar, even by Nelson's erratic standards of communication, and it left a great deal unsaid – but this was understandable. The letter was not in cipher and Nelson would not wish to betray any unnecessary intelligence to the enemy. The truth was that Ambassador Worsley had made a secret agreement with the Venetian Admiral – Dandolo – to hand the entire fleet over to Britain in the event of a French invasion, for the sum of half a million pounds. Nathan's job was to make sure it was worth it. After seeing a number of the ships at the main Venetian base in Corfu, he had concluded that most of them were barely fit for sea, let alone battle. But in any case, by the time he reached Venice, Dandolo had been murdered. And within a few hours of visiting the English Ambassador, Nathan was in the Doge's prison awaiting a similar fate.

But that was by the by. The important thing about Nelson's letter was that it confirmed the order for Nathan to proceed to Venice by whatever means were available to him and in whatever guise should prove necessary. This put Nathan in the clear so far as the *Unicorn* was concerned. He could no longer be charged with desertion.

There still remained the matter of his report concerning French intentions in the Middle East. But his release from prison and the warmth of the Governor's reception indicated that there had been a change of opinion on this issue. Even if they still doubted the truth of the report, their lordships must have decided that Nathan had acted in good faith. Or had they?

Nathan was having difficulty concentrating. His senses were considerably numbed after three months in a prison cell. Indeed, he had been so long without company he was having some difficulty taking in what the Governor was saying to him. He would not have been entirely surprised if it was all suddenly to vanish – the Governor, the crackling log fire, the wine in his glass – and that he would wake up to find himself back in his prison cell, listening for the sound of the swallows.

'So what is to follow?' he enquired, keeping his voice carefully unconcerned.

'I am required by their lordships to provide a passage for you back to England as soon as it may be convenient and a suitable vessel is available to us. In the meantime, I would be honoured if you would remain with me as my guest at Governor House. Though I would entirely understand if you wish to seek private accommodation.'

'So I am to return to England?'

This, in itself, was significant. Clearly Admiral St Vincent had no further use for his services.

'*If* that is your wish.' There was that in the Governor's tone and in the look that accompanied it which did a great deal to sharpen Nathan's blunted sensibilities. Something was afoot – and unless he was very much mistaken, it was about to advance upon him in its usual skulking fashion.

'There is an alternative?'

The Governor sat down again and leaned forward confidentially. 'There is a gentleman I would like you to meet. He has a proposal to make. But I am afraid he may not be entirely – *agreeable* to you.'

Nathan regarded him warily. He seemed remarkably hot under the collar, even for a man in his present situation. 'Not Mr Scrope?'

'Not Mr Scrope, no. But I am given to understand that you have cause for, for some *resentment* where this gentleman is concerned. And that— Well, he has told me to tell you that if you do not desire his company, then he will understand perfectly.'

Nathan strove to recall some of the people who had tried to kill him, or who had subjected him to torture, or given him some other cause for resentment. But the list was endless. 'He is not a Frenchman? Or a Venetian?'

O'Hara gave an awkward laugh. 'No. Neither of those things. He is an American.'

An American.

A swift stab of alarm. But no – it could not be possible. Not again.

The Governor was still talking.

'He has come directly from England and with the full approval of the Admiralty.' He paused for a moment. 'His name is Imlay. Gilbert Imlay.' He reached for the bell-pull. 'Shall we invite him to join us?'

Chapter Eight

The American Agent

———————

Gilbert Imlay. A few more lines at the corners, a little greyer at the edges, but still the same old Imlay with his raffish air of the American frontiersman wandered into my lady's chamber.

'*Bonsoir, mon capitaine*,' he addressed Nathan with a smile and a bow that was somewhat between sheepish and sardonic.

'I think you are in the wrong camp, Imlay,' Nathan remarked more coolly than he was feeling. 'We are the British. I suppose in your profession it is easy to become confused.'

Imlay's smile faltered a little.

'I gather the last time you met was in Lincoln's Inn Fields,' said O'Hara, doing his best to jolly things along a bit. 'Pistols at dawn, was it not? Ha ha. And I think a lady was involved.'

'That was the time before,' Nathan corrected him. 'The last time was in a crypt. And had it not been for Mr Imlay, I had very likely remained there, among the dead.'

Nathan advanced to meet him, extending his hand, and saw a look of relief cross the other man's face.

'I am glad we are still friends,' said Imlay.

'I would not go so far as to say that,' replied Nathan. 'It is as well to ensure there is not a pistol in your hand.'

They had known each other for a little less than four years, but it seemed like a lifetime. Several lifetimes. And yet Nathan was no closer to knowing the real Imlay than when they had first met. It was quite possible that the real Imlay did not exist, just a series of counterfeits.

'I am a man of many parts,' he had informed Nathan once, in what for him was a rare display of candour.

What Nathan knew of him came from many different sources, none of them reliable, least of all Imlay's own account. But it seemed reasonable to assume that at one time or another, and possibly simultaneously, he had been a spy for the Americans, the French, the Spanish and the British.

Their first encounter was in Paris during the Terror – in the Street of Arse-Scratchers, where Nathan was hanging from a lamppost. He had forgotten to wear the obligatory tricolour in his hat, and a mob of vigilantes had been trying to string him up for it, until Imlay persuaded them he was an American and too stupid to know any better.

This had been the high point of their relationship. The lows had come thick and fast. If Imlay had preserved Nathan from a hanging, it seemed at times that it was only to save his neck for the guillotine. But you could never be sure it was Imlay's *fault*, or merely a series of unfortunate events in which he was inextricably, inexplicably involved.

And now here he was again. Apparently in the employ of the British Admiralty, or at least enjoying their confidence.

'Captain Peake and I have had our differences in the past,' Imlay was informing the Governor, as he accepted a glass of wine. 'But we have had some very pleasant times too, along the way, have we not?' he appealed to Nathan archly.

'So, I take it we may now dine together like old friends.' The Governor beamed, though the look he threw towards Nathan was uncertain.

'By your leave, I should first like to hear what is the latest madcap scheme I am expected to find agreeable,' Nathan cautioned him, 'before I am too much under the weather.'

Imlay chuckled good-naturedly, with a glance towards their host as if to say, *See what I have to put up with?*

'We are going to rescue a beautiful damsel from pirates,' he told Nathan. 'What could be more agreeable than that?'

The rest of the story had to wait upon dinner – 'lest it spoil', as O'Hara chided them and he was put to the trouble of finding a new cook.

This might not have been quite the disaster he anticipated.

'I must apologise for the limitations of our cuisine,' he confided as they entered the dining room, 'but at a time of siege we are obliged to make do with what little scraps as are available to us.'

Nathan declined to mention that after several months

in the Governor's prison, a few scraps at a rich man's table would be something of a treat.

They began with a fish soup – with ingredients caught off the New Mole only this morning, the Governor assured them. Its chief ingredients appeared to be crab and bonito – and had it been a little warmer and flavoured with a few herbs, it might have been excellent. This was followed by one of the Governor's hens, a little older and stringier than the Christmas capon, and a salted ham with a mess of potatoes and pickled cabbage – very like the fare dished out in the wardroom of a ship-of-war. For dessert there was a cake of dried fruits and a custard that tasted rather more like a cheese. But whatever the deficiencies of the Governor's larder, or his cook, his cellar was well stocked with Portuguese and Spanish wines, the whites still cool from the ice and straw into which they had been packed in the dark depths of Governor House.

It was, Nathan declared in all honesty, an excellent meal – 'the best I have had for some time,' he added, with a straight face.

Imlay's story was almost as good. For all the flaws of his character, you could never fault Imlay as a story-teller. The question was, of course, how much of it was true.

'I am told that since our last meeting, you have had the pleasure of visiting Venice,' he began, when the servants had cleared away the last of the dishes and left them to their own devices and a decanter of port wine.

Nathan tried not to show his concern. His mission to Venice, as the letter from Nelson had so recently reminded him, was Most Secret. He flicked a glance at the Governor, who nodded wisely. 'Mr Imlay enjoys the complete confidence of their lordships,' he murmured complacently.

'Indeed?' Nathan inclined his head in appreciation of this jest. In fact, his own confidence in their lordships of the Admiralty had never been high and had sunk considerably lower during his months of confinement on the Rock of Gibraltar. The First Lord, Earl Spencer, was probably an improvement on the Earl of Chatham, who had preceded him, but that was not saying a great deal. Chatham had been a soldier; Spencer was a politician. One day, perhaps, they would appoint a sailor to the job, but being in the gift of government it would have been foolish to count on it.

'Well, I would not say their lordships and I agree on everything,' Imlay confessed indulgently, 'but in this matter, I think I may safely say we are in accord.'

'And what does Venice have to do with it?' Nathan enquired, longing, as he often did, to kick him.

'While you were there . . . *if* you were there,' Imlay corrected himself with a small smile, 'you may have had the honour of meeting the American Consul, a Mr Devereux.'

Nathan frowned as if he was trying to recall. In fact, he remembered Mr Devereux perfectly well, though they had only had the pleasure of one brief encounter. It was shortly after his arrival in Venice in the guise of the New York merchant and ship-owner, Mr Nathaniel Turner, and he had gone to pay his respects at the American Consulate on the Grand Canal. But he had no intention of telling Imlay any of this.

'Well, be that as it may,' Imlay continued, 'Mr Devereux

has a daughter, Louisa. His only child and the apple of his eye. Aged seventeen.'

Nathan had a sudden vivid memory of a face peering over a balustrade, just as he was leaving. He had glanced back up the stairs and seen her there, a vision of blonde loveliness in muslin and lace, hastily withdrawn.

'She was packed off to England shortly before the French arrived in Venice,' Imlay continued. 'There was a great deal of disorder in the city at the time, verging on civil war, as you probably know. The Consul's wife had recently died and he was concerned for his daughter's safety. Unfortunately, the ship she sailed in – an American vessel called the *Saratoga* – was taken by pirates off Sicily. I should more properly say corsairs, though there is very little difference in my view. However, they carried a letter of marque from the Pasha of Tripoli licensing them to seize the vessel of any country with which the Pasha considers himself to be at war. Or, at least, not at peace.'

Nathan knew the form, for he had served for well over a year in the Mediterranean before his visit to Venice. 'I had thought the United States had signed a peace treaty with the corsairs,' he ventured. 'The last I heard, they were paying an annual subsidy – which more or less kept their ships free of attack.'

'Rather less than more,' countered Imlay. 'And we had neglected to pay the required bribe to the Pasha of Tripoli – Yusuf Karamanli. You have heard of him, perhaps?'

Nathan confessed that he had not.

'The Karamanli dynasty has been in power for three generations,' Imlay informed him. 'They are the sons of slaves, originally taken from Georgia, in the Caucasus. The present ruler – Yusuf – became Pasha two years ago after murdering his elder brother – in front of their mother, I believe – which is what passes for a typical family fracas in Tripoli. His mother is Georgian, and they still favour Georgian women as their brides. Blonde, blue-eyed, milky-white complexion. I am not sure if Yusuf takes after her in appearance, but I would not be surprised if he favoured the same colouring in his women.'

'You are saying that he kidnapped the Devereux girl for his harem?'

'No. No, I am not saying that at all – though from what I have heard, he would not spurn the opportunity. His chief concern is money. Having recently seized power and being obliged to bribe many of his followers, he is extremely low on funds, so he has taken to pirating. He uses the usual old claptrap with which I am sure you are all too familiar . . .'

' "A permanent state of war exists between the followers of the Prophet and all infidels",' put in the Governor dryly. 'Unless they have had the foresight to make a peace treaty – involving a substantial bribe, of course.'

'It has become a convenient means of raising revenue,' Imlay confirmed. 'When Prince Yusuf came to power, he demanded new treaties with all those nations whose shipping might be said to be "vulnerable". Eight of them complied – for a total sum, I am told, of three hundred thousand piastres. That is to say, about twenty-five thousand English pounds. To be paid annually.'

The Governor gave it as his opinion that this was cheap at half the price.

'Regrettably, President Adams was not of that opinion,' Imlay told him.

'Hence the attack on the *Saratoga*.'

'Was she not armed?' Nathan put in, for he was aware that the corsairs had a greater respect for a decent broadside than for a decent bribe. And they were wary of offending the major maritime powers. Attacks on the shipping of Britain, France and Spain were rare – though this might change now that the British fleet had pulled out of the Mediterranean.

'She was armed – but insufficiently it appears. The ship that took her was the *Meshuda*, of twenty-eight guns and three hundred and sixty men, commanded by a former British seaman – a Scot by the name of Lisle, who jumped ship at Tripoli and turned renegade. He now calls himself Murad Reis and the Pasha has appointed him *Capudan Pasha*, his Admiral of the Fleet. I thought you would like that,' he added, noting the expression on Nathan's face.

'How do you know all this?' Nathan asked, for Imlay had not previously impressed him with his knowledge of the Barbary Coast.

'I have my sources,' Imlay replied with a sly look.

'The British Consulate in Tripoli has become involved in the business,' O'Hara affirmed, though with some reluctance, Nathan thought. 'You might say certain . . . *negotiations* have been entered into.'

'They have asked for half a million dollars in ransom,' Imlay explained. He acknowledged Nathan's expression with a grim smile. 'It amounts to about a tenth of the entire Federal budget for a year, I am told – and has caused considerably more outrage in Congress than the news of the original capture. But, unhappily, the Federal government lacks the means of redress. President Adams has authorised the building of a small Navy to protect our trade, in both the Mediterranean and the Atlantic, but the first ships are still under construction. In my view, they are not likely to be at sea until the end of the century. And in the meantime, the poor wretches from the *Saratoga* are being held in the Red Castle in Tripoli. Apparently they are being reasonably well treated, but this could change at any moment. The Pasha is notoriously unpredictable, I am told, and while his general demeanour is not without charm, he is given to sudden violent rages. If their ransom is not paid, they are likely to be sold on the slave-market and their future would then be very bleak. Very bleak indeed – as I imagine you are aware.'

'Most of the men would end up in the galleys, chained to an oar for the rest of their lives,' the Governor supplied helpfully. 'Or humping stones on a building site. And the women, of course, would be sold into the harems, either as servants or concubines.'

'Or in Miss Devereux's case, I imagine, kept for the Pasha's private enjoyment,' Imlay added, looking at Nathan as if he had a personal interest in the matter. Nathan was puzzled. Was it possible that Imlay believed there had been some intrigue between them while he was in Venice?

And what did he expect Nathan to do about it?

He was not long in doubt.

'As I have already informed the Governor, I have been authorised by the Federal government to negotiate the release of the captives,' Imlay informed him.

'You are going to Tripoli?' Nathan's suspicions increased.

'I am. And to add weight to my powers of persuasion, I am to proceed in a ship-of-war suitably equipped to exact retribution if negotiations break down and the captives are subjected to further torment.'

'An American ship-of-war?'

'In a manner of speaking, yes.'

'But I thought you said the ships were still on the stocks.'

'I did. I meant a private ship-of-war, hired for this particular purpose.'

'And you possess such a vessel?'

'I do. At least, for the duration of hostilities, as it were. It is presently moored in the harbour here in Gibraltar, but in want of a proper crew, I am afraid – and, more particularly, a Captain.'

Nathan's wits had been dulled by his recent incarceration or he would have realised where this was going. But he had been living with his own company – and a map of the cosmos – for far too long.

'You had been better hiring a privateer in Malta,' he advised. 'The Knights of Saint John are very well used to dealing with the corsairs of the Barbary Coast – they have been fighting them for centuries. Indeed, most of them are corsairs themselves – and a sight more predatory than the Moors, from what I have heard. I am assured you would have no difficulty in hiring a fully equipped vessel with both Captain and crew, if you were prepared to make it worth their while. And do not mind working with rogues,' he could not help adding.

Imlay acknowledged this contribution with a tolerant smile. 'I had hoped that *you* might be interested,' he said.

Nathan stared at him for a moment. Then he flicked a glance at O'Hara. The latter's expression was carefully neutral.

'But I am an officer in His Britannic Majesty's Navy,' Nathan pointed out. 'I cannot go harum-scarum about the Barbary Coast in a private ship-of-war, putting the fear of God into the natives.' He glanced at the Governor again. 'Not unless I have been dismissed the service and no one has thought to inform me of it.'

'There is no question of that,' O'Hara hastened to assure him. 'But if the offer is of interest to you, I am informed their lordships will put no impediment in your way.'

Nathan was unimpressed. What was that supposed to mean? He was not dismissed the service, but he might go to hell in a handcart and serve the Devil, so far as their lordships were concerned, so long as he did not knock at *their* door for employment.

'No, it will not do,' he insisted. 'I would have to resign my commission. And that is out of the question. If their lordships wish to get rid of me, they must do it in the proper manner – with a court martial.'

'My dear sir, I assure you there is no question of a court martial, nor of anyone wishing to "get rid of you".' The Governor's voice rose in irritation, as if Nathan's imprisonment had been a slight misunderstanding, an inconvenience which a true gentleman would tolerably overlook. 'The fact is that this mission, if you were to undertake it, would be of considerable service to their lordships. And, of course, to His Majesty's Government.'

'In what way?' Nathan raised a brow. 'There are no British subjects involved.'

'No, but there are British *interests* involved. Very much so. How can I put this to you?' O'Hara replenished his glass in the hope of inspiration. 'We cannot send the fleet back into the Mediterranean,' he went on, 'or even a solitary ship-of-war, not without a single base east of Gibraltar and the fleets of France and Spain – and Venice, for that matter – combined against us.'

This was a soldier speaking, Nathan reflected. He could never imagine Nelson saying that, or even St Vincent. They would happily take the lot on.

Perhaps the Governor had come to a similar conclusion. 'At least not until we know for certain what the French are up to,' he added hastily. 'This gives us an opportunity to find out.'

'I am not sure that I follow you.' Nathan was being obtuse, and he knew it, but he had learned from recent experience. He needed the Governor to spell it out for him. Or preferably write it down with no ambiguity.

'After your mission to Venice,' began Imlay, who had an alarming facility to read Nathan's mind on occasion, 'you sent a report to their lordships concerning French intentions towards the Middle East . . .'

Nathan favoured him with a hard stare. This report had also been headed *Most Secret*. 'What intentions were these?' he enquired.

'That General Bonaparte was contemplating an invasion of Egypt as a stepping stone to India.'

Nathan flicked a glance towards O'Hara but the Governor appeared unmoved by the course the conversation was taking.

'I formed the impression that certain of their lordships were far from convinced by this report,' Imlay continued blithely. 'That they may even have thought you had made it up – or were deliberately misled – and that the French intention was to invade Ireland instead, or even England herself.'

'Just how much *do* you know?' enquired Nathan acidly.

'Their lordships were gracious enough to speak quite freely to me,' Imlay assured him in his most irritating manner. 'I was not told how you came by the information, of course, nor do I wish to know. But it would avoid unnecessary . . . prevarication . . . if you were to acknowledge that I am fully aware of the substance of this report.'

'Oh, I do acknowledge it,' Nathan confirmed. 'I am merely surprised that their lordships felt free to discuss it with a man who not only has no allegiance to the British Crown, but was until very recently in the pay of the French.'

He heard a small gasp from O'Hara. Either he did not know of this, or considered it an improper subject to raise at the dinner-table.

'I pray you will not trouble yourself with the past,' replied Imlay, 'when we have so much that should concern us in the immediate future.'

'But surely it is relevant to know where your true loyalties lie,' Nathan persisted. 'Particularly if we are to work together in the future.'

'My true loyalties are to my country,' Imlay stated.

'Which is not Great Britain.'

'Which is not Great Britain,' Imlay conceded. 'However, recent events have persuaded certain members of my own government that French interests and their own are not necessarily identical.'

'Really? And what has made them come to this astonishing conclusion?'

Despite his tone, Nathan was not at all surprised by Imlay's contention. The French alliance had helped to secure American independence from Great Britain and the two nations had remained on good terms after the war had ended. But of late there had been a distinct cooling in their relations. French privateers had declared open season on American merchant ships in the Atlantic; the slightest suspicion that they were engaged in trade with Britain and they were seized as contraband and hauled into French ports. Stern warnings had been issued that if this continued, it would lead to a state of hostilities.

Even so, it was difficult to see how the French invasion of Egypt might conflict with the interests of the United States.

Nathan took it upon himself to mention this. 'Nor can I imagine their lordships losing much sleep over the fate of a few American sailors in Tripoli,' he added bluntly. 'Or even of a beautiful young woman.'

'Mr Devereux has many friends in England,' the Governor interposed. 'Friends in high places, you might say. But you are right. It is not their lordships' chief concern. Their chief concern is the possibility of a French expedition to the Middle East.'

Nathan was astonished. 'Their lordships' chief concern when I first reported this, almost a year ago, was that I was an agent of the French who had deliberately set out to deceive them.'

'I am not here to answer for their lordships,' O'Hara declared wearily. But then, perhaps recalling the number of times he had been required to answer for them in the past, and doubtless would in the future, he added: 'To be fair, they were considerably diverted at the time by the fear of an invasion of the British Isles. However, they have recently received another report which, to a great extent, tallies with your own. It came from a man who is, I believe, an acquaintance of yours.' He eyed Nathan shrewdly. 'He was until recently the British Consul in Corfu – Spiridion Foresti.'

The name cut through the fog in Nathan's mind like a warm breeze from the South.

Spiridion Foresti.

'Greek by birth, Venetian by nationality, Levantine by disposition, and British by inclination.'

That was how he had described himself to Nathan shortly after they first met in Corfu. Their acquaintance had been brief but they had established an instant rapport. More to the point, Spiridion was valued as a trusted source of intelligence, not only by the British Admiralty but also by every senior diplomat and Naval Commander in the Mediterranean. Nelson had gone so far as to describe him as the best intelligence agent he had ever encountered. But with the fall of Venice, Corfu was now under French occupation, and Nathan had for some time been concerned for his safety.

'You say "until recently".' He frowned. 'Do you know where he is now?'

'The report was sent from Corfu several months ago,' the Governor reported. 'But we have reason to believe that Mr Foresti is now in Tripoli.'

Another piece fell into place.

'He has, as you may know, significant commercial interests in the Levant, and of late he has been much concerned at the activities of French agents in the region. Furthermore, it appears that the Venetian fleet, which is now in French hands, has been ordered to prepare for a major operation in conjunction with the French fleet in Toulon.' He noted Nathan's expression and raised a cautionary hand. 'The report took a considerable time to reach London and the information it contains may well be out of date. Also, there is still the danger that it could be a *ruse de guerre*. We know they have been planning an invasion of Ireland . . .'

'From Toulon?'

The Governor sighed. 'All we know is that some major enterprise is being prepared. Troops and artillery are making their way in large numbers down to the Mediterranean coast. A great quantity of supplies and munitions are also being assembled. But there are a number of possible destinations besides Britain herself. Sicily has been mentioned, or Portugal. However, you can see why their lordships might wish to send an observer – a *trusted* observer – to the region. A man who could be relied upon to take accurate soundings, as it were.'

'And yet they did not find my last soundings particularly accurate.'

Nathan thought about it. All his instincts urged him to refuse. He would be sailing into uncharted waters, almost literally, for he could not call to mind any reliable charts of the coast of Tripoli. And he had much less reason to trust Imlay than he did the charts.

On the other hand, if he did turn it down, and insisted on returning to England, would he ever be given another ship?

'There is one thing that confuses me,' he began. *One thing?* 'If I am to assume this command, what flag will I be sailing under?'

'The American flag,' Imlay replied instantly. He looked to O'Hara for confirmation.

'Well, you cannot very well sail under a British flag,' the Governor conceded, 'not while the fleet is still locked out of the Med. You would inevitably be taken by the French – or the Spanish.'

Nathan might have disputed this, but he had sailed under a false flag before, and there was a more serious issue to be resolved.

'So, am I under the command of their lordships of the Admiralty – or Mr Imlay?'

'Neither,' said O'Hara.

'Both,' said Imlay.

'Neither and both?'

'The matter is very simple.' O'Hara reached for the decanter again, though the colour of his complexion and a tendency to slur his words suggested he had already imbibed considerably more than was good for him. 'You are to take command of a private ship-of-war sailing under the American flag. With Mr Imlay here as the repre . . . as the repre . . .' He gave up. 'As the agent of the ship's owners. You are to convey him to Tripoli where he is to go about his business. But as a loyal subject of King George you are to report whatever you see and hear to their lordships of the Admiralty upon your return. Come, sir, this is your opportunity to prove yourself in the right all along – and their lordships very much in the wrong.'

Despite the drink he had a clear grasp of Nathan's priorities. But Nathan was a long way from admitting it, or of accepting the assignment.

'And what is this "ship" that you have hired?' he enquired of Imlay.

'She is called the *Jean-Bart*,' replied Imlay, looking particularly pleased with himself. 'She is the ship you brought back from your previous mission – to Venice.'

Nathan gazed at him in frank disbelief. 'You have hired her from the Admiralty?' He looked to O'Hara to see what he made of this, but the Governor only inclined his head as if to indicate that their lordships, like the Lord Himself, worked in mysterious ways. It was not uncommon to hire out a King's ship, or even sell it, when the nation was at peace, but Nathan had never heard of such a thing at a time of war, when the Navy needed every piece of flotsam capable of carrying a gun or two.

'Well, perhaps "hired" is not the right word,' Imlay prevaricated. 'For they pointed out that they might never get her back.'

Nathan overlooked this possibility for the moment. 'So you have bought her outright?'

It was as hard to get a straight answer from Imlay as milk from a Billy-goat.

'I suppose I have, although . . .'

'How much for?'

'They wanted twenty thousand but I knocked them down to sixteen,' reported Imlay with modest satisfaction. 'And they said they'd buy her back from me if I returned her in one piece.'

Nathan sniffed. Pirates ain't in it, he thought. But he kept his counsel.

'So where is she now?'

'She is anchored just off the harbour mole,' replied Imlay. 'Why do you not come out with me at first light and run your eye over her? No commitment, mind. But I think I may promise you a pleasant surprise.'

Chapter Nine

The Prize

———◆———

$\mathcal{S}$ he stood off the South Mole in the light of the rising sun. Sails furled, gunports closed, not a sign of life on her decks or on the yards above; the morning mist rising from the placid waters of the bay so that she appeared to be floating on cloud. A ghost ship. The *Jean-Bart*.

The first time Nathan had seen her was in the Tyrrhenian Sea, on his way down to Naples. In a storm. He had been wedged into the crosstrees of the *Unicorn*'s foremast, a good 100 feet above the deck, and the *Jean-Bart* a distant scrap of sail in the driving rain.

'A large corvette, sir, almost as big as a frigate,' Mr Lamb had assured him, with the advantage of his young eyes. 'She is in and out of the waves, sir, and I cannot see if she is flying any colours.'

Nathan was damned if he could see her at all most of

the time. A fresh north-easterly, known in those parts as the Tramontana, was blowing up the Devil of a brew and 'in and out of the waves' was an accurate description. But he was less sure of the midshipman's confident assertion that she was a corvette, a type of vessel unknown in the British Navy, though common enough in the French service.

They had given chase but it was already late afternoon and they lost her as soon as the sky came down. Lamb had been right, though. The next time Nathan had seen her was from the back of a pony, while she rode at anchor in the Bay of Alipa off the west coast of Corfu. She was a French corvette of twenty-four guns. Twenty 9-pounders on her main gundeck and half a dozen 6-pounders on her forecastle and quarterdeck. In the British Navy she would have been called a large sloop or a small frigate. He discovered later that she had been built for the Neapolitan Navy at the start of the war when King Ferdinand had joined the coalition against Revolutionary France. But on her very first cruise she had been taken by a French squadron on one of their rare sorties out of Toulon.

Nathan had taken her back in Alipa Bay, cutting her out with the ship's boats from the *Unicorn* – a desperate hand-to-hand encounter in the moonlight in which almost thirty men had lost their lives on both sides, and as many wounded. He had put his friend Tully in command with a prize crew and left her off Ancona with the *Unicorn* when he set off on his fateful trip to Venice. The Navy had bought her into the service – for the bargain price of £14,000, a quarter of which had gone to Nathan and was now helping sustain his mother's extravagant lifestyle in Soho.

And now here she was in Gibraltar in the service of
Gilbert Imlay – or whoever was paying his bills these days,
for the one thing Nathan was sure of was that Imlay was
not using his own money.

'So may we go aboard?'

'By all means.'

Imlay had the Port Admiral's barge at his disposal and
they rowed the short distance to the sloop which, despite
appearances, was clearly keeping a sharp lookout, for they
were hailed within half a cable's length of her.

The coxswain looked enquiringly at Nathan.

'*Unicorn*,' Nathan replied promptly, for it was
customary to call out the name of a Captain's ship when
he was being brought aboard, and as far as Nathan was
concerned, he was still the Captain of the *Unicorn*, even if
the French had her.

He noted with approval that they had the boarding nets
rigged and hammocks piled in the tops to make a barricade
for their sharpshooters – which was why he had not seen
the lookout from the shore. So whoever had the charge of
her was taking no chance of her being cut out by the
Spaniards, even from under the guns of Gibraltar.

He was greeted by the drawn-out wail of the boatswain's
call as he came aboard, and though there were no side
boys in white gloves or a marine guard with sloped muskets
and stamping feet, there was an officer, of sorts. Possibly
the strangest-looking officer Nathan had ever seen.

He had the face of a bloodhound, or an out-of-condition
mastiff, possessing several chins and more teeth than his
mouth had room for; the narrow eyes almost buried in fat,
his girth enormous, though to be fair, it was not easy to

see where the officer ended and the uniform began. Nor was it a uniform that Nathan had previously encountered on the deck of a British man-of-war, or of any other navy in the civilised world. There was blue in it, and white, as one might expect, and a quantity of tarnished gold, but unlike any other naval officer of Nathan's acquaintance, the man wore a kind of fur cape, or cloak, thrown loosely over his shoulders and trailing almost to his feet. There was a great red sash around his waist in lieu of a belt – possibly the belt had not been made that could circum-navigate such a girth – and under his tricorne hat, which he wore athwart rather than fore-and-aft in the modern manner, there appeared to be a pair of ear flaps, also of fur, rather like ladies wore while skating upon the ice.

Nathan gazed at this apparition, deprived, for the moment, of the power of speech. The officer, too, appeared speechless, though he showed his terrible teeth in what might have been a grin or a snarl and touched his hand to his ridiculous hat. Imlay, however, addressed him famil-iarly enough, though not in a language Nathan understood or recognised. While they conversed, Nathan looked around the deck. About a dozen new members gazed back with a frank curiosity that bordered on insolence. Although they appeared to have no immediate task to hand, they were heavily armed with knives, cutlasses and pikes, as if they had been assembled to repel boarders, or in some strange notion of being a guard of honour.

Then Nathan saw the guns. Was this Imlay's surprise? For instead of the long guns that had been the corvette's main armament when the *Unicorn* had taken her as a prize, she had been fitted out with a couple of dozen carronades – 24-pounders, by the look of them – shining with newness, as if they had just been taken out of their wrappings, straight from the Carron Ironworks.

Nathan regarded them with mixed feelings. Carronades. Short, fat and ugly, they were designed for close engagement; 'smashers' was their more colloquial name in the Navy. They could pound a ship to death with their heavy roundshot and clear a deck with grape soon as look at you – but Nathan favoured them as a supplementary weapon, not as the main armament. The only long guns the *Jean-Bart* had been left were a half-dozen 6-pounders divided between the forecastle and the quarterdeck.

But the guns were not the real surprise. The real surprise was presently emerging from the companionway on the quarterdeck, clearly roused from sleep and still fastening the buttons of his uniform coat.

'Good God!' exclaimed Nathan. 'Martin Tully!'

Tully looked as surprised as he was. He was rendered dead in the water for a moment and then came hurrying forward, his expression torn between delight and concern.

'I am so sorry – I had no idea. If I had known . . .' He shot a glance at Imlay, who was grinning slyly.

'Thought you would be surprised,' he said. 'Just like old times, is it not?'

Nathan sincerely hoped not. They had taken Imlay out with them to the Caribbean in the role of political adviser, in which capacity he had betrayed them to the French, joined in the war against them, and then persuaded their lordships of the Admiralty that it was all in the King's interest. Tully knew him almost as well as Nathan did – if that was any kind of advantage to them both.

'I am very glad to see you, Martin.' Nathan eschewed all formality and shook him by the hand. 'But it is indeed a great surprise. I had been told she had been sold out of the service.'

'So she has, sir, but they needed someone to bring her down to Gibraltar and hand her over to her new command. I had hoped to see you while we were here, but . . .' His eyes strayed almost of their own accord up towards the old Moorish castle sitting on top of the Rock where Nathan had been lately accommodated.

'They have let me out,' Nathan assured him, in case Tully thought he had climbed over the wall. 'And withdrawn all charges against me. No case to answer. All my eye and Betty Martin.'

'Oh, I am so glad to hear it, sir. So glad. None of us believed a word of it, of course. No one. Not that we knew much about it.' He blushed through his dark tan for they both knew you could not lock up a Post Captain for three months without it being a talking-point throughout the fleet, and doubtless some of the speculations concerning his arrest had touched upon the fantastical.

Nathan regarded him keenly. Tully looked healthy enough but there was perhaps something lacking in his usual vivacity. They had known each other since their time on the *Nereus* together, just before the war, chasing smugglers on the south coast of England. Before that, Tully had been a smuggler himself, in his native Channel Isles. He had been pressed into the Navy as an alternative to prison, but had done well enough out of it, rising from assistant sailing master to lieutenant and making at least as much in prize money as he would from cheating the

Revenue Service. But you could usually see the smuggler in him, if you looked carefully enough, as if his time in the King's Navy was something of a joke, on both him and the King. He did not look at all amused now, though. Despite his obvious delight at seeing Nathan, he seemed abnormally anxious. Harassed even. More so than when they had been in battle together. Perhaps he had slept badly, or been hitting the bottle the night before. He had clearly been thrown by Nathan's unexpected arrival.

'I am sorry I was not here to greet you, sir,' he said. 'I am afraid we are all at sixes and sevens.' He shot a glance at Imlay, as if it was a cruel joke not to warn him, which it was.

'And I am sorry to spring myself upon you.' Nathan jerked his head at Imlay disrespectfully. '*He* thought it would be a surprise for us both.'

'I heard the name *Unicorn*,' Tully said, staring briefly out to sea, as if in hope to see their old ship sitting upon the mist off the mole with her plain white figurehead and her thirty-two guns.

'Regrettably she is still in the hands of the French,' Nathan said, 'but I did not know how else to announce myself.'

He hesitated. This was awkward. He was not sure how much he was free to disclose. Probably not much at all. He cursed Imlay privately for being such a fool as not to warn him that Tully was aboard and tell him what he might be permitted to say. It was typical of Imlay, he thought, that within hours of their reunion he was setting Nathan against his friends.

'Perhaps we may talk in private,' Imlay addressed him

now. 'And a coffee would be most welcome,' he instructed Tully, as if he was the landlady of an inn and not the Commander of a sloop-of-war. 'If it is not beyond our primitive resources.'

'I think we can manage that,' replied Tully, catching Nathan's eye. 'If you see your steward before I do, perhaps you might mention it to him.'

'And when your duties allow, perhaps you would care to join us,' Nathan put in firmly, for he was damned if either of them were to be treated as if they were under Imlay's private command.

Imlay frowned in irritation, which far from troubling Nathan afforded him some slight if childish satisfaction. Tully bowed his acknowledgement. 'I will join you shortly,' he agreed.

Nathan followed Imlay into the Captain's quarters which were almost as commodious as those on the *Unicorn*, with one cabin for dining, one for sleeping and a large day cabin running the breadth of the stern, though the space was now shared with two pair of carronades. He remembered sitting here with Spiridion Foresti just after the ship was taken, and washing the blood off his face – someone else's blood on that occasion – and reading the French Captain's orders while he drank the dead man's wine. It was here that he had decided on his ill-fated trip to Venice.

It had been Tully's cabin since, and now, apparently, it was Imlay's. Not that there was much sign of his occupancy. There were charts spread on the table and an oilskin hanging upon a hook, but nothing that might in any way have been construed as domestic or personal. Which did not, of course, surprise Nathan in the least, Imlay being no more inclined to nest-making than the cuckoo.

He could see a large portion of the anchorage through the stern windows, with several gunboats moored alongside a sheer hulk and a large two-decker in the distance, though too far for him to recognise. If he stooped low enough he supposed he would be able to see his former residence at the peak of the Rock.

The steward Tully had referred to appeared upon the instant – an odd-looking cove dressed more like a footman than a mariner in breeches and silk stockings and an old-fashioned periwig. An Englishman apparently, with a North Country accent.

'Some coffee, if you please, Qualtrough,' Imlay instructed him, 'and is it too early to tempt you with breakfast?' he enquired of Nathan considerately.

It was never too early, or late, to tempt Nathan with breakfast but he reluctantly declined, feeling it would put him at a disadvantage. There was much he still required to know and he needed to keep his wits about him, and not feel obliged.

'So who was the officer who greeted us as we came aboard?' he began, as he removed his hat and settled himself, uninvited, at one end of the table.

'That is Belli,' replied Imlay, sitting at the opposite end and beaming agreeably.

'Belly?' Nathan repeated, inaccurately, wondering if this was a private nickname relating to his girth.

'Kapitan-leytnant Grigory Vasilyevich Belli,' stated Imlay impressively, adding unnecessarily: 'He is a Russian.'

'I see,' reflected Nathan, though it was a far-from-accurate account of his understanding in this instance. 'Kapitan-leytnant . . .' he repeated.

'It is the rank of an officer in the Imperial Russian Navy,' Imlay informed him, as if it were no more a surprise to find one in the vicinity of Gibraltar than a swallow, say, on its way to Africa. 'I do not believe there is an equivalent in your own service. Unless it be that of Commander, perhaps.'

'Thank you,' said Nathan. 'So I had assumed.'

He was more familiar with the ranks in the Imperial Russian Navy than Imlay might have supposed, having had them explained to him, with other peculiarities of that institution, by his former first lieutenant aboard the *Unicorn*, Mr Duncan, who had served with the Russian fleet in the Black Sea during the years of peace.

'What is more puzzling to me,' Nathan said, 'is what he is doing aboard an American ship-of-war – unless you have inadvertently misguided me, and she is now in the Russian service.'

'Grigory Vasilyevich is in my service,' Imlay responded, not in the least discomforted by this sally. 'We met in Stockholm when he was in some pecuniary embarrassment and I was able to provide him with some assistance.'

Nathan restrained himself from commenting that this was the reverse of the usual arrangement. 'You were in Stockholm?' he asked instead.

'I was,' confirmed Imlay, but offered no further information on the subject.

'But Lieutenant Belli is, in fact, Russian?'

'He is. He was obliged to seek refuge in Sweden after a disagreement with Admiral Ushakov in which gross insults were exchanged.'

'I see,' Nathan said again. Admiral Ushakov, he recalled, had been the Commander of the Russian Black Sea fleet in the recent war with the Turks. 'And his position on the *Jean-Bart*?'

'He is serving in the capacity of a lieutenant, until Mr Tully hands the ship over, and then he will serve under her new Commander – if they both find this agreeable.'

'He speaks English?'

'Not a great deal, but there are a number of Russians among the crew.' Nathan raised an enquiring brow at this, whereupon Imlay added: 'About a dozen. Personal followers of Grigory Vasilyevich who sailed with him from Saint Petersburg.'

'Sailed with him? So he was in possession of a ship at the time of his . . . decampment?'

'A bomb ketch of the Imperial Russian Navy. It was returned by the Swedes to avoid embarrassment.'

'Very sensibly. Lieutenant-Captain Belli sounds as if he might be something of an embarrassment himself.'

'Oh, not at all. He is a very fine fellow. Very jolly, and so are his followers.'

'And the rest of the crew?'

'There are a few Portuguese we were able to pick up in Lisbon, some Genoese who are, I believe, part of her original crew but are now in my service – and some Americans I brought with me from England.'

'American seamen?'

'Prime seamen. Formerly of the brig *John Harvard* of Boston which was taken by an English cruiser on suspicion of running contraband into France.'

Nathan made no comment on this acquisition other

than to remark that at least some of the crew might speak a version of the King's English.

'I believe they do have that facility,' Imlay confirmed, 'having once been subject to King George, though I can think of little else in the contract that was to their advantage.'

'Apart from defending them against the French and the Indians for the best part of two hundred years,' Nathan reminded him tartly, 'whilst expanding their commerce, increasing their prosperity, and employing their taxes for the common good.' Imlay supplying no counter to this argument more articulate than a derisive snort, Nathan added: 'So what is the entire ship's complement?'

'I believe near sixty.' He noted Nathan's expression. 'Considerably fewer than you have been used to, I would suppose, though it appears perfectly adequate to sail a vessel of this size.'

'But not to fight her.'

'You may rest easy on that score. I have no expectation of having to fight. However, I have plans to increase their number.'

'From where?' Nathan wanted to know.

'From here in Gibraltar.' Then, after a small pause: 'And also from Algiers, which is our next port of call.'

Why Algiers? Nathan wondered. But as he was unlikely to get a straight answer, he asked the question that had been uppermost on his mind since he stepped aboard. 'And who is paying for all of this? The American Government?'

Another small hesitation. 'Not directly.' Then: 'Very well, I will tell you, provided it is kept between ourselves. Most of the funds have been supplied by your friend Mr

SETH HUNTER

170

Devereux, the American Consul in Venice, who is naturally
very concerned for his daughter's safety. And he has the
backing of a number of influential friends in England and
America.'

Before Nathan could push Imlay further on this, the
steward entered with their coffee, Tully at his heels.

'You are sure you do not wish to be private?' Tully said.

'Not at all,' Nathan assured him blithely and in spite of
Imlay's frown. 'It is only by your leave that we have made
free of your cabin, for she is still a King's ship and you her
Commander, I am told – until you choose to hand her
over.'

The sun, suddenly rising from beyond the Rock,
dispelled the final shreds of mist and flooded the cabin
with a golden morning light – Nathan's first morning for
several months outside a prison cell. As he took his first
sip of the steaming hot coffee and stretched his long legs
under the Captain's table, he felt what could almost have
been a surge of happiness. He kicked it firmly back in its
hole. The future, he reminded himself, was still uncertain.
But when was it not?

'So how long were you in Lisbon?' Nathan enquired as
Tully took off his hat and joined them at the table.

'The best part of six months.'

A long time for a ship that had only been at sea four
years. 'But she is a new ship, practically. Built in ninety-
three, was she not?'

'That is right – in the yard at Castellammare in the Bay
of Naples, which has a fine reputation.'

'Finer in many ways than Chatham, I am told.'

Tully shrugged. 'But as much infected with corruption,

I imagine. There was a quantity of green wood in the futtocks and the spirketting, which had caused them to warp considerably in parts.'

'Never!' Nathan exclaimed, for he was always shocked by the perfidy of shipbuilders, whether English or Italian. This latest example of their deceit engrossed the two men for some time, for they could talk of spirketting and futtocks, carlines and cant timbers with as much animation and at as great a length as other men talked of the fashion for high collars and cravats.

'And you have had her fitted out with smashers?' There was just enough of an inflexion in Nathan's tone to imply a criticism, and they both turned their heads to view the most neighbourly of these objects, which stood just a few feet from the end of the table.

'Indeed. It is the practice, I am told, with all the latest sloops. The theory is that it gives them the punch of a frigate at much less expense.'

'If they are permitted to advance close enough to employ them.'

It was a myth, of course, that carronades could be relied upon only at close quarters, since at maximum elevation they could fire almost as far as a long gun – but with nothing like the accuracy, in Nathan's opinion. The two officers discussed this question for some minutes until called to order by a pronounced cough from Imlay, who had endured their debate with a somewhat strained expression.

'May I take it from this impassioned interest in smashers, spirketts and the like that you have decided to accept my offer?' he enquired of Nathan.

Tully shot Nathan a look of sufficient concern to require an assurance from Nathan that he had *not* been dismissed the service, but merely permitted to take a few months leave of absence. 'During which I may, if I wish,' he concluded, 'take service with Imlay here as the Commander of a privateer.'

'Well, if you need another officer,' said Tully, 'I have always wanted to try my hand at privateering.'

'Is that possible?' Nathan looked to Imlay.

'I am sure it can be arranged, if it would help you come to a decision.'

'Do you know what Mr Imlay has in mind?' Nathan asked Tully.

'He knows as much as he needs to know,' Imlay replied swiftly.

Nathan thought it over. The main argument in favour of the venture, so far as he was concerned, was that he might find further evidence of a French attack upon Egypt. But if he did not, if it did turn out to be a *ruse de guerre*, it would only confirm their lordships in their low opinion of him. There were, besides, other considerations.

'I am very reluctant to commit myself without written orders,' he explained to Tully. 'I have just suffered several months in prison on suspicion of consorting with the enemy. If Nelson had not spoken up for me, I would still be there.'

Imlay stood up and crossed to a desk at the far end of the room and returned with a small package and a separate letter, both of which he tossed in Nathan's direction.

'I was instructed to give you these only if you agreed to the commission,' he said, 'but if it helps you make up your mind . . .'

Nathan picked up the letter. The seal was unfamiliar to him. He broke it open and removed a single sheet of paper. It was from Admiral St Vincent, written aboard the *Ville de Paris* off Cadiz and headed *Most Secret and Confidential, To Captain Nathan Peake Esq, Governor's House, Gibraltar.*

That was tactful, Nathan conceded. Addressing it to the Moorish Prison might have caused the Admiral some disquiet.

Sir,

Whereas you presently find yourself without a command, the Lords Commissioners of the Admiralty have conveyed to me their wish that you be granted a leave of absence for an indefinite period, during which time their lordships have been pleased to confirm that you are at liberty to accept any post that is offered you, commensurate with your rank and abilities, by any person or persons whose interests are not opposed to those of His Majesty's Government.

Should any such post arise and the circumstances being favourable, you are to deliver the despatches that accompany this missive to those representatives of His Majesty as you may encounter on your travels and deliver such replies as shall be entrusted to you.

You are further requested and required as an officer of His Majesty's Navy to diligently seek out

*any intelligence of the enemy in whatever region you
are required to visit and to undertake such surveys
and observations as may be useful to those forces at
His Majesty's command,*

*Yours &c
St Vincent*

If this was meant to relieve Nathan's apprehension, it
failed on several counts. He was particularly concerned
that it was not a direct instruction from the Admiralty
or from the Admiral himself. If any problems arose, it
left both parties with ample scope for misunderstanding
or outright denial. Of course, the letter itself provided
some reassurance, but if he lost it, as he had the order
sending him to Venice, he very much doubted if a copy
would be made available. And then there were the
ambiguities.

*. . . any person or persons whose interests are not
opposed to those of His Majesty's Government . . . the
circumstances being favourable . . . those representatives
of His Majesty as you may encounter . . .*

Clearly, St Vincent was being deliberately evasive. Was
this because he feared the letter might fall into the wrong
hands – or from some more sinister motive?

He looked up to see Imlay watching him carefully. He
was holding another letter in both hands, like an offering,
but there was something in his manner that put Nathan
instantly on his guard.

'This also is for you,' said Imlay. 'I was asked to deliver
it personally. But you may wish to read it in private.'

Almost with reluctance he handed it over and then made a small gesture to Tully who looked startled but picked up his hat and, with a concerned glance at Nathan, followed Imlay from the cabin.

Nathan considered the envelope with foreboding, for Imlay's manner indicated the probability of bad news, news of which Imlay himself was aware. He recognised the hand immediately, for though he had received only one letter from her in the past year, he had read it so often it was imprinted on his memory. He broke the seal. It was from Sara. Two pages in her large, clear, confident scrawl. Dated almost two months ago, with a London address. Not his mother's. She wrote:

> *My dear Nathan,*
> *Having just been informed that Imlay is to journey to Gibraltar and has every expectation of meeting with you, I could not miss a sure opportunity of writing, not being certain that any of my previous letters have reached you.*
>
> *If they did, however, you will know the very sad news that Mary Wollstonecraft has died. I am sorry if this comes as a shock to you, for I know that you esteemed her greatly, and that she was a very good friend to you, as she was to me, both in Paris and in London. Although it is several months since she passed away, there is not a day goes by that I do not grieve for her, for I believe her to be the dearest friend I ever had.*

Nathan stared down at the letter.

Mary Wollstonecraft was dead.

He had a sudden mental image of her, flushed and excited, after visiting Thomas Paine in the Luxembourg prison, and in the garden at Neuilly with little Fanny at her breast and the maid Hélène pushing Alex on a swing.

He had been much exasperated with her at times, especially over her relationship with Imlay. Her despair at his infidelity had caused her to make at least two attempts on her own life: once by throwing herself in the Thames, when Nathan had come close to drowning himself in a bid to fish her out. He wondered if she had finally succeeded. But no. He read on:

Mary died in childbirth at her home in Somers Town, with her husband, family and friends at her side, myself among them. The cause of death was given as a poisoning of the blood. The infant survived and is a healthy little girl named Mary, after her mother. I am looking down at her as I write and she is smiling happily up at me from her cot and is the dearest little thing.

If you have received my previous letter, you will know that Mary and Godwin were married in March, since when she and I had been sharing a house in the Polygon, with Godwin occupying the house next door.

Nathan read this sentence twice so as to be sure of taking it in, but was no more enlightened at the second reading. He had no knowledge of this previous letter she referred to, and when he had read of Mary's *husband* being at her side, he had immediately taken this to mean Imlay. But apparently not.

What was this about *sharing a house in the Polygon, with Godwin occupying the house next door.*

The explanation, as such, was swiftly forthcoming:

You may think this eccentric, but both Mary and William were anxious to maintain their independence, and it is no more extraordinary, as they would argue, than for a Duke and a Duchess to maintain their own separate apartments and households while continuing to hold each other in great affection. Indeed, although Godwin had many times called for the Abolition of Matrimony, and their marriage exposed the true nature of Mary's 'Arrangement' with Imlay, on which account she lost a great many of those she counted as friends, they were a very happy couple and often communicated by letter and in person.

Nathan's frown grew a little more perplexed. Had it not been for the tragic nature of the letter, he might have wondered if he was the victim of a tease.

Certainly, Godwin's great love for her is apparent from the extremity of his grief, and I have taken upon myself the care of him and the little ones until he is more able to take an interest in his life and responsibilities.

* * *

Nathan chewed this over for a moment without coming to any definite conclusion.

> *In the circumstances, however, and knowing how much people are inclined to Gossip, especially in London, you must consider yourself to be freed from any understanding or obligation that you may feel towards me, especially as I now have several others for whom I must accept responsibility.*
>
> *It is difficult for me, my dear Nathan, to write of such things as our feelings for each other when we have not spoken of them for so long and in circumstances which have changed very much between us, and in the world. We have been apart for so long and spent so little time together.*
>
> *Please do not be anxious for me. Although I grieve for Mary I am otherwise content and in no want of money or other comforts. Your mother remains very kind and generous. Alex is in good heart and at school in London, and he sends you his greatest respects and hopes for your continued safety and wellbeing.*
>
> *As does your affectionate and special friend,*
>
> *Sara*

Nathan read several of the passages again, trying to discern a hidden meaning. A hint of what she truly meant to convey to him.

Knowing how much people are inclined to Gossip . . .

Gossip about the true nature of her relations with Godwin – or Mary?

Something that she thought would give him cause for distress or offence, however.

... especially as I now have several others for whom I must accept responsibility.

This might be intended as a warning that it was not just she and Alex he would be taking on, but the two little girls, Fanny and Mary. Or it might be an indication of her attachment to Godwin.

... circumstances which have changed very much between us, and in the world ... We have been apart for so long and spent so little time together.

What she meant was – we can no longer feel the same passion for each other as we did in Paris, at the time of the Terror. We no longer even know each other.

Sadly, this was true. And yet. He wanted her and he wanted what they had had then. The same intensity, and longing, and *love*.

And he felt this savage and unreasonable jealousy.

Was she freeing him – or herself? The more he thought about it, the more he was inclined to believe the latter. She wanted this man Godwin. Godwin and a home and family, a ready-made family. Not some distant memory of a few nights' passion in Paris, and a man five years younger than herself, who did not know what he wanted, and probably never would.

There was a tentative knock on the cabin door and Imlay entered. Alone. His face was grave. Nathan indicated the letter. 'It is from Sara,' he said.

Imlay nodded. 'I know,' he said. 'She gave it to me.'

'Then you know about Mary. I am sorry.'

'So am I.' Imlay sat heavily, taking off his hat and

running his hands through his hair. 'He is just a boy, he has never grown up,' Mary had said of him once, but he looked his age now.

It was impossible to guess what his true feelings towards Mary had been. Nathan, having met them both in Paris, was convinced he had set out on a course of seduction partly because of the challenge she represented as a celebrated feminist and writer. But it was not impossible that Imlay had fallen in love with her. He had talked of buying a farm in Kentucky and having six children together. Of living the simple life. A life of principle and high ideals. He might even have believed it at the time. He had the facility of believing in whatever image of himself he wished to put across to people; it was one of the chief reasons they were fooled into believing it themselves.

'You know of this Godwin?' Nathan asked him.

'Yes. William Godwin. He is a writer. Like myself.'

Nathan raised a brow but let this supposition pass unchallenged. 'A writer?'

'More of a journalist, I guess. And I believe he is regarded as something of a philosopher.' His tone verged on the dismissive.

'You were in London when Mary died?'

'No. I heard about it later.'

'So what of the child?'

'Godwin's child?'

'I was thinking more of *your* child. Fanny. The child you had by Mary.'

'I have made what provision I can for her,' Imlay retorted stiffly. 'Sara is looking after her at present. Did she not tell you?'

'Yes. She seems to be looking after all of them. Godwin included.'

'Ah – yes.' A bitter smile. 'Godwin seems to bring out the maternal in women.'

Did he want Nathan to believe there was something between them – Sara and Godwin? Had she confided in Imlay? They had known each other well in Paris. For a time Nathan had wondered if they had been lovers before Mary came into the picture. Or even since, for fidelity had never been Imlay's strong point.

'Why did you give me this now?' Nathan pressed him.

'What was I to do? Withhold it?'

He would have, if it had suited him to do so. But perhaps that was unfair. Imlay had some sense of honour, though it was adaptable to circumstance.

'Well, it seems I have little reason to return to London,' Nathan told him, as he folded the letter carefully in half and returned it to its envelope to read again, no doubt, over and over again in the loneliness of his cabin, or the next prison cell. This was nonsense and he knew it. He had every reason to return to London – apart from his own fear of commitment. 'So, I will take you to Tripoli, God help me.'

'Excellent.' Imlay beamed. 'We will have a splendid time.' His face fell with an almost comic facility. 'It will help us forget our bereavements – and our disappointments.'

'You said I might have Tully as first lieutenant.'

'By all means, by all means.' He fitted his fist into his hand. 'I will speak to the Governor this very morning. I am sure he will be able to arrange it with the Port Admiral.

And if not, a letter to the Commander-in-Chief will secure whatever approvals are necessary.'

'In writing.'

'In writing, as you say.' Though he frowned a little.

'So what other officers do we have, apart from Lieutenant Belli, of course?'

'What other? Ah, I am afraid Lieutenant Belli is our full resource, so far as officers are concerned. Oh, and the midshipman, Lamb.'

'Lamb? Mr Lamb is with you?'

'Yes. He assisted Tully during the refit. I believe he spent last night ashore, but it is quite possible, of course, that he will consent to join us as a volunteer, if you were to put it to him kindly.'

'And what of the hands? You said you had plans to increase their number.'

'I did. I will disclose them to you in a moment. But first, I think this calls for a celebration.' He produced a hip flask and, after wiping out the dregs of their coffee with a napkin, poured a generous quantity into each of their cups.

'I would much rather have breakfast at this time of the morning,' Nathan informed him ungraciously as he peered into the colourless liquid gracing his cup.

'And so you shall, so you shall. But first let us drink to the success of our present venture.'

They clinked their cups together and Nathan sipped cautiously. Not cautiously enough, however, for the fiery liquid caught at the back of his throat and near choked him.

'What in God's name is it?' he demanded, when he had got his breath back.

'Vodka,' Imlay replied, amiably. 'A Russian drink not unlike gin but much purer in content, I am told. Possibly it is an acquired taste.'

Certainly Imlay seemed to have acquired it, for though it caused him to shudder it was with every evidence of enjoyment. 'It is customary to smash the glass after a toast,' he said, 'but as we have only two cups between us, I give you the *Jean-Bart* and all who sail in her.'

'Wait. We cannot call her the *Jean-Bart*.'

'Why not?' Imlay's cup was poised in mid-air.

'Because that is what she was called when she was in the French service. They may not know her by sight, but they may very well know the name – *and* that she was taken prize by the British.'

'I had not thought of that. So what shall we call her?'

Nathan considered. The naming of a ship was not to be taken lightly.

'What about the *Swallow*?' he proposed.

'The *Swallow*?' Imlay mused. 'Well, it is an elegant bird – and swift.'

'It is also a sign of hope, in the maritime world, of a sailor's return,' Nathan said. 'For the swallow, I am told, always returns to its own home, no matter how long its absence and how far the journey.'

He was suddenly overwhelmed by a wave of melancholy so desolate he was scarcely aware of Imlay's response.

'So, the *Swallow* it is.' Imlay raised his cup once more. 'A successful voyage, and a safe return – to whatever we think of as home.'

Part Two

The Shores of Tripoli

———— ◆◆◆ ————

Chapter Ten

The Seraglio

---•◆•---

The life of a slave girl in an Ottoman harem was not so very different from the life of a nun, Caterina reflected, except that you prayed less, ate more, and bathed a great deal more frequently. And though it might have surprised a few people of her acquaintance in Venice, you never saw a man, not even the shadowy figure of a father confessor through a grille.

At other times she was reminded of her childhood, tending to her father's sheep in the hills.

It was rather more enclosed, of course. You never saw the sky, or the sun, or the moon and the stars – all you saw was their light through the narrow windows, high above your head, or reflected off the tiled walls or in the play of shadows on the stone floors. You could not smell the herbs crushed beneath your bare feet or breathe the sun-baked earth and the fresh, clean air. But there was

the same sense of timelessness – of endless days of quietude,
and boredom, and loafing around with very little to do.
Except watch sheep. And the women of the harem were
very like sheep, in Caterina's view, except that they
were lazier, and sillier, and a great deal more inclined to
petulance.

Caterina's understanding of the word 'harem' was that
it meant a safe haven, a forbidden place, sacred and
inviolable. In the best of them, the women were educated
and trained, not only in the skills of being a wife and
mother, but in diplomacy and statecraft. Certain of the
women of the Sultan's harem in Topkapi had achieved so
great an influence they had become the effective rulers of
the Empire.

The harem of Yusuf Pasha, however, was not quite in
this exalted category.

The *seraglio* – the living quarters of the harem –
occupied a labyrinth of rooms on two floors along one
side of the castle, facing towards the sea. Not that the sea
was very much in evidence. Sometimes, you could smell it.
And in some of the rooms you could hear it, especially at
night, the soft murmuring of waves on shingle; the sound
of freedom. But you could not see it. Not if you were a
slave.

There were about thirty women in the harem, not
counting the hostages, and about a dozen young children.
It took Caterina a while to sort out who they were and
how they were related, and even after six months, some of
these attachments were still puzzling to her.

It quickly became apparent, however, that there was a
fairly strict hierarchy and a shifting system of alliances.

At the top of the pecking order was the Pasha's mother, Lilla Kebierra, a faded blonde beauty with an air of tragedy about her, and a withered hand like a claw which she normally kept hidden within her robes.

It was some time before Caterina learned that her hand was not withered but shattered – smashed by a pistol ball fired by her son, the present Pasha, when she had had tried, unsuccessfully, to prevent him from murdering his elder brother. And to make it even worse, this terrible crime had been committed within the sanctuary of the harem itself. There was a room which no one ever entered where the murder had been committed, and it was even said that the floor and furnishings were still soaked in the blood of the murdered prince.

Lilla Kebierra had apparently forgiven Yusuf Pasha this atrocity, or was at least officially reconciled with him. But then, as Caterina's informants told her, what choice did she have?

But although Lilla Kebierra was the official doyen of the harem, the real power lay with the Pasha's wives.

There were two of them. Lilla Hadrami and Lilla Hamdouchi. Lilla Hadrami was white and Lilla Hamdouchi was black. Otherwise, so far as Caterina was concerned, there was not a great deal to choose between them in terms of spite and petty-mindedness.

They were reckoned to be great beauties – at least by the standards of Ottoman high society, if not by Caterina – and they preferred to be surrounded by beautiful things, provided such things could in no way be construed as a threat.

Caterina and Louisa came into this favoured category.

They were without any obvious physical defects or
deformities, but far too thin to be considered alluring by
the Pasha or any of his important male familiars, in the
opinion of the wives. This qualified them as handmaidens.
So instead of being confined to the role of skivvies –
working in the kitchens or cleaning out the bedchambers
and the privies – the two women spent a great deal of their
time in attendance on the wives and their immediate family
circle.

Beneath these close relatives was an amorphous layer
of 'dependants' who were either vaguely related to the
Pasha or were the wives and mothers of men he had
murdered and for whom he had generously taken responsibility. Their role seemed to be to look after the spoiled
brats that passed for children and to organise and discipline
the servants.

The servants were the next layer. They were either
Arabs or Africans and they were exclusively Moslem.
Beneath them, at the very bottom of the heap, were the
slaves, who were all Christian, of course, and did the most
menial tasks. There had been four of them before the
arrival of the hostages – all Italians – and they became
Caterina's chief informants.

It was through them that she learned why Lilla
Kebierra's left hand resembled a claw and why her hatred
of Lilla Hadrami and Lilla Hamdouchi was only surpassed
by their hatred of each other.

For if Lilla Kebierra was unable or unwilling to be
revenged upon her son, she had no such reservations about
his wives. Most of the time she kept her feelings as closely
hidden and as clenched as her shattered hand, but she did

everything she could to make their lives difficult, if not impossible. The two wives distracted themselves from this torment by tormenting each other. And all cloaked in silk and satin and smiles.

So all things considered, the harem of Yusuf Pasha was not so very different from your average convent in Venice.

The problem, from Caterina's point of view, was that she was no longer in a position of authority. And though she was a natural-born conspirator, her opportunities in the closed world of the harem were strictly limited. She could not use her beauty to the same devastating effect as she had in the past; she was a despised Christian; and most difficult of all, she could not speak the language, for though she spoke Spanish and Latin, and French and English almost as well as her native Venetian, she had never learned Turkish or Arabic. There was not the call for it in Venice. And without the books she was unable to master more than a few basics.

The only books available in the harem were of a religious nature, and most of them were in Arabic. There was one Latin translation of the Qur'an – made by Father Ludovico Marracci of Padova – and Caterina did apply herself to this for a while, for she was a great believer in the maxim *Know Thine Enemy* – but in truth it did not tell her a great deal that was useful to her, and as a form of diversion it was not remotely comparable to the amusements that had been available to her in the convent.

She learned much from the four Italian girls, however, and conversed a great deal with Louisa in English. The two captives made as thorough an exploration of the seraglio as was possible, but without finding any obvious

means of escape. The only way in and out was through a
great oak door that was almost permanently locked; the
only times Caterina saw it open – for the admission of
supplies – she noted the heavily armed guards in the
corridor outside. There were plenty of windows, but they
were set high in the walls, and without a rope and a
grappling hook, impossible of access. On the other side of
the walls was the sea – but it must be a 200-feet drop down
the sheer walls of the Red Castle and the rock on which it
was built. But the thought of the sea always gave Caterina
hope. Though she had been born and bred in Verona she
was, by nationality and inclination, a Venetian.

She conversed little with the other Venetians. There
were nineteen of them, all sharing the same crowded
dormitory. They comprised four women from the highest
strata of Venetian society, ten of their servants and
dependants, and five children. The aristocrats treated
Caterina with disdain, though they would not have
done so in Venice. They knew of her reputation there –
that she had been an actress and, some said, a courtesan
before she had become a nun – and they resented the
influence she had formerly possessed. Caterina was in no
way disquieted. For the most part she ignored them as
completely as they ignored her, and took a secret delight
in seeing them trying to make beds or wash dishes in the
kitchens. And yet she could not help but think that if
they could only unite, they might achieve something.
Together with herself and Louisa, and the four Christian
slave girls, they numbered twenty adults. An uprising
was not inconceivable. In her more sanguine moments,
Caterina imagined them taking over the seraglio, locking

the other women in their rooms, scaling the walls and dropping down into the harbour. Then stealing a boat and sailing out to sea.

But those moments were fleeting.

The hostages were closely watched by the Moslem slaves at all times; even at night there was always one of these women on duty in their dormitory. At the slightest alarm Caterina had no doubt that the male guards would come rushing in, as they had at the behest of Yusuf Pasha when he had murdered his elder brother here. Besides, it was impossible for her to trust her fellow captives. Except Louisa.

The chains of slavery had strengthened the bonds forged by the two women on the *Saratoga*. It was as strong a relationship as Caterina had ever known with another woman. In the convent she had always felt a certain detachment from the other nuns, perhaps even distrust, but she experienced a real sense of affection for and protectiveness towards Louisa. She was not sure why this was – perhaps some latent maternal instinct. Louisa had lost her mother quite recently and this made her vulnerable, needful of the advice and support of an older woman. But there was also a sharpness in Louisa, an intellect and a wit, that gave her a status in Caterina's eyes that the nuns of San Paolo had lacked. She made Caterina laugh.

There was, of course, the possibility that captivity had increased Caterina's own sense of vulnerability – her own need for friendship and support, even love. And Louisa was the only person she could really talk to.

They spoke in English, inevitably, since it was the only language Louisa *could* speak. Even after twelve months in

Venice she hardly spoke any of the dialect, though she did know some Latin, which was similar. Officially, they could only converse in their own quarters; while on duty they were not supposed to talk to each other at all. But they found the means to do so in the one place that gave Caterina a feeling of freedom – the *hammam*.

Known previously to her as a Turkish bath, this was on the lower floor of the seraglio at ground level – a tiled oasis boasting a large pool surrounded by luxurious plants which flourished in the humid atmosphere and the light from the high, narrow windows. The women of the harem spent a great deal of their time there and the two new handmaidens were permitted to accompany them. Their duties were not arduous. They were required to help keep the place clean and tidy, pick up the used towels and leave them for the laundress, and occasionally scrub the backs of the Pasha's women with a loufa.

And there were opportunities for promotion. Had Caterina possessed the right skills she might have been employed as a masseuse. Or a fortune-teller – for the hamman was where the women pondered what the future might bring, for themselves and their children.

Caterina did wonder about setting herself up in this capacity. It did not require much in the way of subterfuge and she had inherited certain skills of presentation from her mother, Strega Rosa – but once more the language barrier presented an insuperable problem.

It was a far more basic skill that secured her advancement.

The best thing about the hammam, in Caterina's view, was the pool. She had learned to swim as a child in the

lakes and rivers of the Soave Hills whilst looking after her
father's sheep. Unfortunately the pool was forbidden to
slaves and she could only look on with envy as the women
sedately lowered themselves into the water after taking a
steam bath. But one day, when the women were still in the
steam room, she horrified Louisa by diving in and
swimming to the far side and back. It was only when she
climbed out that she saw Lilla Hadrami standing there
watching her.

The very least she expected was to be exiled to the
kitchens. But the following day one of the servants, Adiba,
who acted as a kind of housekeeper, took her aside and
told her that Lilla Hadrami wished to be taught how to
swim.

And so Caterina's new duties began.

Lilla Hadrami proved an apt pupil, but of course it was
impossible to keep the lessons a secret, and soon they all
wanted to do it – all apart from Lilla Kebierra and a couple
of the older dependants. Caterina soon found herself
teaching the two wives separately on a one-to-one basis
while holding communal classes for the others. She also
taught Louisa. And in return for Caterina's tutoring, the
two handmaidens were permitted the use of the pool when
no one else was using it.

It took them a while to relax with the idea of being
naked, particularly Louisa who was more inhibited – but
once they did, they spent at least one hour a day there,
usually in the evenings. And this was where they did most
of their talking – and plotting.

Caterina had not given up thoughts of escape. The
sound of the sea, especially in the evening and at night,

was a constant enticement to her, a provocation almost. A mass break-out might be out of the question, but with the right tools she was convinced that she and Louisa could do it by themselves. Their hour in the pool at the end of the day provided the opportunity. All they lacked was the means of scaling the walls. They needed a rope and they needed some kind of a hook. Caterina even thought of making use of the hairs she was forever brushing up from the sides of the pool. Although none of the women had any hair on their bodies – they were obliged to be shaved, even in their most intimate parts, using mussel shells and an odious cream that was supposed to stop the hairs from growing again – the hair on their heads, when unbound, hung down to their waists. It should not be impossible to plait the single strands together to form a rope.

Louisa persuaded her otherwise. It would take several months, she argued, and where would they hide it in the meantime?

Caterina forbore to tell her they might well *have* several months. Even years. This was the view of the Italian slave girls who had given up all hope of release or of ever seeing the outside world. What news the captives had of that world – and the progress of negotiations for their release – was brought to them by Miriam, the Jewish woman who was the only outsider permitted regular access to the harem, and who acted as a conduit between the captives and the brokers, who were also Jewish.

Miriam had spent her early years in Livorno, and the Tuscan dialect was close enough to Venetian for Caterina to understand most of what she said. She also understood that the woman's main motive was to discover how much each of the captives was worth – or how much might be extracted from their friends and family to obtain their release. Once a price had been agreed, and approved by the Pasha and his advisers, the brokers would arrange the transfer of funds with their associates in Italy. But the agreeing of a price could take months or even years of hard bargaining.

Of course, Caterina was reluctant to disclose that she had any money at all. As a nun, she assured Miriam, she was constrained by her vow of poverty. Miriam tactfully reminded her of the purse of gold coins that had been found on her when she was captured: thus revealing to Caterina that Miriam and her associates were in the confidence of the Pasha's officials, which was at least useful to know, though it did not inspire confidence in her. Caterina told her that she had been given the purse by one of the other passengers for safekeeping, presuming that as a nun she would not be searched.

It was doubtful if Miriam believed her, but Caterina was determined to maintain the fiction that she was entirely without funds of her own. This was when she was still hopeful that the Church would negotiate her release. It was never a very strong hope and as the months went by, it faded completely.

She had almost reached the point of admitting to a secret but small inheritance, and writing a letter to her bankers in London, when Miriam disclosed that the United States government was prepared to take responsibility, not only for the officers and crew, but for all the passengers who lacked the funds to purchase their own release. Louisa's father had apparently been active in their interests, and agents had been appointed to do the necessary bargaining on the Americans' behalf. Nothing had been agreed as yet, but Miriam expressed confidence that it was only a matter of time.

And then she said something rather strange.

'You have an admirer,' she revealed to Caterina as she prepared to depart, 'here in Tripoli. He asked me to tell you not to lose hope. He is working for your release.'

But despite Caterina's entreaties she would say no more.

So Caterina decided she could hold out for a while longer. It was not as if she was in any great discomfort, or danger. The harem was a much better place to be than the dungeons in the castle basement, or working in a slave gang which, she was assured, was the lot of the male passengers and crew of the *Saratoga* while they waited for the American agent and the Jewish brokers to agree a price.

All she had lost so far, besides her purse, was her freedom.

She spent a good deal of her time wondering about this. What freedom meant to her. What it *was*.

She realised that she had never truly felt free, not even as a child roaming the hills of Treviso with the sheep. It was not as if she had a choice in the matter. She could not decide to do something else. To carry on sleeping in the morning, or read a book. Or even take the sheep to a different pasture without her father's consent. And if she had lost a single sheep, he would have knocked her teeth out. She had had no future, other than the future that her father decided for her.

Then one day, when she was about twelve or thirtee.
she was sitting under an olive tree watching the sheep, or
rather *not* watching them for her eyes were closed and she
was almost asleep, when she heard the sound of a flute.
She did not know then that it was a flute, but she knew it
as some kind of musical instrument: like pan pipes. She
looked up and saw a young man sitting under another
tree, watching her while he played. He was rather a beautiful young man and at first she thought he *was* Pan. Or
some such sprite. But he was not – he was one of a troupe
of travelling players, but Caterina was enchanted nonetheless. And on the spur of the moment, after some further
negotiation between them, she left the sheep and the dogs
and her mother and her father and the life she had led
since she was born, and joined them. And that was how
she became an actress.

But she would not have said she had gained her freedom.
She was still dependent on some man: some lover, like
the flute-player, or some father-figure like the manager
of the troupe, for it was only by his favour – and the
favours she granted him – that she was able to continue
with the life she had chosen and make a little money
from it. And even when she became a famous actress in
Verona, she still counted on the favour of the men who
ran the companies and the theatres and who made the
bookings.

It was the same in the convent, except that she depended
on the favour of women. Women in power, like the
Prioress and the Novice Mistress.

It was only when she gained power for herself that she
achieved something like real freedom. But it was always

.ependent on her guile and cunning – and beauty. It was always dependent on how well she was able to manipulate *men*. Men of power in Church and State.

Freedom was power; freedom was control. And if you ever achieved it, which was unlikely, you could never for one moment relax your guard or you would lose it.

So she found a kind of freedom in being a slave in the harem – the freedom from responsibility and from having to live on her wits. It was like a holiday, and she knew it would not last. Sooner or later a decision would have to be made. If necessary, she would write to her bankers instructing them to negotiate on her behalf. Miriam would see that the letter was sent. Or she could leave it to the Americans. Or her unknown admirer. Or, if they all failed her, she would engineer her own escape.

The more she thought about this, the more it appealed to her – for what would it profit her to purchase her freedom, if it cost her everything she had? In Caterina's estimation there could be no freedom without money. Poverty was the prison she feared the most.

In the meantime, she was in no immediate danger. She might be in the power of the Pasha and his wives, but they were unlikely to do her any harm, not while she was worth something to them.

And then it all changed.

One evening, just before sunset, while she and Louisa were bathing in the pool, she had a feeling she was being watched.

There was a grille high in the wall at one end of the room. Behind it, according to the slave girls, there was a small chamber where Lilla Kebierra sometimes sat and looked down on the other women. It was said that she was looking for a future bride for her son – one of the younger cousins or nieces, perhaps. Someone she could use in her endless war with the two wives he had already.

So naturally Caterina assumed it was Lilla Kebierra looking down at them. But it did not occur to her that it was from anything more than idle curiosity.

Then, the following day, after the usual meagre breakfast with the other captives, Caterina and Louisa received an unexpected supplement. A large dish of bread soaked in milk and sugar.

'What is this?' Caterina demanded of Elizabetta, the slave girl who had set the dish before them.

'It is something nice for you,' said Elizabetta, but she would not meet her eyes. 'On the instruction of Lilla Kebierra.'

Caterina pushed it aside. 'Well, you may thank Lilla Kebierra kindly for me,' she said, 'and tell her that while we appreciate her concern, we have quite enough to eat already.'

Elizabetta looked even more embarrassed. 'Please eat,' she said. 'If you do not, we have been told we must force it down you.'

She abruptly turned on her heel and walked away. Caterina felt Louisa looking at her.

'What was that about?' the girl asked.

'They want to fatten us up,' Caterina told her thoughtfully.

'But why?'

'So we look more like them.'

'But why would they want that?' Louisa had improved

in many ways since her arrival in the harem, but she was still quite naive at times.

Caterina spelled it out for her. 'So we may make suitable brides,' she said, 'for a Pasha.'

Louisa gazed at her in dawning horror. 'What are we to do?' she said.

'At the moment, I have no idea,' Caterina confessed. 'It has been rather sprung on me. I am going to have to think about it.'

In the meantime, they ate the sugared bread soaked in milk. It would have been too humiliating to have it forced down them. Even so, they nearly gagged on it.

Caterina did not have to think for long. She knew what she had to do, but it would take careful planning and the co-operation of their friendly extortionist – and the judicious disposal of a few rosary beads.

Chapter Eleven

The Flight of the Swallow

———◆·◆·◆———

The *Swallow* slipped out of Gibraltar a little before dawn on a murky morning in early April, with every scrap of sail she could carry to make the most of a grudging offshore breeze. She was a fine sailor with a decent crew. She had shown the *Unicorn* a clean pair of heels in the *tramontana* while sailing down to Naples, and the *Unicorn* was no slouch. Nathan could only hope she would see off the Spanish gunboats in the same brisk fashion if they poked their noses out of Algeciras, for the American flag would not save her after the length of time she had spent under the guns of Gibraltar; it would be taken as a *ruse de guerre*, and a poor one at that.

He stood at the quarterdeck rail, feet squarely planted, hands clasped behind him, mouth turned down and his hat pulled low over his frowning brow, the very image of the perfect hang 'em and flog 'em martinet. There was always a chance it might convince them: they were a new crew, they did not know him yet, nor he them.

He was not in the best of moods. They had made a hash of raising the anchor, and it was only Tully's fierce and persistent reproaches that had prevented them from running upon the guard ship at the end of the mole. He thanked God they were not flying the blue ensign and under the Admiral's orders, or he'd have been for the high jump himself. He had caught a jeering verse of 'Yankee Doodle' as they passed the guard ship, and someone on the forecastle had thrown them a biscuit. Which was a little unfair, for there could not have been more than a dozen Americans aboard the ship, for all their Stars and Stripes. The rest were Russian, Portuguese, Genoese and diverse subjects of King George – a term which, as anyone in the Navy knew, covered a multitude of sins.

The original ship's complement – the men who had sailed down from Portugal with Tully – had been increased in quantity, if not in quality, by a trawl of the Governor's prison and the bars along the Gibraltar waterfront; and the Admiral had sent them a draft of 'volunteers' from the fleet – which seemed to consist of every troublemaker and awkward cuss the fleet wished to be rid of. This had brought their number up to a little below 100, but they were of very mixed ability. Perhaps above half of them could be classed as seamen, in that they could hand, reef and steer. The rest were the usual flotsam swept out to sea on a tide of misfortune and misdemeanour. Nothing unusual about that – the King's Navy could scarcely have mustered a squadron without them – but on a King's ship their propensity for mischief was for the most part subdued by the Articles of War, the rope, the lash and a contingent of Marines. The *Swallow*, lacking any of these conveniences, was afflicted with a general spirit of rebellion.

Nathan had never known such an assemblage of sea lawyers, each with an egotistical notion of his own importance and eager to argue his own case, often in an impenetrable tongue. The rest, either through lack of vocabulary or wit, had perfected their own form of protest which Nathan and Tully characterised as 'dumb insolence'. This was the most difficult to check, for with men who had only the smallest grasp of English, it was hard to know if they genuinely did not understand an order or were wilfully resolved to defy it. Both officers were inclined to suspect the latter, but as yet they had come up with no coherent plan to deal with it. It was not easy to impose their authority on such a mixed bunch, each with his own complicated loyalties.

The Americans were Imlay's men. They had previously formed the crew of the *Pride of New Orleans*, an armed brig taken off Ushant by one of the King's cruisers on suspicion of running the British blockade. Imlay had told Nathan the story with frank enjoyment, for he was an old blockade-runner himself. Her papers – and a cursory inspection – had showed her to be carrying a cargo of rice, but on further enquiry this was found to contain a quantity of saltpetre, more familiar to the makers of gunpowder than of puddings. With ship and cargo rightly condemned as contraband, her crew had been kicking their heels in Plymouth when Imlay had snapped them up at the start of his voyage to Gibraltar. He could probably be taken at his word for once, for they were indeed prime seamen. The problem was, they had a great disinclination to take orders from anyone wearing the King's uniform. A good boatswain could probably have knocked them into shape, with the support of his mates and a few lengths of rope's end. Lacking such a creature, Nathan did the next best thing and appointed the biggest and toughest of them as boatswain and permitted him to pick his own mates. He was aware that this could lead to the worst kind of tyranny on the lower deck, but it was the best he could do in the circumstances.

The Russians were a law unto themselves. They had the look of good seamen and certainly knew what they were about, but they had their own particular way of going about it, and appeared impervious to correction or criticism. Of course, they neither spoke nor understood more than a few words of English, or at least maintained that pretence, and a pretty effective pretence it was. Tully put them to working and messing together under the instruction of their own petty officer who answered directly to Lieutenant Belli.

Then there were the Genoese. They had been with the *Jean-Bart* when she was under French command and had readily agreed to continue serving under the British flag when Nathan took her off Corfu. Somehow Tully had managed to keep them from being poached by other ships during the refit, but they were perfectly happy to change their allegiance yet again and serve the Americans, or anyone else for that matter, provided it did not inconvenience them. They were a competent, if arrogant bunch, very much aware of their own abilities and their superiority to all other forms of marine life. Tully put them in the tops, under their own captains, where they formed a kind of aerial tribe, swinging 100 feet above the deck, peering down at the lower orders from their lofty perches and calling to each other in their own strident dialect. They had a tendency to wear colourful neckerchiefs. Nathan and Tully privately called them 'the parrots'.

The Portuguese were also experienced seamen and a few of them even knew enough English to understand what they were being told to do. The problem was that they gave a very strong impression that they thought it was the *wrong* thing to do. Tully could not look at them without a nerve twitching in his cheek. This was unusual in him. He blamed himself for taking them on in the first place when the ship was in Lisbon, but without them he would scarcely have had enough crew to sail her down to Gibraltar. On a British ship-of-war, he would have found a way of dealing with them. As it was, they were an endless source of torment to him. For the time being he had distributed them among the forecastle men and the after-guard. In his smuggling days, he told Nathan nostalgically, he would have picked the biggest of them and beaten him to a pulp – and that would have been an end to it. He was not normally a violent man.

The true-born British subjects were the worst. Those who were not criminally inclined were fit only for Bedlam. Tully distributed the least incompetent among the Portuguese in the hope that their mutual disrespect would distract them from disrespecting their officers. The rest he stuck in the waist where they would do least damage to themselves and the ship. They were, indeed, waisters to a man.

Nathan was better served by the officers. There was Tully, of course, on whom he could rely completely. And Mr Lamb, who had been so eager to serve as a volunteer it had brought a lump to Nathan's throat. Lamb had been with the *Unicorn* when Nathan had taken her over in the Havana in the spring of '95 – a lad of twelve and the youngest of her midshipmen. Now he was fifteen and seemed to have grown a foot taller in the last year. Nathan looked at him sometimes and wondered where the little boy had gone; then Lamb would give a sudden grin and there he was, as if he had been playing hide-and-seek and poked his head out from behind a tree.

They had been accustomed to playing chess together on the *Unicorn*, for Lamb was the only one of the young gentlemen who had the patience for it. Nathan had been irritated at times by his recklessness. There was none of that now. He played a very dogged game indeed, and Nathan was frequently obliged to seek means of distraction.

'So, Mr Lamb, what do you want to do when you grow up?' he asked him, on one such occasion, when he was in danger of losing a rook.

Lamb looked up at him in frank astonishment. 'Sir?'

'When you grow up, Mr Lamb. How do you see yourself, sir? What profession would you assume?'

'I – Oh, you mean if there is peace, sir, and they do not keep me on.' Mr Lamb frowned at this dreadful prospect.

'Well, there is that, but I was thinking more of your own inclination. What would you make of yourself, sir, had you any choice in the matter? Does the Law interest you at all, or the Church?'

Mr Lamb's frown grew more pronounced.

'Well, I – I should like very much to stay in the service, sir, and advance as far as I am able.'

'And how far would that be, sir?'

Mr Lamb blushed but clearly did not want to be thought lacking in ambition. 'I should very much like to rise to a position of command, sir, like yourself.'

'I mean when you *grow up*, Mr Lamb,' insisted Nathan, feigning irritation.

The midshipman was now thoroughly confused. 'I am sorry, sir, I do not know what you mean.'

'Well, to be honest, sir, I was thinking of making you up to acting lieutenant for the duration of the voyage, but I was afraid you would take it ill in me, having your heart set on a chaplaincy.'

'Oh sir! You do not mean it!'

'I did mean it, Mr Lamb, but if I have insulted you I will take it back.'

'Oh no, sir, no, not at . . . That is, it would be an honour, sir, a great honour.'

'You mean you accept?' Astonished.

'Yes, sir. And I promise I will not let you down, sir.'

'I am sure you will not, sir.' Nathan nodded at the board. 'Your move, I believe.'

Mr Lamb advanced a pawn meaninglessly, and Nathan, with a secret smile, moved his rook out of harm's way.

He was less successful in his dealings with Kapitan-leytnant Belli. Though the Russian could speak very little English, they conversed well enough in French, and for all the peculiarities of his dress and manner, he appeared to be a gentleman. He was an experienced seaman, too, and was worshipped by his men; almost literally, for he was as a god to them – *Batiushska* they called him, which Imlay translated as 'Little Father'. The problem was that, like many of his kind, he enjoyed his drink, on and off duty. Vodka normally, but virtually anything alcoholic would do. When he drank, his eyes disappeared into the vastness of his face, which glowed as red as a coachman – which creature he much resembled. Otherwise, it seemed to have no injurious effect. He was no roaring drunk; he did not fall over or carouse or threaten violence; there was no violence in him – if anything, he became more genial – but it would have been unwise to entrust him with the running of the ship, which was a serious disadvantage in an officer.

Nathan was beginning to appreciate why Tully had looked so uncharacteristically careworn on their reunion. The trip down from Lisbon with only one other officer he could rely upon, and that a fifteen-year-old midshipman, must have been taxing in the extreme.

Fortunately, they had taken on another lieutenant at Gibraltar. Mr O'Driscoll was a gentleman from Dublin, in his early thirties, whose last Captain had taken against him, according to the Governor, for the circumstance of his being Irish. This was a not uncommon prejudice in the King's Navy. The loyalty of the Irish – Catholic or Protestant – was held by many officers to be suspect.

'Which is a great nonsense,' O'Hara had declared emphatically. 'That attitude would never be tolerated for an instant in the Army. My goodness, where would we be without an Irishman in the ranks?'

Nonetheless, O'Driscoll had been put ashore at Gibraltar, where he had been kicking his heels for several months in hopes of finding another ship with a more tolerant Commander. Nathan, being half-American and exposed to a similar prejudice, was inclined to be sympathetic. He took him aboard on a trial basis and could find no fault with him during their somewhat limited exercises in Gibraltar Bay. The Dubliner was modest, unassuming, hardworking and efficient, if a little lacking in self-esteem, which was understandable in the circumstances. More importantly, he would enable them to run to three watches, so far as the officers were concerned, giving them the benefit of an eight-hour sleep.

They were pitifully short of warrant officers, but those they did have were as good, or at least as well-qualified, as any Nathan had known on a proper King's ship, with the possible exception of the acting surgeon Mr Kite. Kite had been a loblolly boy on the flagship and had been sent by the Admiral either because he was completely useless or had contrived some other reason to give offence. Fortunately, no one had yet fallen sick. Were they to do so, doubtless Mr Kite would despatch them with at least as much efficiency as most surgeons.

Nathan was more fortunate in his sailing master, Mr Cribb. A laconic young man in his mid-twenties, he was the former mate of the *Pride of New Orleans* and was an excellent navigator, according to Tully, who had tested him out on the voyage down from Lisbon.

The gunner, Mr Wallace, was unusual in that he was not a seaman at all but an employee of the Carron Company. He had been sent down from their foundry in Falkirk to help with the installing of the guns and Imlay had apparently bribed him to remain for the duration of their voyage. His accent was almost as impenetrable as that of the Russians, but he seemed to know what he was doing so far as the guns were concerned – inasmuch as Nathan could tell without seeing him in action. However, it was impossible for him not to miss Mr Clyde, the gunner of the *Unicorn*, who had died in an engagement with privateers off Leghorn, and George Banjo, the giant African who had been set to succeed him until he struck an officer and was obliged to jump ship. In their absence he gave Mr Wallace the benefit of the doubt; a confidence he was not yet prepared to extend to the guns themselves.

The carpenter was also a Scot – Mr Cameron, another old hand from the *Unicorn* who had shifted to the *Jean-Bart* as part of her prize crew and stayed with her for the refit. He was entered on the muster book as a volunteer and was presumably very happy with the £6.12s a month Imlay was paying him, which was almost three times what he had been getting from King George.

The only other officer of warrant rank was the purser, who had been taken on by Tully in Lisbon – a Mr Harvey, half-English, half-Portuguese – the youngest son of a family said to be big in the port-wine trade. On their scant acquaintance, Nathan had formed very little opinion of his character, but unless the man was an out-and-out scoundrel he was prepared to overlook any failings in that quarter, having a great deal more to worry about than the character of the ship's purser.

Mr Harvey appeared to have made a reasonable job of stocking up on supplies, at least on paper and as far as the basics were concerned. According to the ship's books, before leaving Lisbon he had shipped twenty barrels of salt beef, ten each of salt pork, oatmeal, pease and biscuits, and five each of butter and cheese. There was a shortage of fresh lemons and oranges, but he had taken the precaution of shipping a quantity of onions and raisins, which spoke well in his favour.

Nathan had meticulously counted the barrels, though he had no means of knowing what was actually in them. Past experience suggested that at least a fifth of the meat would be rotten, but even so, he calculated that they had sufficient supplies of food for a two-month cruise and it should not be too difficult to obtain fresh supplies during their voyage. The provision of drink was more of a problem. On a King's ship, according to regulations, each seaman was entitled to eight pints of beer a day, or a pint of wine, or half a pint of spirits, and the same would be expected of men serving on a privateer. Beer was out of the question in the Mediterranean and in any case did not keep for more than a couple of weeks. Instead, Mr Harvey had secured ten 30-gallon casks of wine and five of rum which would keep a crew of a hundred going for just thirty-six days – but both he and Imlay seemed confident of securing more supplies on the Barbary Coast, despite the Moslem proscription on alcohol.

All in all, Nathan had a great many causes for complaint. But at least he was more or less satisfied with the ship herself. In fact, the only fault he could find in her was her weaponry, and he put this down to his own prejudice and kept it between himself and Tully; certainly it would have been a mistake to mention it to Mr Wallace.

Nathan had made a thorough inspection of the ship with Tully and the carpenter when he first took command. In dimensions, she was not much smaller than the *Unicorn*, being 135 feet long, 32 feet broad, and 14 feet in draught. Considering the corvette to be a dandified French notion, the Navy had first called her a sloop and then re-gunned her and re-classed her as a sixth-rate frigate. Fully crewed, she would have carried just over 200 officers and men; with fewer than half that, her lower deck felt positively commodious, and of course there were no Marines clump-ing about in their own separate quarters. The gunroom was the only disappointment – certainly for the officers who had to dine there. It was more of a passageway than a room, gloomy and narrow, with the foot of the mizzen-mast through the middle, and the rest of the space taken up by a long table, with the doors of the officers' cabins opening on to the tiny gap on either side.

The Captain's quarters were luxurious by comparison, with three separate cabins and almost enough headroom for Nathan to stand upright in all of them. The day cabin took up the whole width of the stern, with light pouring in not only from the stern windows but through the gunports when they were open. The deck was carpeted with chequered canvas, and the entire space positively gleamed with polished brass and oak. The only problem from Nathan's point of view was that he had to share it with Imlay. The sleeping cabin had been divided in two by a wood and canvas partition and they each slept in cots on either side of it.

They also shared the same servant – the elderly Qualtrough – and a Portuguese cook called Balsemao with two young boys as his assistants. This was by no means an indulgence. Nathan had known frigate Captains who had no fewer than eight servants – and when he was on the

Unicorn he had never had less than three, headed by the formidable Gilbert Gabriel.

Nathan had never missed his old crew quite so much as when the *Swallow* headed out into Gibraltar Bay. They had been so well-drilled, and worked together for so long, he had been able to take the smooth running of the ship very much for granted. This was far from being the case with the *Swallow*. With every man stood to quarters it was alarmingly apparent how short-handed they were. The wind was from the north-west so it was necessary to sail straight out across the bay, almost directly towards Algeciras, before coming about with enough sea room to clear Europa Point – a dangerous manoeuvre at the best of times. Nathan would have liked to have every gun run out and fully crewed – at least on the starboard side – in case they ran into any of the enemy gunboats, but this was impossible with the few men at his disposal. Most of the crew were standing by to brace the yards when they came about, and he could spare no more than a dozen for the guns – barely enough to fight four carronades.

The only thing that cheered him was the weather. It had closed in almost as soon as they cleared the harbour, and instead of becoming lighter as the day went by, the sky appeared to be darkening by the minute. The rain had increased in density, and visibility was down to little more than a couple of hundred yards. Peering into the murk on his starboard quarter, Nathan could see nothing of either Algeciras or the Spanish coast, not even the light at the end of the mole. Although this was very much to his advantage so far as the gunboats were concerned, he would have liked some visual reference before he came round onto the opposite tack. If he turned too soon there was a danger of running onto the Point – an embarrassment which would have made him the laughing-stock of the Navy, if he was unfortunate enough to survive the encounter.

He left it as late as possible, in the hope of seeing the merest glimmer of light from the shore. He could feel the tension in the crew, for even the most lubberly among them knew they were heading straight for the Spanish coast, and when he finally gave the order – and it was executed rather better than he had expected – he gave an inward sigh of relief.

And at that precise moment, just as they were heeling to starboard, there was a startled cry from one of the lookouts and Nathan whipped his head round to see the beak of a massive ship of the line bearing down on them out of the rain, a great red cross emblazoned on her foresail like the curse of God.

For a moment he stood transfixed. The vast spread of canvas seemed to envelop him. He felt like a tiny rodent as some giant predator descends on him from the skies. She was so close he could see every detail of her figurehead: a saintly apparition with fanatical eyes that seemed to bore into his own, the specks of rain and spray on his black beard, the golden cross brandished in both hands and a bishop's mitre balanced ridiculously on his head.

Time stood still. The apparition did not.

'Port your helm!'

Nathan could hear his voice shouting the command, even before his brain began to properly engage with the problem. It was a phrase that came instinctively to mind, as it did to all officers in the King's Navy, though it had long been rendered invalid by the introduction of the wheel.

'Port your helm' meant putting the tiller to port – or larboard. Which would turn the ship in the opposite direction. But modern ships did not have a tiller. They had a wheel, which was connected to the rudder by a system of cables and pulleys so ingenious that if you turned the wheel to starboard, you also turned the ship to starboard. It was nothing short of miraculous, and the Admiralty, lacking an understanding of miracles, had issued no instructions on the subject. Every quartermaster in the Navy knew that 'Port your helm!' meant 'Turn to starboard'. What was the point in changing it?

The trouble, in this instance, was that the quartermaster of the *Swallow* was a Portuguese called Apolinario, and though he was an able seaman and possessed many excellent qualities, including a reasonable knowledge of English, his knowledge of this subtlety was less than perfect.

Possibly he thought Nathan had made a mistake. Possibly the word 'port' evoked in his mind the image of the fortified wine for which his country was justifiably famous. Possibly he had been told the true meaning of the word by Tully but had forgotten. But for whatever reason, he did not respond to Nathan's urgent command as rapidly as might have been desired. He stood staring from Nathan to the oncoming vessel in a kind of fascinated horror.

It was Tully who saved them. With an animal cry he leaped at the immobile helmsman, shouldered him from his station, and spun the wheel.

Slowly, painfully slowly, the bows came round. Far, far

too late. Nathan watched helplessly as the gap between
the two ships narrowed. Other details became apparent.
The double row of gunports. The twin red stripes on the
black hull, like the markings on some exotic insect. The
men aloft and alow staring with the same horrified
intensity as Nathan had seen on the face of the hapless
Apolinario. The large red and yellow flag of Spain at her
stern. The cluster of officers mouthing what might have
been curses or prayers.

They missed her by a good few feet, though for a
moment Nathan thought the bowsprit was going to pass
straight through her stern lantern, and was almost disappointed when it did not. He heard himself utter a strange,
barking laugh. Checked himself. And with clownish
aplomb turned, bowed, and doffed his hat to the Spanish
officers. That and the Stars and Stripes convinced them.
He heard the word '*Americano*', accompanied by several
others he did not understand but which were almost
certainly impolite. He saw the name of her fanatical saint
emblazoned across her stern. *San Leandro*. Then she was
gone into the mist and the rain.

Nathan stood gazing after her for some minutes,
waiting to see if she would turn. But she did not. She must
have been on her way into Algeciras, beating into the wind
as the *Swallow* had on her route out of Gibraltar. He let
out a sigh.

'Well, that was a close one,' said Imlay, coming up to
him and peering into his face suspiciously and not a little
anxious, as if to assure himself that Nathan was still awake
and capable of making a rational decision.

Nathan gave a curt nod. He looked about him.

Apolinario was back at the helm. Tully was reminding him, with emphatic gestures, of the meaning of certain key phrases in the King's English, or at least its maritime equivalent.

Nathan caught the eye of the sailing master, who was looking at least as anxious as Imlay.

'Very well, Mr Cribb,' he told him, 'you may set a course for Algiers.'

They appeared to have missed hitting Europa Point, and so far as he knew there were no other hazards to navigation between here and Africa – besides those they carried aboard.

Chapter Twelve

The Innkeeper of Algiers

———◆———

'No! I will have no more figs!'
Nathan glared down at the overloaded bumboat bobbing beneath his starboard quarter. It contained a very large Arab woman, a very small Arab boy, and a very great quantity of dried fruit. Or decaying vegetable matter; it was hard to tell.

He knew he was sounding like a petulant child, but an hour or so's conversation with the itinerant traders of Algiers had done nothing to improve his temper. Above a score of bumboats pressed in on both sides of the *Swallow*, jostling against each other and subjecting the pristine paintwork of the ship's hull to grievous insult as their occupants engaged in similar transactions with members of the crew — these being conducted in several different tongues at extreme volume and involving a considerable range of goods, mostly edible, though Nathan would have been extremely surprised if women did not figure in them somewhere. He had no doubt that the scene below decks resembled something from Dante's vision of Upper Hell – or the average seaman's vision of Lower Paradise – as it did whenever a ship-of-war moored off a sizeable port and declared itself open for trade.

'Tell her I have enough figs to clear the bowels of Behemoth,' Nathan instructed the dragoman who had been assigned to them by the American Consul in Algiers in the hope, as this gentleman unfortunately put it, that 'it would ease their passage'.

The dragoman frowned over the exact translation of Nathan's directive, but whatever he said it seemed to do the trick. After some muttering, the woman reached under her skirts and produced a live hen which she held up for their inspection.

'Bit skinny,' Nathan told the dragoman begrudgingly. 'Ask her how much.'

They embarked upon another round of negotiations. Normally Nathan would not have jeopardised the dignity of his office in such a manner, but with the purser, the steward, and even the cook ashore with Imlay, he had no other option if he wished to purchase a private stock of supplies while he still had the chance. Since leaving Gibraltar he had been dependent upon Imlay's hospitality, for it had been impossible to obtain anything from the Rock in its present state of siege, and he had a natural reluctance to partake of the supplies of salt beef, pork, pease and oatmeal that were issued to the hands. Imlay had characteristically laid in a sufficient stock of delicacies for himself while at Lisbon, but Nathan was equally loath

to rely upon his charity for the duration of the voyage. For
the same reason he had declined to accept Imlay's offer of
remuneration at the inflated rate he was offering the rest
of the crew, preferring to maintain his dignity as a frigate
captain in the King's Navy on a paltry 11 pounds and 4
shillings a month.

Fortunately, General O'Hara had very generously
advanced him the back pay due to him while he was a
guest in the Governor's prison and he had departed
Gibraltar with seventy-five golden sovereigns jingling in
his purse and a pocketful of loose change. He could afford
the odd chicken.

The dragoman was addressing him. 'She say do the
Effendi want it dead or alive?'

Nathan considered. A live chicken was preferable.
Then he did not have to consume it in the next day or two,
and while it remained alive it might even contrive to lay a
few eggs. But there was no designated Jemmy Ducks
aboard the *Swallow* who could be relied upon to look
after any live animals that were aboard, and if the hen
disappeared into the maws of the ship he would never see
it again; he would have to keep it in his own quarters. His
dignity had suffered a great many setbacks in the past few
months, but he did not think he could tolerate a live hen
running about the Captain's cabin, and Imlay might have
words to say on the subject, besides.

'Dead,' he said, with reluctance.

He watched as the woman wrung its neck and accepted
the offering with distaste before summoning one of the
more reliable of the ship's boys to take it down to his
quarters. The dragoman asked him if there was anything

else he would like, accompanying this suggestion with a significant wink. In fact, there was a great deal that Nathan would have liked, all of it edible, but he was weary of the effort required to obtain it. With a little luck the purser would have purchased a sufficient number of sheep, goats and bullocks during his foray in Algiers for them all to dine off fresh meat for the next day or two. After that, it was figs with everything.

He looked out across the still waters towards the port, about the distance of a long cannon shot off the *Swallow*'s starboard bow. Behind the ramparts of its enclosing walls, the domes and minarets gleamed in the late-afternoon sun. Other details were lost in a shimmering haze of heat.

Algiers. For all his service in the Med, this was Nathan's first visit to the port. But with Spain in the French camp and most of Italy lost, it had become an important source of supply for the British fleet, and all officers were under strict instructions not to give offence to the Pasha-Dey, Baba Hussein. And the Pasha-Dey had duly supplied them with most of what they required, at rates that made his former occupation of piracy redundant.

But Imlay seemed to have no shortage of funds, for once. He had promised to supply the ship not only with fresh meat but also with the additional crew members Nathan required. Quite how remained a mystery. Doubtless there was the usual quota of unemployed seamen in the port, but they would almost certainly be Arab by race and Moslem by religion. Nathan had nothing against either as seamen or as people, but he was not sure how his Genoese and Portuguese crew members would take to them, their countrymen having suffered rather more than

most over the years from the raids of the Algerine Corsairs.
Nor was he at all sure that he could count on their loyalty
if they were required to fight their fellow Moslems in the
service of Yusuf Karamanli.

Imlay had simply told him 'not to worry'.

He had been ashore for most of the day now, visiting
the American Consul Mr Barlow – an acquaintance of his
days in Paris. Barlow had helped to arrange the peace
treaty between Algeria and the United States in '95. As a
result of which, for a payment of about half a million
dollars a year, American shipping was preserved from the
raids of the Algerine corsairs, and the *Swallow* could, with
impunity, sail into Algerine waters. Imlay had been
characteristically cagey about Barlow's role in the present
dispute with the Pasha of Tripoli, but it seemed reasonable
to suppose he was advising Imlay how to make a similar
arrangement.

The only thing that Nathan was sure of was that
there would be something in it for Imlay at the end of the
day.

He took off his hat and wiped a handkerchief over his
sweating brow. As this was a private command, he had
dispensed with the King's uniform for the duration of the
voyage, but even in a cotton shirt and ducks he was still
sweltering in the heat and there was not the slightest of
breezes to alleviate his discomfort. If it was this warm in
late April, he could only hope that he was not forced to
linger off the Barbary Coast through the height of the
summer. Though the heat, he anticipated, would be the
least of his worries.

He gazed with displeasure along the crowded upper

deck of the *Swallow*. Not only was it littered with baskets and bundles of produce – the result of the seamen's negotiations – but diverse articles of apparel hung from washing lines erected between the mainmast and the foremast. The seamen themselves, or at least those who were not having a better time below decks, also hung about, in various stages of undress, taking the sun or otherwise amusing themselves. It would likely have been much the same aboard a King's ship in similar circumstances, but Nathan felt strangely discomforted. There was something different about it from the usual disorder of a washday aboard the *Unicorn*, say, or any other ship-of-war in the King's Navy. Perhaps because there were so few blue jackets and, more to the point, no red ones. No comforting Marine sentry at the con, turning the glass, or at the belfry ringing the bell, or guarding the entrance to his cabin with a loaded musket. And no master-at-arms keeping a wary eye on the sly peccadilloes of the crew. Nathan had been in the Navy since he was thirteen years old, and that sense of discipline, that sense of order, had insinuated itself into his mind to such an extent that when it was not there he felt a distinct sense of unease, almost of offence. Before his present assignment he would have said that he had a natural inclination to unorthodoxy. Now he was not so sure. He felt like a pirate captain – or Captain Bligh in the South Seas tending the simmering crucible of mutiny until it boiled over – and he did not like it.

A cry from the maintop, where Tully had set a watch, alerted him to the approach of another flotilla of small boats from the shore. He thought at first that they were more bumboats and was bracing himself for the invasion when he saw they were led by the ship's launch, which had set off that morning with Imlay and his following. Hopefully, this was bringing them back, for Nathan was anxious for news. He recovered his Dolland glass from where he had hid it in the binnacle, safe from thieving hands, and focused it on the approaching vessel.

Sure enough, there was Imlay, and seated with him in the stern were two gentlemen Nathan had not seen before. One of them wore Arab dress, of no mean substance, from what Nathan could see at this distance, and nor was the man who wore it. He was not quite of Belli's girth but not far short of it. The other man wore a tricorne hat and a blue uniform coat with a smattering of gold lace, so was either a naval officer or a consular official. He was not Joel Barlow, though, whom Nathan had met briefly when he himself was in Paris.

Nathan looked beyond them to the other boats in the flotilla and saw with some anticipation, but also a degree of foreboding, that two of them contained a number of live animals. There were at least half a dozen bullocks and a considerable flock of sheep – or goats, it was hard to tell at this distance – which would have to be accommodated on the *Swallow*'s crowded decks. The other boats seemed to be full of men.

He saw Tully already heading towards him, his face creased with concern.

'Yes, Martin, see if you can clear the decks, will you,' Nathan instructed him, suppressing a twinge of conscience, for this would be no mean feat with the men at Tully's disposal, 'and get rid of this lot.' He waved a dismissive hand at the fleet of bumboats. 'And we had better rig a tackle from the yards to haul the cattle aboard – and a pen to keep them in, until they are slaughtered.'

The next few hours were likely to be fraught, if his previous experience of loading live bullocks was anything to go by, but at least they would have a decent steak to look forward to when they sat down to dinner instead of salt beef and pork.

'Captain Turner, may I present to you His Royal Highness Prince Ahmed of Tripoli. Prince Ahmed, this is my very good friend, Captain Nathaniel Turner.'

Nathan removed his hat and executed a polite bow whilst striving to conceal his bewilderment. The Prince inclined his head graciously. He was a small, plump gentleman of between thirty and forty with a surprisingly pale complexion, a wisp of blond beard – and sad, rather protuberant blue eyes.

'Brother of Yusuf Pasha,' hissed Imlay in his ear as the dragoman translated his introduction for the benefit of their distinguished visitor. But before Nathan could begin to assimilate this intelligence or its portent, the next man had stepped up to the mark.

'And this is Mr James Cathcart, formerly of the USS *Confederacy* and more latterly adviser to the Dey of Algiers.'

'The USS *Confederacy*?' Nathan repeated, permitting a little of his bemusement to show, though in fact the name vaguely rang a bell.

'Thirty-six-gun frigate,' replied Cathcart genially. 'Late of the Continental Navy. Forced to strike to the *Roebuck* and the *Orpheus* off Cape François. I was one of her officers, sir – a midshipman, to be precise – and found myself obliged to spend the next three years on a British prison hulk in the Medway. And I don't mind telling you, sir, all things considered, I had rather be a slave to the Mohammetans.'

Certainly they seemed to have fed him better, Nathan reflected, for he was run considerably to fat. Nathan wondered if he had been castrated, for he had something of the look of a eunuch, though his voice did not seem overly affected by the trauma.

'Ah, yes. Very good,' Nathan murmured blandly. Despite the broad smile on Cathcart's face, he detected a degree of antipathy in his eyes. Clearly, he still harboured some resentment at his treatment by the British authorities, and though Nathan had no personal experience of a prison hulk he had heard enough of conditions aboard them to understand why. He had a distant recollection of the action off Cape François – either he had read about it in his youth or his father had spoken of it. The frigate had been taken into the British Navy and renamed the *Confederate*.

None of which explained what Cathcart was doing here, or how he had come to be adviser to the Dey of Algiers.

But questions of this nature would have to wait upon events. He had visiting royalty to entertain. Fortunately Imlay had brought Qualtrough back with him and Nathan instructed him to prepare some refreshments in the cabin. 'But no alcohol,' he managed to convey in a terse undertone before the steward went below. Qualtrough gave him a look that might have been described as scathing.

Nathan introduced Prince Ahmed to his officers who had all, somehow or other, managed to put their uniform coats on, though otherwise their appearance left a great deal to be desired. The Prince's retinue was altogether more impressive. There were about ten of them, all in flowing robes with a plethora of jewellery and weapons. The rest of the men who had come aboard appeared to be either servants or seamen, many of them Arab but many not. They had also brought a quantity of baggage with them and they stood about the deck, taking stock of their surroundings while the crew of the *Swallow* took stock of them. All in all, Nathan reckoned, there must have been about fifty of them. And out of the corner of his eye, he saw the first bullock swinging up above the level of the deck, its eyes rolling wildly.

'Perhaps,' he said to Imlay, 'we should go below.' He caught Tully's eye and permitted himself the ghost of a smile. 'Carry on, Mr Tully.'

Gradually, in the course of the next half-hour, things became a little clearer.

Ahmed Karamanli Pasha-zade was the second son of the former Pasha of Tripoli, but he had fled the country shortly after the present Pasha had murdered their elder brother, doubtless being anxious to avoid the same fate. Since when he had been in exile, first in Tunis and then Algiers. Now apparently, he was planning to return to Tripoli aboard the *Swallow*, with a view to regaining his lost inheritance.

Several supplementary questions occurred to Nathan at this point, not least the problem of where he was going to accommodate the gentleman and his large retinue in the increasingly crowded lower deck of the *Swallow*. He put this at the head of a long and growing list which he planned to present to Imlay at the first opportunity.

In the meantime, Cathcart was more than happy to fill Nathan in on some of the blanks in his own history. He had been born in County Westmeath, in Ireland, he said, and emigrated to the American colonies at the tender age of twelve – just in time to join the Revolution.

'And how did you contrive to become a prisoner of the Algerines?' Nathan asked him, mainly to divert him from his experiences while in British custody.

'I was aboard the schooner *Maria* out of Boston,' Cathcart replied, 'when we were taken by a corsair. They took me and twenty others as slaves and we've been here ever since. Eleven years.'

'Good God!' Nathan stared at him. The man did not look as if he had endured eleven years of slavery, as Nathan understood the condition. He was not much older than Nathan, and he appeared in the best of health.

'The first years were pretty tough,' Cathcart admitted. 'We were put to work on improving the fortifications down by the harbour, carrying heavy stones and the like. The overseers were plain bastards who'd flog you as soon as look at you – you'd have thought they was in the British Navy – and once I was put to the bastinado. Beaten with a cane on the soles of the feet,' he explained. 'A punishment to which they are much inclined. But then after a while I was picked to work in the palace gardens with the lions and the tigers.'

Nathan bent his head in polite enquiry.

'Oh, aye, lions and tigers – he had them by the dozen,

the old Dey. Antelopes and peacocks, a right royal menagerie. I worked for the *Bostanji-bashi*, the head gardener, and he treated me well enough. Then Pasha Mohammed died and Baba Hussein took over. And one day he's walking in the gardens and we get to talking. I spoke the lingo by then, see, and I always had the gift of the gab in any tongue. Well, with one thing and another he takes a shine to me, and next thing I know I'm working inside the palace. At first I was just one of the clerks, translating documents and the like, but within a year or two I'm one of his top *Hojas*. I advised him on the treaty he made in ninety-six and on account of that, and the money he made out of it, he set me free, and all the others that was taken with me on the old *Maria*. Only by that time I'd put a bit of money aside myself, you see, and I'd found a house with servants, down by the harbour, and acquired a number of taverns.'

'Taverns?' repeated Nathan, casting his eye over their other guests, who were partaking of Qualtrough's non-alcoholic refreshments and the various delicacies that he had provided, which looked suspiciously to Nathan like those he had purchased himself only an hour before from the market traders.

'Oh, the present Dey has no objection to taverns,' insisted Cathcart, 'provided it's Christians what has the running of them. You see before you the biggest innkeeper in Algiers.'

This, presumably, was why Imlay had been so confident about the provision of wines and spirits. But it could not be the only reason that Cathcart was aboard. 'So why then do you wish to accompany us to Tripoli?' Nathan enquired.

'Ah, well, there you go now. Imlay thinks as how I was of such assistance over the treaty with the Dey, that I can be of equal help to him, d'you see, when he tries to deal with the Pasha of Tripoli. And he has promised to see me right over it.'

'And the men you have brought with you?'

'As to that, he said as how you was a bit shorthanded with the crew, Captain, and that we might be able to help you out.'

'But who are they?'

'Oh, most of them are seamen. Least they was, once upon a time. Twelve of them was with me when they took the *Maria*. The rest washed up in Algiers one way or another.'

'You say most of them. What about the rest?'

'The rest of 'em are gunners. Imlay says you are in particular need of gunners.'

'Well, that's true enough, but when you say gunners . . . you mean ship's gunners?'

'Ship's gunners, land gunners, they can fire any type of guns.'

'And what were they doing in Algiers?'

'Well, they was in the service of the Dey for a time, only he had no more need of them once he give up on the corsing, do you see? You might say I helped put them out of business when I helped with the signing of the treaty.'

'So they fought aboard the corsairs?'

'They did, sir, they did. And very well, too, from what I have heard.'

'So how do you think they would feel about fighting the corsairs from Tripoli, if they had to?'

'Oh, they'd have no trouble with that at all, at all. Most of them are from Sicily, do you see, and they'll fight anybody if they are paid enough.'

Nathan pondered this information in silence for a moment. Sicily was part of the Kingdom of Naples, or the Kingdom of the Two Sicilies as some would have it, ruled by the capricious King Ferdinand. The *Swallow* had been built in the King's yard at Castellammare, so Nathan supposed it might be thought appropriate to crew it with his former subjects. 'Taken as slaves, were they?'

'No, no. Never been slaves. They use the slaves for the oars, do you see? Gunners is what you might call a more dedicated profession, but you'd know that, being a Captain in the King's Navy. No, they are more in the way of mercenaries – so you'll have no trouble getting them to fight the corsairs of Tripoli. Not that I expect you'll have to. Not if we do the business with the Pasha.'

Nathan looked about the cabin. Imlay seemed perfectly at home in the role of host and his visitors were quite happily tucking into the refreshments. No one would miss him, Nathan thought, if he went up on deck, for his conscience was troubling him not a little for having left Tully in charge of accommodating the livestock and the additional crewmen. But there was one more thing he wished to know. He dropped his voice a little. 'And Prince Pashaza there, what do you know of him?'

'The Pasha-zade,' Cathcart corrected him mildly. 'It being a title not a name, do you see? It means the son of the Pasha. Ahmed Pasha-zade . . . being as how you always put the title after the name in the Arabic. And strictly speaking there is no P. Which is why some say "the Bashaw".'

Nathan thanked him for this intelligence. 'But why is he here?' he persisted.

'I think you had better ask Mr Imlay that. But no doubt he has his reasons for it.' The Innkeeper of Algiers lifted his empty glass and peered into it a little dismally. 'Now I don't suppose you have any of what you might call a proper beverage, set aside for Christians, if you see what I mean?'

Nathan told him to address himself to Mr Qualtrough.

'If you will excuse me,' he said, 'I think I had better attend to my duties on deck.'

In fact, by the time he emerged, Tully seemed to have matters well in hand. The bullocks and the sheep or goats – even at close quarters it was difficult to be precise as to their identity – were accommodated in pens in the waist, and the men had been put to work clearing up the con-siderable mess they had left on the decks – and even Mr Wallace's precious carronades – in the traumatic process of being hauled aboard.

Nathan joined Tully on the quarterdeck and congratulated him on his efficiency.

'What do you make of the new crewmen?' he asked him.

'Well, they seem to be competent at shovelling up shit,' Tully replied, a little coolly. 'I cannot speak for their other abilities as yet. Doubtless we will soon find out when we put to sea. Sir.'

Nathan perceived that there was a little bridge-building to be done between them.

'I suppose we will have to begin culling tomorrow,' he said, meaning the livestock, and not the crew.

'I expect we will, sir, or we will never be able to work the ship, let alone the guns.'

Nathan left his bridge-building for a more appropriate time and rejoined his visitors below. Cathcart appeared to have taken over as host and, judging from his ebullient manner, had prevailed upon Qualtrough in the matter of drink.

'So there you are,' Imlay greeted him amiably. 'I was wondering where you had got to. I hope you are happier now I have got you some decent seamen.'

'If they *are* decent,' replied Nathan sourly.

'Are you ever happy, Nathan?'

'I have had my moments.'

'One day you must tell me about them. I am sure I would find them stimulating.'

'I would be a little happier if you were to tell me what you intend with the Pasha-zade and his crew.'

'Ah. Yes. Well, I was about to, when we were alone. But as you ask, and as none of them speak a word of English, I will tell you now. Ahmed Pasha-zade is, so to speak, my wild card.'

'Your wild card?'

'My trump, even. If Yusuf Pasha refuses to moderate his terms.'

'And how is Ahmed Pasha-zade going to help?'

'Well, I would have thought that was obvious. He is a rival to the throne. In fact, as the elder brother, he is the rightful heir.'

'So, you are preparing to unleash him on Yusuf Pasha.'

'That is the general idea. I am told he has a great deal of support among the Khuloghlis.'

The implications of this were not immediately apparent to Nathan.

'You might call them the Household Cavalry,' Imlay explained. 'They were instrumental in bringing Yusuf to power but now, I am told, they have had a change of heart.'

'Well, I am glad you are on top of the situation.'

'I am glad you are glad. Is there anything else I can do for you?'

'Yes. You could tell me where I am going to stow him while he is aboard – him and his followers.'

'Ah. Well, as to that, I am afraid we will have to put him here. There is no other option. You cannot very well stick a member of the ruling house of Tripoli down in the bilges with the rats.'

Nathan nodded to himself though he was by no means convinced. 'And will his mates mess with him?'

'His *mates*?' Imlay raised a brow. 'One or two of his bodyguards might – but I am afraid we will have to accommodate the others elsewhere.'

'And what of ourselves?'

A small ironic bow. 'I leave that entirely at your disposal.'

'Then, unless you have any other business in Algiers, and as soon as we have cleared the deck of sheep and bullocks, I believe we will put to sea.'

'As you wish. I shall inform His Royal Highness. Oh, there is just one thing, if you will give me a moment.'

Imlay made his way through the company and returned with a bundle wrapped under his arm.

'This,' he said, 'is our flag.'

Nathan frowned. 'We already have a flag,' he said. They had been flying the Stars and Stripes since leaving Gibraltar. 'It has served us well enough until now.'

'Yes, but it may not be appropriate from now on. We are not, after all, an American national ship. Not in the strict meaning of the word. It would be neither diplomatic nor judicious to arrive in Tripoli flying the official American flag.'

Nathan knew Imlay of old and his suspicions were alerted.

He inspected at the bundle. 'So what flag is this?' He would not have been surprised if it was the skull and crossbones.

'Shall we show them? You take one end and I will take the other.' He raised his voice. 'Your Royal Highness – gentlemen – if you will look this way?'

He nodded to Nathan and they opened the flag between them. It had seven red stripes, like the one they were already flying, but there were no stars. Instead there was a snake, uncoiled as if to strike, and the words *Do Not Tread On Me* written into one of the white spaces.

'What,' said Nathan into the sudden silence, 'is this?'

'It is a rattlesnake,' said Imlay with a smile.

'I can see that,' said Nathan, though in fact the particular breed of snake was previously unknown to him. 'But what is the flag?'

'It is the flag flown by the New Jersey militia when they first went into action against the British Army,' declared Imlay proudly. 'It is the Flag of Freedom.' He fluttered his side of the flag vigorously, so the rattlesnake seemed to ripple.

'Liberty or Death!' he cried out in a loud voice.

'Hurrah!' cried Cathcart.

'Hurrah!' cried the Pasha-zade after a moment's indecision.

'Hurrah!' cried his followers.

Nathan took the flag and went up on deck. The sun was sinking beneath the horizon. The last rays caught the domes and minarets of Algiers. Distantly he thought he could hear the sound of the muezzin. The Moors who had been left on deck were bowing towards the gathering darkness in the east, wherein lay the holy city of Mecca. The bullocks were lowing, the sheep – or goats – bleating. It was all very peaceful. Nathan felt strangely out of place.

He handed the flag to Mr Lamb. 'Hang that up,' he said, 'in place of the one we have already.'

He turned to Tully. 'We had better start killing bullocks,' he said, 'before we lose the light. At dawn we sail for Tripoli.'

Chapter Thirteen

The Room of the Murdered Bey

—————•◦•—————

Caterina first heard it from one of the Italian girls – Elizabetta. There was an American ship-of-war moored out in the Bay. It had brought an emissary, sent by the American President himself, to negotiate the release of the hostages. If the Pasha refused to let them go, then the ship would bombard Tripoli.

Caterina was inclined to be sceptical.

'The Americans have no ships-of-war,' she told Louisa, who was showing signs of excitement. This was another piece of intelligence Caterina owed to her former lover, Admiral Dandolo. 'And even if they have obtained one, it will hardly be enough to take on the whole of Tripoli.'

Caterina was of a phlegmatic disposition, at least so far as some things were concerned. She was not unhopeful, but she did not care to have her hopes raised for insufficient reason. But as the days went by she had to admit to the possibility that something was up. There was a definite air of tension within the seraglio. The two wives betrayed a more than usual degree of malice towards their servants and junior relatives. The hostages they treated with a cold disdain, bordering on contempt, but then this was nothing new. Towards Caterina and Louisa, they maintained a kind of sly watchfulness, like a pair of cats – and just as impenetrable.

Caterina remembered what Miriam had told her about the American agent who had been authorised to conduct negotiations on their behalf. She anticipated the woman's next visit with more interest than usual.

Miriam, when she did arrive, confirmed the rumours, but she was unexpectedly dismissive. Yes, there was an American ship in the bay, but if it was a ship-of-war it was a very small one; yes, it had brought an emissary to agree terms with the Pasha, but he was a very insignificant emissary and talks had broken down almost immediately. The Americans were not prepared to pay the price demanded – an outrageous sum, even by Miriam's inflated standards. And if they threatened to use force, as had been suggested by Miriam's connections in the castle, things would go very hard on the hostages.

This was not at all what Caterina had been hoping to hear.

'Do you have any more good news for us?' she enquired coldly. 'Just to keep our spirits up?'

Miriam regarded her with a curious expression. 'I might,' she said.

There were times when Caterina longed to slap her.

She narrowed her eyes a little to let her know the danger she was in.

'There is a story that is told by the Turks,' Miriam said, 'of a hunter who goes into the forest with his dog. It is a very cold winter's day and there is a heavy frost on the ground. After they have been walking for some little while, the dog finds a bird on the ground with all its feathers frozen.' She smiled at Caterina's expression but continued regardless. 'The bird is unable to fly and it is freezing to death. But there is a pig in the forest who has just emptied its bowels. So the hunter picks up the bird and places it in the warm heap of pig's dung. And after a little while the bird begins to move and flutter its wings.' Caterina appeared about to interrupt at this point and Miriam raised a hand to forestall her. 'And at that moment, a fox jumps out of the forest and gobbles it up.'

Caterina regarded her stonily. 'Doubtless,' she said, 'you are about to explain the meaning of this moving story.'

'It has three meanings. One, that the person who puts you in the shit is not necessarily your enemy. Two, that the person who pulls you out of the shit is not necessarily your friend. And three?' She shrugged. 'It makes no difference either way. *Inshallah* – what will be, will be. It is a very Turkish story.'

'I see. Well, thank you, Miriam, you are a little ray of sunshine today,' Caterina congratulated her. 'And why are you telling me this?'

'Because I am about to do you a service and I want you to know that I cannot say for certain if it will put you in a better place or a worse.'

'Ah. I understand. So what is this service that you are going to do for me – and does it involve pig shit in any way, or any other kind of shit?'

'You remember the interested party of whom I told you?' Miriam enquired.

Caterina agreed that she did, though Miriam had previously referred to him as 'an admirer'. An 'interested party' promised less, in her expectations, than an 'admirer', but even so, it was good to know that *someone* was interested.

'What of him?' she asked.

Miriam dropped her voice even lower so that Caterina was obliged to lean forward to catch what she had to say. This was a not uncommon feature of life in the harem, where much of the dialogue was conducted in whispers, and the only raised voices were those of the wives and the children, but it did not make it any easier to understand what intelligence Miriam had to impart. In Caterina's opinion, as a Venetian, the Tuscan dialect might almost have been designed to conceal one's true meaning. No wonder it had been the language of Machiavelli. But for once Miriam was explicit.

'He wishes to know if you have considered the possibility of escape.'

Caterina tried to read the expression in Miriam's eyes but it was impossible. She could be a cat playing with a mouse. But it was equally impossible not to play along with her.

'I might have,' she replied warily, 'when I first came here.'

'And what did you conclude?'

'That it would require outside assistance.'

'And if such assistance were to be offered?'

'Then it would be churlish to refuse it.' But Caterina had had enough of this game. 'Come to the point, Miriam,' she urged her.

'Very well. This gentleman is prepared to pay a considerable amount of money to contrive your escape.'

Caterina struggled to conceal her surprise at this information. And as she considered it, she spotted an equally puzzling anomaly. 'If he is prepared to pay such a sum to contrive my escape,' she said, 'why not to effect my release?'

Miriam sighed. 'Perhaps because he does not consider your release to be a possibility.'

'How so?'

'Perhaps because he believes the Pasha will not part with you. Perhaps he has heard that the Pasha considers that you are beyond price.'

Caterina studied her carefully for a moment, but Miriam's expression was remote. She recalled the shadowy figure in the chamber above the pool. The confessor figure behind his grille. If she had been more of an innocent she would have blushed.

'And how is this escape to be contrived?' she asked.

'I will bring you further instruction,' said Miriam, 'on my next visit.'

'And this "interested party" – you are not prepared to reveal who it is?'

'I have not been given that authority.'

Caterina's first thought was that it was Peter Lisle – Murad Reis, the Pasha's great Admiral. Admirals seemed to be drawn to her that way. But now she was not so sure. It could, she supposed, be virtually anyone who had seen her at the Pasha's Divan. This was alarming. She did not wish to exchange her present quarters for the life of a concubine in a Bedouin tent, or even the home of a Turkish official.

On the other hand, she did not wish to remain in the harem of al-Saraya al-Hamra for the rest of her life. Or even what she was still pleased to call her youth. Once she was out of here, anything was possible. But she was not going to go alone.

'And what of my friend Louisa?'

Miriam frowned. 'What of her?'

'You do not expect me to leave her here.'

'I do not expect anything. I am only the messenger.'

Caterina shook her head. 'Then you must tell your "interested party" I am not going anywhere without her,' she said.

Miriam did not look at all happy about this, but Caterina would not be moved.

'I will let you know what he says when I return,' Miriam conceded ungraciously.

She was back the very next day. This was a surprise to Caterina, who often did not see her for weeks. 'It is agreed,' she said. 'You *and* your friend.'

'So what must we do?'

'As soon as it is dark, you must make your way to the room of the murdered Bey.'

Not for the first time Caterina suspected that she was the victim of some malicious game. Possibly devised by one of the wives, to humiliate her. Or worse.

'The room of the murdered Bey . . .' she repeated.

'You know where that is?'

'I know where it is. But why there?'

'Because it is the only room in the seraglio that has windows which open onto the sea.'

For the first time, Caterina felt a stirring of excitement, but she tried not to show it in her face.

'That is indeed an advantage,' she said. 'But it must be a hundred feet above the water.'

'More like two hundred,' agreed Miriam complacently.

'So one would need a rope.'

'One would certainly need something. But I imagine that has been thought of.'

Again, Caterina longed to slap her. Instead she said, 'And what if the room is locked?'

'Where there is a lock,' said Miriam, 'there is also a key.' She reached into her voluminous black robes and pressed the object into Caterina's palm.

Caterina quickly hid it within her own robes. She could feel her heart pounding. If this was a trick, she was already hooked. But there was at least one other consideration.

'As soon as it is dark we are confined to our dormitory,' she pointed out. 'And one of the servants is set to guard us until daybreak.'

'The servant has been taken care of,' Miriam assured her.

Caterina stared hard at her. 'All this could not be contrived without a great deal of money,' she remarked.

Miriam permitted herself a small smile. 'You think I would be involved in it,' she said, 'if it did not?'

* * *

'Of course I do not trust her,' Caterina admitted to Louisa when she confided the plan to her in the privacy of the hammam later that afternoon.

'Then why do you even consider it?'

'Because of a story she told me about a hunter and his dog.'

Caterina told Louisa the story. It did not appear to alleviate Lousia's immediate concerns. 'Is Miriam the hunter, or the bird, or the fox, or the heap of you-know-what?' she enquired with a frown.

'I think she is the hunter,' said Caterina, 'but it does not matter. The point is that she told me the story.'

'I still do not understand.'

Caterina sighed. 'I do not think she would tell me such a story if she meant to betray us,' she said.

'So you will go?'

'Only if you will come with me.'

'And if I say no . . . ?'

'Then I will remain here with you – in the harem.'

Louisa considered a little more. 'Very well,' she said. 'I will come with you.'

They retired to bed that night without taking off their clothes and lay awake, under the thin coverings, surreptitiously watching the servant in her chair by the door. Even by the light of the single candle set before her, they could see that she was clearly having problems staying awake. He head kept nodding down towards her ample bosom and eventually she began to make gentle snoring noises.

Caterina turned her head and caught the eye of Louisa, in the bed next to her. Without saying a word they rose and crept towards the door. If any of the other hostages saw them they showed no sign of it, and the servant remained as if drugged, which no doubt she was.

Caterina eased the door open and they slid through the narrow gap into the corridor outside. A flight of stairs led up to the rooms where Lilla Kebierra and the Pasha's wives slept. Moonlight filtered through the high windows. Caterina wondered if Miriam or her unknown accomplices had taken the precaution of drugging others besides the servant on sentry duty. Certainly there was no sign of life. They paused a moment before the door to what had once been Lilla Kebierra's withdrawing room. They both knew the story. And knew that if they were found inside the room – the shrine to the murdered Bey – things would go very hard with them. But there were other, less rational reasons for them to be afraid of entering. Caterina said a silent prayer to the Virgin and opened the door.

The room was generously proportioned and luxuriously furnished. There were no lights burning, but moonlight poured through the large casement windows and they could see quite clearly. It might have been Caterina's imagination but the room smelled of death.

She shook off her apprehension and made her way over to one of the windows. It was a little stiff but eventually she pushed it open – and there, far below her, was the sea. The wonderful, glorious sea, stretching away into the distance with the moonlight painting a wide-open path to the horizon. It was the first glimpse of the outside world Caterina had been afforded for more than six months, and for a few moments she luxuriated in it. She felt the breeze on her face and filled her lungs with air, and smelled the strong, pungent scent of salt water.

And almost on the horizon, directly in the path of the moon, she saw a ship.

It was a three-master with its sails furled. Caterina wondered if this was the ship Elizabetta had told her about, bringing the emissary from the American President. If that were the case, surely they would be wise to wait for the results of his negotiations? But then she remembered what Miriam had said. And it was all too believable that the Pasha wished to keep her here.

But now what were they to do? She leaned out of the window and looked down. There was a sheer drop to the rocks below. It was probably not the 200 feet Miriam had said it was, but it was far enough. She withdrew her head and looked around the room to see if there was any sign of a rope. There was not. Even if there had been, she doubted she would have enough strength in her arms to climb down it, even after all the swimming she had done. And certainly Louisa did not.

It must be a trap. Suddenly it seemed certain. That was why Miriam had told her story about the hunter and his dog. It was not a warning; it was an excuse. Even as the certainty grew, there was a small exclamation from Louisa. Caterina turned sharply and her heart leaped into her throat as she saw the dark figure framed in one of the windows. He was dressed entirely in black with a cloth wrapped around his head and face so that only his eyes were revealed, and they were almost as black as the night. Even as Caterina wondered how he could have got there, he dropped lightly into the room and she saw the rope dangling from above.

Louisa gave another cry and moved towards the door, but the figure was upon her in an instant, seizing her by the shoulders with one hand and placing the other over her mouth. Caterina took a step towards her, but then something made her turn towards the window again, and she saw an identical figure, poised on the sill. He leaped noiselessly into the room and raised an urgent hand to his lips. As Caterina paused, more paralysed by fear than by his instruction, he shrugged a pack off his shoulders and tugged what appeared to be a bundle of clothing from it. He threw it at Caterina's feet and said something in a language she did not understand. Then he made a gesture as of pulling something over his head.

Caterina picked up the bundle. It consisted of a black shift or smock, a pair of loose-fitting pantaloons and a length of cloth that was clearly meant to be wound around her head like a turban. The other man had let go of Louisa and removed something similar from his own pack. Then they both turned their backs and stood there with folded arms, facing towards the window through which they had entered.

Caterina felt hysterical laughter bubbling in her throat. She suppressed it urgently and quickly exchanged her clothes for the ones on the floor. Louisa, after a moment's hesitation, did the same. Then Caterina announced with a discreet cough that they were ready.

The two men moved swiftly towards them and began to fit them out with some kind of a harness which went over their shoulders and buckled at the waist. Then they pulled in the two ropes from the window and tied each of them to a ring in the leather.

They chose Caterina as the first to go, but she shook
her head and pointed to Louisa. She did not want to risk
leaving her behind. Poor Louisa looked terrified, but she
allowed herself to be lifted over the windowsill and gently
lowered down towards the distant sea. It seemed to take a
very long time. Then one of the men nodded to Caterina.

She, too, was helped over the sill. She clung to the edge
as she squirmed round to face the wall. She stared for a
moment into the eyes of her rescuer – or assassin. Their
expression was impenetrable. Then, with a great effort of
will, she let go. And slowly, inch by inch, she was lowered
down the wall. She used her hands and her feet to keep her
face from grazing the stones, almost as if she was crawling
down it. After a few moments, it began to feel exhilarating.
She felt like laughing out loud. She even found the courage
to look down. She could see the rocks, gleaming faintly in
the moonlight, and the white line of surf beneath her feet.
And so she descended, in a series of gentle jerks, until
finally her feet touched solid rock.

She felt strong hands grasping her by the waist and
unbuckling the harness. And as she stepped free, she saw
the boat. A small rowing boat with several more men,
attired in the same black garb – and Louisa seated among
them. Taking care not to slip on the slimy rocks, Caterina
moved towards it.

A man detached himself from the shadows and extended
his hand towards her. He did not wear a turban like the
others, but he was hooded and his face was in shadow.
Caterina took his hand and allowed him to help her aboard
the boat where she joined Louisa in the stern. The two
men who had rescued them were already swarming down

the ropes – much quicker than they had lowered Caterina and Louisa – and as soon as the women were aboard, the crew cast off and began to pull for the open sea.

Caterina turned to the man who had helped her into the boat.

'*Grazie,*' she murmured in the Venetian dialect. '*Grazie mille.*'

To her surprise he answered her in almost the same tongue, but with a heavy and familiar accent.

'It is my pleasure, Signora.'

'Do I know you?' she asked sharply. It was quite clear to her now, that this was not Peter Lisle.

'We met only once,' he said. 'And I regret that the circumstances were not favourable to furthering our acquaintance.'

Then he raised his head to the moonlight and she saw him clearly for the first time. It was then she recognised the handsome but unwelcome features of the man who had been Bonaparte's leading intelligence agent in Venice, Monsieur Xavier Naudé.

Chapter Fourteen

The Consul of the Seven Isles

'Run out your guns!'

For all of his fifteen years in the service, this had presaged the sound that Nathan most loved to hear, at least aboard a ship-of-war – the sound of between ten and twenty heavy cannon being hauled up to the open gun ports. He had heard it likened to the deep-throated growling of a cage-full of wild beasts.

A romantic conceit no doubt, but far preferable to the comparison that now came to mind.

For unlike cannon, which were mounted on proper wheeled trucks of oak and iron, the *Swallow*'s brand-new carronades were bedded to a fancy wooden slide with a groove down the middle to direct the recoil, and the sound they made as they were slid into position reminded him of a piece of chalk rasped across a blackboard at Charterhouse School in London, where he had spent two unhappy years studying the Classics and other subjects that appeared to be of no particular use to him, before his mother had been persuaded to let him join the Navy.

He watched from the quarterdeck rail as the twelve gun crews went through the motions of loading and firing. 'Going through the motions' was all they were able to do most days, for they had been here almost a month now, in the tranquil waters of the Bay of Tripoli, and if he had used powder and shot every time they worked the guns, he would soon have exhausted their meagre supplies.

Even so, Nathan insisted on some form of practice every day, if only to remind the crew they were aboard a ship-of-war and not a pleasure cruiser. And for all his prejudice against them, he had to admit the carronades had some advantage over cannon. They were about a third of the weight, calibre for calibre, and needed about half the amount of powder and half as many men to fire them. Nathan had apportioned their crews along more or less nationalistic lines. The Russians had four guns under the direct command of Lieutenant Belli; the Americans the next four; and the Sicilians the four that were left. After a month or so of practice they could fire three broadsides in less than five minutes, even using live ammunition. But of course, he had no means of knowing how they would perform in battle.

Not that it seemed likely that they would ever be called upon to do so. During all the time they had been off the shores of Tripoli, not a single vessel of the Pasha's fleet had ventured out of the harbour. And even if they had, Imlay had given strict instructions that they were not to be attacked or given the slightest provocation. Not while he still had hopes of succeeding with his negotiations.

He and Cathcart had spent the last few nights ashore and Nathan could only hope that they had made some progress. It was now mid-June and apart from the shortage of powder and shot, he was also worried about running out of food and drink. Cathcart had obtained a quantity of wine from some unknown source ashore and Imlay had said there would be no problem in securing food, albeit at inflated prices, but Nathan thought it would be unwise to count on it. He had enough for another two weeks before he would have to start rationing. And a shortage of supplies was not his only problem.

As if to remind him, here was Qualtrough asking if the Captain would allow the 'Mohammetans' up on deck, now the gunnery practice was finished. With some reluctance Nathan gave his permission, and braced himself for another confrontation with Prince Ahmed and his peripatetic court-in-exile.

Nathan had no idea what Imlay had told the Pasha-zade when he had persuaded him to leave his secure refuge in Algiers, but he had probably not mentioned that he would be kicking his heels aboard a sloop-of-war for the next few weeks off the coast of his erstwhile homeland.

Most of his followers had left on unexplained missions ashore, presumably to take soundings among the populace and prepare the way for his triumphant return. Nathan would have thought the Pasha-zade would have been keen to join them, but for all his obvious frustration he chose to remain aboard the *Swallow* with his diminishing entourage, in stubborn occupation of the Captain's quarters, emerging only to take the air and gaze in a melancholy fashion

towards the distant shore, or to listen with a doleful air of
reproach whilst one of his advisers berated Nathan, or
such of his officers as had the misfortune to be on duty,
with his complaints. The Pasha-zade himself rarely spoke,
at least not while he was on deck. This could be arrogance
but it seemed more like shyness or lack of confidence to
Nathan. The fellow might be a member of a warrior caste,
but you would never have guessed from the look of him.
Imlay called him Ahmed the Terrible – presumably in a
spirit of irony.

There were only two of Ahmed's advisers left, along
with his dragoman, two servants, two bodyguards, and his
personal physician, Omar al-Saayid, who was the only one
of the bunch Nathan had any time for, not only because
he spoke fluent French and had more charm than the rest
put together, but because he had volunteered to be of
assistance to the ship's surgeon. It was more than welcome,
since Mr Kite had been showing increasing signs of panic
since leaving Gibraltar – though nothing like the panic he
induced in his patients. Unfortunately Dr Saayid spoke no
English, but then as this was a deficiency shared by the
majority of the crew, it hardly seemed to matter. Certainly
he seemed to have no problem diagnosing their complaints,
and thus far no one had died of his remedies.

The complaint today was about the rats – apparently
several had been seen on the Pasha-zade's table. Nathan
dealt with this with as much patience as he could contrive.
He advised against leaving any food lying around. It
always attracted rats, he said. Also midshipmen, which
was worse. You could leave poison out, but the rats were
usually too clever to eat it and the midshipmen thrived on

it. In the end you just had to put up with them. They were among the inconveniences of living aboard a ship-of-war, but nothing like as inconvenient as being obliged to command the said ship whilst occupying a cabin the size of a cupboard, immediately adjoining the cabin of an extremely large Russian who snored like a grampus.

If the dragoman understood any of this, which was doubtful, he showed no signs of having done so. Nathan politely touched his hat and returned to the rail to resume his observations of the distant shore, only for his attention to be directed to a small boat approaching from the direction of that shore under a lateen sail. It did not appear to be one of the tartans which supplied them with freshly-caught fish most days of the week, and Nathan raised the glass to his eye in hope that it might be bringing Imlay and Cathcart back from their mission ashore.

It was not. But there were two figures in the stern wearing the dress of rich Levantine merchants or dignitaries, and there was something else about them that engaged his further attention, something vaguely familiar. One of them was a black man and his face was in shadow, but even though he was seated Nathan could see that he was a considerable size. He focused on the other man – and to his surprise and delight, found himself looking upon the unmistakable features of Spiridion Foresti, former British Consul to the Seven Isles, who had sailed with him on the *Unicorn* and helped him to take the *Jean-Bart* from the French.

And unless he was very much mistaken, the man sitting beside him was the former gunner's mate of the *Unicorn*, George Banjo.

* * *

'Well, gentlemen, welcome aboard – though I cannot promise as warm a welcome as on your last visit.'

Nathan greeted his guests on the quarterdeck, where they had fought a bloody hand-to-hand battle to gain control of the sloop when it was in French hands. Banjo had saved his life on that occasion – and not for the first time – but if anything, he looked more nervous now than when he had been laying about him with his machete – as well he might, given the charges that could be laid against him. He wore a turban and had grown a beard, but his massive frame could not be so easily disguised, and it was unlikely that many of his former shipmates would be fooled – certainly not Tully and Lamb, who had recognised him the moment he stepped aboard.

His companion looked more at ease, but then Nathan could hardly imagine a situation when he would not. Spiridion Foresti was, like Gilbert Imlay, a man of many parts. He had been a sailor and soldier and now, Nathan supposed, he must be rated a spy, though in many ways he defied category.

Nathan clapped him on the shoulder. 'It is good to see you, Spiridion. I had almost given you up for lost.'

'I am sorry, my friend. I have only just received your message or I would have been here sooner.'

'They said at the Consulate that you had returned to Corfu.'

'Corfu is in the hands of the French,' Spiridion reminded him. 'If I returned there I would be arrested and very like find myself shot as a spy. However, I may have given that impression. If I disclosed my plans to the people in the

English Consulate, I am afraid it would be all over Tripoli within hours.' He dropped his voice. 'In fact, I have been to Egypt, and if we can speak more privately I will tell you what I discovered there.'

The stern cabin being barred to them by its present occupancy and the gunroom so stifling as to be almost uninhabitable, Nathan proposed they adjourn to the maintop where they stood the best chance of conversing without being overheard. He told Qualtrough to send two of the ship's boys up with a bottle of Portuguese arinto and three glasses.

'And some olives, Qualtrough, if you please,' he said. 'I believe Mr Foresti is partial to olives. If you have not served them all to our other guests.'

'The last I heard of you, you were confined in the Doge's Prison in Venice,' Spiridion observed, when they were comfortably settled in the maintop with the wine poured and the olives in a dish of brine, and a scrap of sail to shield them from the sun. 'But you appear no worse for the experience.'

'Oh, I have been in much more wholesome prisons since,' Nathan assured him. 'I will tell you about it sometime, but now we had better talk of more pressing matters. However, before you tell me about Egypt, may I ask if you have any news of Gilbert Gabriel. You remember him? He was my servant, who accompanied me to Venice.'

'I remember him well,' Spiridion replied. 'I remember the way he fought when we took the *Jean Bart*. But I am afraid I have no news of any consequence. I know that when you were imprisoned in Venice he applied to the

English Ambassador, Sir Richard Worsley, in the hope that he might use what influence he had to obtain your release. But after that . . .' He spread his hands in a gesture of resignation. 'There was a rumour that he was taken up by the authorities and pressed into service aboard one of the galleys, but I was unable to trace him before the French arrived. I am sorry,' he added as he noted Nathan's reaction. 'You were greatly attached to him?'

'I had known him since I was a small child.'

'Well, he stands at least as good a chance of surviving the war in a Venetian galley as he would in the British Navy.'

This was probably true. 'At least you were able to be of service to Mr Banjo here,' Nathan said. 'And I thank you for that.'

It was Nathan who had advised the gunner to jump ship at Corfu, and apply to the Consul for assistance.

'It is I who must thank you, for he has saved my life on more than one occasion since,' Spiridion replied, 'so I hope you are not going to deprive me of his services.'

'I think Mr Banjo may have burned his boats with the Navy,' Nathan acknowledged. In fact, if the gunner ever came aboard a proper King's ship and was recognised as a deserter, they all knew what would happen to him. He sat at some little distance from the two men, in as much as this was possible in the confined area of the maintop, but he followed the conversation with a lively interest.

'But now tell me how you did in Egypt,' Nathan said to Spiridion. 'Was it worth the trip?'

'Very much so, though it would not please our masters in London. Have you ever been there?'

'No. I was never so far east.'

'So what do you know of the country and its rulers?'

'Not a great deal,' Nathan admitted. He did not think it worthwhile to mention that his knowledge came almost entirely from illustrations in the King James's Bible that had lain open in his father's study in Wilmington when he was a child. 'I know that the population is largely Arabic and that it is part of the Ottoman Empire.'

'Well, this is true,' Spiridion conceded. 'Their formal allegiance is to the Sultan in Constantinople. But in actual fact the Turks have about as much influence over Egyptian affairs as they do in Tripoli, which is none at all. The real rulers are the Mamelukes, who are neither Turk nor Arab. You are not familiar with the Mamelukes?'

Nathan shook his head, though the word did, in fact, stir some distant memory.

'It is from the Turkish for "one who is owned". They are a traditional warrior caste in Muslim society, like the *Khuloghlis* in Tripoli – Christian slaves, taken as young boys from the Caucasus, forcibly converted to Islam, and trained as soldiers – cavalry in the case of the Mamelukes, elite cavalry. They are among the finest horsemen in the world. They were originally sent to Egypt and Syria to fight the Crusaders. Saladin himself was one of their number, I believe, though he was never a slave. But they seized power for themselves and have been more or less running the country ever since. They live like satraps with a harem of Egyptian and African women, but they only marry women from the Caucasus – and they never have children by their own wives. If the women conceive, the baby is aborted. Instead, they have a policy of bringing in young boys from the Caucasus at the age of seven or eight and training them as their heirs, in their own image and likeness so to speak.'

'But why not their own sons?'

Spiridion shrugged. 'You would have to ask the Mamelukes that. It is the tradition. They believe it secures them against becoming too like the Arabs, or the Turks – both of whom hate them with an abiding passion, by the way. This is what the French are counting on. They have sent agents into the country to stir up the populace. To tell them the French are coming as allies of the Sultan to liberate them from their Mameluke oppressors.'

'So the French *are* coming?'

'You sound doubtful.'

'Billy Pitt is. He thinks it's all my eye and Betty Martin.'

Spiridion, for all his knowledge of the English and their language, was clearly not familiar with this expression. But Mr Banjo was – he must have heard it many times on the lower deck.

'A nonsense,' he explained. 'A story put about by the French to mask their true intentions.'

'Well, this is possible,' Spiridion conceded, 'but if Pitt is wrong and the French march on India . . . ?'

'They will have to take Egypt first,' Nathan pointed out.

'I doubt that will be as great an inconvenience to them as taking the British Isles.'

'You do not think the Mamelukes will fight?'

'Oh they will fight but –' he shrugged. 'Mr Banjo here has made a study of the Mameluke method of fighting. Perhaps he would be good enough to explain it to you.'

Mr Banjo's interest in military tactics was not a great surprise to Nathan. It was his inclination to debate the subject with his superiors on the *Unicorn* that had led to his downfall.

'They ride their horses toward the enemy at full pelt,' he confided, 'discharging their pistols and carbines, of which they carry a great number. When each gun is fired they drop it to the ground for their servants to pick up, and when they reach the enemy they lay about them with their scimitars, cutting off heads by the score.'

'And what is your opinion of this tactic, Mr Banjo?' enquired Spiridion politely.

'It works very well against the tribes of the desert,' Banjo shrugged.

'And against the French?'

'With muskets and bayonets – and field artillery? And Bonaparte as their commander?' He considered briefly. 'The French will cut them to pieces.'

'Precisely. And then they will march on India to join with the Sultan of Mysore, and together they will drive the British into the sea.' Spiridion noted Nathan's expression. 'Or do you not think so?'

'At present, I am more concerned with how we might persuade Billy Pitt of this danger,' Nathan told him dryly.

'We can only tell him what we know – and of the activities of French agents in Egypt and Tripoli.'

'They are here in Tripoli?'

'They have sent one of their best agents here. Xavier Naudé is his name. His previous posting was Venice, where he created a pro-French interest in the city and stirred up the mob against the Doge. He is doing the same thing here, except that he does not need the mob, for he has more powerful allies – Murad Reis for one – the man you know as Peter Lisle, who is the Admiral of the Pasha's fleet. He has sold Naudé copies of his charts – Murad Reis is famous for his charts, he has some of the best ever made of the Levant. And only last night I heard that Naudé has hired the *Meshuda* to make a survey of the coastline between here and Rosetta on the Nile Delta.'

Nathan stared at him in silence for a moment while a dozen questions ran through his head. He asked only one. 'When?'

'As soon as possible. But Murad Reis is reluctant to leave Tripoli until negotiations with the Americans are concluded. He stands to make a great deal of money from them.'

'Does the Pasha know anything of this?'

'Unfortunately I believe he is a party to it. He thinks the French are the coming power in the region, and that if they were to invade Egypt, he will have them as his neighbours.'

Nathan looked towards the shoreline, curving away to the east until it was lost in the distant haze. It must be almost 1,000 miles to the Nile Delta. A proper survey could take months. But there must be specific points that the French had already identified from the charts. A port or a bay that was big enough and sufficiently sheltered to land an army of around 50,000 men with wagons, guns, limbers and horses.

'I would give anything to see these charts Naudé has purchased,' he reflected.

'I have already named a price,' Spiridion confessed.

'But they are locked in a safe in the French Consulate. It might be easier to obtain the originals from the *Meshuda*.'

Nathan looked at him sharply. 'How?'

'Sooner or later she will put to sea. Do you think you could take her?'

'I would have a damn good try,' Nathan told him, though it occurred to him that Imlay might have something to say about that. He would have a hell of a fight on his hands, too.

He gazed out again towards Tripoli. It was too far to see much detail with the naked eye, but with the glass he could make out the masts of the *Meshuda* in the inner harbour. He had thought at first she was a *xebec*, the traditional fighting ship of the corsairs, but she was a true schooner, with no square sails at all: an unusually large schooner of about 400 tons, built in Philadelphia and originally called the *Betsy*. The corsairs had taken her over a year ago and armed her with twenty-eight guns – only 6-pounders, as far as Nathan could gather, but they would be a match for his carronades at long range, and if he went in close to make the best use of his smashers there was a significant risk of being boarded, which would be no joke with the crew she carried – over 350 by Imlay's account, including a number of Janissaries, all armed to the teeth and outnumbering the *Swallow*'s own crew by more than two-to-one.

He was about to look away when he noticed something else. There was a boat coming out from the harbour; about the size of the *Swallow*'s cutter with a single lateen sail. He raised the glass to his eye and focused on the figures in the stern.

'It's Imlay,' he said.

* * *

They met in the stifling heat of the gunroom, the maintop being considered inappropriate to the seriousness of their discourse and Cathcart too portly to contemplate an ascent.

The negotiations were going nowhere, Imlay reported. The Pasha had modified his original terms, but he was not prepared to go lower than $100,000 for the ship and its cargo, and $100 head money for every man, woman and child aboard – a total of $250,000. Imlay was authorised to go up to $100,000 but not a cent more. There were other terms, besides, which he was not prepared to disclose, but which he described as 'unacceptable'.

'So what are we to do?' demanded Nathan.

'There is only one thing to be done,' replied Imlay. 'We must unleash the dog of War.'

Nathan inclined his head in polite enquiry.

'The Pasha-zade,' Imlay announced. 'Ahmed the Terrible.'

Chapter Fifteen

The Sons of Slaves

———◆———

The *Swallow* lay close inshore, just to the east of Tripoli, as the sun dropped to the west. Some little distance off her starboard bow, just beyond the white strip of beach, was the area known as the *menshia*, the Garden of Tripoli – an oasis of palm and pomegranate and olive trees, where sandy lanes sloped gently down to the sea between hedges of Indian fig and jasmine. It was as peaceful a scene as Nathan could imagine. Earlier he had watched languid oxen circling the open wells to draw water for the plots of green peppers and alfalfa, while Arab farmers on donkeys waved cheerfully towards the foreign sloop riding in the bay. But now there was little movement ashore as darkness fell on the *menshia*.

In the twilight, Nathan could see the lights of small villages and mosques among the trees, and the luxurious villas and stables of the Khuloghlis, the proud sons of slaves who were quartered here in this, the birthplace of Yusuf Pasha and his murdered brother Hassan, and their own Ahmed the Terrible.

Who was now saying his prayers.

Nathan could hear the incantations drifting back from the quarterdeck where the Pasha-zade and his clan had spread their prayer mats. He fancied they had a more fervent air than usual, for tonight Prince Ahmed was to take the decisive step towards reclaiming his lost inheritance. If the reports were true, over 1,000 of his loyal supporters were waiting among those palms and villas for him to lead them into battle. Over 1,000 superb horsemen armed to the teeth, eager to avenge the murder of their beloved Bey at the hands of his own brother. To ride at dawn against the Monster of the Red Castle.

The *Swallow* would play her part, bombarding the fortress by sea as the Khuloghlis attacked by land – and there were promises that the disaffected Moors of Tripoli would rise up and join them as soon as battle was joined.

All in all, it promised to be a right royal mill and Nathan had to admit that after so many weeks of enforced idleness, he was rather looking forward to it. His only complaint, as he put it to Imlay, was that their boy – Ahmed the Terrible – might have shown a bit more enthusiasm about stepping up to the mark. A rousing speech might have been too much to expect, but a touch of bravado would not have gone amiss, a little light dancing on the feet, throwing a few punches, just to let the lads know what they were putting their money on. But he looked like a man who was about to be hanged.

Still, from what Nathan could gather, his father Ali
Pasha had been nothing to shout about either, and he had
ruled for more than forty years with the support of the
Khuloghlis. Everything, apparently, depended on them.
These elite horsemen were the makers and breakers of
dynasties, which was why they were quartered a mile
outside the Menshia Gate and forbidden to enter the city
in any number or with any kind of weapon. If they gave
their support to Ahmed, declared Imlay, it was all up with
Yusuf Pasha.

'*If?*' Nathan had queried sharply at the council of war
called by Imlay in the gunroom of the *Swallow*.

'I mean "when",' Imlay corrected himself. The word in
the street and in the coffee houses was that Yusuf Pasha's
time was up, he declared with his usual air of confidence
– which had never convinced Nathan before and was some
way from convincing him now. But Cathcart was nodding
in agreement. Ahmed's own advisers – the agents who had
been sent ashore – had reported that the Khuloghlis were
ready to receive him with open arms, he said. They had
loved his brother, the murdered Bey, and their hatred for
Yusuf Pasha was at least as intense. Two years ago they
had given him the benefit of the doubt, but he had proved
to be a ruthless and unpredictable tyrant. Now they were
ready for a change.

Spiridion was less optimistic.

'From what I have heard, the Khuloghlis tend to favour
ruthless and unpredictable tyrants,' he informed Nathan
later when they discussed the matter in private. 'They had
rather a strong man than a weak one, even if they feel the
weight of his iron fist.'

The present Bey had something which the locals called *bashasha*, Spiridion said, a word that could not easily be translated into English, but which contained elements of charisma and charm combined with a fierce caprice. It was, one could say, a kind of volatile changeability akin to madness; but in Tripoli and in other of the Barbary Coast states it was seen as a mark of the born leader.

'I know what you mean,' Nathan reflected. 'King George has it in spades. One minute he's all smiles, planting turnips and opening Parliament, the next he's talking to a tree thinking 'tis the King of Prussia. Gives Billy Pitt the shakes but he would rather Farmer George than Prinny any day of the week. Mad as a hatter, of course, but at least he don't rouge his cheeks to look like a girl.'

Spiridion said he didn't know about that but Yusuf Pasha had *bashasha* and his brother Ahmed didn't, and if he had to put money on it, he'd lay it on the Monster.

Whatever happened, it seemed certain that daybreak would bring some kind of a conclusion to the affair, and it promised to be a lively one. The *Swallow* was not yet cleared for action but they had cartridges and 24-pound round shot lined up in the racks next to every gun, with a slow-match in reserve for if the flints failed. Buckets of water had been liberally placed about the decks as a precaution against fire, for it was expected that the fort would use heated shot. Cutlasses had been honed to a razor-edged sharpness, and muskets and pistols stood ready-loaded in case the Pasha sent his gunboats against them – or, even more interestingly, if it became necessary to take a party ashore to rescue the hostages.

All they needed now was for the Pasha-zade to finish praying and put his gloves on.

The sun finally set. Darkness swiftly settled upon land and sea. Ahmed and his followers retired below, hopefully to get ready for the fight. The offshore breeze brought the delicate scene of jasmine from the gardens of the *menshia*. Four bells rang out from the belfry, marking the midpoint of the first watch. The Pasha-zade came back on deck. He had changed out of his flowing robes into a coat of chainmail with a breastplate and a steel helmet and a long curved sword buckled at his waist. For the first time he looked more like the member of a warrior caste, a true Khuloghli. Nathan wondered if a cheer might be appropriate.

Instead he took off his hat and wished the Pasha-zade the best of luck and solemnly shook hands with the doctor, who was going with them.

'We will miss you,' he told him sincerely.

Mr Lamb had brought up the boats from the stern and Nathan and Spiridion watched in silence from the quarterdeck as the Pasha-zade was assisted into Nathan's barge. There was something of an air of gloom about the occasion. Oh, for heaven's sake! Nathan thought. This was no time to be coy. 'Three cheers for the Pasha-zade,' he cried. 'And the doctor,' he added quickly, in the hope of encouraging a better response from his lachrymose crew. 'Hip hip, huzzah!'

And whether it was for the doctor or the Prince, or because they were happy to see them go, the crew sent the boats off in rousing style.

A full moon provided a shimmering pathway to the

beach and Nathan watched them all the way. He could even see the reception committee waiting at the water's edge. A smaller party than he might have hoped for, had he been a prince returning from exile, but doubtless the Pasha-zade's supporters were keeping their strength concealed until dawn.

He watched as the sailors jumped into the gentle surf and ran the boats up onto the beach so the Pasha-zade would not get his feet wet. There was a lot of bowing and scraping from the reception committee and then the liberators headed up the beach towards the gently waving line of palms. They were about halfway there when the sound of a bugle or trumpet alerted Nathan to the presence of a much larger force that had emerged from the trees. There must have been at least 100 of them, all mounted, though it was difficult to be certain against the dark backdrop. Nathan assumed, naturally enough, that they were supporters of the Pasha-zade – a troop of Khuloghli horsemen come to welcome their returning hero.

The returning hero showed no such assurance. To Nathan's consternation, he and his followers began to run back towards the sea, but the boats had left on their return journey and were already about 100 yards from the shore. Even from where he stood, Nathan could hear the agitated cries of the abandoned landing party.

Then there was another blast from the trumpet and the cavalry charged.

Nathan watched in helpless astonishment as they enveloped the Pasha-zade and his men in a tide of plunging and wheeling horses. He saw the flash of swords raised to the moonlight and thought he could hear screams. He turned to see Imlay standing beside him. His face, by the light of the binnacle, appeared more thoughtful than troubled.

'What the hell is going on?' Nathan demanded.

But Imlay seemed less interested in what was happening on the beach than in something over on the far side of the bay towards the port. Nathan followed the direction of his gaze and saw the light at the end of the mole winking on and off, as if someone was passing a cloth back and forth across a lantern.

'Is that a signal?' he asked – and when Imlay made no reply: 'To us?'

'There!' said Imlay, pointing, and Nathan saw the white sails outlined against the battlements of the city wall as a large vessel slipped out of the harbour and headed towards them across the bay. 'The *Saratoga*.' His voice was quietly exultant.

'The *Saratoga*?' Nathan looked from Imlay's face to the distant ship and back. It began to make some kind of sense. 'You arranged it!' His voice was accusatory.

'I agreed to it.' Imlay raised his arm in what was almost a salute towards the emerging vessel. 'And see what we got. The ship, the cargo, the hostages. The lot.'

'For what? Thirty pieces of silver?'

Imlay was unperturbed. 'Oh, the Pasha drives a harder bargain than that,' he said. 'But he took a hundred thousand down and the promise of a subsidy sometime in the future.'

'And those poor bastards on the beach?'

They both looked back towards the shore. It was all over bar the shouting. The cavalry wheeling at the water's edge, shouting their battle cries, their swords gleaming in the moonlight as they waved them triumphantly towards the ship's boats – and perhaps the ship herself, further out into the bay. The boats were about a cable's length from the beach now, the men resting on their oars as Mr Lamb presumably tried to work out what to do next.

Nathan flung out an arm towards them. 'If those men come to any harm . . .' he began.

'They will come to no harm,' Imlay assured him carelessly. 'Provided they do not attempt to intervene.'

'It is a bit late for that.'

It was not possible to see details of the carnage the cavalry had wrought on the beach, but it was reasonable to assume they had taken no prisoners. Nathan thought one of the horsemen was waving a head.

'I am tempted to give them a broadside,' Nathan muttered, for whatever he had thought of the Pasha-zade, he was averse to treachery and greatly saddened and angered by the death of the doctor. 'Just to wipe the smiles off their faces.'

'You will do no such thing,' Imlay instructed him. 'This is no business of ours.'

'No business of ours?' Nathan rounded on him angrily. 'Good God, man, you brought them here. You sent them to their deaths.'

'How was I to know what Yusuf Pasha intended?' Imlay retorted indignantly. 'He could have had them taken prisoner.' He gazed towards the shore. 'He may in fact have done so.'

'Oh, yes.' Nathan's tone was bitter. 'That would fit with what we know of the man's nature.'

'Well, I cannot answer for Yusuf Pasha,' said Imlay
with what might have been a sigh of regret. 'He has his
own way of going about things.'

Nathan turned away, sickened as much by Imlay as
what he had seen on the beach. He might have known, of
course. It was not the first time he had witnessed Imlay's
capacity for double-dealing. He looked back towards the
Saratoga and then noticed something strange. She was
clear of the harbour entrance now and heading in almost a
straight line towards them, but a trick of the moonlight
seemed to have given her a long shadow, stretching back
towards the port. And then the shadow detached itself and
he saw that it was another ship.

'Dear God!' he exclaimed. 'It's the *Meshuda*!'

He looked to Imlay to see if it was part of the plan.
From the expression on his face it was not. 'What are they
up to?' He frowned.

Nathan's head was instantly full of calculations. The
approaching ships were still well over a mile away, nearer
two. If he cut the *Swallow*'s cable now, the offshore breeze
would very likely take her out to sea long before the
Meshuda could bring her guns to bear. There was no time
to pick up the ship's boats, but he could return for them
later. More than anything else, they needed sea room –
room to manoeuvre, to avoid being trapped and boarded
in the shallow, treacherous waters of the bay. Then he
remembered the reefs – the Kaluisa Reefs, an unmarked
bank of shale and rock somewhere between the *Swallow*
and the open sea. But he did not know their exact location
– and in the darkness there was a very great risk he would
not know until his keel grated upon the first rock.

Before he could think of a solution to the problem, the distance between the *Saratoga* and her shadow lengthened, and he saw that the schooner was bearing away to the north, heading for one of the gaps between the long line of islands that extended from the curved beak of the port.

'Where is she going?' he wondered aloud as he watched the triangular sails of the *Meshuda* disappear behind the islands.

'She can go to the Devil for all I care,' said Imlay. 'That signal – it was from one of Cathcart's men, to let us know the hostages were aboard the *Saratoga*.' His features relaxed into a grin. He even clapped Nathan on the shoulder. 'Let her go. We have got everything we wanted. It is over.'

His jubilation lasted a little over an hour until the *Saratoga* came alongside and he learned that he had been short-changed. Two of the hostages were missing, and one of them was Louisa Devereux, the daughter of the American Consul, the man who had put up the money for their entire expedition.

Chapter Sixteen

Kidnapped

———◆———

The fury of a woman scorned was nothing, in Nathan's admittedly limited experience of the condition, to the fury of the double-crosser double-crossed, and a few hours' sleep did nothing to improve Imlay's temper. At times his wrath reached biblical proportions as he vowed to be revenged on the treacherous Pasha, his wives and his children, his oxen and his asses, even down to the seventh generation. He was for sending off an immediate ultimatum, threatening all manner of reprisals unless the missing hostages were returned forthwith.

' "I will do such things",' murmured Nathan to Tully, ' "what they are, yet I know not: but they shall be the terrors of the earth".'

Imlay might not have recognised the quote but he had a clearer idea than King Lear of what terrors to unleash.

They should commence with a close blockade to stop even fishing boats from putting to sea, followed by a bombardment of the port, and if that did not bring the desired result they should send in boats under cover of darkness to fire the ships in the harbour.

Nathan turned away, rolling his eyes at Tully, and even Cathcart counselled a more moderate approach.

'Before we go off on half-cock, I reckon we need to send to the Pasha and tell him that two of the hostages are missing,' he argued. 'Maybe he does not know about it. He has played straight with us on every other issue.'

A head-count had established that all the other prisoners were present and correct. The crew had been put to work as labourers, repairing the harbour defences, and there were some minor injuries and complaints, but most of the hostages were in reasonable shape. So, too, was the *Saratoga* after her long lay-to in Tripoli Harbour, and the cargo appeared to be intact, inasmuch as Captain Fry had been able to tell without a thorough inspection. Some of the women hostages echoed Imlay's desire for revenge, but this was largely on account of being treated as skivvies, the Captain reported. From what he could gather, they had not been violated or otherwise mistreated during their stay in the seraglio. And the two missing women had been accommodated with them until the previous night when they had apparently been moved to other quarters, no one knew where.

'Maybe they got overlooked in the confusion,' Cathcart proposed. 'After all, they are but two out of a hundred or more.'

'Oh, well, that is some consolation, I suppose,' Imlay

remarked with icy sarcasm. 'But perhaps you have overlooked that one of them happens to be Louisa Devereux,
the daughter of the man who is not only paying our wages
but has also raised most of the money for the ransom. And
am I now to go back to him and say, "I am very sorry, sir,
but your daughter has been overlooked in the confusion"?
Pah!'

There was a short but uncomfortable silence. Nathan
broke it by raising the practical difficulty of bombarding
Tripoli with one small sloop, especially as it would be
impossible to approach closer than a mile and a half
without being bombarded in turn by the guns of the fort.

This only drew Imlay's fire upon himself.

'What is the use of an Englishman who will not fight?'
he complained to Cathcart and the world in general. 'It is
like keeping a bulldog that runs shy of the bull.'

'Let us first discover the true situation,' Spiridion
interposed hastily, observing the sudden clenching of
Nathan's jaw, 'before we start a war between the United
States and Tripoli – not to speak of ourselves.'

He proposed that he and Cathcart should go ashore –
Cathcart to make a formal representation to the Pasha
while he made more discreet enquiries of his informants in
the port.

Imlay was far from content, but for want of a better
suggestion he reluctantly agreed.

It was late afternoon before Spiridion returned with
the somewhat confusing news that the women had been
kidnapped.

'Kidnapped?' Imlay's voice was a harsh echo. 'We *know*
they have been kidnapped, goddamn it. That is why I have

just paid one hundred thousand dollars for their ransom.'

'I mean, since they were brought to Tripoli. Two nights ago, in fact.'

Imlay stared at him in astonishment. 'So where are they now?'

'Well, you will not like it,' Spiridion informed him, 'but I have it on good authority that they are aboard the *Meshuda*.'

Imlay did *not* like it. In fact, he demonstrated his dislike by taking off his hat and hurling it upon the deck. Mr Lamb picked it up and thoughtfully dusted it with his sleeve before returning it to him.

'By God, I might have known,' Imlay swore. 'We should never have let her slip away,' he rebuked Nathan bitterly.

Nathan reminded Imlay that it was he himself who had insisted they should let her 'slip away'. 'You said she could go to the Devil for all you cared.'

'But I did not know the women were aboard her,' Imlay wailed. He turned on Spiridion. 'How could they have got out of the castle without anyone knowing? Unless the Pasha is behind it and he has sent them away for safe-keeping – is that it?'

'I suppose that is possible.' Spiridion gazed about the quarterdeck where Mr Lamb, as officer of the watch, and several other English-speakers were pretending they had not the slightest interest in the conversation of their superiors. 'Do you think it is possible to talk more privately?' he requested.

They adjourned to the stern cabin, which the Pasha-zade's unfortunate demise had now restored to them.

'I am told that their escape was contrived by Xavier

Naudé,' Spiridion revealed when they were settled around the table, 'with the undoubted assistance of Murad Reis, or if you prefer, Peter Lisle.'

'I know who Murad Reis is, goddamn it,' Imlay rebuked him, 'but who in God's name is Xavier Naudé?'

'He is the leading French agent in Tripoli,' Nathan supplied calmly. 'And you will oblige me, Imlay, by controlling your temper. We are not your lackeys, even if you would like to think so.'

Imlay glared but then surprised Nathan by apologising with apparent sincerity. 'But it is enough to make a saint cuss,' he declared in a more reasonable tone. 'Why in God's name would the leading French agent in Tripoli wish to abduct Louisa Devereux?'

'I do not think he would, had he any choice in the matter,' Spiridion replied. 'Naudé's interest is in the other woman.'

'I am confused,' Imlay informed him. 'Why would he be interested in either of them?'

'Well, that is something of a mystery,' Spiridion admitted. 'It may be because she is a British agent, but I am told it may be more personal than that. An affair of the heart. She is a very beautiful woman and he is a Frenchman, after all.'

'A British agent?' Imlay wiped a hand over his streaming brow. 'Who in God's name *is* she?'

Spiridion glanced at Nathan. 'Her name is Caterina Caresini,' he revealed, 'and she was until recently the Deputy Prioress of the Convent of San Paolo di Mare in Venice.'

'She was *what*? I think I am going mad,' confessed

Imlay. He appealed to Nathan: 'Do you understand any of this?'

'I was once acquainted with a woman of that name,' Nathan confirmed thoughtfully. 'In Venice.' In fact, their association had been brief but it had made a lasting impression. He frowned suspiciously at Spiridion. 'However, I had no idea she was here in Tripoli.'

'I had no intention of deceiving you,' Spiridion assured him. 'But there was no occasion for me to mention it. It was a great surprise to me when I saw her among the other hostages at the Pasha's Divan. I suppose it was necessary for her to leave Venice in a hurry when the French landed – and unfortunately she picked the wrong ship.'

'Well, I am sorry to be boorish,' Imlay interrupted them, 'but I have not the slightest concern for this woman, whoever she is – nun, spy or the Empress of Ethiopia. Xavier Naudé, whoever *he* is, is welcome to her. Louisa Devereux is all I care about. And how to get her back.'

'We must get them both back,' Spiridion agreed coolly. 'For I have as much an obligation to Sister Caterina as you to Miss Devereux. Which means catching up with her in the *Swallow*,' he said to Nathan. 'Before they reach Egypt.'

'Wait a moment.' Imlay massaged his fevered brows in an attempt to focus his thoughts. 'If Naudé's interest is in this – *nun* – why have they also taken Louisa Devereux, and why is Murad Reis involved?'

Spiridion shrugged. 'I am told the nun, as you call her, insisted upon it. Though it may be that Murad Reis has interests of his own.'

'What interests? You are not saying this is another "affair of the heart"?'

'It is not impossible. But I rather suspect it is more of a financial interest. He probably thinks he deserves more than a small share of the hundred thousand you paid the Pasha and thinks to demand a separate ransom for her.'

Imlay groaned and held his head in his hands. He seemed on the verge of tears.

'But this is speculation,' Spiridion said, with another glance to Nathan. 'All I know for certain is that Monsieur Naudé has hired the *Meshuda*, ostensibly to undertake a survey of the coast between here and the Nile Delta.'

Imlay looked up at him in astonishment, his eyes wild and his voice almost a wail. 'What? *Why?*'

'In preparation for a French landing,' Nathan explained.

'His interest in the women may be something of a diversion,' Spiridion added.

'But what if this whole business is a diversion?' Imlay objected. 'A ruse to send us off on a wild-goose chase after the *Meshuda*. How can you be sure the women have not been concealed in the Red Castle?'

'Because my chief informant helped to organise their escape.'

Now they both stared at him in bemusement.

'You are saying that *you* were behind this?' Imlay challenged him.

'Of course not. I said my informant, not my servant. She is what you might call a *routier* – a freelance. She serves several different masters. One is Naudé, another is myself. She also takes money from the Pasha, or his Grand Kehya. And doubtless others of whom I have less knowledge.'

'And yet you trust her?' Imlay challenged him.

'Oh, I would not say that. But in this instance, yes I do. She has nothing to gain by deceiving me. Her true loyalty is to God and her family – who are of the Jewish persuasion, by the by, with financial interests throughout the Levant and in Italy. I am not sure about God, but certainly her family would not wish to make an enemy of me.'

There was a knock and Qualtrough poked his vulture face around the door to report that the barge was returning with Mr Cathcart.

'Perhaps he has different news,' said Imlay hopefully.

But what little news Cathcart had gleaned only confirmed Spiridion's version of events. He had been unable to speak with the Pasha, but after keeping him waiting for most of the day, the Grand Kehya had informed him that the two women had escaped from the seraglio two nights before.

'He says it was assumed that we had arranged it,' he reported.

Imlay let out an oath. 'The old buzzard! I have a mind to give them a few parting shots before we leave.'

'We are wasting time,' Nathan pointed out. 'The *Meshuda* already has a day's start on us. If we are to stand any chance at all of catching her, we must set sail in the next hour, while we can still see the shoals.'

The two ships crept out of the bay with the benefit of the offshore breeze but under reefed topsails for fear of running upon the rocks, and the sun slipping down behind Tripoli. From Nathan's vantage, the city resembled the backdrop for a stage setting of *The Arabian Nights*, the domes and cupolas, battlements and watch-towers like so many wooden cut-outs against the crimson sky and the first lights flickering in the windows of the houses and along the ramparts of the Red Castle.

Part Three
The Mouth of the Nile

Chapter Seventeen

The Long Chase

———◆———

They parted with the *Saratoga* a little after day-break. It had been decided she would head for Malta, some 200 miles to the north, to replenish her supplies and obtain medical attention for those needing it before resuming her long, interrupted journey to Philadelphia.

While the *Swallow* turned eastward and began her own long journey in search of the *Meshuda*.

Imlay was convinced they were on a fool's errand. 'We can never hope to find her,' he insisted, staring gloomily at the charts. 'She could be heading anywhere in the Eastern Med.'

But Spiridion was confident his information was correct, and that the schooner had been hired by Xavier Naudé to find a beachhead for the French invasion of Egypt.

'That still leaves us a lot of beach between Tripoli and Alexandria,' Nathan pointed out, for though he hated to agree with Imlay, he was inclined to share his doubts.

'About a thousand miles,' Spiridion acknowledged. 'But why march a thousand miles through a desert when you can sail straight to Alexandria – barely a hundred miles from Cairo. A five- or six-day march along the Nile, say, with a fleet of boats to carry your supplies. That would be my choice, and I cannot believe I am a better General than Bonaparte.'

The map argued his case more eloquently than words, but Nathan was not entirely convinced.

'I thought Naudé came to Tripoli to make a treaty with Yusuf Pasha?' he said.

'This was one of his reasons,' Spiridion agreed thoughtfully. 'What of it?'

'So what if Yusuf has offered the use of his own ports – Tobruk perhaps, right here on the Egyptian border.' Nathan indicated its position on the map. It was still a fair way from Cairo – about 400 miles, he reckoned, as the crow flies, but at least they could disembark in an orderly fashion at a friendly port. 'Bonaparte might prefer that to wading ashore on an open beach,' he observed, 'with the Mamelukes waiting for him, sharpening their blades.'

'Indeed,' Spiridion nodded. 'But if that were the case, Naudé would have no need to conduct a survey. Murad Reis would supply him with all the charts he requires. No, my friend, in my view the *Meshuda* will head straight for Alexandria and conduct a leisurely survey of the beaches between El Alamein and Rosetta.' He described an arc with his finger, covering a distance of around 100 miles. 'And that is where we will find her.'

He made it sound relatively easy. 'Why leisurely?' Nathan queried.

'Because they have two of the most beautiful women in Venice at their disposal,' Spiridion declared morosely. 'Why would they wish to hurry?'

Nathan could think of several reasons, not least the temper of an impatient Bonaparte back in Paris, or Toulon, or wherever he was at the present moment in time.

'How long will it take to reach Alexandria?' Imlay asked him – as if Nathan were a coachman delivering the Royal Mail.

'Depends on the wind,' Nathan told him with shrug. But seeing Imlay's expression, he relented a little. 'The prevailing wind being westerly,' he informed him, 'if it remains light and from the present quarter, we might expect to sight Pompey's Pillar in anything between eight to ten days.'

Imlay echoed these figures with dismay.

'If it is any consolation, I do not suppose the *Meshuda* will be any quicker,' Nathan assured him dryly.

'Well then,' Imlay sighed, 'if we are all agreed, let us set a course for Alexandria. And with good fortune we may overhaul her on the way.'

It was never a good idea, in Nathan's experience, to presume upon the wind. Within a few hours of their parting from the *Saratoga* it had dropped to a mocking whisper that left the sails flapping limply at the yards and the crew almost as lifeless in the heat of the afternoon sun.

Below decks it was like an oven, and the only relief that could be obtained was under the canvas awnings Tully had rigged between the masts, with the fire engine playing water on them from time to time so that, as Nathan put it, 'at least we may be wet whilst we fry.'

But Tully could do nothing about the wind. The first day, they barely moved. As the sun set, they could still see the sails of the *Saratoga* on the northern horizon. The next day they made barely ten miles between dawn and dusk. Overnight the wind picked up a little but by morning, perversely, as if playing with them, it had backed to the south-east and came on so strongly they were obliged to strike down the topgallants and struggle on under reefed topsails with the boats brought aboard, everything battened down, and the sea breaking over the decks.

Nathan's only consolation was that as conditions worsened, the attitude of the crew improved perceptibly. Even his waisters showed a dogged resource he had not expected of them as they endured a constant battering of wind and rain, fighting their way along the decks with the water pouring off their sou'westers, clutching at the lifelines as the sea threatened to carry them off wholesale, and the wind howling through the rigging like a demented wolfpack on the rampage. Time and time again he struggled to bring the ship's head round to the east, only to be beaten back by the sea. Twice they were almost broached. As if scenting victory, the wind increased in violence, obliging them to run before it on bare poles or with the merest scrap of a staysail to keep their stern to the wind. For three days it harried them without mercy, driving them further and further to the north-west.

'At this rate,' Nathan complained to Tully, 'we will soon be back in Gibraltar.'

'If we are so lucky,' Tully muttered, with an eye to the scudding clouds.

The sky remained overcast night and day. Being denied the facility of a horizon or a single celestial body from which to take a reading, they could only judge their position by dead reckoning, or even more primitive guesswork. Tully and the sailing master, Cribb, feared they might run upon the south-western coast of Crete or one of its outlying islands. Nathan put them further to the west, just off the tip of the Morea. And Spiridion, who had a more supernatural view of the world and its winds, believed that, with a malign sense of irony, it might drive them onto the shores of Zante, his birthplace in the Ionian Sea.

In fact, when the sky cleared sufficiently to take a reading, all four of them agreed within a small margin of error that they were at 35° 27' North, 22° 24' East – which put them about 100 miles to the west of Crete and about the same distance south of Cape Tainaron on the Morea.

'So we were both right,' Nathan remarked to Tully, not without a degree of complacency for he was aware of his deficiencies in the matter of navigation, especially when it was based on pure instinct, unsupported by his painstaking mathematics.

'It could have been worse,' Tully commented.

In truth, it was a lot better than Nathan had expected, for although they had been driven much further north than he would have wished, they were only 300 or so miles from Alexandria, and if the wind would only maintain its

present speed and direction, they might hope to reach the
port within three to four days. But being the wind, of
course, this was no more likely than a mule might grow
wings and fly. It did, in fact, veer westward overnight, but
dropped away altogether by daybreak, leaving them
stranded off the southern coast of Crete. And off Crete
they remained for the best part of a week; the wind, when
it could be bothered to blow at all, herding them slowly
and sullenly along the length of the island, making scarcely
thirty miles from noon to noon.

It was an island Spiridion knew well, though he called
it by its Venetian name of Candia. Once the cradle of
Minoan civilisation, it had been part of the Venetian
maritime empire for 400 years until it fell to the Turks,
since when many of its inhabitants, who were Greek in
origin, had converted to Islam. But they were friendly
enough, according to Spiridion who did a great deal of
trade with them, and he was able to replenish their
dwindling supplies in Selino with the tacit consent of his
friend the Turkish Governor, who had been oiled by a
large bribe. They were even able to replenish their supplies
of wine, acquiring a local variety mixed with pine needles
which was something of an acquired taste but which the
crew tolerated with admirable fortitude. It proved an
excellent accompaniment to the fish, and even turtles,
which were plentiful in these waters. Indeed, with food,
wine, sunshine and calm seas, it might have been an idyllic
cruise – and for most of the crew it probably was – but
Imlay was in a fever of impatience to catch the *Meshuda*
and Nathan even more anxious to report back on what he
had learned of the French intentions. It was only Spiridion's

insistence that they needed the *Meshuda*'s charts that kept him from abandoning the chase there and then, and turning back for Gibraltar, though it would have gone hard between him and Imlay.

Finally, after five days of crawling along 'that damnable shore' as Nathan described it, the wind picked up, and for the first time in almost two weeks, the *Swallow* began to spread her wings and fly, with studding sails spread aloft and alow, a bow wave at her head and a long creamy wake spreading back to the rapidly dwindling island at her stern.

But they had lost a great deal of time, and after studying the map, Spiridion prevailed upon Nathan to set his course south-east by east, heading directly for the little port of Rosetta, some forty miles east of Alexandria on the Nile Delta.

'For in my view that is the most likely place for the French to land,' he argued, 'and if I am wrong and the *Meshuda* is not there, then we can head westward towards El Alamein and hope to run into her on the way.'

And so, on the morning of 18 June, twenty-one days after leaving Tripoli, they entered a wide bay Spiridion pronounced as Abukir – the Bay of the Castle.

They approached from the north-west with the wind on their starboard quarter, but blowing so mild and desultorily, their stately progress seemed hardly to break the surface of the water. The sky was a cloudless blue and the sun rising behind them bathed the long sandy shore in an indolent golden haze.

They could see the castle – more of a small fort of some

antiquity – on the western and nearmost headland, with the Ottoman flag drooping listlessly from the flagpole. There were about a dozen cannon on the ramparts facing out to sea, though Spiridion doubted if they were less than 100 years old and had probably never been fired in anger. There seemed to be little for them to protect besides the ruins of ancient Canopus, a small distance inshore, and a few isolated clumps of palm, and nothing of any substance on the sea but a solitary coastal trader of a type Spiridion called a Scandaroon. There were a few fishing boats dragged up on to the beaches but no sign of any fishermen.

Directly ahead was a small island – shown on the chart as two adjoining islands with a narrow channel between and called by a single name: the Isle of Abukir. Between that and the headland was a line of breakers indicating a hidden spit of sand, cutting off access to the bay. The curving coastline beyond was broken by a small rivermouth which Spiridion said was the mouth of the Nile, or at least one of its many mouths in the Delta, and the current, though invisible, stirred up a great quantity of sand so that the waters closest to the shore were as murky as a millpond and almost as flat. And almost certainly not as deep, Spiridion had warned them. He also advised against placing too much trust in the chart – their *only* chart of the coastline in these parts – which had been brought from Algiers by Cathcart. The shoals were constantly shifting, he said, owing to the force of the winter gales and the volume of water being emitted from the Nile when it was in flood.

Apart from the coaster and the fishing boats there was little sign of life either at sea or ashore. Directly opposite the island, on the farther side of the bay, there was a distinctive hill like the hump of a camel, rising out of the flatness of the shore and topped by a substantial building of stone which Nathan thought was another fort but which Spiridion said was a caravanserai – a kind of hostelry for the caravans that trekked across the deserts between Alexandria and points East – Persia, India and beyond. In times past they had brought the silks and spices that made Venice the great trading power of the world, but now the caravanserai looked as deserted as the rest of that forsaken shore.

There seemed little point in lingering, the fort so moribund Nathan was reluctant to waste powder in a formal salute, but then, as he was about to give the order to wear away and begin trawling the coast closer to Alexandria, there was a shout from the lookout in the foretop and he followed the direction of his outstretched arm and saw the bare poles of a three-master just beyond the headland, previously masked by the bulk of the fort.

She was schooner-rigged with a green flag at her mizzen and thirteen gunports painted along her sides. And as Nathan studied her through his glass, conviction grew to certainty. She was the *Meshuda*.

Chapter Eighteen

Close Quarter Action

———◆•◆•◆———

*N*athan studied the schooner through his glass as the *Swallow* rode the gentle swell in the mouth of the bay. Their approach had provoked a bustle of activity on board the *Meshuda*, but no obvious signs of panic. She did not cut her cables and make a dash for the open sea. She did not waste powder and shot in a vain attempt to deter them at such a range. But her guns were run out and she swung at her anchor to follow the *Swallow*'s every move – a sure sign that she was moored on a spring cable. She had boarding nets rigged along both sides and her tops were crammed with men armed with muskets and swivel guns. She looked a tough nut to crack, but the real problem, from Nathan's point of view, was the bay itself.

The schooner was moored in what looked like clear water about halfway between the headland and the mouth of the Nile. But according to Cathcart's chart she was very close to a large sandbank, barely two fathoms under the surface and extending over much of the inner bay. Spiridion supposed that she must be in one of the channels created by the interplay of tide and current; such tide as there was in this part of the world. But to reach her would require a local pilot, or a much more accurate chart than the one they possessed. The *Swallow*'s draught was a mere fourteen feet, but even where they were now, well out to sea, they could see the seabed quite clearly beneath their keel.

The only alternative was to fire on her from long range, or attempt to cut her out with small boats – by night. Both of which raised serious tactical problems.

Nathan had been agreeably surprised by the range of the carronades. At the maximum elevation of 11 degrees, with a full charge of powder, they could hurl a 24-pound round shot to a distance of about 2,000 yards, almost as far as cannon of the same calibre. But they were woefully inaccurate. In the admittedly few live practices he had permitted – firing at a raft made of empty rum casks – they had come nowhere near to hitting the target at even half that range. Their chances of hitting the *Meshuda* from the outer reaches of the bay were minimal, and the schooner could fire almost as far and with much greater accuracy with her 6-pounders.

Then there was the question of the fort.

The Turkish Commander was unlikely to remain neutral while an unknown man-of-war attacked a Muslim vessel anchored peaceably in his own waters – especially as she was flying an Ottoman flag. And Murad Reis would hardly have told them he was conducting a survey for the French.

Nathan viewed the guns through his glass. They were probably culverins, he thought, firing an 18-pound shot. With the advantage of their height above the water they would easily reach him at 2,000 yards, and the effect on the thin timbers of the sloop, especially if the shot was heated, did not bear thinking about.

The only other approach – a night attack with the ship's boats – was fraught with difficulties of its own. There was no chance of taking the *Meshuda* by surprise – not now – and according to Spiridion she carried a crew of well over 300, twice as many as the *Swallow* – veteran fighters, who specialised in boarding operations. Nathan's own crew were fine enough sailors, but they were untrained and untested in battle. They would be cut to pieces.

'We have to find some way of bringing her out,' he said to Tully.

But he was damned if he could think of one.

Imlay, of course, had his own half-baked solution. 'If it looked as if we were making an attack, prepared for battle, guns run out and all – might it not spur them into some kind of a response?' he proposed. And before Nathan could make a sufficiently scathing reply, he went on: 'Surely they would not wish to remain at anchor. They would cut their cable and try to find sea room. Just as you did – or intended to do – when you thought the *Meshuda* might catch us moored off the *menshia* in the Bay of Tripoli.'

'This is true,' Nathan conceded, 'but unlike us in the Bay of Tripoli, the *Meshuda* is moored on a spring cable.'

He saw that this meant nothing to Imlay. 'This enables her to swing at her mooring,' he explained patiently. 'She could cover any approach we make and hit us again and again with her broadside before we could bring our own guns to bear.' And in case this did not impress him: 'Besides which, if she lies where she is at present, she is covered by the guns in the fort. Between them they would pound us to pieces before we approached within a half-mile of her. And if we were to run aground, heaven help us. She would come out then all right, and we would be helpless to defend ourselves.'

But even as he spoke, the germ of an idea was forming in his mind. He rejected it at once. It was absurd. Tantamount to suicide. But it refused to be so lightly dismissed.

He leaned over the rail and peered into the translucent depths below the keel. He could see the seabed with remarkable clarity, the gently waving seaweed, the colourful fish darting to and fro, even a crab scuttling across the sandy bottom – a hermit crab, carrying its home on its back, like a barnacle with spider's legs. It stirred a dim, half-forgotten memory from his time as a midshipman in the South Seas.

And suddenly he knew how it could be done.

He gave orders to take them out to sea, far out of the sight of prying eyes. Then he explained to Tully what he had in mind.

It was mid-afternoon before they headed back into the bay – with the gun crews at the guns and the topmen in the tops and a solitary seaman in the bows swinging the lead. The wind remained steady from the west, blowing almost

directly across the bay but still so mild as to scarcely ruffle
the surface of the water. The only hint of a breaker was
where the sea broke on the rocks between the islands and
the headland, and a very small hint it was, like the lazy
curling of a lip. But it showed how shallow the waters
were thereabouts. Hopefully they were almost as shallow
on the seaward side of the islands. Nathan's plan depended
on it.

At about 2,000 yards, seeing that the shoals had not
deterred them, the fort fired a warning shot. It sank about
a cable's length off their starboard bow. Nathan gave the
order for the gun crews to lie down beside the guns. But
his prime concern was not the shot from the fort, not as
yet.

'Four fathoms five,' sang out the seaman with the lead.

They were now almost directly in line with the fort,
with the twin islands almost masking them from the guns.

'Very well, Mr Cribb,' Nathan nodded to the sailing
master.

The Genoese and the Portuguese worked efficiently
enough but Nathan was gnawing on his bottom lip as he
watched them, willing them to work faster, and restraining
an urge to bawl them out for their indolence or impudence,
or both, for they still chattered away like parrots, even
with the prospect of dying in the next few hours.

'Four fathoms four,' came the voice from the bows.

Up came the maintopsail. Up came the foresail and the
foretopsail.

'Four fathoms two.'

Down came the forestaysail and the mainstaysail.

'Three fathoms five.'

They were almost past the islands now and the *Meshuda* was exactly where they had left her, with her guns still run out and her boarding nets rigged.

Nathan leaned over the starboard rail and peered down into the clear blue waters. Was he wrong? Had he stayed too far out? Then he saw the sudden swirl of sand and felt the slight tremor under his feet.

'Port your helm!'

She was very sluggish answering, but round she came until the bowsprit was pointing almost directly at the mouth of the Nile, with the *Meshuda* lying at an angle of about 45 degrees off their starboard bow. Still coming round – too far now. He opened his mouth to instruct the helmsman.

'Three fathoms three.'

Then she struck.

They had taken the precaution of doubling the stays, but the foretopgallant mast broke away at once, toppling almost elegantly forward across the bows and bringing down jib and staysails with it in a hopeless tangle of canvas and rigging. Nathan feared that the maintopgallant would follow, but it held and the Genoese were already hauling in the remaining canvas at maintop and mizzen with the waisters under Mr Lamb hacking away at the shambles in the bows.

The islands masked them from the fort but not from the *Meshuda* and she fired almost immediately – a rippling broadside that fell a little short of their bow, a single shot skipping up and ringing off the bower anchor.

Now came the real test. Was she going to stay there, potting shots at them at long range, or was she going to

come out? It was all down to the vanity – or the courage
– of one man. Peter Lisle, the former seaman turned
Admiral of the Fleet.

'Oh, he will come out,' Spiridion had declared confidently. 'He is a corsair and a Scot, he will not be able to
resist. Think of the glory, bringing you back in triumph
into Tripoli.'

Nathan stared out across the bay towards the schooner,
wondering what he might do in the same circumstances.

'Start out the water,' he said to Tully. If Lisle saw that
they were trying to lighten the ship, it might convince him
they truly were aground. If ditching the water did not
wash, they might have to sacrifice a couple of guns.

Another broadside. This time two or three shots struck
the hull, but they were firing at extreme range and the shot
bounced harmlessly back into the sea.

Then Spiridion let out a shout. The canvas was
mushrooming out from the *Meshuda*'s spars and stays,
and through his glass Nathan could see the long teams on
her decks hauling on the halyards.

'She has slipped her cable,' O'Driscoll announced,
unnecessarily.

They watched as she began to move slowly off her
mooring, heading away from them at first with the wind
directly abaft, but then round came her bows and out she
came.

Nathan fought down the sudden euphoria; there was a
long way to go before he could allow himself to feel
exultant. And for a few minutes indeed he thought she
was steering clear of them, heading for the far side of the
bay. He brought the glass up to his eye, focusing on the

figures at her stern. He could not make out Lisle, among the group of officers – if they *were* officers, for they seemed to wear no particular uniform. He imagined the debate they must be having. To play safe and steer for the open sea, or take the prize that was so temptingly offered. He caught Spiridion's eye but the Greek's face was expressionless. Confident, assailed by doubt? It was impossible to tell. Then he saw the ghost of a grim smile, and looking back towards the *Meshuda* he saw that her bows had come round and she was heading straight towards them.

His exultation was shortlived. An instant later, the two long nines at her bows opened fire – with remarkable accuracy at 1,000 yards or more. The first shots skimmed the water a few yards off his larboard bow, but the next smashed into the rail just abaft the mainmast, hurling lethal splinters about the gundeck. Nathan heard the screams and the groans of the wounded and watched them carried below to the tender mercies of Mr Kite. Others, beyond his torment, were thrown overboard without ceremony. But the men kept their nerve, waiting, silent and remarkably steady, beside the guns.

And the others, with their axes, poised and ready, in the waist.

Nathan could see Mr Wallace, the engineer from the Carron Company who was acting as their gunner, and it occurred to him that this was probably the first time he had been in action. He looked tense, but then so did they all, and beside him, among the starboard carronades, was the immensely reassuring presence of George Banjo, who had slipped easily into his old role of gunner's mate.

On she came.

'Stand by,' he murmured to Tully, more like a prayer than an order. 'Any moment now.'

From where he stood he could see along the length of her gundeck and it was crowded with men. So many, there must be ten to each gun and as many in the tops with their muskets and their swivels. He had doubted Spiridion's figures, wondering how they could cram so many into such a small vessel, but somehow they had, and here they all were, standing by to fire their broadsides or to board. Or both.

And on she came . . .

Surely Lisle would not risk coming too close for fear of grounding. She would cut across their bows and rake the *Swallow* with her broadside until she struck, or was so knocked about there would be no fight left in her.

Nathan waited, with every nerve screaming at him to give the order. But he had to let her come so close there was no turning back: back into the shoals of the bay where he could not follow. Two hundred yards. One hundred . . . He could see the faces of the gunners at the long nines in her bow. They fired again – at point-blank range now, the long plume of flame almost scorching the *Swallow*'s rail. One shot came straight through it, showering the quarter-deck with splinters and striking the 6-pounder on the larboard side, knocking it clean from its mount. Another came so close to Nathan it thrummed the air about his ear, and as he looked round in clownish bemusement, he saw that it had taken off the head of one of the quarter-masters behind him, the body still standing upright with the blood spurting from the severed neck, until the knees buckled and the corpse collapsed onto the deck like a puppet whose strings have been cut.

Nathan looked back at the advancing schooner.

'Now,' he said softly – almost resignedly, to Tully.

It had taken them the best part of the day to prepare, hove to in the heat of the midday sun just out of sight of the shore.

'Just like a keelhauling,' he had said to Tully, as if he did it all the time.

He had seen it done only once, in fact, when he was a midshipman in the South Seas – carried out on a Dutch ship, for it was illegal in the King's Navy. A terrible business, the memory of which had stayed with him for days: the victim tied to a line and dragged under the keel and up the other side, emerging like some nightmare creature of the deep with the skin hanging in shreds from his back, lacerated by the barnacles on the ship's hull.

But it was a lot easier to keelhaul a man than an 18-foot gig.

First they had dropped four cables over the bow, working them aft until they were hanging under the middle of the ship. Then they had hauled the gig up from the stern, tying more lines to the thwarts on both sides and opening the seacock until she filled with water. Then they dragged her under the keel, half the crew pulling on one side, the rest letting out the cables on the other – constructing a false keel that extended their own by a good few feet.

It took them four hours to make it secure. It took less than a minute for the axemen in the waist to cut it free.

* * *

Nathan felt the movement instantly as the *Swallow* shed her false keel, and the topsails, instantly loosed from the yard, flapped and filled. He was alive now, all dullness gone, as alive as his ship, rushing to the quarterdeck rail to shout encouragement to his men as they leaped to their feet and bent over the waiting carronades.

Slowly but surely the wind brought their bows round to larboard, the *Meshuda* so close now Nathan could have thrown a stone and hit her bow. He had a moment's doubt – thinking about the two women, hoping they had been stowed safely below the waterline, but it was too late to worry about that now.

He gave the nod to Tully. 'Fire as you bear!' and heard the command echoed down the length of the gundeck before he was deafened by the roar of the first carronade.

It is doubtful if anyone aboard the *Meshuda* realised the corvette had come free of the sands. The smoke was still wreathing about her bows as the first shot hit her. And as the wind continued to bring the *Swallow*'s head round towards the open sea, all twelve of her starboard carronades poured their fire into the schooner.

It was not until the smoke had cleared that Nathan was able to see the damage they had done. The hollow shot fired by the carronades was designed to break up on impact, showering the enemy deck with wood and metal. But at such close quarters it had punched jagged holes in her hull, knocking several gunports into one. The devastation on the gundeck must have been dreadful. Some of the guns had fired back, but not many, and Nathan could see no obvious signs of damage aboard the *Swallow*.

Someone on the schooner's quarterdeck – Lisle himself, perhaps – must have finally realised what had happened and ordered the helmsmen to bear away. She answered well enough at first, but the *Swallow* was still coming round with the wind, gathering pace as she did so, and the two vessels were running side by side when the corvette fired her second broadside.

If Nathan still entertained a prejudice against carronades, he suspended it for the duration. At close range they gave the little sloop almost as much firepower as a ship of the line – which presumably was the purpose of installing them in preference to long guns. Mr Wallace was dancing with glee or astonishment – or both – and Nathan was about to issue a sharp reprimand when he remembered that this was the first time the man had seen his precious ordnance fired in anger. Thankfully, George Banjo was dashing from breech to breech, in that curious gait beloved of gunners, like a large ungainly bird, unused to walking, constantly doubling at the waist to peer through the gunports or check a powder charge or a flintlock. Lamb was doing the same thing, up with the forward guns, and Lieutenant-Captain Belli – where *was* Lieutenant-Captain Belli? Then he saw him, or rather what was left of him, stretched out on the gundeck with half his head missing and two of his Russians wailing over the ruin. Nathan opened his mouth to shout at them to carry him below, and then snapped it shut. They would not understand him, nor would they be able to carry the officer below, not unless they took a half-dozen men from the guns.

The *Meshuda* was drawing away from them now. Nathan doubted if she was a faster sailor, not with the

wind on her beam, but the *Swallow* was still struggling to
gain momentum from her standing start. Lisle clearly
sought to take advantage of this, for instead of veering
further to leeward, the schooner began to turn into the
wind, and Nathan saw that he planned to cut across their
bows and rake them with his remaining guns.

'But two can play at that,' Nathan said to himself. He
grabbed the sailing master by the shoulder to catch his
attention, for they were both deafened by the guns, and
shouted instructions in his ear. Tully heard enough to have
the gun crews racing across the deck, and they already had
the larboard guns run out and aimed as the *Swallow* cut
across the schooner's wake. This time the smoke was
blown forward and Nathan had a clear view of the effect,
as one by one his cannonades discharged into the
Meshuda's stern.

The first six were double-shotted and at that range they
simply blew the stern apart, smashing through the windows
and the ornate gilt scrolling and hurtling the length of her
gundeck. The next six fired grapeshot – 200 musket balls
to every gun, released from their canvas bags at the
moment of firing. Nathan could see clear through the
gaping holes, and even in the fury of battle he winced at
the havoc they had caused.

But ironically it was the 6-pounders on the quarterdeck
that did the most damage, for one of them carried away
the helm, killing or maiming the two quartermasters and
cutting the cable between wheel and rudder so she could
no longer steer.

The *Swallow* came up on her starboard side and Nathan
ordered his men to hold their fire, willing the schooner to

strike for it was plain that she could not bring her broadside to bear. Lisle's men were still firing back with the swivel guns in the tops – and with some effect, for they were firing straight down onto the corvette's exposed gundeck. Men were going down like skittles and with a shock that was like a physical blow, Nathan saw that one of them was Lamb. He started forward but Tully reached the boy first and lifted his head gently from the deck.

'Load up with chain,' Nathan ordered, almost sorrowfully. 'Maximum elevation.' And they fired the next broadside into the masts, clearing the marksmen out of the tops and tearing through the rigging like a gale through a forest.

And so the *Meshuda* drifted, rudderless, her sails in tatters, onto the bank.

Chapter Nineteen

The Butcher's Bill

―――――•◆•―――――

Nathan backed the mizzen and they lay off the *Meshuda*'s bow at a distance of a pistol shot, while they swabbed out the *Swallow*'s guns and reloaded. But there was no fight left in in the schooner, and the wailing of the wounded, carried across to them on the wind, was piteous to hear. Nathan had Cathcart hail them in English, Turkish and Arabic, calling on them to strike. And to his immense relief the green flag came down from the mizzen and it was ended.

He left Tully in command and took his barge over, with the launch and the cutter, all loaded to the gunwales with armed men for fear of treachery, but it was not guns they needed now, and all the swabs in the world would not have mopped up the blood on that benighted deck. Nathan had never seen anything like it, not even in the two great battles he had fought with Jervis and with Hood.

He stood gazing around him, stupefied, at the debris of dismounted guns and shattered timbers. The bodies and body parts, the severed heads, arms, legs ... And the crawling, crying wounded, the arms stretched out, the screams and lamentations, the frantic petition to Allah, Allah ... Allah the merciful. And the others who simply looked at them, dully or accusingly, helplessly or with eyes filled with hate.

He remembered Mr Wallace dancing with joy when he saw the effect on the schooner's timbers. Well, he should see the effect now on human flesh.

And yet Wallace could not be blamed for this. Wallace was as much a machine as the carronades themselves. It was the ship's Captain who gave the order.

Nathan stumbled towards the quarterdeck, watching where he put his feet, avoiding the eyes of the men who still had eyes to see.

Imlay was already there, talking to someone – and in English – a short, stocky man with a reddish beard, dressed all in white: white shirt, white pants, even a white turban round his head, spotless white amidst all that blood and gore. Nathan stared in astonishment and something like awe, as if he had been chasing a myth all that way from Tripoli, and not a living man.

Murad Reis, Admiral of the Fleet, formerly Able Seaman Peter Lisle of His Britannic Majesty's Navy.

He gave Nathan an elaborate bow that might have been ironic, and Nathan nodded stiffly, wondering if he should hang him now or later, for he was a deserter and a renegade – and someone had to pay for the carnage on that ship. But Peter Lisle could wait. There were other priorities.

They found her in the orlop, beneath the waterline, where she had been stowed for the duration of the battle. Louisa Jane Devereux of Virginia. Dressed, for some reason, in men's clothing and, in contrast to Lisle, all in black, with a turban wound round the blonde tresses that Nathan had last seen hanging down from the balustrade of the American Consul's house in Venice. Her face was less perfect now – rather grubby, in fact – and she was crouched against the bulwarks like a trembling animal, a fist pressed into her mouth and her eyes uncommonly bright. An animal, or a creature from Bedlam.

Imlay spoke to her gently. He was an American, he said, sent by her father and the President to rescue her. She was safe now, in good hands, and soon she would be reunited with her father in Naples. This was the first Nathan had heard of it, but he gave Imlay the benefit of the doubt for once.

Spiridion had rounded on Lisle. 'Where is the other woman?' he snapped.

The Scot shrugged. 'Naudé took her,' he said.

'Naudé took her? Took her where?'

'To Cairo.'

'Cairo? Why?'

'Why? You must ask the Frenchman that. And the woman.'

Spiridion leaned towards him. His voice was now almost as soft as Imlay's. 'I am asking you, Lisle. And by God, you had better tell me.'

He was a much bigger man than the Scot but there was no fear in the man's eyes. If anything, it was a look of bored contempt.

'That is all I can tell you,' he said. 'He said he was going to Cairo and that he was taking her with him.'

'And she went willingly?'

'I heard no complaint.'

'So why did you bring them here from Tripoli?' Nathan demanded.

'Because I was paid to,' Lisle said simply. 'By the Frenchman. And they made no complaint about that, either.' He looked at the woman on the floor. 'Not until you came along.'

'So why did you come here?' Nathan persevered. 'To Abukir?'

Another insolent shrug, or perhaps it was simply disinterested.

'Because the Frenchman wanted to come here,' he said, 'and he was paying.'

They made him take them to his cabin and there were the charts spread across his table – detailed soundings of Abukir and another beach called Marabut, closer to Alexandria. But nothing else. If there were any written orders, they did not find them, and Lisle claimed to be entirely ignorant of the French intentions.

The 'Frenchman', as he persisted in calling Naudé, had engaged them to conduct a hydrographical survey – he had no idea of the reason why.

Nathan did not believe him, but he did not hang him. There had been enough deaths for one day. He left him there with his ship – and the dead and the dying and the wounded. In truth, he did not know what else to do with them. The schooner was too badly holed to take as a prize so far from home, even if they could have dragged her off

the bank. Had she been a French ship he might have
burned her to the waterline where she lay, but he still
served King George, and King George was not at war with
the Pasha of Tripoli. Besides, he had the wounded to
consider, and at least they had a surgeon aboard the
Meshuda who looked like he was trying not to kill them.

'What is the butcher's bill?' he asked Tully as soon as
he came aboard the *Swallow*.

'Four dead, six wounded.'

'Four? Only four?' It seemed impossible after the
slaughter he had seen aboard the *Meshuda*. 'And Mr
Lamb?'

'He is alive, but . . .'

Nathan made his way down to the cockpit in the orlop.
He could hear the screams long before he reached it. Three
men were trying to hold down one of their shipmates
while Kite sawed off his leg below the knee. Lamb was
half-sitting against a bulkhead with his head turned away,
ashen-faced, his expression twisted in horror or pain or
both. He had a blood-soaked rag pressed to his shoulder.
Nathan went to him and carefully eased it away. There
was an ugly hole in the skin, just below the collarbone. A
musket-ball, most like. He moved the boy forward slightly
to examine his back, but there was no exit wound. The
ball was still inside him.

Nathan leaned him gently back against the bulkhead.

'You will be all right,' he said as convincingly as he
could. Then, lowering his voice, 'I will not let that butcher
near you.'

He found a clean bandage and bound up the wound as
best he could.

'Just bide there a while,' he told the boy, as if he might consider taking a stroll. 'I will be back soon with someone who can attend to you.'

But who else was there? He could not take the surgeon from the wounded in the *Meshuda*, even if he was willing to leave his crewmates.

He put the question to Spiridion when he returned to the quarterdeck. But for once the Greek was at a loss. 'You might try the fort,' he said. 'But I do not think it would be wise.'

Nathan did not think so either. There had already been several speculative shots from the guns in the fort. Well short and wildly off target, but he would not care to test them by going closer.

'Your best hope is Candia,' Spiridion told him. 'There are a number of doctors there – Greeks for the most part, and Venetians who have fled from the French. But you will have to bribe the Turkish Governor, I think. And it could take you a week to reach there if the wind does not pick up.'

The wind had dropped almost to nothing, but something strange seemed to have happened to the sky. It was no longer blue but curiously opaque, though there was not a cloud in sight, and the sun appeared as if veiled – Nathan could look on it without shielding his eyes. Spiridion had noticed it, too.

'This I do not like,' he said. 'Perhaps you had better move further out to sea.'

'You think there is a storm coming?'

Spiridion frowned. 'Possibly. A kind of a storm.' He seemed strangely distracted.

'Well, there is no reason for us to stay here,' said Nathan. He looked around for Imlay but he was nowhere to be seen. He had not seen him, in fact, since they came back from the *Meshuda* with the Consul's daughter. 'Pass the word for Mr Imlay,' he said to one of the boys. He saw Tully talking to Cribb over on the opposite rail and made to move towards them. But Spiridion caught at his sleeve.

'I have a favour to ask,' he said. 'Will you let me have a boat, so that I might go ashore?' He looked away towards the distant beach. 'I think there is time.'

Nathan was bemused. 'Time for what? I thought you said it would not be wise to go ashore.'

'I have to follow Naudé to Cairo.' Spiridion dropped his voice. 'I have to find out what has happened to Suora Caterina.'

'Ah.' Nathan nodded. Sister Caterina. He had almost forgotten her. 'Do you not think Suora Caterina can look after herself?' he enquired, for his experience of her in Venice, though brief, had assured him that she was a woman of some resource.

But Spiridion thought not; not in this instance. He did not believe she had chosen to accompany the Frenchman of her own free will. 'And she has no friends in Cairo,' he said. He felt it was his duty to help her if he could.

Nathan could not help wondering if there was more to this than loyalty to a fellow agent, but he knew better than to ask, or to try and talk him out of it.

'But how will you get to Cairo?' he asked him.

'I will apply to the caravanserai for a mount.' Spiridion nodded towards the stone building he had pointed out

earlier on the far side of the bay on its little hump of hill.
'I am perfectly able to take care of myself,' he assured
Nathan. 'And of course, I will have Mr Banjo to assist
me.'

Of course. Nathan could hardly keep Banjo aboard the
Swallow, though he would dearly have liked to.

So he gave them a boat and wished them well, though
he felt a great sense of loneliness as he watched them go,
wondering if he would ever see either of them again.

He became aware of Imlay at his side.

'I have sent Miss Devereaux below,' he said, 'with
Qualtrough to attend to her.'

'How is she?'

'Very shocked, very low. It has been a terrible ordeal
for her. I have put her in your cabin – I hope you do not
mind.'

Nathan wondered what was wrong with Imlay's cabin,
but he let it pass.

'The men behaved very well,' said Imlay, looking down
at them in the waist as they secured the guns, 'do you not
think?'

'Very well,' agreed Nathan, his mind on other things.
He felt the hint of a breeze on his cheek, but not from the
west. It had backed right round to the south-east. Cribb
had felt it, too, and was giving orders to trim the sails.

'And not for God, I think,' Imlay went on, 'nor King
and Country, like your British seafarers.'

'Some of them are British,' Nathan pointed out.

'But not many – and not under a British flag.' He gazed
up at the rattlesnake writhing now among the red stripes
at their stern, as the wind lifted it. 'Nor did they fight for

Freedom,' he said. He looked at Nathan. 'So what did they fight for? Their pay – or the sheer joy of fighting?'

'Or the sheer hell of it,' said Nathan. He had no idea what men fought for. He wondered sometimes what *he* fought for. But now was not the time. He raised his eyes to the sky. It was darker; darker than it had any business to be at this time of day, and the sun a pale, veiled countenance, dropping to the west. 'You tell me.'

'Oh, I merely ask the question. I do not know the answer.' Imlay beamed amiably. 'But we won,' he said, 'that is the important thing. I believe you sent for me?'

'Yes.' Nathan told him of his intention to sail for Crete and why.

It was not well received.

'I told Louisa I would take her back to her father,' said Imlay. 'In Naples.'

'And so we will. But first we must go to Crete to treat our wounded.'

'Well, I suppose it is on the way,' conceded Imlay doubtfully.

Nathan left him standing there with his scowling face and crossed the deck to join Tully and Cribb. He was halfway there when a sudden gust of wind laid them hard over and he finished at a run, clutching at the rail. Cribb was already roaring at the topmen to take in sail. There was another gust, not so strong, but Nathan felt the heat of it on his face, as if he had opened an oven door.

'Dear God,' said Tully, staring off towards the shore. 'What has happened to the horizon?'

Chapter Twenty

A Wind of the Desert

———•◦•———

*I*t was like a wall of sand rolling across the desert and into the sea. And with it came the wind.

The *khamsin*, Cathcart called it, a wind out of the desert. And it seemed to bring most of the desert with it.

They had barely reefed sail and got the boats aboard when it struck them. A blast from Hell that heeled them over almost onto their beam ends and then drove them before it into the open sea – at least so Nathan hoped, for it was like navigating in a fog, save that the air was thick with stinging sand. First it wiped out the sun, then the sky, then the mastheads until he could see no more than a few feet before his face. The crew staggered blindly about the deck or sought what shelter they could, neckerchiefs tied round nose, mouth, even eyes. Nathan, who had no handkerchief, could only crouch in the lee of the binnacle, with his hand clamped about his face to filter the gritty particles.

But these were just the outriders of the storm. Within minutes, the wall of sand was upon them and Nathan could barely see the compass with his nose pressed up against the glass.

He spared a thought for the stranded schooner and wondered if she could survive, but there was no way of reaching her, or even finding her in such a storm. He could only hope that she was close enough to the land, and in shallow enough water, to endure the pounding of the waves. The *Swallow*'s own fate was, besides, precarious. They were still without jib or staysail, both of which had been carried away by the falling topgallant, and the two quartermasters were fighting desperately to keep her head out to sea and stop her yawing to leeward. How they could breathe in this, let alone steer, was a mystery to Nathan, who was stooped beside them, one hand to his face, the other gripping the binnacle, less for support than reassurance that there was something solid, something real in that intangible world of wind and sand and salt spray.

He had no sense of direction, or time, or distance. He could barely breathe. He felt a wave of panic and struggled to his feet, staggering like a blind man, hands stretched out before him. Someone seized him and thrust something into his groping hands – a towel or turban, soaked in water – and Nathan wrapped it gratefully around his face and head, leaving a small gap for his eyes. He tried to thank this unknown Samaritan but found he could not speak, even if the man could hear him. He was wearing a similar guise but Nathan somehow knew it was Tully. So they sheltered together in the lee of the binnacle, while the ship plunged madly on.

And then the rain came down. A red rain, thick with the sand of the desert, so that it seemed to be raining blood. As if in Divine Judgement on the slaughter they had wrought upon the *Meshuda*.

But at least it cleared the air a little, though they could see nothing resembling a horizon. The land had vanished completely and they were surrounded by a heaving if strangely sluggish sea. They could take no kind of a reading, but from the chronometer Nathan judged they must be five or six leagues north of Alexandria.

And then he saw them. Dim shapes moving through the yellow murk off the larboard bow. He thought at first it was a trick of the imagination, or the storm, a phantom fleet that came and went in the mist of sand and rain. Even when others saw them, pointing and shouting in his face, he could not rid his mind of the suspicion that they were some mischief of the desert, something like a mirage, projected far out to sea. It was only when he heard the sound of the guns – signal guns fired singly and at intervals – that he accepted them as real. And then a beam of sunlight pierced the clouds and he saw the French tricolour streaming bravely from the stern of a giant three-decker.

His eyes met Tully's and he saw the same baffled sense of wonderment. They looked again. In and out of the mist the great ships moved: three-deckers, two-deckers, frigates and sloops, transports – clumsy, lumbering beasts in a sea of blood, with here and there a flash of fire from the signal guns. And so many. They stretched away into the distance, filling the vacuum between the *Swallow* and what should have been the horizon. Scores of them. Hundreds even. Not just a fleet but an armada, close-hauled on a course that would bring the first of them to Alexandria before dawn.

'So you were right,' said Imlay, at his shoulder. 'There is your proof.'

The invasion fleet. The very calamity he had warned against, and not an English ship within 2,000 miles of ocean that could stop them.

Chapter Twenty-one

The Angel of Death

————•◦•————

For two hours they watched the great fleet pass by, the nearest ships at a distance of about half a mile. And even when night fell, they saw the lights twinkling in the darkness, like a moving city in the sea. They had counted more than 200 sail, and Nathan reckoned that as many more must have passed by unseen.

'What will you do?' asked Imlay. Perhaps he was thinking Nathan would insist on making straight for Gibraltar. But what was the point? It could take them a month to reach the Rock; longer still for Jervis to bring the fleet from Cadiz, even if he had the authority to quit his station.

'There is nothing I *can* do,' Nathan told him, but it did not stop him thinking about it. All he could do was ensure they knew about it in England as fast as possible. Egypt did not matter, not to England. It would only matter if

Bonaparte used Egypt as a base to march overland to India. But he would not do that in a hurry. It had taken Alexander eight years. Even if Bonaparte marched in a straight line for 2,000 miles, even if he did not have to fight the Turks and the Persians every step of the way, it would take him at least six months, more like a year. Time enough to send a fleet and an army round Cape Horn if necessary, or at least to warn the Governor-General in Calcutta.

The more Nathan thought about it, the more he was inclined to continue with his journey northward – to Crete and then to Naples where he could report to Sir William Hamilton, the British Envoy there, and let him deal with it. If Hamilton sent a courier overland, travelling poste through Switzerland and Germany, the news could be in London within a fortnight.

But Nathan had sent the news of Bonaparte's intentions to England over a year ago and they had failed to act on it.

There was little satisfaction, Nathan discovered, in being proved right.

He lingered at the stern, looking back into the darkness towards the coast of Egypt. What a gamble, though, what an incredible roll of the dice. Four hundred ships, and God knows how many men – thirty or even forty thousand – launched across the sea to a distant shore, far from France, far from the main theatre of conflict. Only Bonaparte had the nerve for that – or the folly – or the vision. If he lost them, France would surely lose the war. But if he won . . .

He had done it before – in Italy. Nothing like as spectacular a gamble as this, but all the same . . . Two years ago, when he was appointed to command the ragtag Army of Italy, there were few in England, or Austria, or even in France, who believed he could get it to fight, much less take it across the Alps, win a half-dozen battles, conquer half of Italy and force the Austrians to make a humiliating peace for fear of losing Vienna. If he did the same in Egypt . . . Well, Billy Pitt might be compelled to throw in the towel. For if the British lost India, there was the end to Empire.

And that little man with his sallow complexion and his greasy locks would be the new Alexander – with the world at his feet. Who would have thought it? Certainly not Nathan, when he had first run into him in Paris in '95 – the little *chef de brigade* in his shabby uniform, looking for a job. And only Sergeant Junot to run his errands for him, and keep the wolves from the door.

Nathan turned away from the rail. He was exhausted. His eyes were red with sand and smoke, his legs like lead. Let Bonaparte have Egypt – he was welcome to it. He could have India, too. All Nathan wanted was his cabin and his cot and eight hours of uninterrupted sleep. It was only as he stumbled down the companionway that he remembered: Miss Louisa Devereux of Virginia had his cabin, goddamn her – and goddamn Imlay for giving it to her. Wearily, he turned away and blundered down another deck to the gunroom to see what was available to him there.

For two days the wind served them well, blowing considerately and with some consistency from the south-south-east, and with sufficient force to move them along at a pace that even the impatient Imlay found acceptable.

Frequent castings of the log revealed that they were making between four and six knots from hour to hour – and in the right direction for once. The first day, from sunrise to sunrise, they covered a little over 120 miles, almost 150. Nathan remarked to Tully, with the usual caveats and cautions, that if the wind sustained them for a further twenty-four hours, he could not help 'but think we might sight the mountains of Crete a little before sunrise upon the morrow'.

Unfortunately, this exchange was overheard by Mr Cathcart who, not being an officer, felt free to inform them, with a great air of scholarship, that the word *khamsin* in the Arabic meant fifty, because it was a wind that invariably blew for fifty days.

Although Nathan received the news with his usual courtesy, he wished Cathcart had kept it to himself. Winds, in his experience, being of a generally cantankerous nature, were wont to take any such prediction as an impertinence, and to demonstrate their wilfulness by doing the exact opposite of what was supposed of them. The khamsin proved no exception to this rule. Within a few hours of Cathcart's indiscretion it had dropped away to a mere zephyr and it proceeded to blow fitfully for the rest of the day. The following day it failed them completely and they lay becalmed for hours on end under the blazing sun.

In similar circumstance, with a Navy crew, Nathan might have put them to the boats. Sooner or later, if the wind continued to fail them, he knew he would have to, for their water supply was now running dangerously low. But he held off as long as possible. The mood among the crew had taken a considerable turn for the worse since the battle with the *Meshuda*. They were sullen and recalcitrant, particularly the Russians. Their beloved leader had been buried at sea, as soon as the khamsin permitted, along with the others who had died, and after a final outpouring of grief, his followers had relapsed into a collective ill-humour, enlivened by several instances of drunkenness which Nathan felt obliged to ignore for the time being. It was impossible to reason or remonstrate with them, for they barely spoke a few words of English between them and nothing of any other language. The rest of the crew steered clear of them for fear of provoking a row, and the mood between the Russians and the Americans was especially bad. It was only a matter of time before there was a fight and then Nathan would be compelled to take action – though without two score Marines at his disposal he was not optimistic of the outcome. He longed for the voyage to end.

'What are you going to do with them when we reach Gibraltar?' he asked Imlay.

But Imlay did not know.

'As far as I can gather, they do not wish to return to Russia,' he said, 'for they fear to be hanged as deserters. And I do not know where else they might settle.'

'Then I think you will have them for life,' Nathan told him heartlessly.

He had no doubt what *he* would do with them. He would happily surrender them to the first British cruiser he encountered and let the Navy knock them into shape. He was not in the best of humours himself.

He paid several visits to the sickbay to see how the wounded did. Two of them had died: the one whose leg

Kite had amputated and another who had taken a bullet in the chest. Three others, who had suffered only slightly from splinter wounds, appeared well on the way to recovery. Mr Lamb continued to give concern.

Nathan visited him as often as he could – he was down to two officers now and obliged to keep a watch himself – but though the boy was putting a brave face on it, he was obviously in a bad way.

Kite said he feared that pieces of clothing had been carried into the wound and that it had become infected.

'His only chance is to probe for the ball,' he confided to Nathan.

Nathan had heard this before, but he knew from hard experience that probing invariably led to death, even when carried out by someone other than Mr Kite. Unless a ball of lead was lodged in some vital organ, when death was in any case inevitable, it was far better to leave it inside a man. One thing he knew for certain, if he let Kite dig around with a knife, the boy would die – and in a great deal of pain.

On the morning of the third day, to his considerable surprise, he found Louisa Devereux in the sick bay, apparently attending to the wounded.

Nathan had not seen her since she came aboard and his enquiries had been met with Imlay's assurance that she was 'getting her strength back' and must not be disturbed. Mr Qualtrough had taken her in a little food from time to time, but she spent the greater part of her time asleep. But here she was sitting beside Mr Lamb with a basin on her knee, applying a cold compress to his fevered brow.

'She wanted to make herself useful,' Kite told him – somewhat resentfully, Nathan thought.

But at least Mr Lamb appreciated it.

'She is an angel,' he informed Nathan, with a ghastly grimace of a smile.

Nathan smiled and nodded, while privately wondering if she might prove to be the Angel of Death, for the boy's condition gave him considerable cause for concern. In appearance, too, she looked the part; she still wore the black Arab clothing they had found her in, and her face was as white as the boy's. But he was impressed that she was here at all.

'We will soon be in Crete,' he assured Lamb before he left. 'And the Greeks, you know, are noted for the excellence of their physicians. Hippocrates himself was one.'

But the wind, or rather the lack of it, continued to frustrate them. For two long days they barely moved at all. Tully did his trick with the awnings and the fire engine, and Nathan had a sail slung over the side to the depth of four feet so that the off-duty watch might bathe, even those that could not swim. Most preferred to put out lines and fish. They were down to salt beef and pork and Nathan was worried about their reserves of water, not to speak of alcohol.

On the fifth day, the wind picked up a little and partway through the forenoon watch the foretop lookout alerted them to an approaching sail two points off the larboard bow – the first they had seen since their encounter with the French off Alexandria. But this was no Frenchman. As the two ships converged, Nathan announced, to the great delight of Imlay and the other Americans, that she flew the Stars and Stripes.

Chapter Twenty-two

The Phantom Fleet

———— ✦ ————

'The Flag of Freedom, by God! Well, I'll be damned, I have not seen that since the war with the British.'

Captain Hosanna Poe was a big, bluff New Englander in his fifties whose pleasure at meeting up with an American vessel so far from home was matched only by his astonishment that she was a ship-of-war. His own command was the *Algonquin* brig, out of Plymouth, Massachusetts – bound for Aleppo, he told them, with a cargo of grain and molasses.

'We called it the Navy jack in those days,' he said, still gazing up at the flag. 'But that was when we *had* a Navy. I cannot conceal my satisfaction, gentlemen, to be standing aboard a fighting ship once more, manned by my own countrymen.'

Nathan did not trouble to correct him in this

presumption, and if the Captain had noted the preponder-ance of Italians, Portuguese, Russians and Englishmen among the crew he did not allude to it.

'We have nothing to hide,' Imlay had protested, when Nathan warned him of the possible embarrassment of the encounter. Personally Nathan would have settled for the exchange of news and compliments at the length of a pistol shot – but Imlay must needs invite the Captain and his officers for dinner.

'We will not, of course, mention that you and several of your associates are in the service of King George,' Imlay proposed, 'but I am assured Captain Poe and his men will be delighted to hear of the success of our mission against the Barbary corsairs.'

This was inevitable.

'It is the greatest victory for American arms since we kicked the British out of Yorktown,' Captain Poe declared. 'Allow me to shake you by the hand, sir.' Seizing Nathan by this implement, he pumped it so vigorously it was a wonder Nathan did not gush water like Tully's fire engine.

At Imlay's request the Captain brought his doctor with him, but the latter shook his head gravely over Lamb's wound and confirmed Nathan in his belief that the wound was best not disturbed. 'For they always die, you know,' he murmured confidentially, 'once they have been put to the probe.'

Nathan had been 'put to the probe' himself, after the Battle of Castiglioni, and been saved by the expertise of a French surgeon sent by Bonaparte himself, but he understood this to be the exception rather than the rule. Certainly it would have been fatal to let Kite try his hand at it, and Dr Beamish was 'more physician than surgeon', he assured Nathan with a great air of consequence.

'No, you had best let him sweat it out,' he added, 'for I never met a surgeon yet that was not a butcher, and the fellow who is attending to him, he is an Englishman, is he not?'

Nathan admitted that this was indeed the case. As was his patient.

'We have a number of Englishmen among the crew,' Imlay confessed in a tone of apology. 'Deserters for the most part, or fugitives from the British concept of justice.'

Dinner, Nathan reflected, was going to be a trial.

Imlay's Portuguese cook, Balsemao, had done his best at short notice with the limited fare at his disposal. He had made a large fish pie from the most recent of their catch, with a ragoût of salt-pork and pease to follow; and for pudding they were to have a figgy-dowdy – a great favourite of the service, consisting of ship's biscuit, pounded into crumbs by a marlin-spike and reconstituted with a mixture of pork fat and dried fruit soaked in grog. Imlay appeared less than impressed with this menu, but contributed a dozen bottles of wine from his private stash in the hold.

'If we cannot be genteel,' he submitted, 'we can at least be merry.'

Privately Nathan considered that it would take a great deal more than twelve bottles, but he kept his peace. He felt obliged to invite Tully and O'Driscoll to the feast, warning them of the need to put aside their loyalties to King and Country for its duration. They seemed rather amused than not at being taken for fugitives from British justice, and were ready to play their part – rather too enthusiastically in Nathan's opinion, with O'Driscoll giving his impression of a bog Irishman and Tully speaking in a fake French accent. But whatever suspicions their visitors might have entertained were entirely erased by the appearance of Miss Devereux.

She was wearing a dress made of red sailcloth, which the sailmaker had apparently knocked up for her, with a fringed shawl of the same material draped over her shoulders. Her golden hair was woven into a long pigtail, happily not tarred, which she hung over her left shoulder, and she had contrived to bring some colour into her lips, probably by biting them, for they looked faintly, and desirably, swollen. She looked as stunning as when Nathan had first seen her on the Grand Canal in Venice and the company was duly stunned.

Inevitably the conversation turned to her capture by the corsairs and her enforced stay in Tripoli as a hostage, and for the best part of the meal she entertained them with a description of the Pasha's harem and the various customs and practices she had encountered during her prolonged stay there.

Nathan observed her thoughtfully from his position at the opposite end of the table. He was surprised as much by her exuberance as he was by her appearance, for she had looked like a bedraggled urchin when she first came aboard. There were certain women, he reflected, who could transform themselves from hoyden to society beauty whenever it was required of them, and Miss Devereux clearly came into this category. He could not help comparing her to Sara, who was a good fifteen years older and a great deal more damaged by her experiences, but blessed with the same ability to adapt herself to vastly different circumstances and environments.

But it was best not to dwell on Sara, not if he did not wish to arouse his demons to further torment.

'Do you not think so, Captain?'

With a jolt Nathan realised she was addressing him directly, and with a twinkle of what might be mischief in her eye, but although he had been staring at her with what passed for rapt attention, he had not the faintest idea what she was talking about, or where the conversation had taken them.

He inclined his head in pretended consideration. 'As to that, I will have to reserve my judgement,' he said.

She seemed a little disappointed at this but the rest of the company resumed their conversation as if he had not spoken at all and he was able to catch up a little. It appeared that they had been discussing her dramatic escape from the harem and the part played in this by the mysterious Frenchman, Monsieur Naudé. The Americans had been shocked at her assertion that Naudé had fallen in love with her beautiful companion, Sister Caterina, though it was not clear if this was because Sister Caterina was a nun or because they could not imagine anyone more captivating than Miss Devereux herself. She had further provoked them by proposing that Frenchmen were of a more romantic and reckless a disposition than Americans – hence her remark to Nathan.

He wondered now at that glint of mischief in her eye. Either she was flirting with him or she had reason to believe he was not who he said he was. He was trying to think of a remark convincing enough to establish his credentials, when Captain Poe remarked that whatever Monsieur Naudé's motives in rescuing them from the corsairs, it was interesting that he had taken them to Egypt.

Nathan was moved to ask him why.

'Why, because it is rumoured that the French have determined to invade the country,' the Captain replied, 'and have put out with a great fleet from Toulon.'

Nathan was shocked. 'And where did you hear this rumour?' He struggled to keep his voice normal.

'Oh, it was current in Gibraltar when we were there,' declared the Captain dismissively, 'and we heard it again in Carloforte, when we called there for fresh water.'

'Carloforte?' Nathan strove to place it on the charts.

'On the island of San Pietro, that lies off Sardinia,' replied the Captain's mate, a red-haired gentleman by the name of Finlay who had not previously said a word beyond a mumbled request for the salt.

That such rumours had circulated in Gibraltar was distressing, if not entirely surprising, but Nathan was at a loss to discover how they might have reached a small island off Sardinia. The Captain's explanation, however, was a much greater surprise.

'The British had been there,' he said. 'Indeed, we just missed them, for which I was exceedingly thankful. They would have stripped me of half my crew, the scoundrels.'

'The British? What do you mean?' Nathan challenged him with more aggression than he had intended.

'Why, the British fleet, of course.' Captain Poe frowned at Nathan's tone. 'But there is no reason for alarm, sir, for it was in the last week of May.'

'In May?' Nathan's voice rose even higher. Two months ago. It was not possible. Unwarily, he said as much.

'Well, I am only repeating what was said to us.' The Captain, a little put out, gazed about the table for confirmation, and Mr Finlay and Mr Beamish nodded obligingly. Imlay shot Nathan a warning glance.

'I am sorry. I do not mean to give you the lie,' said Nathan, 'but I understood the British fleet had abandoned the Mediterranean.'

The Captain shrugged. 'Well, I am not privy to the decisions of the British Admiralty. All I can tell you was what I was told when I was in Carloforte.'

'And did they give you any idea of their number?'

'As to that, they were not precise. I gather that some remained out to sea. They were caught in a tempest, I was told, and the flagship dismasted.'

'The flagship?'

'The *Vanguard*, I believe. She was in the port for some days undergoing repairs.'

The *Vanguard*. Third-rater, of seventy-four guns, laid down in Deptford before the war – but who had her now? Nathan was damned if he knew, but she was not at the Battle of St Vincent, nor the Siege of Cadiz – though she may well have joined the fleet since.

Had the Admiralty sent a squadron back into the Med? No, it could not be true. If an English Admiral had news of Bonaparte's destination in May, even late May, he would have intercepted the French long before they reached Alexandria . . . unless he had been defeated, which was unthinkable. But how had they known the name of the ship?

'And did you discover who commanded this mysterious fleet?' he asked the Captain.

'I did. According to my informants, his name was Nelson.'

'Nelson!'

'You have heard of him, perhaps?' The Captain raised a heavy brow.

'Of course I have heard of him, but ...' He caught Imlay's eye again. The Americans – and Louisa Devereux in particular – were all looking at him curiously.

He had been about to say that Nelson had lost his arm at Tenerife and been invalided out of the service, but the Captain of an American privateer was unlikely to be so well informed. It confirmed Nathan in his suspicions, however. The story was arrant nonsense. This really was a phantom fleet.

'Is there a particular reason for your interest, Captain?' Poe enquired.

'Only that if there is a British fleet in the Mediterranean, we would wish to avoid running into it,' replied Imlay, 'and for the same reasons as you, Captain. We are not greatly desirous of losing our best men to the British Navy.'

'Well, bad cess to them, wherever they be.' Captain Poe raised his glass. 'Let us hope the Frenchies make fools of them as they did in the last war, and we can all go about our business in peace.'

'Oi'll drink to that, Captain,' cried O'Driscoll vigorously, raising his own and treating the company to an exaggerated wink.

'I had thought the French were making more trouble

for us than the English at present,' put in Imlay. 'Or is that not your opinion, Captain?'

'As to that, I will tell you my opinion, sir,' replied the Captain. 'And it is that I would not trust either of them as far as I could spit. Begging your pardon, Miss. But if I had to choose between them, then I would choose the Frenchies, at least the present lot, for it is my belief that for all their failings – and they have many, I'll not deny – they are inclined to favour Freedom over Tyranny and the Rights of Man over the Pride of Kings and Princes.'

'And Popes,' cried O'Driscoll in a loud voice. 'Don't forget the Popes.'

'No, I do not forget them, sir,' replied Captain Poe in the silence that followed this contribution, 'and Bonaparte has served out the present Pope very much as he deserves, I believe, in his march through Italy. But I recall now that you are Irish, sir, so I hope I have not given offence.'

'Irish but not Papist, sir. No, by God, and I'll fight any man who says I am.' He glared around the table belligerently but his lips twitched a little when he caught Nathan's eye. Nathan was not amused. O'Driscoll was topping the Irishman a deal too much in his opinion, and was, besides, in danger of losing his bearings. If he was not a Papist, or inclined to their cause, what did he think the Americans would make of him, save a loyal subject of King George?

'Well, and I am pleased to hear it, sir,' declared Poe, 'for I'll not deny I am a Presbyterian myself – not that I'd hold a man's religion against him,' he added hastily, in case there were those around the table of a less exalted persuasion.

'So, Captain, I take it you are in favour of Bonaparte and his march through Italy?' enquired Louisa Devereux before Nathan could move the conversation into less troubled waters. In the King's Navy there was an unwritten rule that you did not discuss sex, religion or politics at the dinner-table. It made for very dull conversation at times but at least it cut down on the potential for violence.

'Well, I have heard that it has brought Freedom to a great many people,' said the Captain, 'who were otherwise in thrall to Tyranny. And you cannot deny that Bonaparte is known throughout the peninsula as the Liberator.'

'Well, certainly he has liberated a great many treasures and sent them back to Paris for safekeeping,' Miss Devereux declared, 'but I am not sure the Venetians would agree that their liberty has been secured by handing them over to the Austrians and ending a thousand years of independence.'

Nathan looked at her in surprise. Were these her own ideas, he wondered, or was this the influence of Sister Caterina Caresini – after six months of shared captivity in the seraglio of Tripoli? But whatever stimulus she was under it had brought a very attractive flush to her features.

'Well, as to that, Miss, I do not know,' Captain Poe conceded with ill grace. 'All I am saying is that they know how to deal with kings and princes and the like.'

'By cutting off their heads, do you mean?'

'I think what the Captain means . . .' began Imlay, who was looking a trifle alarmed at the turn the conversation was taking. But Miss Devereux would not be diverted.

'I take it you do not think much of kings, sir?' she addressed the Captain.

'To tell the truth, Miss, I try not to think of them at all,' he assured her. 'But when I do, I prefer to think of them with their heads off rather than on.' At which amusing image, he gave a good-natured chuckle.

'And queens, too, I suppose,' Louisa replied, 'for I recall that Queen Marie Antoinette was served the same way . . . but pray tell me, sir, what does it achieve, all this cutting off of heads and spilling of blood?'

'Freedom!' Mr Finlay had found his voice again, and apparently a cause worthy of giving voice to. He banged his glass down on the table with a force that spilled a considerable amount of wine over the rim. 'Freedom is what it achieves.'

'Life, liberty and the pursuit of happiness,' Dr Beamish informed Miss Devereux rather more serenely. 'As is enshrined in our Constitution.'

'And the right to keep slaves? Is that enshrined in our Constitution? I cannot remember.' Miss Devereux gazed brightly around the table as if for assurance.

'I believe we fudged that one,' put in Imlay hastily, 'but let us not quarrel, gentlemen, or lady,' with a bow towards Miss Devereux, 'for we are all friends under the Flag of Freedom, are we not?'

Before this contentious notion could be put to the test, Qualtrough entered the cabin with the figgy-dowdy on a large silver platter, the effect of which was by no means spoiled, at least in Nathan's opinion, by Miss Devereux's clapping her hands and exclaiming: 'My goodness, the head of John the Baptist!'

Unhappily, this coincided with a violent heel to starboard and Qualtrough, no doubt distracted by this irreverence, heeled with it, permitting the figgy-dowdy to slide to the deck where it exploded like a grenado. In the silence that followed this disaster, one of the ship's boys thrust his head around the door to relay Mr Cribb's compliments and inform the Captain that the wind was freshening to such an extent that he was obliged to take in sail.

Nathan seized the opportunity to escape the shambles that was left of their dinner. One glance aloft and another at the sea apprised him of the changed situation, and if he was in any doubt of what it portended, Mr Cribb's face settled it for him. He saw their visitors into the waiting launch with almost indecent haste – though he had an idea that they were not entirely averse to quitting so subversive an environment – and the *Swallow* proceeded under considerably reduced sail on her interrupted journey to the north-west, leaving the *Algonquin* a swiftly vanishing memory in the distance.

The wind continued to freshen. Within an hour of dinner they were fairly flying along under topsails and a reefed fore course, and the casting of the ship's log confirmed a speed in excess of 10 knots, which earned a grudging cheer from those of the crew that were on deck. At the close of the second dog watch, they sighted the island of Koufonissi, and an hour or so later, a little before sunset, the mountains of Crete itself could be clearly discerned off the starboard bow.

The wind dropped considerably as they rounded the eastern end of the island and it took them two more days to reach the port of Candia, halfway along the northern coast; two more to find a suitable doctor: Dr Marangakis, the best doctor on the island, Nathan was assured by the British Consul, with certificates from the Universities of Padua and Modena. By the time he came aboard, Nathan feared that certificates from Hippocrates himself would not have helped. The patient looked more than weak; he looked like a corpse.

'I will have to operate,' the doctor declared when he had emerged from the sickbay, 'without further delay.'

'He is very weak,' Nathan replied doubtfully. 'Is there nothing else you can do?'

The doctor subjected him to a cold stare. He was a small, prickly man with a long nose, a lugubrious countenance, a bald head and black whiskers. Too black for a man who looked to be well over fifty; they looked dyed to Nathan, who did not trust doctors at the best of times and was not prepared to relax this prejudice for a doctor who dyed his whiskers.

But he had little choice in the matter.

'It is very likely that a quantity of clothing has been carried into the wound,' Dr Marangakis confirmed, 'and unless it is removed he is very likely to die within the next day or two.'

'And if you do remove it?'

The answer was difficult for Nathan to follow, since Dr Marangakis spoke neither English nor French and they conversed in a mixture of Latin and Classical Greek which had not been Nathan's strongest subjects at school, but he gathered that at least the patient had the ghost of a chance, which was a great deal more than he had if the wound continued to fester.

'Would it help if you were to apply honey,' Nathan enquired helpfully, 'to reduce the possibility of infection?'

This had been the somewhat startling remedy applied to Nathan in the hospital on Lake Garda after a similar procedure, and he had made a full recovery. The suggestion was greeted with icy disdain.

'It would help a great deal more if I was permitted to practise my profession without advice from the unqualified,' the doctor countered, 'or to operate upon the patient in my own surgery. However, I fear that it would be fatal to move him. I will have to do my best in the pig-sty where you have seen fit to deposit him.'

He had brought the tools of his trade with him, but he insisted on having his own assistants ferried out from the port and would not have Mr Kite or any of the *Swallow*'s crew in attendance, not even Miss Devereux who had offered to do what little she could, even if it was only to mop the sweat off the patient's brow.

This process took the rest of the day and involved a further outlay of gold coin. The operation itself lasted above an hour. Upon its completion, Dr Marangakis announced that he had removed the musket ball and a small piece of clothing that had been carried into the wound. He had also drained off a quantity of pus, but he feared the infection might have passed into the bloodstream, in which case he entertained little hope of the patient's survival. It might help, however, if he remained in the care of a proper physician, and not some butcher's boy who was only good for hacking up dead meat.

Nathan considered this proposal gravely. Every instinct protested against delay, but with the French at Alexandria, he conceded that time was no longer such an issue, and they owed it to Lamb to at least give him a chance of recovery.

So the *Swallow* remained at her mooring off the mole, and Nathan took advantage of their extended stay at the port to replenish their supplies of food and fresh water. He also gave permission for the crew to go ashore in relays, there being little risk of their jumping ship with the wages Imlay was paying them, and the port authorities being nothing loath for them to empty their pockets in the various establishments provided for this purpose.

Nathan had little to do on the *Swallow* and so on the second day he decided to join this exodus, though he told himself he would content himself with viewing the less venal attractions of the port. This resolve was enhanced when, just as he was settling himself in the stern of his barge, Miss Devereux leaned over the rail and begged leave to accompany him. Since the operation, she had resumed her role as nurse, but the patient had recovered sufficiently to swallow a small amount of gruel, she said, before falling into a deep and apparently peaceful sleep. She required only sufficient time to change.

Nathan's pleasure at her company was tempered only by the thought of presenting her to the population of Candia attired in crimson sailcloth. He need not have worried. The sailmaker had created a more modest version in white canvas, with a matching hat and parasol to shade her from the sun. And so, with a small escort of Janissaries provided by the Turkish authorities, and the Consul's dragoman to translate for them, they set off on a tour of the port.

In classical times, Candia had been one of the great

commercial centres of the Mediterranean, and it had continued to thrive for many centuries under the successive control of Byzantines, Ottomans and Venetians. But early in the present century it had been retaken by the Ottomans after a twenty-one-year siege – the longest in history, according to the Consul – when over 100,000 people had died, and since then it had slipped into decline. The harbour had been allowed to silt up and most of the sea-going trade had moved to Chania on the west of the island. There were indications of its former greatness, however, in the massive Venetian fortress of Rocca al Mare which guarded the harbour entrance, and in the faded grandeur of the villas built for Venetian nobles and merchants along the waterfront.

They strolled here for a while before venturing inland where they discovered a small marketplace, where Louisa bought some pastries filled with honey which she thought might tempt Mr Lamb.

Mr Lamb would be a great deal more tempted by the presence of his nurse, Nathan suspected. He was only fifteen but he had shot up remarkably in recent months.

'I suppose you will find life quite dull after all your adventures,' he remarked, when they walked on.

'Yes, but I am going to write a book about them,' she declared confidently. 'As soon as we arrive in Naples.'

'A book!' Nathan gazed at her in consternation. 'Do you think that is wise?' he protested. And when she appeared puzzled by this response. 'I mean, what will your father think of that?'

'I really have no idea,' she said. 'I suppose he will not approve.'

Having met her father in Venice, Nathan felt bound to agree.

'And do you often do things he does not approve of?'

'Never. But you see, I wanted to stay in Venice, and he decided to send me away. So he can hardly complain.'

Nathan thought this unduly sanguine, but he held his peace. 'But what exactly do you intend to write about?' he enquired in the same censorious tone.

'I assure you there is no shortage of interesting material,' she asserted stoutly. 'Unless you do not consider it interesting to be captured by Barbary pirates and sold on the slave-market and forced to submit to the indignities of life in a Turkish harem.'

'I . . . I really had no idea,' Nathan stammered, wondering at these unnamed indignities. He found that he was blushing. 'I mean – that you were sold on the slavemarket.'

'Well, that is an exaggeration, I suppose, but I would have been if we had not been rescued. And we were all lined up, you know, for inspection, in the Pasha's palace before we were packed off to his harem. And that is very like the slave-market.'

'I am so very sorry . . .' Nathan was lost for words.

'Oh, it was not so very bad,' she conceded. 'In fact, it was quite pleasant most of the time. Apart from the wives. And the other hostages.' She shuddered.

'So what were,' Nathan did not know how to put it, 'these *indignities* that you intend to write about?'

'Oh, you know, the usual things,' she declared airily. 'It is what people expect, is it not?'

Nathan could think of no immediate riposte.

'It will not *all* be untrue,' she asserted stoutly. 'Some of the things that happened to me are truer than fiction.'

His continuing frown betrayed a lack of conviction.

'Sister Caterina?' she reminded him. 'The beautiful nun who was my only friend? And how we used to bathe together in the pool of the hamman – *naked* – under the watchful gaze of the Pasha.'

'My God!' Nathan had a sudden memory of Mr Devereux of Virginia in his study above the Grand Canal railing against the iniquities of the decadent Venetians.

'And the Red Castle and all the blood that was spilled there?' his daughter continued relentlessly. 'And the room one was forbidden to enter where the heir to the throne was foully murdered by his own brother *in the arms of their mother.* And then his body hacked to pieces by the slaves.'

She mistook his startled expression for one of disbelief. 'It is quite true, I assure you – I saw the bloodstains. We used the same room to make our escape, with the help of hired assassins. At least, that is the way they were dressed. *And* they made us strip in front of them and change into the same clothing. I would like to know if that is not an indignity,' she rebuked him sternly. 'And then we were obliged to climb down a rope for hundreds of feet above the shark-infested sea.'

'Are there sharks in Tripoli Harbour?' It seemed a small detail but he thought to mention it.

'I do not know. Good heavens, *you* are the sailor! Anyway, Naudé said there were sharks. Only that might have been to stop us jumping overboard,' she conceded regretfully.

'Did you think of jumping overboard?'

'Of course I did –' indignantly – 'when I realised he was taking us back to the *Meshuda* and not the *Swallow*. Not that we knew it was the *Swallow* at the time, of course, but we knew it was American and thought it was you who had rescued us. We had no idea it was the French.'

'And was it really because this man Naudé had fallen in love with your companion?' Nathan said, if only to detract from this apparent failure on his part.

'Oh yes, I do assure you. If you saw her you would understand.'

Nathan had not told her that he and Sister Caterina were acquainted.

'The French spy and the nun – you could not make that up.' She grinned triumphantly. 'And of course, there is the battle with the *Swallow* in the Bay of Abukir. That will be the climax of the whole thing. And the handsome American sea captain who rescued me,' she added coyly. 'I might have an illustration of that for the frontispiece, you carrying me off in your arms. Or else Sister Caterina and me being sold in the slave-market. Which do you think is best?'

Nathan was unable to express an opinion on the subject.

'Either way it will sell thousands of copies,' she continued, 'and I shall be rich.'

'I thought you *were* rich,' he said, finding his voice. 'I mean, I thought your father was.'

'Oh, he is. Well, perhaps not quite so rich now he has had to pay all that money to get me back again. But I mean I will be rich on my own account. Not just an heiress.'

Nathan was feeling a little unsteady on his feet –

doubtless the effect of walking on a stable surface after so many weeks at sea – and they found somewhere to sit outside one of the coffee houses under the shade of a plane tree where, in the absence of anything stronger, they drank sherbet lemon and watched the world go by. It went by very slowly and did not seem to be doing very much in particular.

'You would not think that we were at war,' remarked Nathan, after a period of reflective silence, forgetting for the moment that he was supposed to be an American and a neutral.

'I am not at war,' she assured him. 'And they are not. *We* are very much at peace, thank you.'

Sometimes she reminded him not of Sara but of his mother. He lapsed into a gloomy silence. It was Louisa who broke it.

'Never mind,' she said, 'you will probably not be at war forever.'

'No,' he said. His gloom was unrelieved.

'So what will you do when you are not?' she said.

He blew out his breath, his shoulders slumped. 'I have no idea,' he said.

'Well, never mind,' she said, patting his hand in motherly sympathy. 'Perhaps you will marry an heiress.'

When they returned to the ship, Tully was waiting to greet them. Nathan could see by his expression that the news was bad.

'I am truly sorry,' he said, 'but Mr Lamb ...'

Louisa let out a wail and they watched her stumble below.

'He died in his sleep,' Tully murmured gently to Nathan, 'a little while after you went ashore.'

Nathan felt the tears flood to his eyes. He stooped to pick up something that had dropped from Louisa's hands. It was the bag of pastries she had bought in the marketplace.

'There is more news,' Tully told him. 'A wine-brig just put in from Corfu and we exchanged news with the Captain. He says he came across a great battle fleet two days ago in the Ionian Sea, some fifty miles south-west of Zante. Thirteen ships of the line flying the British flag, sailing due east towards the Morea.'

Chapter Twenty-three

The Blue Admiral

—◆—

athan shook his head in bemusement as he gazed down at the chart. A most excellent chart from William Heather's *Mediterranean Pilot* of 1795, it showed the Ionian Sea and its numerous islands, with the surrounding coastline of Italy and Greece. But no matter how long and how hard he looked at it, Nathan could think of no plausible reason for a British battle fleet to be heading towards the Morea – an obscure peninsula under Ottoman rule halfway between Sicily and the Turkish mainland.

The Greek Captain who had reported this phenomenon had permitted Tully to examine his ship's log where he had entered his own position at the time of the sighting – longitude 10° 30′ East, latitude 37° 5′ North which put them some 250 nautical miles to the north-west of Candia. But that was two days since. If the fleet had continued on the same course, it would take them into the Gulf of Coron.

But why?

'We are not at war with the Ottomans, are we?' Nathan mused aloud. 'Have I missed something since we were in Tripoli?'

Neither Tully, O'Driscoll nor Cribb appeared to think he had. But Nathan could agonise over this all day and well into the night and still be none the wiser. 'Are all the hands aboard?' he asked Tully, and when he was assured that they were: 'Then make ready to sail. Mr Cribb, set us a course for the Gulf of Coron.'

He made his way to the upper deck, to make this decision known to Imlay. He anticipated strong opposition and strong opposition was what he got.

'On no account,' Imlay protested. 'What? In search of a fleet that may not exist? And even if it does, will be long gone by the time we get there.'

'It is but a little out of our way,' Nathan argued reasonably. 'And if the wind holds, we may be there by the day after tomorrow.'

'And if they are not there?'

'Then we will crack on to the Strait of Messina,' Nathan assured him, 'and thence to Naples.'

For once the wind did not fail them and Nathan's prediction proved to be correct. Midway through the forenoon on the second day after leaving Candia they rounded Cape Matapan and saw the Gulf of Coron before them, shimmering in the fierce light of the summer sun.

And there, almost lost in the haze at the far side of the bay, was their phantom fleet.

* * *

'Good God!' It seemed as if Nathan was the ghost, judging from the startled reaction to his appearance aboard the flagship. Even the boatswain's call was stunned into silence and Captain Berry fair goggled at him in astonishment.

'What in the Devil's name are you doing here?' he demanded, having apparently decided that the Devil was a more appropriate invocation than the Almighty where Nathan was concerned. 'And what is that damned flag you are flying? We had thought it was the Stars and Stripes, but I am told it is some kind of a snake.'

'A rattlesnake. And it is the Flag of Freedom. I am surprised you did not know that,' Nathan replied tartly, for though Berry was now made Captain – and apparently Flag Captain at that – he had been a lieutenant when they had last met, and they were pretty much the same age. 'As to what I am doing here,' he went on, 'I could ask the same of you, Edward, for the French ain't here, you know, they are in Alexandria. And have been for the past three weeks.'

This caused even more of a sensation than his appearance and he was obliged to give a full account of himself.

When he had finished, Berry looked a trifle pale in the gills. 'You had best tell this to the Admiral,' he said, 'for we have been searching for them for the last two months and he is brought so low I fear for his sanity.'

'The Admiral?' Nathan cocked a brow.

'Why Nelson, of course.' Berry looked surprised but then took in Nathan's expression. 'Did you not know?'

'I heard a rumour to that effect but I had thought he was back in England nursing his wounds.'

'He was.' Berry dropped his voice. 'But then the First Lord sent him back to St Vincent in the *Vanguard*. And St Vincent sent him into the Med to sort out Bonaparte. We've been looking for him ever since.'

Nathan leaned on the rail and gazed down the long line of ships. Thirteen ships of the line, most of them 74s, and one small brig, all flying the blue ensign which he had assumed, when he first saw it, was the flag of Admiral St Vincent.

'But what brought you to the Bay of Coron?' he persisted. 'And where are all your frigates?'

Berry sighed. 'I had better take you to the Admiral,' he said, 'and he can tell you himself. But Peake . . .' he looked Nathan straight in the eye and lowered his voice '. . . you will find the Admiral greatly changed from when you last saw him. I fear he has had too many disappointments for the good of his health. He starts at any familiar sound – and his heart . . . Well, I am not a medical man, but the doctor says he must not be over-excited.' Nathan stared at him in astonishment. 'Come, I will take you to him and you can tell him your news. But break it to him gently, if you will, and pray do not ask him where are all his frigates.'

Nelson was in his day cabin, where he had apparently been receiving medication, for the doctor was on the way out as the two Captains came in. Despite Berry's warning, Nathan was shocked by the Admiral's appearance. He seemed a decade older than when they had last met, though it was not much more than a year ago; his face was pale and gaunt, even his good eye seemed to have lost its lustre, and the sleeve of his missing arm was pinned across his breast.

'Look what the cat brought in,' declared Berry with a poor attempt at humour. 'And wait till you hear what he has to tell you.'

Nelson regarded Nathan bleakly. For a moment there was no recognition in his face, then it lit up a little, but it was like the face of an old man clutching at a distant memory.

'Why, Peake. The *Unicorn*, is it not? Have you brought me some frigates at last?'

Nathan's heart sank. The Admiral appeared to have lost his wits as well as his right arm. Before he could inform Nelson that the *Unicorn* had been lost to the French nearly two years ago, Berry went on: 'He has brought you something better than frigates. Tell him,' he urged Nathan, but with a warning look.

In as flat a tone as he could contrive, Nathan recounted what he had seen off the coast of Alexandria. He tried to keep the slightest degree of excitement or urgency out of his voice, but to his alarm Nelson began to rub his forehead vigorously with the knuckles of his remaining hand.

'When was this, you say?' He uttered the question through gritted teeth as if in an extremity of pain.

'The evening of the thirtieth of June,' Nathan told him, and was even more alarmed when Nelson let out a howl like a wolf and beat his fist on the table with such violence it brought a cup crashing to the floor.

'The thirtieth of June,' he repeated in a manic falsetto. 'Do you hear this, Berry? *The thirtieth of June.*'

Nathan threw a helpless glance at Berry and saw that he had his eyes closed and was swaying rather more than the movement of the ship necessitated. He wondered if they had both gone mad.

'I am sorry,' he said. 'I did not mean it to distress you.'

'Tell him, Berry,' commanded Nelson.

Berry opened his eyes. 'We left Alexandria on the evening of the twenty-ninth,' he said flatly. 'There was not a single French ship in sight.'

'You were at Alexandria?' Nathan looked from one to the other, but neither replied. 'But – the sea was filled with them. We counted over two hundred sail. I do not know how—' He was about to say 'how you could have missed them' but caught himself up in time.

It was apparent, however, that his meaning was clear.

'I suppose it was the khamsin,' he finished lamely. 'You could scarce see your hand in front of your face.'

'And yet *you* saw them, Captain,' Nelson pointed out. 'Two hundred sail, you say?'

'About that. Insofar as we could judge.'

'I think your judgement is about two hundred short, would you not agree, Berry?' Nelson's tone was deceptively light. 'There were four hundred at Malta. And we missed them there, too – by about the same distance.'

He let out something like a sob and covered his face with his hand.

Gradually, in fits and starts, the two men relayed a story of mishap and misunderstanding that almost had Nathan crying, let alone the Admiral.

Their troubles had begun back in May, off the coast of Sardinia, when they were beset by a severe storm – as bad a storm, Nelson said, as he had ever endured, even in the Caribbean. The squadron was scattered, each ship fighting desperately for its own survival. The *Vanguard* was dismasted and left wallowing helplessly off the rugged coastline. Fortunately, as the storm abated, the *Alexander* managed to get a line aboard and tow her to the small island of San Pietro where, miraculously, the crew had her seaworthy again, with a jury rig, in a matter of days.

'It would have taken a British dockyard months,' said Nelson with a mixture of pride and bitterness.

A secret rendezvous had been agreed before the squadron was scattered, but though the heavier ships had survived the storm, there was no sign of the four frigates.

'We learned later that they had returned to Gibraltar,' Berry reported glumly.

They were left with only one small brig – the *Mutine* under Captain Hardy – to scout for them.

Worse was to come. A day later they met with a merchantman from Marseille and learned that Bonaparte had sailed from Toulon over a week before, taking with him thirteen ships of the line and over four hundred transports. But there was no clue as to where they were headed, and without frigates – the eyes of the fleet – the chances of finding them were slight.

On 22 June, Hardy, who had been sent off in the brig, reported that they had landed at Malta about a week earlier – and left a few days later, heading east. This finally persuaded Nelson that they were bound for Egypt.

'As you advised us about a year ago,' he said to Nathan. Nathan winced as if it was a rebuke, and perhaps it was.

So the squadron sailed east, sending Hardy ahead to look into Alexandria. On 29 June he reported back. The roads, he said, were empty.

It was the same evening that Nathan had sighted the French fleet in the murk of the khamsin.

'So you must have been just a few miles to the east,' he mused, perhaps unwisely. He did not like to ask where they had been going, but Nelson told him anyway.

'On our way to fucking Asia,' he snarled, through gritted teeth.

They had first gone to Aleppo, Berry supplied, and then the Gulf of Antalya and then back up along the coast of Asia Minor to Crete.

'Chasing shadows and rumours across the Levant,' he added softly.

Nelson's great fear was that the threat to Egypt had been a ruse to divert him far to the east while Bonaparte landed his troops in Sicily. So he hurried back towards Italy – only to find he was wrong again.

It was this, he said, that had broken his heart.

'So what have you been doing, sir?' he enquired of Nathan in the same suspiciously light tone. 'Pray entertain us with a full account of it, for we are dearly in need of entertainment, are we not, Berry?'

'Perhaps later,' Berry advised Nathan, in case he should presume to take this instruction literally. 'Shall I prepare the fleet for sea, sir?' he enquired of his Admiral with the gentleness normally preserved for the old and infirm.

'Why not? We may as well check out this latest "rumour".' Nelson's glare at Nathan was even fiercer for having only one eye to give it vigour, rather like the glare of a Cyclops. 'For it is better than chasing back to Gibraltar for fear they may be on their way to England.'

* * *

Nathan returned to the *Swallow* to inform Imlay of the change of plan.

Imlay, however, would have none of it.

'*You* may go where you damn well please,' he declared, 'but *we* are going to Naples and there is an end to it.'

The argument raged fast and furious and they might have come to blows, had it not been for the intervention of Miss Devereux, who was brought out of her cabin by the row. But even her pleas failed to move Imlay. It was her father who was paying for this expedition, he informed them, and not Captain Peake, nor Admiral Nelson, nor any other Briton that he knew of, and it was her father who had the prior claim on them. Captain Peake might go to the Devil for all he cared, but he would not take the *Swallow* with him, nor any of its crew, save those in the service of King George. And if Captain Peake wished to dispute it, they might settle it with swords or pistols at any time of his choosing.

Nathan was tempted to take him up on the offer, but it would not do. They could not fight a duel in front of the entire crew, most of whom would very likely be in Imlay's corner. His only other recourse was to appeal to Nelson, but Nelson might be reluctant to seize what was, technically speaking, a private ship-of-war in the service of the American President, with all the diplomatic complications that would ensue, especially with so much else on his mind.

So in the end there was nothing for it but to quit his command.

He had all hands piped on deck and addressed them one last time.

'Men – as many of you know, I am a British officer,' he began. They stared back at him without expression. 'And as such I am bound by my oath to King George – and my own inclination – to offer my services to Admiral Nelson in his pursuit of the French. I expect many of you feel the same way . . .' He paused and surveyed the stony faces before him. There was no immediate sign that they were moved by the same considerations. He doubted, in fact, if half of them understood more than a few words of what he was saying. He sighed. 'However, you have all signed on for the duration of the voyage, and until the *Swallow* returns to Gibraltar your duty is clear – you must remain with the ship and serve Mr Imlay here as you have served me.'

He nodded towards Imlay who stood, stiff and formal, at his side. He thought he saw relief on some of the faces before him. Others stared back with the same incomprehension as before.

'It only remains for me to thank you all – every one of you – from the bottom of my heart, for the loyalty and devotion you have shown to me and to the ship and to your shipmates over the past months, and especially during the battle with the *Meshuda*. Thank you – and a safe voyage.'

He nodded to the boatswain, but before he could give the order to dismiss, Nathan heard another voice pipe up from among the body of men in the waist, a voice with a distinct American accent.

'Three cheers for the Captain. Hip, hip – huzzah!'

And to Nathan's frank amazement the entire crew, American, Russian, Italian, Portuguese – even the British

– raised their disparate voices in three hearty cheers.

Nathan felt his eyes prick with tears and turned away with a curt nod to Imlay – though even he looked moved, Nathan thought, as he made his way below.

He found Louisa Devereux in the stern cabin. Her eyes, too, were suspiciously red.

'I wish you a safe voyage to Naples,' he began formally, 'and a happy reunion with your papa.'

He was rewarded with a glare almost as savage as Nelson's. 'Why did Imlay call you Captain Peake?' Her voice was accusing.

'Because that is my name,' he confessed. 'Captain Turner is what you might call a *nom de guerre*.'

'So you are English?'

'I am.' He thought of explaining that his mother was American and that he had relatives in New York, but this would, he thought, be an unworthy distraction.

'I thought you were,' she declared, though with little satisfaction. 'An English naval officer?'

'Post Captain.'

'So will you come to Naples when you have finished fighting your wars?' she asked him bluntly. 'Or will I have to find you in England?'

He was so unhappy it took him a moment to take in the significance of what she had said. Then he took her in his arms. It would have been ungallant not to, though he knew it was unwise. It was probably less wise to kiss her, but he did it anyway. Tears were always so seductive, he had always thought, at least in a woman. He told himself that she would forget him within days of arriving in Naples.

* * *

Before he left, he packed the charts they had taken from the *Meshuda*. Legally speaking, they probably belonged to Imlay, or Mr Devereux, or the American President, but Nathan was damned if he was going to leave them behind after all the trouble they had caused him.

Tully and O'Driscoll were waiting for him on the quarterdeck with their bags packed. As King's officers they were bound to accompany him – and he expected nothing less. And so they took off their hats, made their bows to Imlay, shook hands with Mr Cribb and the rest of the warrant officers, and stepped into the waiting barge.

'I expect,' said Imlay, just before Nathan disappeared over the rail, 'that we shall meet again, sooner or later.'

'I expect we shall,' replied Nathan in the same resigned tone. Then Imlay put out his hand and Nathan took it. It was, he thought, like shaking hands with his own destiny.

Berry offered Nathan accommodation in the *Vanguard*, but the two lieutenants were packed off to the *Orion* and the *Zealous*, both of whose Captains had need of officers. Nathan experienced a familiar sense of desolation as he watched Tully ferried over to the *Orion* and felt as alone again, and as lonely, as he had felt in the Moorish prison on the Rock of Gibraltar or on the deck of the flagship off Cadiz with the four men hanging from the yards.

'Captain's compliments,' said a small unbroken voice at the approximate level of his waist and he looked down to see one of the younger servants looking up at him, 'and he would be obliged for the pleasure of your company, sir, in his day cabin.'

Captain Berry's day cabin was immediately below the Admiral's and almost as well-appointed, with a view of the mountains of the Morea through the great stern windows. Unexpectedly he was alone apart from his steward, who poured from a freshly opened bottle of Madeira before he was dismissed.

'So how did you find the Admiral?' Berry wanted to know, after the conventional toasts.

'Well, as you advised, he has changed a great deal from when we were at Cadiz,' Nathan replied warily. 'But then the loss of his arm . . .'

'I vow he would lose the other for a sight of the French fleet on the open sea,' put in Berry abruptly. 'But these constant setbacks, they are driving him to madness.'

'He expects too much of himself,' observed Nathan, drawing on his seniority as a member of Nelson's squadron in the Gulf of Genoa back in '95, for Berry had joined them a year later in San Fiorenzo.

'Aye, I grant you that, but then he feels a lot is expected of him.' Berry kept his voice low, for the stern windows were open and voices carried, even in as big a ship as the *Vanguard*. 'He was appointed to this command over the heads of a great many more senior officers – and many who think themselves far more deserving. They will be only too glad to see him fail.'

'Even if it means a French victory?'

'You know as well as I that there are plenty who put their careers before their country. And if the French do win, they will blame Nelson for it.'

'I do not see how Nelson can be held to account,' said Nathan after a moment. 'Their lordships were much opposed to the notion that Bonaparte had Egypt in his sights. They were convinced it was a ruse.'

Berry nodded. He must have known of Nathan's own difficulties in that regard.

'It is not as if he did not go there,' Nathan went on. 'He just got there too soon.'

'Aye, but bad luck is as often held against one as bad judgement,' observed Berry, 'especially in a Commander.'

This was true. Bonaparte thought luck was the most important attribute a General could have. But Nathan thought it prudent to keep this wisdom to himself.

'Well,' said Berry, raising his glass, 'let us hope your phantoms are still in Alexandria when we get there –' so now they were *his* phantoms, thought Nathan, and presumably he would be blamed for their absence – 'and do not slip by us once more in the night, on their way to Corfu.'

'Corfu?' Nathan looked startled. 'Why Corfu?'

'Because it is as secure an anchorage as you will find in these waters, the main base of the Venetian fleet – and now in French hands. As you would know, of course,' he added significantly.

Nathan said nothing, but he wondered how many of his acquaintance knew of his nefarious activities in Venice.

'And why would the French fleet remain in Alexandria,' Berry persisted, 'once they have delivered the Army?'

Nathan frowned. 'Is that why you were in the Bay of Coron?'

'We thought it was well placed to intercept them if that was where they were headed.' He shrugged. 'But you know the Admiral. He is mad to be at them. Could you not see it in his face?' He considered a moment and then he glanced at the deck above his head. 'I only hope it does not betray him to a greater madness.'

The wind had shifted westward and they made good time on the return to Alexandria, sighting Pompey's Pillar in clear weather soon after noon on the first day of August. It was Nathan's birthday – but there was no present for him. The harbour was full of shipping, and not a single one of them French.

'Dear God,' murmured Berry in an undertone, looking across to the lonely figure of his Admiral staring towards the shore. 'He will kill himself.'

'He is as likely to kill *me*,' confided Nathan, who felt his responsibility keenly.

They turned eastward along the coast with little hope of a result, and at 1.30 p.m. Nathan sat down in the *Vanguard*'s wardroom to as miserable a dinner as he could remember. The assembled officers ate in a wretched silence, in which requests to pass the salt or the gravy, or 'Could I trouble you for the pickle, sir,' rang out like the tolling of the death-cart at a time of plague. Then, just as the cloth was being removed, a very small midshipman came running in with a message from the officer of the watch.

'Signal from the *Zealous*,' he squeaked, without delivering himself of the usual compliments. ' "Enemy in sight!" '

Chapter Twenty-four

The Shoals of Abukir

———◦•◦•◦———

They were in the Bay of Abukir. Thirteen of them, moored in a single line, the nearest very close to the island where Nathan had first sighted the *Meshuda*, the rest curving away to the south-east, right up against the edge of the Inner Shoal. As near invincible a line of battle as Nathan could have imagined, for an approaching enemy would be obliged to run directly into the fire of some 500 cannon on the ships alone – with more guns mounted on the island and in the fort on the headland, which was now occupied by the French.

And then there were the shoals.

Nelson called a council of war in his cabin to which all the Captains were invited – his band of brothers. The sight of the French fleet had worked wonders for his state of mind. He was more like the Nelson of old, the Nelson Nathan remembered from the Bay of Cadiz. But there was something almost feverish about his excitement, something not altogether reassuring.

The Captains had been asked to bring any charts they had of Abukir Bay. There were three. One – the only one that was English – showed the whole region from Alexandria to Aleppo, but Abukir was no more than a small indentation in the coastline with no markings of any kind. Ben Hallowell had a small sketch of the bay taken from a French prize, but it was not much better. And there was another French map torn from an atlas. There were very few soundings and those they had they did not trust.

Nelson lost a little of his exuberance.

'Do we have no better than this?' he demanded. 'And is there no chance of obtaining a pilot?'

'Captain Peake knows something of the bay,' Berry ventured with a glance at Nathan, who had told him of his battle with the *Meshuda*. Every eye now turned to him. Nathan knew many of the Captains personally, the rest by name and reputation, and he knew they must all be curious to know what he was doing there. They would all be aware of his arrest and imprisonment. Some would also know, or guess, that he had other duties beside that of a ship's Captain.

'I also have a chart,' he nodded, 'of sorts.'

He unrolled the chart he had taken from the *Meshuda* and spread it on the table. There was a collective intake of breath as they gathered round. It showed the entire bay, from Abukir Island in the west to Rosetta in the east, with the shoal waters clearly outlined and the soundings marked in fathoms.

'You have been here?' Nelson queried him sharply. 'In this very bay?'

Nathan acknowledged that he had. As the Captains listened in silence, he described some of the obstacles he had encountered during his battle with the *Meshuda*.

The silence continued for a long moment after he had finished speaking. Nathan thought he might have given offence by his presumption, for besides Berry he was the most junior officer present – and a frigate Captain at that. Then Nelson spoke.

'What would you say is the draught of a French two-decker?' he asked the company at large.

They agreed that it would be about 23 feet – much the same as their own.

'And the length?'

Someone rather hesitantly proposed that it must be about the same length as a British two-decker, which was about 170 feet, if you did not take the bowsprit into account.

'And I am sure you will have observed that they are moored by the head only,' said Nelson. 'So they will swing with the wind and the current. Yes?'

He gazed around the table and there were several nods in agreement, though it was clear to Nathan that most of them, like him, did not have the faintest idea what Nelson was talking about.

Then Nathan got it. If the French ships were moored by the bow only – and not at bow and stern – they must be able to swing their own length without danger of running aground. His voice was joined by several others who had come to the same conclusion.

'Which is room enough, do you not think,' Nelson continued, 'for our seventy-fours to sail right around their line and up the other side?'

'By God it is!' exclaimed Berry. 'We will come up on their blind side.' He blushed furiously when he realised what he had said, but Nelson appeared not to have noticed, or if he did, not to care.

'Not all of us,' he corrected him. 'The first five will suffice. The rest, led by *Vanguard*, will bear up to seaward.'

'We will take them on both sides,' declared Berry, in case the Admiral had not made it plain enough for them.

'But – do you mean us to pass right down the line?' This from Sam Hood – and he had a point, for it would expose each of them to the fire of the entire French fleet.

'No. We will engage the van and the centre only,' Nelson assured him. 'We will bring the whole weight of our attack against the first seven in the line and overwhelm them before the ships at the rear can come to their assistance. They will, as you can see, have the wind against them. Each ship will anchor beside her opponent – by the stern only, mind, so the head does not drift up into the wind. Is that clear?'

It was clear enough to Nathan. He only wished he had a ship.

'And I assume we are to attack at dawn?' said a voice. Nathan did not know whose it was, but it was a silly question. The sun was already low in the sky and at that latitude there was very little in the way of twilight. It would be properly dark in an hour or so.

'By God we will not,' said Nelson. They all looked at him. One or two were smiling. The others looked as startled as Nathan was. He caught Berry's eye and recalled his words.

'I only hope it does not betray him to a greater madness.'

Nelson was looking straight at him. 'You trust this chart?' he said, placing his hand upon it as if it was a Bible.

Nathan swallowed. He was inclined to prevaricate but knew it would not do, not when he had laid the chart so brazenly before them. He nodded, with a much greater confidence than he felt.

'Very well then, we will go straight at 'em.' Nelson looked around the circle of faces and smiled. 'Do not worry about the dark, gentlemen. It will be light enough when five hundred guns are firing at us. Thank you – and may God be with you all.'

Whether or not God was with them, for once the wind was. A steady onshore breeze carried them clear into the mouth of the bay under a full press of sail. Nathan, with no particular duties, took himself aloft to observe the French preparations.

The battle fleet stretched across the bay in one long line for about a mile, with less than half a cable's length between each ship. And in the shallower waters beyond were the frigates – three, no, four of them – and two smaller vessels. Nathan focused on each of them in turn. *Yes.* He felt his heart lurch. She was tucked away at the rear of the French line, right up against the Inner Shoal. She had a slightly different rig, but he was sure of it. The *Unicorn*. He gazed at her for some time while various conflicting emotions chased across his mind. The strongest was the continuing sense of loss – and regret for leaving her in the care of his first lieutenant while he played games of cloak and sword in Venice.

And yet it was his exploits in Venice that had surely led him here, where there was at least some hope of winning her back.

He turned his attention back to the main battle fleet – the chief obstacle to this ambition. Thirteen sail of the line. Exactly the same number as the British fleet, save that three of Nelson's ships – *Swiftsure*, *Alexander* and *Culloden* – had yet to join them. They had been sent on scouting missions and were still several miles behind. Nelson, of course, would not wait for them.

Nathan wondered again at the Admiral's state of mind. He had an impatience for death or glory that was akin to Bonaparte's, but if anything, more frenzied. Perhaps because he was seventeen or eighteen years older than Bonaparte and in poor health. And, of course, there was the frustration of that long, desperate chase.

'By this time tomorrow I shall have gained a peerage – or a tomb in Westminster Abbey,' he had told Berry as he rose from dinner.

Either way, he must be confident of victory, for their lordships would not care to bury him at Westminster if he led his men to defeat. And for most of those men, of course, the alternatives were much less glorious. A pocketful of prize money and the thanks of a grateful nation – or a watery grave off the coast of Egypt. And God help you if you were wounded.

Nathan focused his mind and his glass on the line of French ships. There was a great deal of activity both in and out of the water. Scores of boats were moving about from ship to ship and also between the ships and the shore – and all loaded with men. Why? Nathan could see no obvious reason for these transfers. But every ship had her guns run out, all along the line, and there was little movement aloft. It was clear that they meant to meet the British attack where they lay – at anchor.

He felt the ship heel unexpectedly to leeward and wrapped his arm more firmly about the futtock shroud. They were hauling sharply to the wind to weather the foul ground to seaward of the island, where the *Meshuda* had gone aground. Even from where he sat, 100 feet above the deck, Nathan could hear the voice of the seaman in the bows casting the lead. *Fifteen fathoms, thirteen, eleven . . .*

He studied the gap between the nearest Frenchman and the island. Scarcely more than a cable's length – 250 yards, perhaps, and most of it shoal water. Was there room enough to pass? And even if there was, they would take a terrific pounding from the guns on the island. Nathan could see the gun crews there, stacking up the reserves of powder and shot, and there was enough smoke in the air to suggest that they were heating it up. Red-hot shot. If a single British ship ran aground, it would all be over, for there was no room for any other to pass.

Zealous was leading the line, but *Goliath* was coming up beside her on her larboard bow, as if racing her for the honour. By God, they were never going to run through the gap two abreast . . . He could see the lofty figure of Sam Hood at the con of the *Zealous*, cool as you please, doffing his hat to Tom Foley on the *Goliath*. Like a pair of swells at the races. And then the wind took the hat and blew it overboard.

Then, from behind the French line, a small brig appeared under full sail, heading straight for them – or as straight as the wind would allow – as if she planned to take on the entire British fleet. What could she be playing at? Then Nathan realised. She was trying to lure them onto the shoals. He almost shouted a warning, though they could not possibly have heard him.

The brig was almost within gunshot now, but neither of the British ships took the slightest notice of her. They continued to run on, neck and neck, heading for the gap at the front of the French line.

Then suddenly the French opened fire. One moment they were sitting there, like ducks in a row, the next the whole French van exploded in a fury of fire and smoke. As the long rolling roar died away, Nathan trained his glass on the *Zealous*. Several large holes had appeared in her topsails. They looked like cabbage leaves when the caterpillars have been at them. The French were aiming high, as usual, and with chain shot, doing their damnedest to wreck the rigging before the British were in a position to fire back. It made sense of a sort, for in these waters, even if they brought down a single spar, it might easily cause a ship to run aground. But their gunnery was poor. They were firing most of the shot into thin air – Nathan could see the splashes where it was falling back into the sea. He checked his watch. Almost half after six, the fiery sun sliding beneath the westerly horizon and leaving a crimson stain that seemed to spread across the surface of the sea towards the scene of battle. Nathan wondered if he would live to see it rise. He trained his glass once more on the gundeck of the nearest Frenchman and saw something else, something he had not noticed before.

They had only run out the guns on the seaward side. The guns facing landward were obscured by piles of what looked like luggage. Boxes and bags – even furniture. What in God's name were they up to? The guns were there, but almost hidden by all this junk. Certainly they were not manned, or even unloosed, and the gunports were firmly closed. He looked at the next ship in line, and the next, and the next. They were all the same. They were so sure they could not be attacked from any direction but the sea, they had used the landward side to stack furniture.

He slid down the backstay so fast he near took the skin off his palms. But when he reported what he had discovered, he found they knew it already. Nelson had spotted it from well out to sea, even from the deck and with only one eye to see by.

'They will live to regret it,' he said.

'Is there anything I can do?' Nathan asked Berry, feeling like a junior midshipman, just come aboard, though even snotties usually had some duty or other to take their minds off the thought of imminent death or mutilation.

'You have done enough with your chart,' Berry assured him. 'I do not know how we could have proceeded without you.' Then, after a small pause . . . 'But if you have nothing better to do, you can stand as close to the Admiral as he will permit, for he is only a little fellow, you know, and you are such a great lofty lout, you may be able to take some of the heat from him.'

He left Nathan to make of this what he would. In truth, it was not greatly to his satisfaction. Something of the sort had been said to him before – at the Battle of St Vincent, when Nelson was only a Captain. This, it seemed, was to be his role in life for as long as he was without a ship – to stand next to Nelson whenever he was in action, to deflect or absorb whatever pieces of iron, timber or other deadly weaponry were flung at him.

After taking a few moments to reflect upon this imposition, he climbed a little way up the starboard mizzen shrouds to see what was happening at the head of the British line. *Goliath* had taken the lead and was almost through the gap. The lead French ship was firing at her with every gun she could bring to bear, but the guns on the island remained strangely silent. And now she was crossing the French line, raking the lead ship with her broadside. But something checked her. Was she aground? No. Her sheet anchor seemed to have come loose and it must be dragging along the bottom – Nathan could see men struggling to cast it loose from the cathead. But it slowed her down considerably, and Hood seized his chance and pushed *Zealous* ahead of her, bringing her up on the inner side of the French line and pouring his broadside into the lead ship at pointblank range.

Goliath passed behind her – so close as to almost scrape her sides – and lay along the next French ship in line. And three others followed them round – *Orion, Theseus* and *Audacious*. The whole of the French van was now wreathed in smoke and flame.

And then *Vanguard* brought her starboard broadside to bear – and they were in the thick of it.

They moored beside the third ship in the French line – Nathan could not see her name but she was a two-decker, a 74, so they were equally matched. But the next ship was still not engaged and she had come round slightly on her cable to bring the whole of her broadside to bear on the British flagship. A hail of shot swept the gundeck and for a while they were hard pressed. Then *Minotaur* raced past them on the seaward side to join the fight, and through the smoke Nathan saw another British 74, on the inshore side of the line, pounding the first of their opponents at very close range. There were eight British ships now engaged, attacking the first five French ships in the line from both sides. And on the landward side, so far as Nathan could see, the French did not have a single gun in action.

It was dark now. But Nelson was right – the French line seemed to be lit by a giant flickering bonfire, darting flashes of flame in every direction. You almost choked on the smoke, eyes streaming, ears deafened by the constant roar of the guns. Shouting, sweating faces loomed like apparitions, or figures from some ghastly carnival, sometimes pouring with blood, always shouting, unheard. Instructions were given by bawling directly in someone's ear or making frantic signs which were as often as not misunderstood. Nelson had his head bent over the chart from the *Meshuda*, studying it by the light of the binnacle. Nathan moved slightly towards him, remembering Berry's instruction, though he felt fairly confident that no sharpshooter would be able to pick out the Admiral through the smoke and the gloom. And in that moment Nelson was hit.

Nathan actually saw the shot strike him, high in the forehead. It was a piece of *langridge* – the scrap metal the French used to rip the British sails apart. Inexplicably, they were still using it, though it hardly mattered at this stage of the battle.

'Oh Christ,' Nathan said as he bent over him. There was a great gash in his forehead – Nathan could see the white gleam of bone – both eyes were gone and his face was drenched in blood.

But his lips were moving and Nathan put his ear close to them so he could hear.

'I am killed,' he whispered. 'Remember me to my wife.'

Chapter Twenty-five

Victory

———◦•◦•◦———

hey appeared within seconds. Nelson's people,
the men who followed him from ship to ship.
Shocked, disbelieving, united in their grief. They
raised him gently from the deck. His face and chest were
drenched with blood and it was still pumping out through
that ghastly wound. It looked as if he had been scalped. A
great flap of skin hung over his eyes, and by the light of
the guns Nathan thought he could see his brains through
the blood.

'Take him below,' said Berry. He gave Nathan a look
of agonised reproach.

They both followed the cortège below, down into the
orlop and through to the cockpit. It was crowded with
wounded men, sitting or lying amidst a shambles of the
dead and the dying, with a team of sawbones doing their
best – or worst – by the light of the swaying lanterns.

'Jefferson may be able to save him yet,' said Berry.

Jefferson, Nathan recalled, was the principal surgeon. A good surgeon, by all accounts, unlike most of them. But he could not perform miracles.

'I'll not be served first,' croaked the corpse, and they almost dropped him.

Nathan stared at that impossible mask of blood and torn flesh, and the lips moved again.

'I'll await my turn, along with the others.'

Happily no one took a blind bit of notice, and after poking around in the wound and lifting up the flap of skin, Dr Jefferson announced that the wound was superficial and there was 'no immediate danger'.

There was wide rejoicing among his followers, but Nelson had difficulty in believing it, even when Jefferson stitched him up and wrapped a bandage around the wound. He asked if they would send for the chaplain, and also for his secretary, Mr Comyn, so that he might dictate a last message for his wife. He was clearly in a great deal of distress, possibly because the bandage covered his eyes and he was in total darkness, hearing only the screams of the wounded and the roar of the guns.

But now there was another sound. Very like cheering.

'Go and ask Berry what is happening,' Nelson commanded one of his followers, for the Captain had returned to the quarterdeck.

Moments later, Berry himself came and knelt down by the Admiral's side.

He had 'pleasing intelligence' to report, he said. The *Spartiate* had ceased firing. He had sent the first lieutenant with a party of Marines to take possession of her – 'and he sent back this'.

He pressed the hilt of a sword into the Admiral's hand.

'It is the French commander's,' he announced, as Nelson ran his fingers down the steel, 'and I have received news that the *Aquilon* and the *Peuple Souverain* have also struck.'

He looked around at the throng of people gathered about the wounded Admiral and raised his voice: 'It would appear that victory has already declared itself in our favour.'

The impact of this speech and the cheering that followed was somewhat spoiled by Dr Jefferson's brisk request that the Admiral being in no immediate danger, perhaps they would care to remove him, and themselves, from the cockpit so that he could get on with his work.

After some discussion among the Admiral's servants, it was decided to carry him to the breadroom, which was thought to be spacious enough for his needs and far removed from the din of battle so that he might dictate his letters in peace.

Nathan left them to it and followed Berry back on deck. It seemed to be a good deal brighter than when he had left it. Then he saw that the French flagship appeared to be on fire. By its ruddy light, and the continuous flash of the guns, he gazed upon a scene that he knew would stay in his mind for as long as he lived. Ship upon ship lay dead in the water, many dismasted, their hulls riddled with shot, the sea around them heaving with debris: spars, whole masts and sodden canvas, shattered launches, half-filled with water, bodies and blood.

The British line seemed as badly damaged as the French – and Nathan could see the *Bellerophon* – the old 'Billy Ruffian' as she was known by the hands – drifting helplessly away to the north with all of her masts gone. Nelson had ordered his Captains to fly the white ensign instead of the blue so it might be the better seen in the poor light, and it was still streaming from the flagpole at her stern. Then, from out of the darkness in her wake came two more ships, also flying the white ensign but quite undamaged: the *Swiftsure* and the *Alexander*, the two 74s Nelson had left behind. They headed straight for the centre of the French line and began to pour their broadsides into the burning three-decker.

'By God, what is this?' demanded a familiar voice.

Nathan turned. Nelson had come on deck. His head was still wrapped in bandages and the whole of his upper body was soaked in blood. He looked like a walking corpse, but he had pulled up a corner of his bandage so he could see out of his good eye and he was looking towards the growing conflagration in the French centre.

'It is the *Orient*, sir,' said Berry, 'the French flagship.'

'They said on the *Spartiate* that she was repainting,' said someone else. 'Her poop was full of oil jars and buckets of paint.'

'Send Galway with the ship's boats,' Nelson instructed the Flag Captain. 'Tell him to lay off her and save all the men we can.'

'There is only one boat left, sir,' Berry told him. 'The rest are riddled with shot.'

'Then send that. And let us hope others do the same.'

But it was too late. The flames grew ever more fierce, racing up her tarred rigging and along her newly painted sides. By the light of the fire, Nathan could see almost the whole of the French line stretching off to the far side of the bay. Six ships had struck their colours. He could even see the names at the stern. *Conquérant, Guerrier, Spartiate* . . . warlike names, inspiring names. Then the *Orient* blew up.

The explosion was so massive, they heard later that the French troops heard it in Rosetta, ten miles away. Nearer to hand it was like a thunderclap from Hell. It seemed to stun both fleets into silence. The firing stopped completely. Total darkness reigned. And in the darkness, from the sky, the debris fell. Masts and yards, charred cables and timbers, fragments of metal, and the burned and shattered bodies . . .

The battle resumed within minutes and went on, spasmodically, through the night. Nathan joined Lieutenant Galway in the launch and spent the hours till dawn helping to pluck men out of the water. They picked up seventy who had jumped before the explosion and were clinging to the wreckage. The total crew, they said, had been over a thousand.

Nathan was still in the launch at first light, a little after four. By then most of those they pulled from the water were dead. And they were surrounded by dead and dying ships. No fewer than seven had struck their colours and two more had drifted into the shoals. Shattered and dismasted, they reminded Nathan of the prison hulks he had seen as a child among the shoals and marshes of the Medway.

But the Medway had never seen such a sun. It rose from the sea like the God of Judgement on the last day of the Apocalypse: blazing, angry, red as blood, hurling its fiery rays like spears through the lingering smoke. And as if in defiance, the firing resumed.

The French ships at the rear of the line had scarcely seen action, and now they poured their fire into the British ships nearest to them – the battered *Alexander* and *Majestic*. It would have gone very badly for them, but as Nathan watched helplessly from the launch, two ships emerged from the smoky morning haze like vengeful angels, belching flame, and to his astonishment Nathan recognised them as *Theseus* and *Goliath*, two of the first ships to have entered the battle, still miraculously under sail.

The French swiftly broke off the engagement and fled for the mouth of the bay. Two of them made it – the *Guillaume Tell* and the *Généreux*. A third, the *Timoléon*, ran aground with such force it dislodged the foremast, and then, as the pursuers closed in on her, the crew set her on fire and took to the boats.

The last French ship to hold out was the *Tonnant*. She had been dismasted during the night but her Commander, mortally wounded with both legs blown off, had ordered his men to nail the tricolour to the mast and stand him in a barrel of bran to staunch the blood. And so she had fought on, but now as she tried to follow the fleeing *Timoléon* under a jury rig, she too ran upon the sands and there, her Captain dead and her decks crowded with 1,600 survivors from the rest of the fleet, she finally surrendered.

An hour later, the *Timoléon* exploded. She was the eleventh French ship of the line to be destroyed or captured in the course of the battle. The greatest British victory, Berry announced, since the defeat of the Spanish Armada.

'What happened to the frigates?' Nathan asked him, and when Berry looked at him blankly: 'The French frigates.'

Berry's expression cleared but he did not seem greatly interested. 'One has been taken, I believe, and another ran aground. The other two have escaped, but it is of no consequence, set against the magnitude of our victory.'

No. Of no consequence whatsoever. Nathan ran up the shrouds to look out over the shoals towards the frigate that was aground, not far out from the shore. She had lost her mizzen and most of her mainmast, and was so battered about he could not tell if it was the *Unicorn* or not. Then, as he looked, he saw the smoke and the flames rising from her waist.

He found Galway slumped over one of the carronades on the quarterdeck, his eyes shut fast and his mouth hanging slack. Mercilessly Nathan shook him awake.

'Can I borrow the launch?' he shouted in his ear, for they were both still deafened by the guns. He explained why he needed it and Galway wearily nodded his assent and went back to sleep.

The frigate was burning fiercely before Nathan was halfway there and he met Lieutenant Hoste of the *Theseus* coming back from her. Captain Miller had sent him to take possession, he said, but the crew had set her alight.

'What ship was she?' Nathan asked, staring over towards the burning vessel.

'The *Artémise*, thirty-two,' Hoste replied indifferently, 'but I believe she was one of ours originally. Taken off Toulon in ninety-six.'

Nathan made the men sit at the oars while he watched her burn to the waterline. The last he saw of her was her bowsprit, sticking up out of the water, like a crooked cross, and a charred figurehead that could have been anything.

They were pulling back for the *Vanguard* when he saw another boat heading out from the shore. She was a local craft, a felucca under a single sail, and there was a figure up in the bows waving across the water to him and shouting.

Nathan ordered the men to rest on the oars again, and as the boat came up he saw that it was Spiridion Foresti, back from the dead.

Chapter Twenty-six

A Passage to India

———◆◆◆———

'I could not find her,' Spiridion admitted gloomily. 'There is no news either of Caterina or of Naudé. They have vanished into the sands of the desert. Or the Bedouin have taken them, which amounts to the same thing.'

The news he did bring was of Bonaparte and the French Army.

'They landed on the beach at Marabut, a day after we left you,' he told Nathan as they sat in the stern of the felucca amid the shoals of Abukir. 'We were on our way to Alexandria when we ran straight into a patrol of Chasseurs, and they made me go with them as guide.'

'And George Banjo?' Nathan asked him, for the gunner was not with him and he feared the worst.

'He is at the caravanserai.' He directed Nathan's attention towards the stone building on the far side of the bay where they had taken him in the ship's launch a little over a month ago. 'I thought it better that he did not come with me in case he was taken up for a deserter.'

'There is little chance of that,' Nathan told him. 'We have rather more on our mind at present than to be worried about a deserter, even if he were to be recognised, which is unlikely.'

They sat there, gazing at the wrecked and shattered ships all around them.

'It is a famous victory,' Spiridion said, shaking his head in wonder. 'But now you have burned their boats, I am afraid they will never leave.'

'Then we will have to let the Mamelukes deal with them.'

'The Mamelukes are history,' Spiridion informed him. 'Bonaparte has served them as he served Venice – but with a great deal more bloodshed.'

The French had marched inland towards Cairo, he said, following the route of the Nile, and the Mamelukes had come out to meet them under their General, Murad Bey, in the shadow of the Pyramids.

'When he heard they had no cavalry, Murad Bey laughed out loud,' Spiridion recounted, for like all Greeks he loved to tell a good story. 'He said he would slice through them like watermelons. But these watermelons had muskets and bayonets, and howitzers. The French formed up in squares, ten men deep, with the artillery behind them. But the Mamelukes charged anyway, not knowing how else to fight.

'It was as I said it would be, when we were in Tripoli,' he reminded Nathan. 'They were cut to pieces. Those that were left fled south, and I expect they are fleeing still. And Bonaparte is in Cairo, playing the Great Liberator, as he did in Italy. Come to free the people from tyranny.'

'But – it cannot be over, surely? Not after one battle?'

'Well, it is over for the Mamelukes,' Spiridion assured him, 'for I doubt there were more than twelve thousand in the whole of the country, and most of them died at the Pyramids. But he may have problems yet. The Egyptians are glad to be rid of the Mamelukes, that is for sure, but they are not so sure that they want the French to take their place. And of course, there are the Turks to be reckoned with. They are even less happy to have Bonaparte in Egypt.'

'And will he march on India?'

'What else can he do, now that you have destroyed his fleet?'

'But was not that always the plan?'

'Who knows? The men in Paris – maybe they just wanted him out of France – him and his Army. I think they will be very happy that you have destroyed his ships so he cannot get back there in a hurry. And they will be even happier if he vanishes into the desert, like poor Caterina.'

'Will you go on looking for her?' Nathan asked him.

'No. With the French here it is too dangerous for me. There are men with Bonaparte who know that I work for the British. No, now that you have destroyed his fleet, I think I will go back to Corfu and join the Resistance. But first I must speak to your Admiral, and tell him what I have learned of the French intentions.'

* * *

But Nelson was in no fit state to receive visitors, even ones as important as Spiridion Foresti, and it was two days before the Greek was able to make his report. In the meantime there was work to be done. They had to effect what repairs they could to the battered ships, cater for thousands of French prisoners, tend to the wounded – and bury the dead.

The British had lost fewer than 200 men in the battle, but more than 1,700 Frenchmen had died and almost twice as many had been wounded. There was a great need to dispose of the corpses, and they could not be buried in the shallow waters of the Bay of Abukir. Most were interred beneath the sands of Abukir Island, where the work parties sweated under the Egyptian sun, plagued by the millions of flies.

Nathan, with his knowledge of French, was put in charge of conducting the prisoners ashore under a Marine guard and arranging their transfer under parole to the French garrison at Rosetta. It was no easy task, for they were shadowed by parties of marauding Bedouin, eager for plunder, not to speak of the usual hordes of flies. On the evening of the second day after the battle, he was returning to Abukir when a midshipman came riding up on a mule and told him the Admiral wished to speak with him.

He knew Nelson was sending Berry off in the *Leander*, the fleet's only forth-rate, to take news of their victory to England – she was already making ready to sail on the far side of the bay. However, it was rumoured that the Admiral was keen to send another officer with him, to carry a copy of the report to Sir William Hamilton in

Naples for despatch overland. So when Nathan was sent for, he had hopes that the choice had fallen upon him.

He found Nelson in his day cabin with his secretary and Spiridion Foresti. The Admiral looked very weak and more than a little feverish, but he managed a bleak smile when Nathan was shown into the cabin.

'Ah, Peake, I am glad they were able to find you. I had thought you had gone gallivanting off with the French again.'

Nathan managed a smile that was only slightly less bleak. Nelson waved him to a chair.

'I have been having a very interesting talk with your friend Mr Foresti here,' he said, 'and it is in my mind to send you to India.'

It took a moment for this to sink in.

'It seems only fair,' Nelson went on, 'as you were the first to alert us to Bonaparte's intentions, that you should have the honour of conveying the news of our victory to the Governor-General in Calcutta – and to warn him that Bonaparte may march upon India to join with the Sultan of Mysore against the British interest.' In the absence of a response he added after a moment, 'Or do you not think so?'

Nathan was lost for words. He threw a wild glance at Spiridion whose expression was ambiguous. The Sultan of Mysore, the Governor-General in Calcutta, India . . . India! What was India to do with him? He clung to the only straw of sanity – his diminishing hope of obtaining a new ship. One of the French prizes, perhaps. One of the smaller ones.

'A very great honour, indeed, sir,' he heard himself saying. 'Only that . . .'

'Only that?' Nelson put a hand to his head as if the sudden raising of his eyebrows had burst a stitch.

'I – I was hopeful of obtaining another ship, sir,' Nathan stammered. 'I am – that is, since I lost the *Unicorn* . . .'

Nelson exchanged a glance with Spiridion.

'A ship?' he repeated in tones of wonder, as if it had been a flying machine. 'Is that conceivable, Mr Foresti? I would have thought he would have to travel overland – by camel perhaps – at least until he reaches the Red Sea when he might pick up a dhow.'

'By camel?' Again Nathan looked at Spiridion. Were they making game of him? Spiridion said nothing.

'Well, it will take you far too long to travel by way of the Cape, you know,' Nelson proposed not unkindly, 'and I can think of no other way. Unless you have it in mind to dig a canal.'

Nathan was in no mood for humour. He thought of the year he had just endured – the long months of imprisonment at Gibraltar, the months of serving under Imlay and the Flag of Freedom. Was this the price of being proved right – to be sent off on a camel in the general direction of India? He was almost overwhelmed by his sense of injustice.

Nelson was still speaking. 'However, we may be able to employ your talents in some other way. What do you think, Mr Foresti?'

Spiridion inclined his head as if in consideration of this dubious possibility, as Nelson reached for a paper lying upon the table.

'I have here a recent despatch forwarded to me from

Calcutta. It appears that there are a number of French privateers operating from the island of Réunion in the Indian Ocean, and the Company is anxious for the safety of their shipping through the Straits of Sumatra. There is also a fear that Bonaparte might attempt to force a passage to India by way of the Arabian Sea.' He paused for a moment and observed Nathan through his good eye. 'Although there are no King's ships at present in the Indian Ocean, the East India Company possesses a small squadron of its own at Madras. I cannot give you the precise details but I believe it includes a former French ship of the line, the *Pondicherry* of fifty-four guns, two very fine sloops of twenty guns or more, and some smaller armed brigs and suchlike. The Company has been petitioning their lordships for some time to propose a serving officer as Commodore, and if you are agreeable I should be very happy to recommend you to the Governor-General as the ideal candidate for the post. What do you say, sir, does it suit you or no?'

Epilogue

The Nun's Journey

———◆●◆———

*I*t was the Devil of a journey. The camels evil-eyed and spitting, their drivers cursing and grumbling, forever demanding more pay, or drink, or women. No relief from sun or sand, the flies and the smell of excrement. And the nights cold and dark, huddled into a blanket next to a smoking fire of camel dung.

There were no towns, and the villages they came across were small and filthy.

She wished, many times, she was back in the harem. Swimming in the pool while the light faded from the windows and the Italian girls brought sherbet in tall glasses.

She discounted her memories of the stale bread soaked in milk and sugar, and the Pasha's wives, and the Pasha himself watching them from behind the grille. And her dreams of freedom.

The food on the journey was, besides, not much better, and she was no freer now than she had been then.

She thought many times of escape, but they were shadowed every step of the way by the Bedouin, and on the whole she preferred to take her chances with Naudé and the men he had hired as guards in Cairo.

He came to her many times, especially at night, but she could hardly bring herself to speak to him, much less let him into her bed. Not that she had a bed.

He maintained a form of chivalry and did not impose himself on her. He seemed to have hopes that sooner or later she would give herself to him voluntarily.

And sooner or later she probably would, she thought. But not on that journey, among the camels and the flies and the filth.

'I will make it up to you,' he said, 'when we arrive in India. You will be a princess. You will have a palace with servants, and silken dresses, and ride on elephants.'

'Is it better than riding on a camel?' she asked him sourly.

He was a hopeless romantic; and dangerous.

'I do not want to be a princess,' she said, 'if it means being kept by a man.'

'Surely it is better than being kept as a slave,' he said, 'or a nun.'

He seemed to think he had saved her from a life of penury or worse.

'I was not just *any* nun,' she said. 'I was Suora Caterina Caresini, Deputy Prioress of the Convent of San Paolo di Mare in Venice, do you not remember? A woman of power and influence – until *you* came along.'

'You were a hireling,' he said, 'in the pay of the British.'

'Well, at least they paid me,' she said. 'And did not drag me off to India with a promise that I might ride on an elephant.'

She had not told him about the wealth she had accrued in the vaults of Coutts & Company of London, though it seemed increasingly unlikely that she would ever lay her hands on it. For how could she ever prove that it was hers?

But she could not help wondering, as she swayed across the sands of Egypt and Arabia on her camel, if they had a branch in India.

Acknowledgements

With most sincere thanks to Martin Fletcher and his colleagues at Headline Review for giving me the pleasure of writing this series, and to all who have helped me with the research, especially the staff at the National Archives in Kew and at the Caird Library in the National Maritime Museum in Greenwich. Also to Andrew Wilson at Sky News for his help with contacts and logistics in the Middle East; to Nick Moll for his guidance on the migration of birds, especially swallows; to Cate Olsen and Nash Robbins of the Much Ado Bookshop in Alfriston for finding me such invaluable reference books on the history and sieges of Gibraltar and on the corsairs of the Barbary Coast; to the Maritime Bookshop in Greenwich for finding me the obscure but incredibly detailed *Naval Wars in the Levant 1559–1853* by R. C. Anderson published by Liverpool University Press in 1952; to Ayse Tekçan for her folk story about the hunter and the bird; to Bill Cran and Clive Syddall of Paladin Invision for giving me the opportunity to study the workings of the harem at Topkapi Palace in Istanbul while making the series *Harem* for Channel Four; and to Sharon Goulds for making my stay on the island of San Pietro a great deal more pleasurable than it would have been without her.

History

—◦●◦—

As usual I've based the latest Nathan Peake novel around real historical events and characters, so readers might like to know where fact and fiction merge – and where they part company.

The Fall of Venice, which starts the novel, happened in the spring of 1797, when the city was occupied by the French under Bonaparte. It was the first time that Venice had fallen to an invader, and put an end to its thousand-year history as an independent republic. Sister Caterina Caresini is, unfortunately, a figment of my suspect imagination. You can read more about her – and Venice – in my previous Nathan Peake novel *The Winds of Folly*.

The hanging of the four 'mutineers' and the bombardment of Cadiz really took place. Nathan's objections mirror those of serving officers at the time; both Jervis and Nelson were criticised for their part in the bombardment, though it was, in fact, ordered by the British Admiralty in the hope of forcing the Spanish fleet to come out and fight. However, it's also true that Nelson sent a note to the Spanish Admiral warning him that it was about to happen and telling him to evacuate the civilians. War was obviously less barbaric in those days.

The Moorish Castle in Gibraltar is a real place and is still there – you can visit it, if you don't mind the climb. Alternatively, you can see a picture of it on the back of a Gibraltar five-pound note. It was used as a prison until 2010.

General Charles O'Hara, the Lieutenant Governor of Gibraltar, is a real-life character and it is true that he had the distinction of being taken prisoner by two of the greatest political and military leaders in history – Washington and Napoleon. The son of an Irish lord and the latter's Portuguese mistress, he was variously described by his contemporaries as charming, garrulous, eccentric and larger than life – but suffered a ludicrous caricature as an upper-class English officer in the film *The Patriot*, starring Mel Gibson.

The story of the migrating swallows is, I think, particularly interesting from an historical point of view. It was only when I was writing this that I thought I had better check to see if people knew about the migration of birds in 1797. It turned out that they didn't – but that they were thinking about it. Until then, it was widely believed that the birds hibernated – under water.

Absurd though this seems, in those days it would have been a lot more believable than the notion that they could fly from England to Africa and back without getting lost. One of the first to suggest this as a possibility was the Reverend John White, who saw it happening during his stint as Chaplain to the garrison of Gibraltar. He was unable to convince his more famous brother, Gilbert, however, who continued to believe to his dying day that the swallows spent the winter months in ponds.

As for the corvette *Swallow* and its mission to Tripoli, this is based on the operations of the newly established US Navy and Marines in the First Barbary War of 1801–05. Yusuf Karamanli and his two brothers – Hassan and Ahmed – are historical characters, as are James Leander Cathcart, Xavier Naudé and Peter Lisle aka Murad Reis. I hope I haven't been too unjust to them. Having said that, Yusuf appears to have been an eighteenth-century version of Gaddafi, who not only seized power by murdering his older brother in their mother's harem – in the way I have described – but went on to terrorise his people and whoever else was unfortunate enough to fall into his power. But, like Gaddafi, he did have charisma. This is not a recommendation. However, to read more about him, and the war with the US, I recommend *A Nest of Corsairs: The Fighting Karamanlis of the Barbary Coast* by the former British diplomat Seton Dearden.

Life inside the harem is described from personal experience, although it is based not on the harem in the Red Castle but on the Great Sultan's harem in Topkapi. I spent a very happy few weeks there filming the docudrama series *Harem* for Channel Four in 2003. It hadn't changed much, not by the time we'd finished with it.

Spiridion Foresti is a real character. He was British Consul in Corfu but was kicked out when the French came. I have no idea if he was ever in the Levant, but it wouldn't surprise me. Nelson said he was the best intelligence agent he had ever met. Though now I come to think about it, I'm not sure they actually did meet. Their correspondence is well worth a read, however. You can find it in the National Archives at Kew.

Gilbert Imlay is another real-life character. And he, too, was a spook. He was probably born in Philadelphia around 1753. As a youth, he was employed in the family shipping business which was largely centred on the rum trade – a euphemism for smuggling in the West Indies, though rum probably came into it somewhere. During the American War of Independence he served in Washington's army – as pay officer for the New Jersey Line, an early example of the credulity of his fellows, for who in his right mind would have entrusted Imlay with his pay? He deserted after a few months and his activities for the rest of the war are shrouded in mystery. His family were convinced to their dying day that he had been an agent for the British – or certainly an informer – and they never spoken to him again. But others reckoned he was working for General Washington all along: one of a select band of brothers known as Washington's Boys who were paid out of the General's own pocket – or at least out of secret funds provided by Congress for whatever nefarious purposes the General and his Boys had in mind. A kind of embryonic CIA.

After the War of Independence, Imlay turned up in London, with a book he'd written based on his experiences on the American frontier: *A Topographical Description of the Western Territory of North America*, which was published by Debrett 'to wide acclaim'. He followed this up with a novel called *The Emigrants*. Less widely acclaimed, it contained scenes of rape, wife-beating and brutal attacks by native Americans. Imlay said his purpose was to encourage emigration.

Certainly it made him something of a celebrity for a time and he became a popular guest on the London salon circuit. Then came the French Revolution and he took himself off to Paris where the action was – and the money. He worked as a shipping agent running goods past the British blockade for a handsome profit and helped himself to the Bourbon silver, i.e. the property of Louis XVI and Marie Antoinette. He was also some kind of a diplomat and probably a spy. I've seen copies of his reports – in Paris and Havana – proposing French operations in Spanish Louisiana, which certainly show he was up to no good. While he was in Paris he became the lover of Mary Wollstonecraft, the pioneer English feminist, and fathered her child, Fanny. His behaviour towards her was such that she twice tried to commit suicide. He eventually got her off his back by sending her to Sweden, with their one-year-old daughter, to find a treasure ship he'd lost, with the Bourbon dinner service on board.

You couldn't make it up.

However, I *have* made up his adventures in the Levant. I doubt I have been unjust to his character but if I have, he deserves it.

A note on the Levant, by the way. The Levant is now taken to mean the Eastern Mediterranean, from the Bosphorus to the Nile, but in the eighteenth century it was used to describe the much wider region covered by the Ottoman Empire, including the Greek islands and the eastern provinces of North Africa, including Egypt.

And turning to Egypt – Nathan's intelligence of the French invasion plans are derived from the secret intelligence reports of Spiridion Foresti and Sir Sidney Smith, an

English naval Captain who had been taken prisoner by the French and learned of the plans while he was in Paris. It is also an historical fact that their lordships discounted these reports – preferring to believe that the French intended to invade Sicily or Portugal or the British Isles themselves. This was one of the reasons Nelson was reduced to chasing shadows across the Mediterranean.

I suppose the idea that the French were planning to invade Egypt was as nonsensical to their lordships as the notion that swallows flew to Africa for the winter. And they had a point, at least as far as the French were concerned. It made no strategic sense at all – unless Bonaparte seriously thought he could march an army of 60,000 men 2,000 miles through hostile territory, desert and mountain without a reliable chain of supply. Maybe he did. Generals are not always noted for their sanity.

Here are some telling notes from his diary:

January 1st, 1798, Paris: Paris has a short memory. If I remain longer doing nothing, I am lost. In this great Babylon, one reputation quickly succeeds another. After I have been seen three times at the theatre, I shall not be looked at again. I shall therefore not go there very frequently.

January 29th: I will not remain here; there is nothing to be done. They will listen to nothing. All things fade here, and my reputation is almost forgotten; this little Europe affords too slight a scope; I must go to the Orient; all great reputations have been won there. If the success of an expedition to England

*should prove doubtful, as I fear, the army of England
will become the army of the East, and I shall go to
Egypt. The Orient awaits a man!*

The French government, of course, was glad to see the
back of him. Fearing a military coup, they did not really
care where he went so long as it was out of France – taking
his army with him. Egypt seemed just about right.

Which brings me to the Battle of the Nile.

I think I've described this accurately, even if from the
POV of a fictitious participant. I had the pleasure of
working on another docudrama about the life of Nelson,
again for Channel Four, in 2005 – which gave me the
opportunity to study the battle in detail and to film a
reconstruction. Where I've departed from the known facts
is in including the presence of the frigate *Unicorn* and in
having Nathan bring the news of the French fleet to
Nelson, as well as presenting him with a chart of the Bay
of Abukir which he had taken from the *Meshuda*.

It is true, however, that Nelson was in the Bay of Coron
at the time, and that the news was brought to him by an
'unidentified vessel' which had spotted the French fleet off
Alexandria. It is also true that Nelson was in a wretched
state of health, physically and mentally, having spent two
months in a futile search for the French, a search that had
taken him to almost every part of the Eastern Mediterranean. He later admitted that those long, fraught weeks
of high tension, doubt and disappointment had knocked
years off his life, and there were those at the time who
feared for his sanity.

But then, no sane person would have ordered a night

attack on a superior enemy force in a well-defended position in the shoal waters of the Bay of Aboukir.

Certainly, it was the last thing the French Admiral expected. He had sent half his crews ashore to forage for food and water, and he thought he had at least eight hours to prepare for an attack the following day. If Nelson had been entirely sane, he might have waited until dawn, when the French would have been in a far better state to fight him.

As for the charts – it was later reported that Nelson had three charts of the area, none of them very good or trustworthy, and that his success in navigating the shoal waters of the bay was down to a combination of luck and skill. However, the French were astonished at the confidence with which the British ships entered the bay, avoiding the shoal waters with remarkable accuracy. Only one British ship – the *Culloden* – went aground. This *might* have been luck, but the French certainly believed that Nelson had the benefit of expert advice, possibly from some local pilots he took off a wine-brig. It is also true that he was studying a chart of the bay at the time he was hit in the head.

The battle was proclaimed throughout Europe – apart from in France, of course – as a great British victory. It was, and it led to the creation of a Second Coalition against the French, including Austria, Britain and Russia. But it tends to be forgotten that Nelson's mission was to stop the French from reaching their target – and in that he failed. Twice, he missed the French Armada at sea, if only by a whisker. When he finally caught up with them, they had already landed Bonaparte and his army in Egypt, and

Bonaparte had no further use for the fleet that had escorted them there. The French army went on to win several more battles against the Turks and the Mamelukes, and when Bonaparte wanted to come back to France he did so – in two frigates. He seized power in a military coup, smashed the new coalition in one decisive campaign and forced a humiliating peace on England.

Arguably, the greatest consequence of the Battle of the Nile was in India. Immediately after the battle, Nelson sent one of his officers to Bombay with news of his victory, coupled with the warning that Bonaparte might attempt to march east and join with Britain's great enemy, Tipu Sahib, the Tiger of Mysore. After a number of adventures the officer, Lieutenant Duval, reached Bombay, where his news spurred a young Anglo-Irish officer into action. The resulting campaign saved India for the British. The officer was Arthur Wellesley, later the Duke of Wellington.

But that is another story.

Printed in the USA
CPSIA information can be obtained
at www.ICGtesting.com
LVHW041057010424
776066LV00019B/62